Kinfolk

Martin Woodward

Tiger Hole Publishing

USA

ISBN: 0615481051
ISBN-13: 9780615481050

DEDICATION

For Sue and Jenelle,
Always in my heart.

Martin Woodward

Acknowledgements

Oh, yes. I had help. My thanks to Fay Downy, David Samson, Jo Woodward, and Dr. Akis Kalaitzidis for their help and support.

Foreword

In May of 2010, a major news outlet posted a brief article announcing that genomic research scientists in Maryland had managed to create a living organism by mixing a homebrew of chemicals. Holy Cow.

No one paid any attention.

Now, we have hobby drones for the public and military robots that are just steps away from full autonomy. That's not to mention biological 3D printing and robotic cells that assemble themselves into a single robot *and experiment on their own to evolve improved models.*

Still, our media and legislatures are oblivious to the portents.

The Alpha predators in this book (not counting the humans) were nowhere near possible when I began sketching the outline for *Kinfolk.* Things have changed. Technology capable of the feats in this story is no doubt on its way. Creation and genetic modification research programs are full speed ahead in many countries—some in secret. With governments and corporations in charge, an accidental release event is all but certain.

So, take heed. When you hear something scratching at the door in the night, it may not be the cat.

PROLOGUE

The storm ended in early evening. Near the wooded lakeshore, a boar raccoon, gray around his scarred muzzle, emerged from the hollow of a tree. The raccoon padded through the fresh mud puddles following a faint path. At the edge of the lake, in a shallow pool hidden by a tangled willow thicket, the raccoon stopped, its nose lifted. An unusual, pungent scent drifted from the pool. Two large metal objects rested near the shore, half-out of the water. One had legs and a head; the other, did not. He had seen other large metal things before, far away on the dry streams of flat rock where they ran fast and killed prey, but did not eat. One of them had killed his mother. The black birds ate her body by the side of the dry stream.

The old raccoon sat on the shore, listening and sampling the air. Only the hum from the metal things, a faint sound like a beehive, was present. The voices of the frogs and insects were absent from the pool and willow thicket. The air, washed clean by the passing storm, was sharp with a myriad of scents. He separated and catalogued the scents:

wet wood and sodden vegetation, a deer that had paused to drink but did not, traces of decaying meat which he attributed to a bobcat, dead at the water's edge, and several desiccated mice that lay on the thick film of algae covering the pool. There was the metal smell of the things themselves, and a new scent that pervaded all else. Several moments passed, and the metal things did not move.

With caution, the raccoon approached the water, still sniffing, sure now; the odd smell had the essence of food underlying its stronger, bitter property. He discovered it was the algae on the pool that gave off the pungent odor, an almost metallic bite masking the sweeter scent of young life growing in translucent globules floating just beneath it. The raccoon's stomach rumbled with hunger.

Wading into the pool, pushing through the thick coat of algae, he retrieved a small globe, handling the unfamiliar texture gingerly. He washed away the sticky algae and nipped at the globe twitching in his paws, his sharp incisors cutting through its thick membrane. Rich broth spilled into his mouth. He ate the globe and the small, unformed creature inside, finding the taste reminiscent of duck eggs he stole from nests in the spring. The raccoon cast around for his next course, sniffing at but passing up several large globules under the algae and settling on another smaller globule similar to his first. As he wiped away the dark algae from the globe, his paws began to sting. He dropped the globe and looked at it, shaking his paws. The globe lay on the algae, a non-threat. The raccoon growled as the stinging intensified. He stuffed his paws into his mouth and tried to chew away the increasing pain but without success. Panicked, he fought his way through the algae, slipping on the pool bottom slick with a growth of slime. The stinging seeped through his fur, attacking his skin like red ants. He turned and bit at his algae-covered side, searching for the ants that tormented him.

He dashed for the shore and collapsed there, vomiting his last meal between his teeth in terrific spasms, lying in it, unable to move. Mercifully, his skin became numb, and he could no longer feel the maddening pain or the dark coat of algae as it continued injecting toxins through his skin. His vision blurred, and the night became darker. His heart slowed; his breathing became labored as his lungs grew weak under the paralysis that crept through his body. Somewhere in the trees, a whip-poor-will began to sing, registering as a faint patina in the raccoon's last moment of consciousness. Before the night bird finished its song, the raccoon's nervous system failed completely, and he died.

1

Is there a Monster in Table Rock Lake?

The Sheriff's Department is investigating claims by a swimmer that she was attacked by an unidentified creature in Table Rock Lake last Sunday, July 28. Diane Green, an English teacher from North Ridge High School, Little Rock, Arkansas, claims she was swimming near Willow Point when she was severely bitten by an unknown creature. Friends transported her to King County Hospital where she received sixteen stitches.

This incident follows a report filed two weeks earlier by Jim Dodge and Randy Morris, motorcyclists' from St. Louis. The men were swimming at the Cow Creek boat ramp as part of their club's End-of-Summer Rendezvous when they allege something in the water attacked them. This occurrence took place at about ten p.m. on August 15, and left both Dodge and Morris with abrasions and puncture wounds on their legs and sides. Both men admitted they had been drinking but insisted that a large aggressive animal had been with them in the water.

Sheriff Sam Gordon declined to comment on the alleged attacks beyond saying that both events were still under investigation.

Asked in a phone interview if she thought a connection existed between the attacks and this summer's historically low fish count, Sheila Darnell, Fisheries Biologist with the Missouri Department of Conservation, said that she doubted it. "We are still researching the cause for this summer's sudden population drop in several species of lake fish," she said, "As for a large predatory fish or animal attacking swimmers, it is extremely unlikely that such a creature is in Table Rock Lake. No native species of any kind exists in this region that would attack human beings in such a manner." Ms. Darnell did admit that someone could have released a non-native species into the lake. "We'll know more when the bite information taken from this latest victim's wound is analyzed."

The rest of the article made guesses at the identity of the culprit and cited similar unexplained attacks in world lakes. It even referenced the Loch Ness Monster.

Lee Picket scanned for the by-line.

"Reaching for it, Ms. Jordan," he said. "Sell those newspapers."

Lee put aside *The New Le Beau Examiner* and looked out the window of his cabin where he had all but quarantined himself, writing hard on the first draft of his novel. He had a good view of Table Rock Lake glittering in the morning sun, his cabin the last of five limestone cabins supplementing the main lodge lined along the small shoreline bluff. He had been a week at the Prescott Lodge and Sanctuary and still could not believe his good fortune. The place was perfect. He was the only guest at the lodge. Weird, but so had been the phone call from Celia Prescott, one of the wealthiest widows in Missouri, inviting him to stay, recuperate, and concentrate on his writing. He had yet to meet her, Celia being in Florida all week visiting friends. Her absence had let him explore the lodge and lakeshore, and work on his book uninterrupted.

The staff, Darla the cook, Anita the maid, and Red the maintenance man, were pleasant, but did not go out of their way to engage him in conversation. Perhaps Celia had warned them to leave the writer alone. Last night, Celia had returned but did not visit him. Sydney Tatum, Celia's live-in assistant, an unadorned surprise in her mid-twenties, had checked with him to see if he needed anything. Otherwise, they had left him to himself.

The clock on the stove in the kitchenette read 9:55 A.M. Sydney would soon be here to collect him for his meeting with Celia. He shut down his computer and slipped on a tan sports jacket despite the warm morning.

Standing on his little stone patio, the fresh air and the view made him glad he had come here. He loved the lake and hills, the hills shaggy with oaks and hickories, sassafras and black walnut. New Le Beau, the nearest town, was far across the lake, accessible by a twenty-minute boat ride on the pontoon boat or a forty-five minute drive-around via a gravel road, a county blacktop, and a narrow bridge.

He had remarked on the remoteness to Red when the maintenance man had first showed him around the lodge and grounds. "Celia likes it that way," Red had said. "It's just us on this side of the lake for miles. The rest of the north shore on this arm belongs to the Army Corps of Engineers." Lee found he was beginning to like Red, quiet but easy to talk to, a black guy from Kansas City.

Movement at the lodge's main porch caught his eye. Sydney had just come out, poised on the top step, delicate against the massive stone building. Moments later, she greeted him on the steps, Sydney wearing a blue print skirt and white pullover this morning. She led him through the great room toward a central staircase. Halfway through the great room, she gave him a cautious look.

"You don't look like a cop," she said. Then, "I'm sorry. I didn't mean to be that personal. It's just that meeting you last night, I expected . . ."

"I'm an *ex*-cop. Why? What did you expect?"

She had expected someone heavier, not as slim, older maybe. He had the right height, what was he, six feet? She just thought of cops as being heavier, that's all. She thought he looked a little like Leonardo DiCaprio, the younger version. He was not sure how he felt about that, Leonardo DiCaprio not being his first choice for his movie star look-alike. He liked to think he was more of an Errol Flynn type, a Hollywood classic.

"Old Hollywood," Sydney said. "Black and white or color?"

They stopped at the second door at the top of the lodge's central stairs. She spoke into a wall-mounted intercom.

"Celia?"

Lee liked her eyes. Sydney had great blue eyes. She was about his age, he thought, somewhere in the twenty-seven to thirty age group.

A moment later, the speaker vibrated with a high, steady voice. "Come in."

He followed Sydney into the room, appreciating the way she moved, her shoulders a little narrower than her hips. Feminine, but not flaunting it.

The room was a surprise. Any Park Avenue resident would have been at home in the apartment. Rich carpet spanned the floor; colorful abstract paintings hung against golden, fabric-covered walls. To his left a double door opened into a painting studio, an easel with a half-finished painting facing a north window. At the far end of the room they were in, a large window with extravagant draperies framed a trim iron-haired woman in a motorized wheelchair. She sat hunched behind a fat telescope, the telescope trained on something out the window.

Without looking up, the woman, Celia Prescott, Lee guessed shrewdly, motioned to them with one hand. "Come quickly, Mr. Picket."

He hurried around the table. She grabbed his sleeve and pulled him down to the telescope, giving up her place at the eyepiece. "Look there, do you see him? Do you? Just to the left of that big tree in the water."

It took a moment for Lee to find the focus in the sight picture. The wooded shoreline near the far end of the crescent bay came into view. By an old Johnboat half-hidden by a fallen tree, a man stood talking, to himself apparently. The man wore faded overalls and what appeared to be—no shit—a raccoon skin cap.

"Do you see him?" she asked again.

"The man?" As Lee spoke, Davy Crockett pushed the boat into the water, raccoon tail swinging, and climbed aboard. "He's leaving."

"He'll be back."

Lee looked up from the telescope. In the distance, the boat was the size of a minnow. The telescope had plenty of power. Celia Prescott spoke from behind him.

"That was Luther Creed."

The boat moved across the bay, heading under the power of a small outboard motor toward a far wooded point. Lee turned, struck by the disgust in the lady's tone.

"We don't like Luther Creed?"

Celia Prescott leaned back in her wheelchair, all one-hundred-five, rail-thin pounds of her. She wore a yellow pull-over and black slacks that matched her sharp eyes. She reminded Lee of an undersized hornet. He was willing to bet she could still sting.

"Mr. Picket," she said, "Luther Creed has poached my property for several decades."

"I see."

"Not by half, you don't. Have a seat."

Salty.

The electric motor hummed as she guided her chair to a large glass table with a laptop computer, an intercom and telephone setup—command central.

"I would like to call you 'Lee,' if you do not mind. And you may call me, 'Celia.'"

Lee relaxed. He was going to like Celia Prescott.

She leaned forward. "I do not know if your friend Sherry told you, but I do not operate this lodge for income. It is for my friends to enjoy and acts as a support base for my many interests, such as the writer's retreat Sherry attended. I believe that without the Arts, human beings are merely animals that have learned to use the toilet."

"I hadn't thought of it quite like that," Lee said.

"I also support charitable causes." She patted the arm of her wheelchair. "More-so since my accident."

Her accident. Lee thought back, Sherry giving him the background info on the Prescotts when the lodge offer came through. Edward, Celia's husband, had started Prescott Scientific. They made high tech scientific instruments of some kind and branched into research contracting. Edward and Celia had been in an auto accident—a year ago? They had a daughter working with the company in Kansas City, his old territory, but he had yet to meet her.

"When Sherry told me about you, I thought it natural to offer you a place to work on your novel."

"I appreciate that."

"This lodge and its surrounding sanctuary is my Shangri-La. However, it is plagued by petty evils. Luther Creed and his loathsome brother, Corliss, are two immediate examples."

"I think I see where this is going." He checked Sydney, who let slip a Cheshire Cat smile that said, yeah, it's a set-up.

"I want to offer you a job, Lee," Celia said, "As an ex-police officer, you have the qualifications. I will give you free reign. You set your own hours, buy what equipment you need, do whatever you think best to control trespassers on the sanctuary, in particular, the Creeds."

Lee thought about the insurance money he had squirreled away and the monthly short-term disability check that would stop in less than a year. He hoped to finish his novel and get it to an agent before the money ran out. Celia's offer could relieve the already growing pressure to beat that clock. "Carte blanche, huh?"

"Within reason, yes."

"I set my own hours?"

"I am only interested in results. If you can keep the sanctuary secure with just a few hours per week, that's fine. However, if the job requires fifty hours per week then I hope to rely on your judgment and work ethic to see it through."

"And the benefits?"

"Room and board, use of all lodge facilities, and an expense account."

"That sounds reasonable."

"I think so. Lee, you have two-thousand acres of Ozark hills to watch over. Whatever equipment you need, ask Sydney to get for you. If it is something unusually expensive, talk to me first. Within a week, I'd like your recommendations for security improvements."

"That shouldn't be a problem. Are there any areas in particular you want addressed?"

"Yes." Celia looked out the window. "You see that island opposite us?"

Lee stood to get a better view. Table Rock Lake swept in a deep curve around to form another point. An island stood close to the tip, so close it almost appeared connected.

"A short bridge runs to it," Celia said.

"Is it part of the sanctuary?"

"No, and that is the problem. That is Creed Island, ancestral home to the entire clan of ne'r-do-wells. The Creeds have been a thorn in my side and the county's side, for years. There are only the two boys left now, and their mother, but they hunt and poach on the sanctuary with impunity. Corliss, I am happy to say, is currently enjoying county hospitality for some petty crime he's committed. Luther, as you observed through the telescope, is my current concern. I'm sure he is taking game out-of-season and on sanctuary property."

There it was, the catch: persistent trespassers. "What about Missouri Conservation, or the Sheriff's Department? Are they aware of the problem?"

"We've tried the Operation Game Thief task force. They set up a sting operation twice without result. The Sheriff's Department has been out numerous times, but they don't stay long. Luther Creed is a half-wit, but apparently, he is graced with idiot-savant skills when it comes to woods craft. The rangers have tried several times to catch him poaching, but have so far captured only his traps and snares, with no evidence linking them to him. They said it could take months to catch him. They claim not to have the manpower."

Lee nodded. "Is this man dangerous?"

Sydney and Celia glanced at each other. Celia answered. "The Creed name is synonymous with crime and violence in this county. During Prohibition, two Creed men were convicted of murdering government agents. I do not know how many have been convicted of manslaughter and rape, but I would say several. The Creeds live by the feud."

"But, Luther?"

Sydney answered. "As far as Luther goes, he has never been arrested for anything. I think he is relatively peaceful. Corliss may be a different matter. I don't think he's stable."

"And he's in jail?"

"Due to get out soon, I think," Celia said. "Do you have a gun?"

His back stiffened. The thought of carrying again had not occurred to him, but now the idea, what, scared him? He put the issue on a mental back burner. "I have a pistol."

The intercom buzzed.

Celia depressed a button on the intercom. "Come in."

Darla, the cook, pushed her way inside with a serving cart of coffee, tea, and cake. Sydney met her at the door and brought in the cart. Lee saw Darla, plump and fortyish in an apron, her spectacular golden hair swept up and tied in place. Sydney helped set the cups on the table, then shooed Darla out the door and followed her, leaving Lee alone with Celia. A pre-arrangement, he thought, these two women staging him. He settled for black coffee, Celia pouring.

"Mrs. Prescott, ah, Celia. Suppose I take care of the Creed problem, I won't be doing myself out of a job, will I?"

Celia sipped from her tea, her firm lips leaving little rose-colored prints on her cup. "I think I can find enough to keep you busy."

Lee waited, sensing she had more to say but was searching for an opening. Nearly a full minute passed before she spoke.

"I want you to watch my daughter," Celia said. "She has been here too often this summer, and then she takes too many boat rides. I would like to know what she's up to, where she goes and who she sees."

"Your daughter?"

"Jessica. She is now President of Prescott Scientific Solutions, her father's company. *Our* company. She lives in Kansas City. However, her behavior has changed. She has been visiting here far more often than usual, missing work at her office, not that it matters. Between us, we are the major shareholders with seventy-two percent of the company stock. In the past, I've been lucky to see her once a summer, and then only for an extended weekend. Now she comes nearly every week and stays several days, slipping off in the boat." Celia frowned. "We have always been close, always talked things over. That has changed. And, as far as I know, she is not dating in Kansas City. No, I am certain she is keeping something from me."

"This is a bit much. Chasing off trespassers and catching poachers is one thing, but spying on family members isn't—"

"I just added three-thousand dollars a month to your

offer. Now, does spying still trouble your sensibilities?"

***

Later, leaning on the dock rail beside Sydney, trying to forget how easily he had lowered his ethical standard, Lee studied the lake, the sun on the far side sinking in thick purple clouds. Table Rock was a long, twisting lake with a thousand little coves and bays, and long arms that reached deep into secret hollows among the timbered hills. Across and angled from the lodge, about two miles away, the town of New Le Beau huddled on the shore, trapped between the water and the leafy ridges.

Sydney, quiet since they had come down, crossed her arms and glanced back toward the lodge. From where they stood on the dock, under the short bluff that sheltered the boathouse, only the roof of the lodge was visible. On the dock, he could see the bluff diminish as it followed the crescent sweep of the shore, eventually vanishing into a brief bit of beach where Sydney said Celia had truckloads of sand dumped every few years. The boathouse needed paint and smelled of oily water, damp wood, and the faint bite of gasoline from the five-hundred gallon tank on the end of the dock.

"I'm surprised the EPA lets you get away with that fuel tank," Lee said. "Surely there's a code against that much gas stored over the water."

"It has a basin under it. Besides, who's going to tell? This is the Prescott lodge." Sydney shrugged. "Wealth and respectability have privileges."

The large pontoon boat with "Prescott Sanctuary" stenciled on its sides in maroon letters, floated in its slip. It had a fifty-horse Mercury outboard on the back for push. Twenty minutes ago, Lee had helped Red tie off the boat when he had come back with Darla, the cook, and several boxes of groceries. "I like that boat," Lee said. "It looks friendly."

"Our water taxi and work boat. Red makes two regular trips a day for Darla and Anita who park in town. Jessica likes to use the other boat, that Bayliner."

"I haven't met her yet." Lee pulled a cigar from his pocket, a full-bodied Maduro. "You mind if I smoke? I permit myself one in the evening, my little reward."

Her blue eyes focused on him. "Kind of like a ritual, huh, help put things in order at the end of the day?"

"I guess, yeah." He pulled the cigar from its tube, trimmed the end off with his small knife.

"Jessica is usually gone most of the time. But, this summer she's taken a sudden interest in boating. Stays out for hours. Celia thinks she's up to something."

"Maybe she has a boyfriend."

He lit the cigar with a match from the little waterproof canister he carried, giving Sydney time to think that over.

"Why would she hide that, a boyfriend? Unless he was, you know, unsuitable somehow."

"Hmm." He drew on the cigar, the smoke rich, earthy, a hint of cedar and spice on his tongue. "When do I get to meet her?"

"This weekend. But lately, she can show up anytime."

"You don't seem too excited."

"I prefer to have one boss, not two."

"Jessica's a type 'A,' huh?"

"More like a grade 'A', but you can judge that for yourself." Sydney nodded at the lake. "You know, they killed off old Le Beau when they built the dam and flooded the valley. That was . . . 1958."

"What did they do with the buildings?"

"I think they moved a church or two, oh, and a cemetery. Old Le Beau is halfway out and nearly two-hundred feet down. Buildings, homes, roads, everything, still there."

Lee thought about that, fish swimming in and out of dark windows, dead human secrets trapped forever in the cold waters. "Must have been something, watching the water take the town."

"I hear it took months."

They stared at the lake. Clouds obscured the setting sun now, thick bands of them on the horizon all but smothering the light behind them. A single amber ray escaped the clouds but vanished a brief moment later.

"This place keeps its own time and its own secrets," Sydney said. "This is an old land, but it's potent, like it's been boiled down to essence."

Lee shifted, looking at her, this woman suddenly becoming more interesting, a new aspect showing in her personality.

She continued. "I never really knew the full meaning of the word 'melancholy' until I came here. You stay here long enough, you'll feel it, kind of a bittersweet sadness. It's like watching a rainbow glowing over a cemetery, you know, a feeling you get like that?"

"I like that, the rainbow-cemetery simile. Maybe you should be the writer."

"I'm not joking. This is a great place, a special place, but it can be dangerous. It's elemental. What's going on with the Creeds? You should be careful."

"I was a Kansas City cop, remember. I can handle it." Kansas City made him think about the maintenance man, Robert "Red" Redmond. "Isn't Red from KC?"

His cigar smoke drifted between them.

"Yep. He's been with us almost two years."

"I just wondered. He seems a bit . . . misplaced."

19

"Probably the only black man in twenty miles. Red's good. He's one of Celia's projects. She found him in Kansas City at Crown Center during one of her fundraisers. A purse-snatcher grabbed her purse. Red saw it happen. He tripped the man and got her purse back for her. He was there filling out job applications at the shops. Celia asked if he would relocate to the lake, and here he is."

"A stranger in a strange land." Lee looked across the crescent sweep of the sanctuary shoreline. Creed's Island was a murky hump in the distance. He nodded in that direction. "They ever show a light over there?"

2

Table Rock Lake

Startled by movement in the shallow water, Luther Creed banged his bare knee on the gunwale of his Johnboat. He massaged the injury through the tear in his faded overalls. Something on the lake floor moved again. The light breeze dancing into the cove rippled the water and made it hard to see down there. He put down the cane fishing pole and slipped his paddle into the water. He could just touch the bottom. His reflection looked back at him, his face fractured in a shifting parody of himself: gray whiskers and big, bright eyes, a battered coonskin cap on his head.

"Han'some boy," he crooned. "Han'some boy."

There. Beneath his reflection, the something moved again. It wasn't no fish, neither. It was a *thing.* Looked like a big rubber fry pan.

"Gonna get you."

Kneeling, moving the boat over the thing, Luther took a firm grip on the paddle and hooked his tongue in the corner of his mouth. He could just see the thing lying on the mucky lake floor. Holding his breath, he centered the paddle over the creature.

Now!

Luther drove the paddle down onto the thing, felt it punch hard then soft through the flesh. The strange critter squirmed and wiggled, vibrating the paddle as it tried to get free.

"Got you! I got you!"

The boat tipped. Luther fell into the lake, swallowing a good bit of water. While he was under, he grabbed the thing with his free hand so it could not wriggle off the paddle. He came up coughing, spluttering, and shook the water from his eyes. The sodden tail of the 'coonskin cap slapped him in the mouth. Smack.

He raised the thing from the water where it flopped slowly on the paddle blade, dying. It made a wet, chirping sound. A dark liquid Luther took to be blood ran down the paddle and dripped into the lake. The thing was shaped like a fry pan all right, only it was flat and meaty, its smooth skin a dark mottled green on top. As far as he could tell, it had no eyes, only a small mouth on the pale bottom side. Luther shook it on the paddle, watched it jiggle helplessly.

"No bones?" He thought about that. "No bones. Jellyfish!"

He reached out and felt the quivering flesh, quite pleased. "Caught me a jellyfish!"

He tossed the jellyfish, paddle and all, into the boat. Of course, he had heard of jellyfish, but he had never seen one.

"Oh, gotta tell Mama." He smiled, and with some difficulty climbed into the boat, almost capsizing it. He shook the jellyfish off the paddle, letting it fall to the bottom of the boat where it twitched feebly. He noted it smelled fishy, but with a boggy odor that reminded him of crawdads, too. Luther straightened as gust of wind pushed at him. Nasty looking storm clouds gathered in the west, all purple and dark and heavy.

"Better git." He turned the boat towards his family's island. "Hmm-humh. Better

git."

***

The first gust of the storm hit when Arletha Creed was in the cellar. She heard the door, propped open by its swing arm, rattle and creak on its hinges. She had known the storm was coming. The flies had bit like devils all day, right through her old blue dress, and the birds had traveled west to east, both a sure sign of bad weather on the way. Her own body had told her, too, hadn't it? It was the reason she had come down here in the dark, to get some apple cider vinegar for her bath. That would take care of the arthritis, that and a cup of burdock tea. Set her up real fine for the night. She wanted to hurry so as not to be caught by the rain.

She set the kerosene lantern on the pickle barrel and massaged her back. The air was dense in the cellar, a presence around her. That was another way she would have known the bad weather was coming, by the way the cellar smelled, strong and musty.

"Going to be a doozy," she murmured.

Rough oak shelves, laden with years of garden truck preserved in Mason jars by her own hand, lined the walls made of native limestone quarried by Great-granddaddy Creed. Standing there among the shelves made her feel wealthy. Arletha could look at each jar and recall the year. Two-thousand-and-twelve had been a good year for persimmons. In two-thousand-and-thirteen, she had put up one hundred and sixty jars of green beans. Only a dozen jars remained from that crop now, sitting beside this year's meager batch of fifty-three. The bugs were getting the lion's share this year.

She sighed and reached a dusty gallon jug of apple cider vinegar off the stained shelf. Jars of pickled pig's feet sat on the next shelf. The uncertain lantern light gave the tatters of gray-white flesh suspended in the brine the illusion of movement. Only five jars left. That was all right. Come fall, they would butcher at the first good frost. Used to be the whole family would set out a long table line, the men would kill a pig on one end, scald the hair off and quarter the carcass, and then send it down the tables. By the time it got to the end, the women would have the meat all parceled out, the head saved for headcheese and mincemeat, and the fat rendering down for lard. Lord, those were the times, back when they were all alive, her husband Jubal, and the others. Now, it was only her and her boys, and Corliss would likely find an excuse not to be around; that would leave her and

Luther to butcher by themselves.

She had not told a soul how much she missed the rest of the family and the old times. Even when Jubal was away at prison, she always knew he was coming home. Jubal and his crazy brothers had all taken a run at her back when she was Arletha McAllister, wild as a fox, still a silly girl at fifteen. Then, there was her first little boy, Danny. Poor Danny, crippled and wheelchair bound, missing since 1979.

With the apple cider vinegar in one hand and the lantern in the other, she moved up the steps. Her seventy-six-year-old bones ached. Soon, she would likely be seeing Jubal and the others herself. What would she say to him if Danny met her on the other side? A chill tapped her spine like a cold finger. She jerked around, looking for someone to be standing there. She was still alone in the cellar.

"Was his fault," she whispered. "He run off. What was I to do?"

Wind moaned by the opening above, shaking the wooden door, threatening to rip it from the hinges. Beyond the doorway, tumbling clouds darkened the sky. She moved up the steps, the jug of vinegar heavy in her hand. Just as she could see the house, another gust of wind slammed against the open door, shifting it back and allowing the prop to fall away. The door dropped, hitting her hard on the top of her head. Arletha staggered. The jug fell from her hand and bounced down the steps, shattering on the last step, exploding in a splash of dark, reeking vinegar.

Her knees wobbled and her vision darkened. Arletha

faltered down the steps, the lantern rocking wildly in her weak grip. She saw the pickle barrel and managed to set the lantern down on its dusty top.

"Oh," she said, and slid down the barrel.

The dirt floor was cool beneath her dress, the barrel rough against her face. Darkness pushed at her mind. She wondered if her boys would find her. They were good boys. Luther was simple, just that Corliss was high-strung, was all and . . .

Blackness filled her mind; she felt it as a pressure collecting under the portion of her skull where the cellar door had struck. Arletha relaxed against the pickle barrel, and she slept.

***

Must be Global Warming, Lee thought, trying to ignore the soupy nausea in his stomach, the boat ride too rough in this storm. He hoped he could find Jessica Prescott out here before he tossed his cookies, look weak in front of the maintenance man, Red now piloting the pontoon boat.

"That's it, man," Red said, turning the boat in the choppy water and rain, the waves shoving hard against the broadside. Dead ahead in a small cove, the lights of a large houseboat showed, blurry and liquid in the dark.

Red fought the steering wheel, the big pontoon boat

bucking in the storm waves. Rain beat down on the lake, the wind slinging some of it under their canvas canopy, keeping their rain ponchos wet. Lee pointed his powerful halogen light toward the houseboat. The beam found the lodge's Bayliner bumping alongside the bigger boat, doing some damage in the rough water.

"You've got good eyes," he said.

"It's how I stay alive." Red slowed the throttle. Red, lean and graying in his early forties, pulled the hood of his poncho back to peer through the rain. He wore a Kansas City Chiefs do-rag and a gold ear stud. "What's Jessica doin' at this boat? Wrecking the runabout. She ain't got enough bumpers on it. Look what it's doing to her boyfriend's yacht."

"It's a houseboat. What makes you think it's her boyfriend's?"

"What else she be doin' out here, a storm like this?" Red cut loose a blast on the horn, making Lee jump as the unexpected sound jolted into his nervous system. "She ought to know her momma's wondering where she's at. Rude bitch."

"You always bad-mouth the boss's daughter?"

"You ain't met her yet, Marshal."

Lee looked at him.

Red shrugged. "Her momma knows how she is."

They got within hailing distance, the water not so rough

here in the little cove, and the maintenance man yelled out, "Miss Prescott! You in there? It's me, Red."

Lightning flashed above them, the rolling thunder vibrating in Lee's chest. The air was sharp with the electric smell of ozone. No one appeared on the larger boat.

The thought that maybe things weren't just right ran through Lee's mind and slithered down to his stomach joining the motion sickness. "Red, I think—"

Sudden light spilled from the houseboat's opening aft door. A woman peered from the doorway. Lee lowered his beam, letting it shine on the pontoon boat, letting her see it belonged to the lodge.

"Red?" she called.

"Yes, ma'am. You're mother was getting worried, you out in the weather like this. We come to get you. You okay?"

"Ah, my boat quit running. This gentleman here was kind enough to let me tie up and wait out the storm. Who's that with you?"

To Lee, the woman was a silhouette, tall and slim, athletic, maybe wearing shorts and a sport shirt. He answered for Red, raising his voice over the rain and waves.

"My name is Lee Picket. Your mother hired me to run lodge security." He stepped out to the forward deck, the rain hitting hard and mean on his poncho. "Catch this line. We'll tie-up and see if we can get your boat running."

She came out, a blurry figure in the rain and gloom, her brusque manner showing her displeasure about getting wet. She caught the line and secured it to a deck cleat, retreating when she finished to the shelter of the open door. Lee turned to Red. "Should we drop anchor, too?"

"If we can find the bottom." Red killed the engine and came forward, grinning, blinking against the rain. In a low voice he said, "I'll do it. You go on up an' meet Ms. Corp'rate Queen."

Lee timed the rise of the deck with the swells, leaped and caught the handrail when the decks were near level with each other. He climbed over the houseboat's rail, noticing some of it was missing from the aft end. The doors on the end were large and double, big enough to have party people running in and out. He stepped inside one of them and stopped, not wanting to drip all over everything, and closed the door behind him. Chilled air struck him, raising goose bumps on his exposed flesh. The larger boat tamed the wave motion to a moderate roll, but still made balance a conscious issue. Jessica Prescott stood in front of him, giving him the once-over. Her dark hair, wet now, was shoulder length, the bangs trimmed straight across her broad forehead. She had high cheekbones and a firm, no-nonsense mouth that was not smiling just now. Lee guessed she was still unhappy about getting wet.

He was right about her clothes. Her white sport shirt and green shorts were wet from the rain. Her bare arms and legs showed the long efficient muscles of a swimmer. She was twenty-seven-years old according to her mother. He held out his hand. "I'm Lee. Glad to meet you."

She took his hand with a firm grip, gave it an up-down pump, and dropped it. "I'm Ms. Prescott. Security? I heard you were a writer."

"Your mother made me a deal I couldn't refuse."

"And you're Johnny-on-the-spot already, saving the damsel in distress. How gallant."

She kept her tone just one notch under true sarcasm in the irritating fashion some of the cultural elite adopted when an outright expression of contempt would be socially unacceptable. He would let it ride for now, not get off on the wrong foot with her.

"Thanks, but it was Red who did all the work. I don't know my way around the lake yet."

"So? I'm sure that will change."

Watching her, a slight frown passing across her brow, Lee wondered if she had a sweeter side and did not wear that hard look all the time. Jessica turned and motioned to a slight, white-haired man wearing horn-rimmed eyeglasses and one of those smock-type shirts so popular in retirement communities, the kind with the waist-level pockets in them, this one a pastel blue. "This is Dr. Kane. He found me floating off the point and towed me here."

Dr. Kane came from behind a stack of some kind of electronic gear, a couple of computers, and a lot more stuff that Lee did not recognize. The man had to be over seventy, but still had some juice in his step, walking light, like a dancer. "Mr. Picket? How good of you to come to Ms.

Prescott's rescue. I'm afraid I haven't been much, ah, help to her."

They shook hands. Dr. Kane's grip was weak and dry. Lee said, "Again, it was Red who deserves the thanks."

"So modest," Jessica said.

Red stepped inside. Water ran off his face and plastic poncho. "Ms. Prescott, looks like the storm will be breaking up soon. You mind if we wait to take a look at your boat?"

She looked at Dr. Kane. Lee thought he saw just the slightest hint of caution in her glance. "Doctor?"

Dr. Kane moved back to his table. "That would be fine."

He pulled a white bed sheet over most of the electronic devices.

Lee shivered in the cool air, wondering what Dr. Kane needed with all the gadgets. "I guess all that gear puts out a lot of heat, huh? You keep it cool in here."

"That's right." Dr. Kane looked at him. His mustache twitched. "I don't mean to be rude, but if you will excuse me . . . um . . . nature calls. Please, make yourselves at home."

"Sure."

The doctor disappeared down the narrow hallway. Lee heard a door shut. He looked at the covered equipment, then at Jessica who had found a seat on a couch cluttered with technical books and files.

"That," Lee said, nodding at the mound of equipment on the table, "must be the biggest fish-finder I've ever seen."

Red found one of his cigarettes was still dry, paused, the slim white cylinder between his ebony fingers. "You think he mind if I smoke?"

Lee glanced at him and shrugged, his mind on Jessica and the doctor.

Jessica said to Lee, "He said it was some kind of sonar experiment. He's been down here all summer, trying to get it to work."

"Hmm." Lee moved over to the couch, letting his fingers trail across some of the files there. "He have partners, did he say?"

"I don't," a slight crease furrowed her brow, "I don't know. He didn't say. Why do you ask?"

Lee tapped a stack of papers. "These memos are addressed to a Dr. Chilson. I just wondered if Dr. Kane had a partner."

"He didn't say. Don't snoop through his papers like that. You're dripping on them." Getting a bit huffy, now. "He was kind enough to help me and I don't think we need to pry into his business. Red, don't smoke in here."

"The man say to make ourselves at home."

Jessica glared at him. Red touched his forehead and

stepped outside with his lit cigarette, staying in the questionable shelter of the awning. He shut the door behind him. The cabin grew quiet but for the rattling of rain against the windows and roof, the dull knock of waves against the hull.

Lee looked around the cabin. Beneath all the scientific gear, the book and paper clutter, quality craftsmanship and fabric showed through. Not a discount special, this boat. Who knew what all the gadgetry on the table cost? The old man, or whoever was sponsoring him, had funding. Jessica bounced her foot in little impatient kicks.

"Does the storm make you nervous?" Lee asked. "You look pale."

"No. How upset is my mother?"

"Not upset, just concerned."

"You should know, Mister Picket, that Mother over-reacts. The next time she asks you to track me down, don't. I can take care of myself. There is no need for you to waste your time jumping through her hoops."

"A phone call would have given your mother a little peace of mind, and helped me and Red find you."

"Cell phones don't work out here."

"What you need are some radios then, like those two on the table."

"Oh?" She glanced at the hand-helds.

"Yeah. We should get a radio base station for the lodge. Things like you getting stranded and not being able to contact us wouldn't happen." Lee stepped forward, turned a ball cap that hung carelessly on a wall rack by the door, reading the logo and checking the size.

"Radios have a hard time working on this part of the lake, too," Jessica said. "But, you could not have known that."

Somewhere forward a door opened, and the sound of approaching footsteps announced the return of Dr. Kane. "I believe," he said, "the storm is dwindling somewhat."

"Sounds like it," Lee said. "Doctor, you think the Braves will go all the way this year?"

"The Braves?"

"Yeah, the baseball team from Atlanta?"

"I suppose so." The good doctor seemed confused, a faint frown on his face.

"You do follow them, don't you?"

"Err, no. Why do you ask?"

"I saw the Braves' cap and thought you must be a fan." Lee nodded at the hat rack.

"No, oh, no. A friend of mine gave that to me."

Red stepped through the door. "Hey. The rain's stopping."

"Good." Jessica stood. "See what you can do for my boat. If you can't get it going, we'll have to tow it home. Let's go. Out, you two. We've intruded on Dr. Kane long enough."

But for scattered droplets, the rain had stopped and the wind had diminished, calming the waves. Not being much more than a lube and oil man and knowing nothing about marine engines, Lee stayed out of the way and held the light for Red.

"First things, first," Red said, and turned the key in the ignition.

The deck vibrated as the engine rumble to life. It purred smoothly.

"Ain't nothing wrong with this engine," Red said. He shook his head. "Maybe it was a fuel problem. Sometimes a lil' water or dirt gets in there and jams it up. I'll have to check the filter tomorrow."

They said their goodbyes. Dr. Kane, white hair glowing like a nimbus in the boat lights, waved them off. Jessica zoomed away in the Bayliner, not having more time for either Lee or Red. Her running lights trailed into the night.

As they splashed through the dying waves, the lights of the lodge and dock coming into distant view, Red asked Lee what he thought of Jessica Prescott.

"I think," Lee said, watching Jessica far ahead under the lodge dock lights, "your original assessment is correct. She's one chilly babe."

***

Arletha could not remember why she was in the cellar until the smell of vinegar jarred her memory. Her head ached something terrible, and her skirt clung wet and clammy to her legs where it had soaked up the vinegar. She lay still for a moment, staring at the shadows cast among the shelves by the lantern light. Thunder boomed in the world beyond the cellar, for the moment drowning out the sound of rain pummeling the door. She felt lightness in her body; her arthritis pain was gone.

She tried to rise, but fell back, too weak to stand. She would rest a bit and wait out the storm. The lantern was still going, so she could not have been asleep long. Maybe Luther would come looking for her. Corliss, she knew, would not think about her until it suited him. He had become much like his pa, too wrapped up in his notions and the outside world to think of family matters.

Arletha rested her head against the wall and relaxed. Her gaze wandered among the jars of preserves. The children of her labor, they never disappointed her. The apples, crisp brown jewels suspended in amber, the green beans, slender digits snapped and broken to fit the jars, all memories of summers past.

She remembered when Jubal, not long after they were married, had caught her down here one muggy June day. He had gotten his way then, lifting up her skirt and taking her from behind like an animal, his hands rough and firm, holding her hips as he slapped into her, the cool stone steps hard on her hands and knees. The memory sent a flicker of heat through her heart.

Dear Jubal, her man, murdered with his brothers by that wicked Mr. Prescott. No proof, of course, but she knew. He had killed them over the blackmail. Jubal and the boy's had demanded more money for helping Mr. Prescott persuade balky landowners who did not want to sell. Well, Corliss had settled with *him*. She just wished it had not taken years of her nagging at him to right the wrong. Finally, Corliss fixed the brakes on Prescott's Lincoln and off the road he went. Almost got Prescott's bitch in the bargain, but she only come out a cripple.

Heh! *Foxed 'em, we did.*

Still, she missed Jubal and the others, and the way things used to have been.

Nausea rippled through her belly. Arletha closed her eyes so she would not see the cellar spin. The air grew cold against her skin. Heat flashed through her body then evaporated, leaving her shivering. When the dizziness subsided, she opened her eyes.

The light was different in the cellar. It glowed green and fungal, throwing a thin, unhealthy sheen over the shelves and jars, the dirt floor, everything. Her breath congealed in the air, then dissipated in spectral shreds before her eyes.

The ground trembled slightly. For a moment, she fancied the dirt beneath her squirmed with life. She stared hard at the jars on the shelves. Had there been movement in some of them?

Yes! The pig's feet. They had moved. Arletha closed her eyes, opened them. What was in the jar now pulsated, shifting its shape in sporadic agony. Fascinated, she watched, thinking how impossible it was but seeing it happen, the preserved flesh coming alive. In the other jars, the pickled flesh shifted too, becoming something besides pig's feet.

"Lord," she whispered.

Jubal's face appeared in the nearest jar pressing against the glass, his eyes closed in sleep, not death. Or, so she thought. She dared to look into the other jars. The faces of Jubal's brothers floated in the dark brine, some still looking a bit like pig knuckles. Her heart pounded, insistent in her chest. Though it hurt to do it, she shook her head to clear her vision. Hardly daring to, she looked again at the jars. The faces were still there, suspended in their murky fluid. She stared, fascinated.

It had to be a sign. But, of what?

In the nearest jar, Jubal opened his eyes.

She shrieked.

Fresh air rushed down the steps as the cellar door opened. She turned, looking up to see Luther coming down the root-cellar steps, a kerosene lantern in one hand lighting his way, his other hand out in front of him like he was warding off cobwebs. One of the galluses on his bib overalls dangled and danced behind him, ting-a-linging as he brushed the stone wall.

"Mama! Mama what happened?"

Arletha looked back at the jars on the shelves. The faces were gone. Pig's feet once again floated in the brine.

Luther's muddy bare feet slapped on the stone as he landed heavily beside her. He sat his lantern beside hers on the barrel, and knelt, helping her to sit. His clothes were damp. He smelled of fish. "Mama, you hurt?"

"My head hurts some," she said. The vision of Jubal's face still haunted her. She stared at the jars, wanting to see him again, yet frightened with the thought. "I seen your pa. He was just here with me."

"What?" Luther drew back, threw a hasty glance into the shadows lurking under the storage shelves. "Where?"

"Up there in one o' them jars. Uther, Jessie, an' Horace an' Hank," she said, pointing at the shelf. "They was all here. But, gone now."

"Well, that's good. Mama, I found me a jellyfish. Hey! Your head's bleedin'."

"It was a sign, it was. Help me up. You can tend me up to the house."

He did as she asked, lifting her easily, his arms lean, hard as hickory limbs around her. His gray whiskers scratched her face as he spoke. "I was goin' to wait, let you see it, but Mama, the eagers got ahold of me and I couldn't help but to skin it. You know how I am. Why is your dress all wet? You smell of vinegar."

"It was a sign. I know what for." Trembling, she touched Luther's chest. "Boy, your pa's comin' back. Him and his brothers."

"Pa's comin' home? But he . . . he's dead."

"Sure he is, but not for much longer. He's goin' arise like Jesus himself!"

"You talk like Reverend Hickey does on his radio show. Mama, this jellyfish hadn't got no eyes, nor bones, and I'm not goin' to trade the skin neither. I'll keep it as a curiosity, like Cousin Rafe keeps his 'pendix in a jar."

Arletha lifted her lantern, the wooden handle warm and reassuring in her hand. She touched her wounded and aching head, felt the blood sticky, already drying in her course hair. "Oh, stop your jabberin' and come on. We got some work to do."

"I kept the meat," Luther said, taking his lantern and following her. "It's all skooshy an' see-through, and you'll likely say 'give it to the hogs,' but maybe we can try cookin' it. How come you to break that vinegar jar? Smells to heaven down here."

Arletha felt a sharp pain in her head and stopped, leaning against the wall, keeping her eyes closed. Night air came down the steps; cool, smelling of dead fishin' worms and rain. The pain throbbed now, in the front part of her head just under her skull. Beside her, Luther said, "What?

Mama, you okay?"

"Just wait," she said, holding still. The vision of Jubal's face in the jar came to her. In a moment, the vision and pain subsided. She moved up the steps, her legs weak now. She steadied herself in the mud outside. Darkness had fallen. "Close that door behind you, boy, and run that bar through the latch."

"Yes. Ma'am." He paused to comply, and then fell into step beside her. "You 'fraid the coons'll get in there again?"

Their lanterns pitched their shadows back and forth along the ground as they walked, the house ahead silent and watching. The wind whispered in the old white oak that sheltered the house.

"The sky's clearing," Arletha said, "and the frogs, hear them singing 'hallelujah?' Them's good signs, too. I got to be right about your pa, what he wants me to do."

"I stayed in the barn while it stormed, all the time you were down there. I'm glad Pa didn't come to see *me*. What kind of work we goin' to do?"

"Some witchin' work, boy, some witchin' work. Your pa an' the others need our help to come back."

"Oh." Luther scratched his chin, his fingers rasping through his whiskers.

We goin' to eat, first?"

3

On the Yamaha ATV that had arrived that morning, Lee followed the faint trail through the woods. Eventually, the trail lost itself to saplings and deadfalls. He discovered if he took it slow, the bouncing did not hurt his back. The warm sun, the sight and smell of the woods had him feeling introspective, looking at his new life, his new routine. It felt right. Tour the lodge grounds before breakfast to see if anything amiss had occurred in the night, and then write until lunch. Afternoons, attend to minor security duties, including keeping tabs on Jessica, but as she had returned to Prescott Scientific Solutions in Kansas City, that game was on hold. Nights, more writing, but make one last round of the lodge before bed, usually around midnight.

These afternoon excursions were enlightening; he had hiked miles of trails crisscrossing the sanctuary, the trips revealing the sheer size of the territory under his protection. Two-thousand acres seemed like ten thousand when most of it consisted of steep timbered ridges, rocky bluffs, and deep hollows. The new ATV would help with that problem. Familiar now with the lay of the land, he was paying his first visit to Creed Island.

The trail ended at the tip of a ridge, counterpoint to the lodge a mile away on an opposite point with a wide bay between, the lodge and island jutting like the swept horns of a bull into Table Rock Lake. Heavy and dark, the creosote timbers and iron beams of Creed's bridge threw angled reflections on the forty feet of water separating the Prescott Sanctuary and Creed's Island. Weeds grew in the cracks of the planking, betraying a lack of vehicle traffic on the span. Someone had wired a cow skull to the right-hand bridge post, faded red paint on its broad forehead forming two dripping words: Stay Out.

Lee cut the engine, felt the vibration die under his rump and legs. He sat back, watching the man on the other side of the bridge working away at something, the man ignoring him. A blue and white kingfisher flew from the bridge's top beam with a rattling cry of irritation. The man wore bib overalls, was shirtless and barefoot, and sported, despite the morning heat, a coonskin cap. The cap's tail swung and flopped on his neck and shoulders as he bent over the carcass of a large animal at the lake's weedy edge. Lee saw pink flesh and white fat tissue come loose and away under the man's knife, the man doing a little butchering this morning.

"Good morning," Lee called.

The man looked up, Lee seeing a thatch of gray whiskers and feral eyes. "Y'ain't comin' over, Warden. This my property. Y' cain't come over."

The child-like, stubborn tone was a surprise.

"I'm not a game warden." Lee got off the ATV to let the man see he was dressed in blue shorts and a short-sleeved maroon pullover, no badge and no gun. "I'm working for Celia Prescott. I'm Lee Picket."

The man stood, his body hard and lean under the straps of his overalls, the knife dripping gore in his hand. "I don't know you. You say you workin' for the cripple lady?"

"That's right. I'm watching over her land, making sure nobody poaches the animals or does harm to it. I'm to keep trespassers off."

That brought a grin. "Sure, y' got to do that."

"Are you Luther?"

"Yep. You know me?"

"I've heard of you. They say you know your way around the woods."

"I guess. I'm kind o' busy, Mister. Sun's gettin' hot an' the flies are out." He grinned again, showing an empty socket in his upper front gums. "Don't want the meat to spoil."

"Yeah, you don't want that." From where he stood and from what Luther had done to it, the carcass was unrecognizable. A pile of purple-pink intestines lay half in the water, staining the lake with rainbow ribbons of grease. Minnows rippled and dimpled the water there as they nipped at the loops of floating entrails. The animal could have been anything from a large dog to a small person. Lee raised his eyes, not wanting to look at the mess any longer than necessary. "What kind of animal is that, anyway?"

"This here?" Luther pointed to the half-butchered ruin

with his knife, in case Lee might be talking about some other animal. "It's an ally-gator. Ain't that something?"

Ally-gator.

"It sure is, and in Missouri, too." Lee stepped onto the bridge. "I didn't think they got this far north."

"This the first one I seen."

"I'll bet. Do you mind if I come over and take a closer look?"

"Oh, no. Y' cain't come over, Mama don't allow strangers on the island."

"I just told you who I am. We're not strangers anymore."

Luther stared into space, appearing to think it over, but he shook his head. "Don't try an' fox me, you. That ain't what I mean. Y'cain't come over. It's pain-of-death."

Lee pushed his hands out. "Okay, okay. If those are the rules, I'll live by them. But, Luther? I want you to abide by Mrs. Prescott's rules and stay off her property, okay? It's important."

"Mama says that's our land too. It got stole from us. I got to hunt. Them ghost roads are ours anyway, I know that for sure. We got the right-o-way, the law says so."

"Ghost roads, what are they, Luther?"

"Well, you just rode down one, don't you know that?

They's old loggin' trails that go out to the Prescott road an' other places about. Nobody uses 'em now, 'cept me an' the ghosts. They use 'em at night. I don't like to go around after dark, because of them." Absently, he wiped the knife blade on the leg of his overalls, leaving a streak of blood. He looked down at the pile of raw meat and bones and grunted, as if he had forgotten it was there. "I got to hurry now, sun's comin' on. You s'cuse me."

Lee watched Luther bend to his work once more, guiding the knife blade through meat and sinew with deft and practiced ease. Shore weeds obscured much of the carcass, but Lee thought he saw a long, skeletal tail, one that could belong to a large reptile, but he was not sure. That was impossible of course. Luther kept busy, his cap's coon tail rolling back and forth on his neck, sopping up sweat and shooing flies in a jaunty fashion.

"Hey, Luther?"

Luther stopped again, giving Lee his full attention. He held the knife in one hand, a scrap of meat in the other. "What?"

"Do you know Jessica, Mrs. Prescott's daughter?"

"I know her when I see her."

"You ever see her on the lake? She likes to drive around in that big boat."

"That fancy one, yep. She goes over to that floating house all the time."

"A houseboat?"

"That's it, the big one's been here all summer, has that old man on it. He's always putting lines in the water and drivin' all over the lake. She goes over to visit with him." His eyes fell on the carcass, and then bounced up to Lee again showing a gleam even across the water. "You ever take the skin off a critter, Mister?"

"Just some small game, rabbits and a few squirrels when I was a boy."

"Ain't it a hoot?"

Luther attended the carcass again, leaving Lee to think back, try to remember if he got any particular kick out of skinning the few animals he had taken as game. No. Mostly he had been a little grossed-out, the greasy feel and the sharp scent of the raw flesh making him hurry to finish the task.

He swung a leg over the ATV and settled into the seat. "See you later, Luther."

Luther did not seem to hear him. Lee started the ATV, turned it around and drove back down the trail he had followed all the way from the lodge road. He shook his head and said under the growl of the engine, "Ally-gators and ghost roads."

***

47

Late that afternoon, Lee briefed Celia. Warm light oozed through draperies in the apartment's big west windows in a suffused glow, backlighting Celia in subdued radiance while she sipped her tea and selected a scone from a plate in the center of her table. She sat back in her wheelchair, chewing a small bite of the pastry with intentional thoroughness, her eyes unfocused as if she were digesting the update he had just given her on his meeting with Luther Creed.

Lee had decided not to tell Celia his suspicions about her daughter and Dr. Kane on the boat. His suspicion was vague anyway, only a sense that Jessica and Dr. Kane were not the strangers they pretended. What he had them on at most was a suspicion of being suspicious. So, he kept his mouth closed about it, looking at Celia now from across her nerve-center table, alone with her in a private meeting after Sydney and Red had concluded their portions of the weekly staff meeting.

"I would like to let Red know what I'm doing, keeping tabs on Jessica. Would you mind? I've been studying him. I think he is trustworthy and smart. I could use an extra set of eyes and ears."

Celia smiled at him and took a sip of tea.

"You already have him doing that, huh?"

"Casually. I did not give him a commission like yours."

"Okay, then" Lee said, "on to other business. What about Luther's insistence that he is allowed use of the sanctuary property?"

"He is talking about the easement from their island to the gravel road. It's all in the sales agreement."

"An easement. So legally, Luther, any of the Creeds, can use the trail?"

"That's right."

"That puts a spin on things. Legally, they can come practically to your backdoor."

"Yes." Celia sighed. Her fingertips roamed the rim of her teacup. "Jubal Creed was the father and a vile, lazy, dangerous man. A moonshiner, thief, and God knows what else. He spent the money the government paid him for the land that the lake consumed. Douglas bought the rest of their land, with the exception of their island, just before it went on the county auction block for unpaid back taxes, some three-hundred acres. He paid them a more than fair price. They were content because they continued to use the land as if it were still theirs."

Lee waited, watching Celia go back to the time it was all happening, some memory tugging down the corners of her mouth and compressing her lips. She broke another piece off her scone but left it on her plate.

"Douglas tried to move them off gently, and tried to make up for their loss. He gave them work and paid to have the road to their place kept up. However, they became a nuisance, showing up at the back door at odd hours half-drunk and wanting handouts of one kind or another. One of them, Jessie Creed, stalked one of our maids, eventually running her off." She sighed. "Building the lodge and creating the sanctuary was part of our retirement plan. I was to see that it became the ideal retreat, but with Douglas gone so much of the time, I wasn't strong enough to handle the Creeds alone. The county officials were not effective for the vague crimes committed by that clan."

The light in the windows behind Celia was brighter now. She seemed to draw strength from the glow. Idly, she turned the cup in her saucer.

"The situation came to a head when Douglas discovered that Jubal kept a moonshine still on our property. Douglas had the sheriff come in and arrest Jubal and his four brothers. That's when the feud began in earnest."

"How bad did it get?"

"Bad. Jubal threatened to gun-down Douglas as soon as he got out of prison. For the years Jubal and his brothers were away, I had to replace five windows in the lodge. You see, some of the clan took potshots to let us know they still cared. Some mornings we would go out and find our boats sunk. They would pull the drain plugs overnight. We gave up keeping dogs here. They would disappear or turn up poisoned."

"You think Luther's behind that?"

"I understand the Creed's barn is covered with animal skins. By all accounts, Luther is quite a trapper."

"So, what happened?"

"Jubal and his brothers escaped from prison three

months after their conviction. No one has seen any of them since."

Lee considered that. "Vanished completely?"

"Completely. Federal investigators know they escaped in a garbage truck, but that is all."

"What about Arletha?"

"She claims they never showed up or contacted her."

"Hmm. I can't imagine five guys with their personalities could hide very long, no matter where they went."

"It is a mystery." Celia took an appointment book from the table and began flipping pages. "Is there anything else, Lee? I have some other things I have to do soon."

Lee stood. "That was it. Thanks for the tea."

****

Standing easy on the Bayliner's deck, Table Rock Lake calm under the angular rays of the setting sun, Lee took the binoculars from his eyes and put them on the console, looping the strap around the mounted compass to hold them in-place. The boat floated just off the wooded shoreline, the bug song loud at this range, the crickets just tuning up to replace the shrieking cicada day shift. He took a swig from his beer, English today, a Newcastle ale with some real taste to it, and said to Red, "I guess the guy's legit. All he's done this afternoon is drag the lake with that gear in the water. I guess he *is* testing that new sonar or whatever it is he's working on."

It was the second time he had held surveillance on the diminutive Dr. Kane and his houseboat. This time was more of an excuse to go fishing than real work. Whatever the old gentleman was up too, it did not seem sinister.

Red, wearing a scarlet do-rag and wrap-around sunglasses, shifted his attention off the red and white bobber that marked the spot where his worm dangled two feet below the water's surface, the worm impaled on a number six fish hook. He watched the distant houseboat making headway toward a wooded cove. "Look like he callin' it quits for the day."

Lee picked up his rod and reel and stepped to his seat at the rear of the boat where he took a red plastic worm off the leader and snapped on a new lure. He looked at the houseboat again, catching a last glimpse before it vanished into the cove. With a long cast, he dropped the lure within two feet of a fallen dead tree, its bare, branchy crown half-submerged in the lake. Slowly, with gentle jerks and brief pauses, trying to make the lure appear like a wounded minnow, he worked it back to the boat.

"I still can't help but think he and Jessica knew each other," he said, referring to the time he and Red had found them together in the storm. "I just can't imagine why they'd need to keep that secret. What's the motive?"

Red grinned. "Maybe he's getting it up for her, old dude taking her on the sly."

"You're a lot of help." Lee brought the lure up, cast it out again.

"Hey, I been helpin' you with this stake-out, ain't I?"

"Been helping drink my beer, anyway. You're lucky I got you out of work. It's not everybody I take into confidence this way."

"Man, I live at that lodge, on-call twenny-four-seven. The lady an' Sydney know when they call me at one o'clock in the morning to fix something's busted, I'm there, no bitch, no bones. I take an afternoon off, they don't say nothing, long as my work's up to speed."

Lee worked his lure up to the boat, pulled a weed from the wicked set of treble hooks, and cast it again, coming down near what looked like a sweet spot, a big patch of water brush and tangled driftwood. He felt good, at peace with the sun and water. He considered having his evening cigar early, top off this perfect moment. "I guess some guys step in honey."

"Your ass! I ain't seen you work yet, Marshal, just wander around the woods, riding that four-wheeler or taking boat rides—and gettin' paid for it. Or, hole-up in your cabin, tappity-tappin' at that computer of yours. No, you the one with the honey job, busted-ass ex-cop. I still have to work for a livin'."

"Yeah?" Lee tugged at his lure, caught on something in

the weeds near the shore. "We all got to pay our dues sometime."

His casual remark struck him. Yes, we all got to pay dues. But, what price redemption?

Red took a pull on his beer, set the bottle back between his legs, his orange silk jogging shorts getting wet from the condensation on the glass. "I paid my dues, man. I paid my dues."

Lee whipped the fishing rod back and forth, but to no avail. The lure was caught fast. He looked at Red.

"You suppose you can get the boat closer? My lure's hung up in the brush and I don't want to lose it."

Red propped his sunglasses on his head, blinking, and reeled in his line, saying, "Bust my chops, then want my help."

"It's a six dollar lure."

"That so?" Red stepped on the trolling motor pedal. "If you use real worms 'stead of those store-bought jerry-poppers, we wouldn't have this hassle, just cut the line and tie on a new hook."

As the boat moved closer to shore, Lee reeled in the slack fishing line. As the bow nosed into the driftwood, a dragonfly left its perch on a skeletal branch and zoomed away over their heads, its crystalline wings clattering like a mechanical toy. With steady, gentle pressure, he pulled on the three-pound test filament, watching the area it where it entered the water. Something weighty rose to the surface.

Lee froze. His lure was snagged in rotten black cloth covering a bare, sun-bleached collarbone, there just a few feet from him in the water.

Red said, "Damn."

Shock tingled though Lee like a mild electric current. He wrapped the fishing line around a cleat, letting the human remains snagged on his lure sink just to the surface. The skull, with tatters of rotted scalp still floating from it, bobbed just beneath the water, mercifully facedown. The faint, sweet-sour odor of decayed flesh arose from the corpse.

Lee reached for the two-way radio clipped to his belt, fighting a queasy sensation in his stomach. This rotted corpse carried a greater sensory assault than the other bodies he had seen as a police officer. He said to Red, the man still looking at the tragic debris in the lake, "I hope you didn't have plans tonight."

***

Later, with darkness pressing against the lodge windows, Lee's discovery of the body still stitched a thread of disquiet between his shoulder blades. He was conscious of how the lodge's large kitchen caught his words and tossed them back at him. "The Water Patrol isn't sure how long the body has been in the lake," he said.

Celia and Sydney were both dressed for bed, Celia with her wheelchair pulled close, listening attentively, and Sydney staying quiet in that careful way he was just beginning to appreciate. He tried not to look at Sydney, Sydney wearing a silky blue dressing gown that enhanced beyond measure her ripe curves. God, did he want to look, lose himself in the beauty and nurturing promise of her gender and forget the gruesome afternoon. He forced himself back to business. "But, they think the body has been in the lake a couple of months."

Red had begged off the meeting and had retired to his room, muttering about a long shower and a bottle of Crown Royal waiting for him. The kitchen clock read eleven thirty-two.

Sydney shifted, placed her slender hands on the table as if she were about to take notes. "Do they know how he died?"

"It's going to take a full forensic investigation to determine that. There wasn't much left of the body after this much time has passed."

"Oh."

"Well," Celia said, "you and Red have certainly had an exciting night. Poor Red, he seemed a bit shaken. It must have been a terrible thing to find."

A voice from the doorway asked, "Find what?"

They turned. Jessica Prescott stood poised there, an overnight bag in one hand and a garment bag in the other.

Celia said, "Jessica, what a surprise. You're coming in very late, dear."

"I decided at the last minute to come down. Now, what happened?"

"Lee and Red found a body," Sydney said, "in the lake this evening, over on the Broken Creek Arm. They've only just gotten back."

"Well," Jessica said, giving Lee an appraising stare, "you've been a busy boy."

She wore red shorts and a sleeveless, red and white striped shirt, with sandals on her feet. Her hair was mussed, Lee guessed from riding with the top down in her BMW sports coup. He was surprised she would take the car down the long, rough gravel road when she could have parked it in town and had Red meet her with the boat. She blew a strand of hair off her face. "Anyone we know?"

"I conducted an informal examination while we were waiting for the authorities," Lee said, trying to hold at bay the sensory memory of the stench and feel of the wet rags clinging to the corpse. "Keep it under your hat until the authorities can inform the next-of-kin."

They all nodded at him.

"I found a wallet in what was left of the victim's pants," Lee continued. "According to his driver's license, work I.D., and several credit cards, he was Dr. Peter Fraily, Director of Biological Research at Greenbough Energy. He worked at that lab that blew up in Kansas City early this summer."

Jessica stared at him, mouth open. For just a moment, she had that deer-in-the-headlights look. "Oh."

"We lost people in that," Celia said, quietly.

"I'm sorry," Lee said, and then to Jessica, "Is this someone you knew?"

"No."

"You just had that look when I mentioned his name."

"Did you find anything else?"

"Like what?"

Jessica straightened her shoulders and looked at Celia. "I've had a tiring day, Mother. I'm going to bed."

"How long will you be staying, dear?"

"A week, maybe longer. I don't know. I brought my laptop, so I can work from here. Good night."

They all murmured, "Goodnight."

Jessica turned and vanished from the doorway. Lee heard her overnight bag scuff against the wall as she climbed the stairs.

"She's a quiet girl," he said. "I didn't hear her come in."

"She's always been that way," Celia said. "I never

know when she'll appear."

Lee smiled. "Maybe we should bell the cat."

4

Luther Creed noticed the smell when he was tying the heavy nylon trotline to one of the water willows that grew thick against the tail of the backwater. The starchy-sweet smell, like a cross between crab apple blossoms and battery acid, stayed in his nostrils as he baited the last of the steel hooks with a small green sunfish, working the hook through the fish under her dorsal fin, letting her flutter in his hand in silent pain. Underlying the odd scent, the smell of decaying flesh, dry, salty and over-sweet, floated on the air, the invisible residue of death. Something else was odd: He noticed the willow thicket was quiet, no bugs or frogs screeching in there, no birds singing.

It was as if the whole willow thicket had died.

He dropped the baited hook into the water and used the boat paddle to push his flat-bottomed Johnboat into the willow thicket, ignoring the branches that scraped at him, one knocking his coonskin cap from his head. The cap lay on the weathered deck boards, the raccoon's empty eye sockets staring up at him, the way its lips had dried and set making it seem to leer.

"Shut up," Luther told it, grinning. "You 'ol sassy coon."

The boat stopped, caught by a barricade of stubborn branches. Luther leaned hard on the paddle, his muscles jumping under his overall straps, and the boat lurched forward, clearing the water willows and sliding into a small, algae-encrusted lagoon.

Urine spurted down his leg. Near the shore, a metal monster basked in the sun.

"Hey!" Instinctively, Luther raised the paddle like a club.

The monster did not move. Algae webbed its banded belly and legs. A large metal tank-like thing rested behind the monster. The tank thing was busted open at the leading end, what looked like plastic tubes all snarled out of it like entrails, everything caught up in the algae. Luther had a notion the monster had dragged the barrel through a break in the willows on the other side of the pool and tore it open on a snag or rock over there.

The thick algae brought his boat to a gentle stop. Luther remained on-guard, the paddle cocked over his shoulder like a baseball bat, studying the situation. The monster made a faint humming sound, and he realized that it was a machine of some kind, maybe one of them UFO's people made such fuss about. It did not look like anything he had seen before, that was certain. He lowered the paddle, noticing as he looked around there were things of different sizes bobbed up under the algae, looking like they were made of clear jelly. Most of the things were small, ranging from about the size of a chicken egg to a softball in size. A few were melon-sized. But, there were five big blobs grouped together right beside him. Also, there were dead animals all around, mice, birds, a bobcat, and a big raccoon up on the shore, its fur a mess, covered with dried algae. Luther picked up his cap and set it on his head, wondering if he could salvage the coon's fur.

Probably not, it looked an awful mess. And, it would stink.

The mechanical monster remained motionless.

Luther sat still. If he was still and quiet, sometimes he could think pretty good, but he had to sit and let the thoughts find him or it would not work. A horsefly bit him, stinging like the devil. He slapped it, felt its papery body crush under his palm.

All the dead critters at the shore got his curiosity up. Maybe little green men came out of the monster and ray-gunned them. He almost laughed, but controlled himself. A Thought was coming.

One time his brother Corliss had left a batch of corn they had salted with rat poison out in the barn, just being lazy; he was supposed to put it in the tin trashcan for safekeeping. Three days later, Luther had found not only rats and mice, but also a squirrel, birds, and three of their own chickens, all dead from eating the poisoned corn. The dead critters around the pool reminded him of that time.

"Sure," he whispered, "you been poisoned."

He recollected never having seen algae quite like the scum here, the strange, rough texture and the dark green and gray patterns it made. He lifted some with his paddle and sniffed. Starchy smell. He dropped the gloppy stuff back into the water.

He leaned over the side to get a better look at one of the big blobs, this one about the size of a young boy, floating just under the algae. He used the paddle to scrape away some of the algae and felt the blob had a tough membrane protecting it, like the capsule on the medicine he had to take when he got that bad fever. Something inside the jelly moved a bit. Shading the water with his cap, he made out a few details of the thing inside. With a rush, he realized he was looking at an animal, at a blurry face that looked human, kind of. He sat straight up in the boat.

"Jeezy-bell," he said, staring at the other shapes in the pool.

He leaned to get a closer look at the critter in the capsule. This time he used the paddle and poked at the thing. A ripple ran through the jelly, and the whole sack rolled a bit. Luther held his breath; he could see better now, the head and features. The face seemed human but with the look of a cat. He thought, overall, it was a pleasant face. Maybe it was one of the outer space people.

"Han'some boy," he said, and stroked it with the tip of his paddle.

He was still staring at it when it opened its eyes.

***

Red brought the pontoon boat into the dock, Lee going forward to tie it to a cleat under the lodges' roofed dock. Hot, this afternoon, Lee feeling their time ill spent; spying on Creed Island was getting stale. He looked at Red, at the sweat trickling down his face past a welt on his cheek where a horsefly had nailed him, Red not having much to say after that. They had spent three hours crouched in the brush across from the island, catching sight of Luther and his mother, Arletha, only twice. Luther had gone to and from the barn, and Arletha visited the shabby outhouse. Exciting stuff. Red switched off the engine and put the keys in his pocket. Lee stepped onto the dock. The shifting reflections on the dark water, the bite of the outboard's dying breath, and the occasional whiff of dead fish matched his mood.

"That was fun," Red said. "Call me, 'you want to do that again in about six months."

"Yeah. I don't want to spoil you."

They parted with brief goodbyes. Red went straight to the lodge, lighting his cigarette on the way. Lee walked around to the line of cabins. The sun, low in the west, cast long shadows in front of him on the cracked walkway. Late summer roses, their flowers hanging like faded rubies amid green leaves, dominated the air with their heavy scent. Cicadas shrieked their endless cacophony in the canopy of red oaks and hickories. There was a bottle of Black Seal Rum in his cabin. To each man, his poison.

Movement ahead attracted his attention. Jessica

Prescott left the lodge's back door, not seeing him. She walked straight across the yard to one of the five cabins, knocked, waited, then unlocked the door and stepped inside.

Lee stopped. "Damn."

It was *his* cabin.

When he reached his door, he opened it just enough to peek inside, taking care not to make a noise.

Jessica, dressed in shorts and a pullover, had her back toward him, leaning on the small dining table where his computer sat. His manuscript lay before her, naked and unprotected in its first draft. She had pulled up the title sheet with her slender fingers and was reading page one.

He stepped in and closed the door behind him. "Help you with something?"

She turned, surprise living and dying on her face in the space of a heartbeat. Her feet shifted for better purchase, as if she were on a playing field. "As a matter of fact, you can. Forget the deal my mother made you and write full time."

"After one page, you think it's that good?"

Jessica leaned on the table, her polished nails like drops of blood on her fingertips. "I don't like people taking advantage of my mother or following me. That is part of the bargain isn't it, to keep track of me?"

"I don't think anyone takes advantage of your mother."

"You don't know her. Let me acquaint you with some

information you may find useful in your decision-making. First, my mother thinks I'm still fifteen-years-old and need to be chaperoned everywhere I go."

"So does mine."

"Funny. Secondly, this lodge doesn't need a security officer. It is an unnecessary expense."

"If what your mother tells me about the Creeds is true, I'm not so sure."

"The Creeds have become the focus of all Mother's neuroses. Don't give those poor hillbillies a second thought."

Lee studied Jessica, her poised stance and tight lips. "You mother makes what, five, ten-thousand dollars a day without even getting out of bed?"

When she did not reply, Lee continued. "No. It isn't the payroll or your mother that's bothering you, lady. It's something else. Why don't you tell me what it is?"

"Oh, don't flatter yourself."

"No, really. I'm interested. Why all the drama? What are you and Dr. Kane up to?"

She focused on him, a cold gaze he imagined she turned on her subordinates and peers alike at Prescott Scientific Solutions. "Very well. I don't want someone with your background on the job. If you can't protect your partner, how can you protect anyone else? Your negligence may have killed him, not to mention the boy."

Lee's heart beat faster; his vision darkened at the edges. There was no escaping the incident that had changed his life. "Internal Investigations cleared me."

"Where there is smoke, there is fire. I don't want a trigger-happy cowboy shooting any of our guests."

"Okay." Lee heard his voice tighten. "You've done your homework. Good girl."

He sat on the edge of the table. His world shrank to Jessica's eyes; everything else went blurry. The precise brows over her eyes arched.

She said, "No comment?"

"If you're truly interested, I'll let you know how it was, just to set the record straight."

"If you feel you need to."

Lee picked up his story, trimmed to a summary by countless repetitions. "That night we'd stopped a car for speeding, in the 'hood, up on College, around the thirty-five-hundred block, a car full of kids."

The hot Kansas City summer night surrounded him again, a breathless atmosphere summoned from his nightmares. The siren cut off abruptly, leaving a dying echo ricocheting between the crumbling houses and their scabrous slate siding.

"Matt, my partner, took the driver's side. I took the passenger side. We got the kids out, all teenage boys, Gangsta wanta-bees. The driver was the oldest. He was seventeen." There it was in his mind, the dark street, the sour stink of beer and sweat on the boys, and the night air, humid and sticky on his skin. They had stopped in front of a vacant lot, weeds growing rampant over the blackened concrete bones of an old foundation. "Matt frisked the driver and found a bag of meth on him. He cuffed the kid and sat him on the sidewalk, then started with the others. One of them started giving me a ration, acting like he's going to rabbit. The kid Matt's frisking, just a pup, somehow came off the car. I don't know where he had the pistol hidden, but he managed to put two rounds into Matt's vest and knock him back."

"He shot at me then, hit me just under my vest." He felt it again, dimly, the hammer-like blow to his lower abdomen, the air punched out of him, and the pain as the bullet lodged near his spine like a hot coal, his legs going dead and dropping him to the pavement. "Matt got off a couple of shots, but they missed. The kid's next shot took Matt in the throat, and he went down. Lying on my side, I shot the kid five times. It was the adrenalin."

That was what he told himself, too, adrenalin, not panic or revenge.

The kid had fallen into the gutter. His foot had twitched as if he was tapping out a beat. Tap, tap, tap. Tap, tap, tap. Lee still heard it in his dreams. In his dreams too, he still relived the moment when he realized what he had done, the moment he had put the pistol to his own head, mad with anguish. He had not told the psychiatrist about the impulse; he would never tell anyone.

"Turns out," Lee said, his voice tight in his throat, "the boy was only fourteen."

"That's a sad story.

Lee stared at her and continued flatly. "There was an uproar in the community and in the department. A top civic leader called me a bloodthirsty racist. Matt had a wife and two kids."

"I sympathize. Mr. Picket, the bottom line is: I don't want you here."

Lee walked to the door, held it open, tired, no patience left for dealing with this cold and arrogant woman. "Lady, we're just not going to get anywhere. Time for you to leave."

"I'm fair. I'll throw in a thousand dollars for your resignation. Call it a severance package."

"It's not going to look good, me turkey-walking you out of here in front of whatever staff is watching."

"What?" Her back straightened; her eyes blazed. "Who the hell do you think you are, talking to me like that?"

To hell with the consequences.

Lee crossed the room in three swift strides. He grabbed Jessica by her neck, feeling the strength there, and the waistband of her shorts. Hoisting her almost off her feet, he trotted her through the door on her tiptoes and into the driveway where he let her go without warning. She stumbled but kept her balance. She turned. Shadows from the oak trees striped her face with dark ribbons.

"You . . . you can't . . ." She caught her breath. "You son-of-a-bitch! Whatever deal you had with Mother is over. You pack your things and—"

Lee took a step toward her. "I'll walk you all the way home."

She stood rigid, her mouth open, her eyes blazing.

"You have any problems with me," he said, "you talk to your mother. She says 'Go,' I'm gone. Otherwise, stay out of my way."

Jessica's eyes flashed. Her mouth snapped shut. She whirled and stamped toward the lodge, her shoulders a stiff horizontal plane.

****

"That metal thing's gone, Mama," Luther said. He sat in the bow of his old Johnboat and back-paddled to stop the boat in the center of the algae-slimed willow lagoon. The big mechanical thing was gone. Only the drumming of a distant woodpecker and the white noise of buzzing cicadas reached the stagnant pool. Sweat trickled down his neck, the sun hot today.

Mama, sitting in the back of the boat, pulled a leafy willow twig from her white hair and said, "I knowed you was making it up. You just ain't right, boy."

"But Mama, it was here. Right here! Look-it over there. See them tracks? It must of took off."

"It ain't your fault, son." Mama sighed. "It's your weak mind leads you to seeing things wrong and telling tales. Leastwise, you didn't make up the smell. It surely stinks here."

Luther felt a slow, burning weight sink down inside him, pulling him after it, making him feel small. He felt that weight every time his stupid mind got him to make a fool of himself. This time the machine had tricked him, but it was no use to tell that to Mama. She had seen him wrong and stupid too many times to believe him now. He pulled his coonskin cap down hard on his head. His eyes dropped to the pool, to the algae scum on the still surface. He brightened.

"Look, Mama. There's the jelly-sacks I told you about."

Mama looked over the side to see one of the large capsules floating beside the boat just under the algae, the cat-human face smeared and blurry under its jelly shell. Mama gasped, clasped a hand to her sagging bosoms. Light from the water's surface made her face shine.

"God's Power!"

"I tol' you!" Luther said, feeling the glow of righteousness kindle within him. "It's all just like I said. And that machine was here, too! 'Don't you b'lieve me? Over yonder's the tracks. Look on the shore, tracks."

"Boy," she said, her tar drop eyes searching over the algae, "how many of these big things you say there were?"

"Five of 'em. Five big 'uns just like that. There's the other two over there."

"You know what you found?" She looked hard at the pool, her lips moving as she counted the five large capsules in the water. She tottered forward in the boat, raising her old print dress to cross the middle bench seat where she sat abruptly, rocking the boat and clutching Luther's arm to steady herself. Her voice sank to a whisper. "You recollect our ritual?"

"The magic ritual?" He thought hard, and the memory flickered up from the depths of his mind. Not long after she had fallen in the cellar they had stood by a fire in the woods, in a circle of char-blacken stones. Mama had mumbled strange words and tossed handfuls of doctor weeds into the fire. He had killed a piglet, and she had cut out its woman parts, feeding them to the eager, hissing flames.

He said, "You mean the ritual your vision told you to do?"

"Yes, that night we sacrificed to the spirit world, you 'member why we did that?"

"You said it was for Pa an' the uncles."

"That's right!" Mama nodded, her mouth stretching tight on her wrinkled face. Luther could see her skull beneath, and he did not like it. She licked her lips. "It was to get our family back! Don't you see?"

He tried to remember what they had started talking about. Hadn't it been about the jelly-sacks? "I don't reckon I do, Mama."

She squeezed his arm with surprising force and waved at the pool. "These are them."

He looked at the lumps under the algae, trying to understand. "Them?"

"Boy," she said, and took the paddle from him. She leaned over the side and scraped away the green goo obscuring the face in the first sack, the algae stringing from the paddle like strands of moldy noodles. "Don't you know your own pa?"

Luther stared at the face under the transparent membrane. The eyes opened, and he drew back.

"See!" Mama said. "He knows we're here."

She leaned over the side, scraping away more of the algae. Luther thought she would fall out if she were not careful.

"Jubal," she said, fondness tempering her tone, "I come for you."

The critter in the sack, Luther guessed somehow now his pa, began to tremble. Its hands pushed up and raked at the membrane, opening long slits in the tough skin. Mud

73

boiled up from the bottom as the critter rolled and jerked in the shallow water, trying to free itself, arms and head straining to escape the ruined container. Its strange head cleared the surface, slinging water droplets like falling diamonds in the sunlight. Luther heard it gasp for breath before it fell back into the water.

He jumped when Mama prodded him in the ribs with the paddle.

"Luther! Don't sit there like a lump. Help your pa out, a'fore he drowns."

***

The air coming through Lee's cabin window screen carried the warmth of the noonday sun but also concealed a hint of chill within its softness. His writing was not going well. When Celia offered him the security position, he had rolled over like a Kansas City hooker, the cop in him still unburied, an inconvenient corpse cluttering up his psychological parlor. But, there was another reason he had taken the job. It had come to him last night; he needed to *do* something. He needed to do good deeds, feel worthy. Polish up that armor, take up a cause, rescue the damsel, find a way to make things right. Because, Darkness had fallen on the world, and he needed to fix that. Almost unconsciously, he shut down the computer and drifted into the kitchen where he washed down another painkiller.

Painkiller. Yes, that was a good word for it. Only, lately it was not just for his back injury, was it? The little white pills killed other pain as well; they gave a man a little float, a little distance between himself and . . . the Darkness.

The mother in the courtroom: *You killed my Baby!*

A teenager with a gun, but still someone's Baby.

Matts' widow, Gina, seeing it in her eyes: *Why didn't you save him, Lee? Why?*

Dark emotions. He had told the psychologist he was cured, that he was fine. He had believed it himself. However, the Darkness was a tricky bastard, climbing into his baggage and following him to the Ozarks.

Still brooding, he laced on a pair of hiking boots and changed shirts, replacing the blue Polo with a long-sleeved camouflage jersey. He looped the camera, his new toy, over his neck, its shiny body and the barrel of the 200 mm zoom lens now spray-painted with a tan and green camouflage pattern. Before leaving the cabin, he stuffed a camouflage head net and the brown plastic prescription bottle deep in his jean's pocket.

The sky overhead was a pure cerulean blue. The sun hung at zenith, a ball of unbearable white light. The lodge's small parking lot was empty but for Jessica's electric red BMW, its flawless complexion coated with dust from the unpaved road. At the far end of the lodge, Red stood on an extension ladder, perched under the eaves with a screw gun in his hand and a long piece of wood trim bowing away from the wall. Lee waved and kept going, intent on escaping for the afternoon. He did not make it. Someone called his name as he walked toward the maintenance building where he kept the ATV. Celia Prescott, Sydney Tatum, and a woman Lee did not know were having lunch on the lodge's back patio. Celia waved him over. The sun struck shards of light from her diamond ring, exploding like tiny flares around her fingers.

He thought of the scene last night, Jessica in his cabin. Celia would know by now.

"Ladies," he said, arriving at their table and giving them a nod. The remains of their lunch littered the table, an empty bottle of Chardonnay between them. "It's a fine day, isn't it?"

"It is," Celia said, turning her wheelchair to better see him, the little servo motors humming beneath her. She met his gaze. "Lee, I want you to meet Elizabeth Jordan. She's a reporter for *The Le Beau Examiner*. Elizabeth, this is Lee Picket. He's a writer, too."

There, he knew Celia had too much class to bust his chops in public. Or, perhaps Jessica had not told her about their adventure.

"I'm Liz," the woman said as they shook hands. Her hand was small and soft. "What do you write?"

"So far, a first-draft police mystery."

She looked at him. Liz Jordan had delicate crow's feet at the corners of her brown eyes and creases that bracketed her mouth like a pair of faint parenthesis. He guessed Liz

Jordan was pushing thirty-five. She had square shoulders under a blue blouse, wide hips and sensuous legs under a summer skirt printed with minuscule roses. A reporter's tablet lay open beside her bare right elbow, scribbled with spidery handwriting.

"*The Examiner* is just my day job," she said. "I freelance to make ends meet. Regional magazines for the most part, and some for the airlines."

"Interesting."

"Sometimes."

"Elizabeth is doing an article about my fund-raiser coming up in October," Celia said.

Lee nodded. "The one you told me about, the one for crippled children?"

"Under-privileged, physically challenged children, yes," Celia said. "I am hosting a party for a group of children and some major contributors, a get-together of sorts, October ninth. You haven't forgotten about it?"

"It's on my calendar," he said.

Sydney spoke. "Are you going for a walk?"

"Looks like he's going into combat," Liz said.

"Thought I'd take the ATV, cruise over and see what the Creeds are up to."

"The Creeds!" Liz said. "King County's secret shame.

You know, it's rumored they eat human flesh?"

"Elizabeth!" Celia said.

"Well, it is." She looked at Lee. "Not that I believe it, but there was a time when any missing child report would send the sheriff to the Creed's place. We used to scare each other when we were kids with Creed stories. You know, how the Creed boys crept around at night, peeking into windows and stealing children. I used to see Arletha Creed as that old witch in *Hansel and Gretel*."

"The police ever find a connection?" Lee asked.

"No, but that hasn't stopped the talk. You know how a small town can be."

"I know how a big town can be."

"Doesn't Corliss get out of jail soon?" Sydney asked.

"Corliss?" Liz said. "He gets out tomorrow. He was serving a short stretch for disturbing the peace. Or, was it some type of assault? I forget."

They all looked at her.

"I cover the courts, too," she said. "I keep tabs on all potential news makers in the county. That boy has 'scoop' written all over his face. If you ever meet him, you'll know what I mean.

"Tough customer, huh?" Lee said.

"Corliss is an evil person, and I mean that in the biblical

sense." Liz studied his face. "There's nothing in his eyes, nothing. It's like looking down a black water well."

"Hmm. I can't wait." Lee turned to Celia, "I haven't seen Jessica today."

Celia put down her lemonade. Her tone was non-committal. "She said she had some business in town. She took the speedboat and left early. She didn't say how long she plans to stay this time."

"She's a busy girl," he said. "Well, I want to put a few hours in the woods before the mosquitoes get too thick. Liz, it was good to meet you."

"Stop by the lodge tonight, Lee," Celia said. "I have something to discuss with you."

There it is, Lee thought. "Sure," he said, and then looked at Sydney. "Bye, Syd."

"Bye." Her voice was soft.

He had taken a dozen steps when Liz called after him.

"Hey! You haven't run across anything unusual in the lake have you?"

"Like what?"

"Alligators, anything like that?"

Now, he remembered why her name had seemed familiar. "Really, Ms. Jordan. You know the alligator story is just someone's idea of a practical joke, just like your story about the fisherman who found a piranha in the lake."

"There have been three verified bite incidents and we have two missing persons who were last seen on the lake. Something is attacking swimmers. People are starting to talk about a Table Rock Lake Monster."

"Well," Lee replied. "If I see anything unusual, you'll be the first to know."

"I would appreciate it."

"Sure," Lee said. He cast a last glance at Sydney, catching the curve of her cheek and the softness in her eyes before turning toward the maintenance shed and the vehicle that would carry him away from the craziness.

***

Celia's voice crackled through the intercom. "The door's open."

Lee entered the apartment, knowing the meeting would be about Jessica. He pulled at his shirt, the fabric damp and uncomfortable against his skin. Like the band of a hat that was a size too small, a tight strap of pressure encircled his head, squeezing pain behind his eyes. Celia sat in her wheelchair behind her command table. Had his back hurt bad enough to take two painkillers washed down with rum?

Why did he decide to take two shots of rum? Was he afraid of this old woman in a wheelchair? As he approached, he thought she looked a little pale above her maroon dressing gown. Maybe she was afraid of him. No, not him, but something.

Everyone had a tiger on their back-trail.

"Celia," he said, dropping into a chair at the table, "I wish you'd lock up, at least at night."

He wondered if her iron-streaked hair ever had the audacity to misbehave, or if she held it in place by shear willpower. She reached for a silver coffee service at her right, her hands like frail liver-spotted puppets, and began arranging the cups and saucers, setting them up for use.

"Good evening to you, too." She smiled. "I appreciate your concern, Lee. However, since you've taken the job, I feel safer now. Coffee?"

"No, thank you. Look, anybody can cruise up here on a boat, or you could get a truckload of drunken Bubbas' come down the road. Not to mention the Creeds."

"Would you prefer a beer?" Her tone was cool. She settled her hands on the table. "You seem to have had a few."

His spine stiffened.

"Would you like to postpone our meeting?" she said.

"I'm fine."

"You're sweating."

"It's hot in here."

"The air conditioning keeps this room a steady seventy-four degrees."

"I'm fine, Celia." He resisted the urge to wipe the sweat from his brow. This scene was too raw. Where was the float? Damn, two pills and some rum, and still no floaty feeling. "If you want to postpone the meeting, that's up to you."

She stared at him. "Jessica tells me you assaulted her in your cabin yesterday. Is that true?"

He felt more heat in his face.

"I found her snooping in my cabin. I escorted her out the door."

A clock ticked from somewhere in the depths of the apartment. Celia's perfume, a resolute, lavender-scented presence this evening, reached him, reinforcing her gaze as it held steady on his face. Her dark eyes glittered, unreadable. The clock ticked ten times before she spoke.

"I would have liked to have seen that."

He relaxed. "She was put-out in more ways than one."

"She'll get over it. If I thought for a moment you had behaved badly, we would have had this conversation yesterday." Celia folded her hands on the table in front of her. "Now, what have you been up to?"

"Just what you saw this afternoon, a little sneakin' and peekin' at Creed Island. You can't imagine what I saw today." Lee noticed the air conditioning seemed to be working now. The invisible pressure band around his head lessened. "I scoped Alretha and Luther with my camera zoom. They seemed to be stocking up their root cellar. Both of them had their hands bandaged for some reason. Weirdest, Luther killed a chicken and took its blood down the cellar in a coffee can.

"He took the blood down to the cellar? What on earth for?"

"I have no idea. They are very strange people."

"Disgusting."

"Yeah, until I saw that, I thought they were just laying-in stores for the winter or something. Anyway, Corliss is supposed to come home tomorrow. I'll keep an eye on him, too."

Feeling better now, he warmed to the conversation. "Also, Jessica took a boat ride this afternoon. I saw her when I was coming back from peeking at the Creeds."

Celia sat back, her lips pursed, questions in her eyes.

Lee plucked at his shirt. It itched now that the heat had finally left him, and the drying sweat made him want to scratch. He felt a little dizzy, too, but a good kind, as if a fever had just left him. Maybe the prescription was kicking in. "I think she's still meeting with this Dr. Kane."

Celia poured herself a cup of coffee, her face expressionless. "Are you sure you don't want some?"

"Uh, no, thanks."

Celia raised her cup and blew across it. Pale wisps of steam swirled away and vanished like brief, tattered ghosts. "By the way, why *was* Jessica in your cabin? Did she say?"

"She offered me money to leave."

"She told me she you had wanted to talk to her. Hmm. Jessica can be very persuasive or very intimidating with the stick when the carrot doesn't work. I appreciate you staying." She tapped a faultless fingernail against her porcelain cup. "I know her. She is up to something. That's why she wants to get rid of you."

At that moment, Lee heard the door open behind him. He cursed silently. He was fool enough to be caught sitting with his back to the door. He turned in time to see Jessica stride into the apartment, her long dark hair pinned up. She looked scrubbed and clean in silky summer sleeping shorts, her firm flesh in tan contrast to the delicate pink material.

"Oh," she said, coming to the table without slowing, "have I interrupted something?"

Lee turned to Celia. "This is what I meant about locking your door."

Jessica crossed her arms, a silky, pink-clad icon of confidence. "Mr. Pickett, you're being dismissed because of your own hostile actions. You brought this on yourself."

"I'll apologize if you will," he said, surprised by his own admission. *Damn.* But, he did not care, starting to feel the float now.

"I will not apologize for being battered about like a common-law wife. You are lucky I don't press charges."

"Ouch," he said.

"Jessica," Celia said. "Lee is staying on."

"What! He assaults me and you let him get away with it? He's a brute and a mercenary. He's only here to take advantage of your weakness, Mother."

"Mercenary?" Lee said.

"What are you doing with this . . ." Celia looked at Lee for confirmation, ". . . Dr. Kane?"

Jessica's mouth snapped shut. Her eyes darted from her mother to Lee, then back to her mother. "What?"

"Don't act so shocked, dear. I'm sure one of the reasons you want Lee to leave is because you suspect I hired him to keep watch on you."

Lee could smell Jessica now, a light tropical tang mixed with her own clean, fresh-from-the-shower scent. She stood with her bare legs braced, her hands clenched, reminding him of a kick-boxer.

He said, "Whatever it is you are doing, you're attracting attention. There was a guy at the city dock today asking about you. Red said he looked like he came from corporate

HQ, or was perhaps a cop of some kind."

"You didn't tell me this," Celia said to him.

"I was coming to it."

"What guy?" A crease appeared on Jessica's brow.

"He had black hair, was about my size, maybe a little bigger. Mustache. According to Red, he asked too many questions. Sound like anybody you know?"

"No. What was his name? Where was he from?"

"He didn't give a name, but he said he was an old family friend and that he'd be stopping by for a visit."

"Damn."

Celia's voice was gentle. "Are you in trouble, Baby?"

Jessica stared at her.

"Yeah, she is." Lee stood, comfortable now, and pulled a chair from the table. "Why don't you have a seat and tell us about it."

Slowly, Jessica sat in the offered chair. She held the table's edge as if to keep it in position.

"Believe it or not," he said, keeping his voice gentle, "we're on your side."

Her eyes found his. He saw the decision come to her, the flying thoughts behind her eyes locking into place with almost audible clicks, like the spinning wheels coming to rest in a mechanical slot machine.

"Very well. Since you both seem so interested in my affairs, I'll tell you who the man was on the city dock. It's likely he was a spy."

Celia remained silent, her eyes on her daughter.

"Like from a foreign power?" Lee asked.

"No. An industrial spy working for any number of other tech companies. Or, he may be freelance. Dr. Kane and I are working on a secret project for Prescott Scientific Solutions, cutting edge technology that our competitors would love to obtain."

"Is this something dangerous?" Celia asked. "Are you in any kind of danger?"

"The technology is worth millions. It's possible someone would kill for it."

Lee said, "What kind of technology are we talking about?"

"Maybe you didn't hear me. It's secret."

"That sonar?"

"It's *secret*."

"All right, fine." Lee looked at them. "Where do we go from here?"

"I need to speak with Dr. Kane," Jessica said. "Then

we can set up a meeting and construct a plan."

"Tomorrow?" Celia asked.

"Tomorrow night," Jessica answered.

"Red will have to know," Lee said.

Jessica stared at him. "I don't see why."

"Because he is no fool, and we'll need him to keep us apprised of any more snoops."

"Sydney as well," Celia added. "For the same reasons."

"I don't think Sydney can keep a secret. And as far as Red is concerned, I don't really want to put my trust in one of your adopted strays, Mother."

"Do you think I would hire someone without first having them checked out?" Celia smiled. "You may be surprised about Mr. Redmond."

"Wonderful. I'm sure he was a choirboy and served soup at the mission house. My point is the fewer people who know about our little secret, the better."

Lee looked at Celia. "Are we finished? All this love is too much for me."

"We are. But, I want you two to get along. Jessica, Lee is here for your protection as well as mine. Try to remember that."

"That will be easier to do if he stops manhandling me."

Lee looked at the fire in Jessica's eyes, a thousand responses coming to him and none of them suitable. He shook his head, silent. No, the lady never let up.

5

Lee leaned back in his folding chair on the lodge dock. Clouds, big fluffy ones, had stolen into the afternoon sky, floating high and brilliant white in the vast blue remoteness. The lake mimicked the sky with liquid reflections, a feast for the visual palette. Lee turned to look at Red, the man taking a sip from his can of beer, his eyes unfocused, likely mulling over Lee's account of last night's meeting with Celia and Jessica. It was a blue jeans and tee shirt day, Lee's tee a plain blue Hanes with a pocket. Red's shirt was red with a silk-screened bust of Socrates, the words "The unexamined life is not worth living" stenciled below it. This guy from the K.C. badlands, Lee thought, up on philosophy.

"I knew some shit was going on," Red said at last, leaning on the dock rail and nodding at Dr. Kane's houseboat anchored thirty feet off the lodge dock. "Corporate spying out here in the woods. Just can't escape corporations. They're everywhere, man. Got the world in a choke-hold."

Lee popped the top on a beer, wincing as his back gave a twinge. Helping Red move Dr. Kane's belongings to the lodge, room number six, and the scientific gear to the maintenance building, had been unwise. He wanted another pill, but not with Red standing there. "Yeah," he said, "we'll have to keep Dr. Kane under wraps as much as possible, keep his sonar tests to a minimum. Remember, to the rest of the staff and any future guests, he is one of the Prescott's old family friends."

"Check."

"And let me know if anyone suspicious comes around."

"Check. Anything else, Marshal?"

"Thanks for your help."

"Cross my palm with silver, show you're sincere."

"Would you settle for a good cigar?"

Lee heard feet scuffing the steps behind them. Sydney was coming down, her breasts bouncing some beneath the thin sleeveless top she wore, the fabric green with faint white lines running through it. She looked fresh and healthy in tan shorts and sturdy hiking boots, her honey-colored hair pulled back off her neck. She reminded him of an archeology student out for a dig, not that he had seen many archeology students, but his idea of them. On the dock beside them now, she arrived like a scented breeze. Her polished fingernails and lipstick conflicted with his archeology student impression.

"Well, Dr. Kane is installed," she said, leaning on the rail between them, a little breathy from coming too fast down the steps. "He's adorable. He calls me 'My Dear.'"

Red lit a cigarette. "He's a strange old dude."

"I think he's sweet."

Red grunted and blew smoke into the air. His gaze followed a boat far across the lake.

"Anyway," Sydney said, "all this intrigue is exciting. Don't you think so, Lee?"

"A thrill a minute. Would you like a beer?"

"I'm serious."

"Me, too." He toed the cooler at his feet. "Only one left."

Sydney made a sour face at him. "Mr. Picket, you are too young to be jaded."

"The Chinese have a curse," Red said, still looking at the lake. "May you live in interesting times."

Lee looked at Red. The man ignored him.

"You're both killjoys," Sydney said. "I think I'll find something else to do with my afternoon. Celia has one of her headaches. She doesn't have them often, but when she does, she wants everybody *out*."

Lee twisted a little in his chair, trying to find the optimum position that would ease his back. Red took a swig of beer.

Sydney turned her back and leaned on the rail, looking at Lee. "She lays in bed with the drapes drawn and God help whoever disturbs her. She's fired me once today, and Darla twice, just for checking if she needed anything. She's had them ever since her accident."

"Migraines?" Lee asked.

"Migraines. So, either of you going into town today?"

Red nodded at the gas tank on the end of the dock. "I got to fuel the boats, replace some shingles on cabin three before it decides to rain."

"You're drinking beer and you're going up on a roof?"

"I can have one beer and still climb."

"Don't let Celia know. I'll catch an earful." Briefly, she raised both arms to adjust and pat at her hair-tie. "What about you, Lee? Can I persuade you into taking me to town? I've got a few things I could pick up for myself and the lodge."

"I was going to make a round of the sanctuary, see if Luther Creed is still setting traps. Maybe catch a glimpse of the infamous Corliss."

"Oh." She brightened. "Can I go with you?"

"I thought you wanted a ride to town?"

"I'm just bored. Anything to get out of here for a while."

"It's a long ride on a bumpy road, and it'll be hot and buggy."

"I can handle it."

"We get back in there, you can't change your mind."

"Take her back, Marshal." Red flicked his cigarette butt into the water. "You afraid she'll bite?"

Sydney stood waiting, honey-blond, expectant, and curvy.

"All women bite," Lee said, "sooner or later."

"I only know two reasons for biting," Sydney said.

Lee met her gaze; she turned and looked at the lake as if the exchange had not occurred. Still, the ancient gauntlet had been thrown.

Red grinned at him.

***

They followed the ghost roads through the woods, Sydney riding behind him on the ATV, her arms around his waist. Tree shadows rippled over them like torn ribbons. The air smelled of leaf loam and hot engine. Lee parked the ATV, and they traveled on foot the last half mile toward Creed Island, to his observation post under the old hickory tree. He wanted to catch a glimpse of Corliss if he was home, and size up the new player.

They kept their voices low.

At the tree, he pointed the best viewpoint out to Sydney, handing her the binoculars so she could see how the Creeds lived as if they were stuck in the 1890's, with kerosene lanterns and a hand-pumped water well. He was busy clearing a spot for himself a few yards away in the thin undergrowth when he heard the dreadful mechanical click as a trigger plate gave way. Sydney cried out.

He turned instantly.

Sydney was on the ground, her face white with pain. He fell to his knees beside her. She gasped when he put pressure on the large animal trap, trying to loosen its jaws from around her ankle. He could not get his hands in to get any leverage to open the trap. Sweat dripped from his face.

"It's too strong," he said, trying to keep the edge of hysteria he felt from his voice. "I can't get a grip. I'll have to find a stick and pry it apart."

The woods around them had gone quiet. The mid-afternoon sun filtered through a million leaves, giving the air an aquamarine tint. Sydney's breathing quickened; she was going into shock. He looked through the trees and across the small bay to Creed Island, wondering fleetingly if her cry of pain and surprise had carried that far.

"Stay here," he said, realizing at a sublevel how idiotic the words sounded. Where was she going, her foot caught in an anchored steel trap? "I've got to find a something to pry with."

He thrashed through the undergrowth, his haste making him clumsy, tripping on roots and rocks hidden in the dead leaves. At last, he found a suitable branch on a windfall limb. With some difficulty, he broke it off and rushed back to Sydney. Her lips were pursed and white with pain.

"Try to breathe slowly," he said. "I'll have this off in a minute."

On the ground beside her, his hands slick with sweat, Lee wedged the stick between the jaws of the trap and pried against them. They gave enough for him to work his fingers through the upper jaws. With an effort, he pushed them open, releasing her ankle from their grip.

Sydney moaned and pulled free of the trap. Lee let the jaws spring shut, their serrated edges gnashing together like the teeth of a wild beast. His hands trembled as he took her foot and inspected it gently. The metal jaws had fastened on the padded upper edge of her hiking boot, which spared her the full force of the trap. Her skin was unbroken. Lee breathed a fraction easier.

"Does it feel broken?" he asked. "Can you move it at all?"

"I'll try." She inhaled sharply. "Okay, it hurts."

"Christ, I'm sorry, Sydney. I had no idea this would . . . who the hell . . ." A bolt of anger shot through him as the obvious culprit emerged. "Luther. Son-of-a-*bitch*."

The voice came from behind them, rough and close. "I ain't have nuthin' to do with that."

Lee whirled. Luther Creed stepped from behind the black bole of a gum tree, the tail of his coonskin cap swaying as he moved. The muscles of his bare shoulders moved like animals beneath the straps of his faded overalls. The dark, work-grimed handle of a skinning knife jutted from a side tool pocket on his right thigh. Luther grimaced, showing the conspicuous gaps in his upper gums.

"Weren't my fault," he said. "I never wanted to do it."

Before Lee could react, another man stepped from behind a tree to the left of Luther. This one was a younger, more heavily muscled version of Luther, Lee noted, but for one thing. This man had eyes like Arletha Creed, black, soulless buttons under a heavy brow. The words of the reporter, Elizabeth Jordan, came to him, describing Corliss Creed. "There's nothing in his eyes, nothing. It's like looking down a black water well."

Her description was accurate.

Corliss wore blue jeans and a green print western shirt with the sleeves torn off. When he moved, the crepe soles of his battered brown work boots made no sound in the leaf mold. He touched the brim of his dirty white straw cowboy hat, the edges worked and crimped hard so they curled radically to the crown.

A white hat, Lee thought, a good guy. One of life's little jokes.

Corliss worked his jaws on a lump of tobacco. "Looks like y'all found some trouble."

"You did this," Lee said. He felt his back stiffen with the realization that here was a natural enemy, his moral opposite.

"Can't say as we did." Corliss looked up into the trees, dropped his gaze to the lake shining through the leaves, innocent, just out for an afternoon stroll, maybe a faithful member of Percy Throckmorton's Bird Watchers Club looking for a rare thrush. "Anybody could have set that ol' got-cher-foot. Could have been here for years. Probl'y set to catch a chicken thief, like a weasel or somethin'."

Lee looked at Sydney, saw fear mixing with the pain in her eyes, her mouth open in an unasked question. He followed the trap's short anchor chain and wrenched the stake from the ground, the sudden strain hitting him in the lower back like a steel band snapping. The pain, the heat, and the situation made him light-headed. He raised the trap, wanting to shake it at Corliss. "If your prints are on this, your stay home will be a short one."

"They ain't on it." Corliss spat a stream of brown tobacco juice into the buck brush and put more bass in his voice. "But you need to be more respectful of folks, son, talkin' guff like that to me."

Lee liked the weight of the trap in his hand, the way the heavy jaws at the end of three feet of chain made an improvised medieval mace. "You and your brother are trespassing."

Corliss reached behind his back and drew a Bowie knife from his belt. The blade was fully twelve-inches long, two-inches broad at its widest point, the tip dropped and sharpened on both the top and bottom edges, designed to gut a man with one stroke. He made a show of pretending to clean his fingernails with the huge knife.

Luther said, his eyes shifting from Lee to his brother, "We was jus' goin', wasn't we, Corliss? Mama'll be havin' dinner on in a bit, an' I got chores yet to do."

"The neighborly thing," Corliss said, eyeing Sydney, "would be to he'p get this little girl up to the house where she can rest a bit. How 'bout it, darlin'?"

"Lee?" Sydney said, looking up, fear building in her eyes.

Getting some of his strength back now, Lee flipped the trap over his shoulder where he let it hang down his back, an implied threat. He wondered if Luther would come into it on his brother's side if it came down to a fight.

He said, "Luther, your little brother is about to get into trouble again. You'd better get him home."

"You talk mighty big, city boy," Corliss said, lowering the knife to his side, the blade horizontal in his fist, ready for work. His fingers shifted on the handle, finding a better grip. "They done tol' me how you come down here tearing up our traps and insultin' our mama. You some kind of hot shit, think you can't wake up at the bottom of the lake? You stay out of our business."

"Don't you kill him, Corliss!" Luther stamped his foot and stomped several yards away where he turned, coon tail swinging around his head; he pointed an index finger at his brother. Lee noticed Luther's hand was blotched pink with new skin, as if healing from a bad burn. "This ain't right, an' you know it. Look-it what you done, made me set that trap and now this pretty lady's hurt."

"My brother ain't quite right in the head," Corliss said. "He hears the trees talkin' and skins out animals 'cause he likes the way the hides look all stretched out. You cain't b'lieve a word he says."

"You going?" Lee said, feeling the trap chain grow slick in his sweaty hand. He tried not to look at the knife in Corliss's hand, or think about the damage it could do. He was not at all sure of the outcome should the man decide to take him on.

"*I'm* goin'," Luther said. He walked a few feet and turned, looking at Sydney. "Sorry lady, Ma'am."

Corliss watched his brother disappear into the trees. Lee saw a degree of resolution leave the man's face.

"Corliss, I think that's your cue."

"Think you're so smart?" The man's eyes were twin pots of tar, flat and dead. "We ain't finished, you an' me."

"Probably not."

"Boy, I'm going to break you over like a shotgun and load a magnum shell up your ass."

Lee kept his eyes locked on Corliss. He heard Sydney whimper as she shifted her weight behind him. Corliss spat jet of tobacco juice toward them; Lee could smell it, a sour brown stream splattering into the leaves. Then Corliss turned and strode away, buck brush and gooseberry scraping against his jeans. In moments, the leafy curtain of trees swallowed him from sight.

Lee dropped the trap. It lay on the ground like the skeleton of an alien predator. He knelt beside Sydney. "You okay?"

"No." Tears suddenly rimmed her eyes. "Can you get me out of here, please?"

***

His run-in with Lee Picket still hovering in the back of his mind, Corliss Creed stepped out onto the porch, working his teeth over with the bare end of a kitchen match, scrubbing away the residue of his mother's cooking, the meal not too good this evening. The cuisine got like that when something was on her mind. Or, maybe her clutch was finally beginning to slip, and she was just losing her shit. Whatever it was caused her to burn the bacon, he didn't ask. If she was finally on the way out, he'd live with it, maybe make like she was still alive and keep cashing the Social Security checks. And if not, if it were something concerned him, she would tell after she had chewed it over enough. He sat down in a creaky cane chair that was twice his age, leaned back and crossed his ankles on the rail, the laces of his scuffed work boots untied and loose in their brass eyelets. The sun was almost down beyond the lake, a red ball in a bleeding sky. Time bring on the night shift, swap out the swallows for the bats, the dogs for the cats.

How about that shit? Made me a rhyme.

It was good to be back, wearing his own clothes, sleeping in his own bed, no thick-necked guards messing with his head. King County Lock-up, what a joke. Not that Booneville was tough, his stay on the State there easy, stay away from the meth-heads and ganged-up punks eager to prove their horsepower. Not like the things he had heard about Leavenworth Federal, the place he may wind up if the Feds caught him with his crop.

The yard in front of him was peaceful, the soft gloom of twilight stealing from the trees, pooling around the barn and smoke shack, rising up like a dark mist and hiding the sharp edges of the dead farm machinery rusting in the weeds. Shit, when he was a boy he used to play on the rusted bones of that 1937 Farmall tractor up there by the tree line, the rubber tires all but gone now. Good ol' days. He raised his nose. A cool breeze trickled through the trees; the crisp smell of the lake washed the sour smell of the hog pen back to the barn. But, a whiff of charred garbage spoiled the moment, arriving from the fifty-five gallon burn barrel that was upwind, unburned garbage spilling out its rusted base.

Corliss sighed. One of these days, he'd have to get Luther to move that sum-bitch downwind of the house.

And, he noted for the umpteenth time, he needed to get Luther to replace the rotting planks covering the old cistern before somebody fell in. It sat halfway to the cellar, where the first Creed shack had stood way back in 1910 or some shit, before Great-uncle Somebody burned it down smoking in bed. Corliss hated that cistern. Every summer of his young life, Mama made him water the garden out of it, drop down a galvanized bucket and haul it up, heavy, and carry it out to the garden, water the plants one at a time. What bullshit. Soon as he was big enough not to be whipped, he quit doing it.

Pa, supposed to have been killed by the sheriff and Mr. Prescott back then, what Mama had always said, telling him and Luther that since they were kids. However, for the past several years Corliss had entertained the notion that maybe Pa simply run off, maybe with a woman. The kink in that was all his uncles had vanished too. Hell, they'd broke out of jail together. Maybe they were all living it up down in Mexico, rolling with some hot little pepper-bellies every night, knocking back mescal and inhaling some righteous Mex weed. Maybe they didn't have a reason to come back, sure as hell not to this dump.

Thinking about the Mexican weed threw a craving on him. So did the thought of dark-eyed senoritas, imagining them eager in those peasant blouses, their tits bunched up and luscious, but he had no fix for that urge just now. Maybe later he'd step out behind the barn, take matters in hand, take the edge off.

Corliss tapped a hand-rolled joint from his pack of generic cigarettes, wetted it for luck, and stuck it between his lips. With his thumbnail, he popped a flame from the dry head of the kitchen match and lit the homegrown marijuana, a little Ozark Gold he tended from one of several patches he had scattered in small hidden clearings around the lake. He had to keep the plots small and covered over with camouflage netting because the State Police could spot that shit flying over with infrared cameras, the cheating bastards. The pot was one of his on-going business ventures. Like the bible said (so he had heard), as ye sew, so shall ye reap. He took a good toke and held it, feeling the thick smoke expand in his lungs and work its magic, thinking it would soon be time for him to do some reaping, get his crop to market.

The screen door slapped behind him.

"Mama don't like you doin' that," Luther said. He held the pig bucket in one hand. A pair of flies zeroed in on the table scraps inside, eager for a last meal before nightfall.

Corliss let out the smoke in a sudden huff, blinking it from his eyes. "When I'm home, I do as I please. 'Sides, she don't say nothin' about it no more."

"But, she don't want you doin' it."

Luther's problem: He would always be a mama's boy. Corliss took another toke, feeling that first little tingle that would soon creep up his scalp like slow moving ants and make his eyelids squinch down. His big brother stood watching him, the empty eye sockets of his coonskin cap staring too. One of the straps on Luther's overalls, undone, hung down behind him, making him look like a little boy despite the lean muscle on his arms, the deep creases and a three-day growth of gray whiskers on his face.

Corliss exhaled. "Are you too stupid to fix up your

britches right, or are you makin' some kind of fashion statement?"

"What?" Luther looked down at his overalls. His free hand moseyed over to check the button-up fly.

"Nuthin'." Corliss spat over the porch rail. It had been like this all his life, Luther too dumb to know shit from shingles. "I swear to God, boy, you ain't no fun. Don't even know when somebody's fuckin' with you. You ain't right by half."

"You the one ain't right, smokin' that stuff agin her wishes."

"Hey, lick the skull, bitch." He'd picked up that one in lock-up this last time, from a Kansas City biker busted for meth, which, as it happens, was another business venture he was considering, crystal meth the popular head-fix these days. He had seen what meth did to people, turn their brains to mush and their teeth to rotting stubs, but hey, he'd sell it if they bought it. He drew hard on the joint, burning it halfway down. Yeah. *Lick the skull.* Let his goofy fucking brother figure out that one.

"*You* lick it," Luther said.

The screen door creaked open. Mama hobbled out, a loaf of fresh homemade bread tucked under her arm.

"You boy's stop it. And Corliss, you stop baitin' him so. You know it's how he is."

Corliss dropped his feet off the rail and let the front legs of the chair hit hard on the porch floor. "Well, s'cuse me for drawin' breath!"

"Now, don't carry on that way. You know what I mean."

"You always liked him best. *Oh, we got to treat Luther special, he's a retard.*" He pinched the fire off the joint, ignoring the small pain the action cost him. Mama stood looking at him, those black eyes of hers steady on him, staring like judgment day. Old anger flickered through him, silent, like heat lightening. "If he'd a been a dog, he'd of been drowned at birth."

"Corliss!"

"It's all right, Mama," Luther said, his voice quiet. "He don't bother me none."

"I just don't know what's gettin' into you, Corliss. You're jus' gettin' so mean and lazy."

"Lazy! I been in the County. You mind if I relax a little?"

"You let that boy go today, that Lee Picket, without a scratch on him."

"Mama, he had a woman with him. What was I supposed to do, cut him up in front of her? Then I'd have a witness to get rid of."

"Your pa would have found a way."

He had heard that all his life. His Pa, Superman an'

Jesus all rolled into one, smitin' revenuers and walkin' on water. He sighed, tired of the ghost. "Pa ain't here no more, Mama." He was tempted to say, "He's down to Mexico getting his knob polished every night by some tequila-mouthed senorita." But, he didn't. Couldn't quite bring himself to talk to Mama that way.

For a moment, they all were still, then Corliss put the half-smoked joint back in his cigarette pack and slipped the pack into his shirt pocket. Mama put a hand on his shoulder. He could scarcely feel its weight.

"Let's show him our surprise," she said to Luther.

"What surprise?" Corliss said.

He followed them out to the root cellar.

The stench of animal waste and wet straw permeated the cellar, making the cool air thick and heavy. Unconsciously, Corliss breathed through his mouth, staring at the creatures huddled together in a makeshift wooden crate, the crate open on the side. They stared back at him, their eyes a faint luminescent yellow in the lantern light. Mama stood on his left, a smile on her thin lips, her hands pinching a ball of bread from the loaf. Luther stood to the right, holding the kerosene lantern up so they could see. Aided by the effects of the Ozark Gold humming in his blood, a sense of unreality rippled through Corliss.

"What the fuck are they," he said, "some kind of monkey?"

"Watch that mouth of your'n," Mama said. "I don't

107

want them pickin' up bad language right out the gate."

He thought about asking how the hell they could pick up bad language, but decided not to get wrapped up in one of Mama's bent notions. "Well, what are they?"

She beamed at him. "It's your pa, and his brothers."

Corliss wet his lips, now feeling for damn sure like he was in a dream, with the cellar a formless, shadowed backdrop and the flickering lantern light shining on the strange animals. Grouped the way they were, with the crate and straw, they looked like the nativity scenes around the churches at Christmas time. He could feel the cellar air creeping inside his clothes too, cold, sticky with moisture. He never did like the cellar, all those things in the jars, and shit, he could only half-see back up under the shelves. Pitch black back there. Had Mama said these things were his pa and uncles?

"Pa," he said, trying to get his mind on what she meant by that. Maybe he misheard her.

"My witchin' brought him back to us, him and the others." She stepped forward and held out her age-spotted hand. The largest of the creatures left the huddle and put its paw out, taking her hand. But, it wasn't a paw. Corliss saw it had four fingers and a thumb, just like a person's. Out in the light more, he saw that fine fuzz grew all over the thing, the color of it hard to pin down, like it was changing. Mama continued. "This is him, Jubal, your pa."

She gave the thing the ball of bread. It took the offering and ate it slowly. Mama tossed more bread to the creatures

108

still in the crate. Corliss watched in fascination as they ate the bread, mouthing it as if it were unfamiliar, sucking their teeth. He noticed they looked at Luther's bucket several times. They had been getting the pig scraps.

"Mama, this—"

"Jessie's the one with the bent ear," she said, pointing into the crate, "and the other one is Uther. Those other two, see how much they look alike? They're Hank and Horace. Hank's the one on the left. You can tell because he squints like he did before."

Corliss stared at the thing holding Mama's hand. He saw right off he was wrong about them being monkeys. They were built more like people, with long legs and feet that would likely fit a pair of shoes, little toes, no monkey thumb sticking out. Small, neat ears lay close to their heads, positioned the same as on people. No hair on them, just that odd fuzz. They were boys, though, had their equipment swinging free, the fuzz growing thicker in the crotch. Their faces were oddly human, with something of the cat in them, maybe around the eyes and mouth. Dress them up, and they would almost pass for people, at least in the dark. As he watched, the thing with Mama changed color. In the crate, the mottled, yellowish hue it had been matched the straw bedding and tawny pine of the surrounding wood. This color now leeched away and became a tricky, shifting pattern of darkness, like moving oil trapped under its skin. The fuzz changed color with the skin.

"Ain't that pretty,' Luther said. He licked his lips. "They do that no matter where you set them. That's special skin it is, real pretty."

Mama said, her voice sharp with warning, "Luther, you quit what you're thinkin'. This here's your pa, and them others is your uncles. You tack jus' one of them to the barn and I'll have *your* hide."

"What are you talkin' about!" Corliss said, his voice loud in the cellar, Mama and his brother standing there talking . . . craziness.

The thing with Mama growled softly, turning its yellow eyes on him, the thing standing a little more than waist high and weighing seventy, maybe eighty pounds. Nothing to fool with, Corliss decided. He'd seen it had a pretty good set of choppers in its mouth and short, sharp-looking claws on its fingertips.

"Now behave, Jubal," Mama said.

The thing retreated to the crate where it resumed its place with the others. They murmured to each other, making little moans and growls, looking at Corliss. Pa's skin, *the thing's* skin, Corliss reminded himself, shimmered, and slowly returned to match the colors of the crate. The damned thing even copycatted the shadows and light where it struck the crate and background.

"I don't b'lieve they like you, Corliss," Luther said.

"Well, fuck them. The feeling's mutual. What the hell you doing with them, anyway? Where'd they come from?"

"I told you about that language," Mama said.

"Mama, they're animals! They cain't understand what we're saying. God-damn. Whyn't you get a TV, watch the *Discovery Channel* once in a while?" He had seen that show while in lock-up, fucking crocodiles dragging full-grown zebras into the water, all that nature shit.

"They's your pa and his brothers, come back from the grave. And they know what's being said."

Luther dug into his bucket and tossed a hunk of raw meat to them. The one Mama wanted to believe was Pa caught it, and then passed it on to one of the others, Horace or Hank, Corliss wasn't sure which.

Horace or—shit! They had him thinking crazy, now.

Luther threw another piece of meat into the crate. The thing Mama called Pa caught it again and passed it down the line to the other twin, the squinty one. Corliss started.

"Damn, those ain't table scraps! That's good beef."

Mama said, "You don't 'spect to feed family hog slop, do you?"

"They ain't family!"

"They eat bread and milk, too," Luther said, setting the bucket at the crate and letting the little bastards dig in on their own. "And taters, and just about anything. But, they like meat the best. Look at 'em go."

The creatures ate noisily, moaning and muttering to each other as if they were having their own little dinner party. Juice from the raw beef stained their chins red.

"Now, mind your manners," Mama said to them.

They looked at her, then resumed their meal, but at a slower pace.

"Don't tell me they understand you," Corliss said, fighting the idea. His buzz was a long way gone now, but he still felt high and a little bit queasy.

"They forgot quite a bit since they been gone," Mama said. "They're like new-borned babies. I got to teach them everything. But it's coming back to them fast."

"All right. Where did you find them?"

"I told you, boy. I witched them back."

"It's true, Corliss," Luther said. "I was with her. We killed a pig and everything. It was while you were off to jail. Mama had the r'tual, and a little while later, I found them in the lake, all bundled up like frog eggs."

A thought struggled in the back of Corliss's mind. "In the lake, you say?"

"Over by that willow pool. They was a metal thing there, too, looked like some kind of alien spaceship or something, but it's gone now."

"A space ship, huh?" In his mind's eye, Corliss was with that science guy again in the moonlight, the bulky metal tank behind him making the boat ride low in the water, dangerous low, the guy chewing him out, saying he should have gotten a bigger boat, Corliss saying, shit, he didn't know the thing would be the size of a fucking Volkswagon.

He saw the boat sinking then, taking the screaming science guy, the container, and the sweet five-thousand-dollar deal with it.

Luther was looking at him, nodding, saying, "Yep, a space ship."

Corliss looked at the creatures eating. "Is that strange little dude still on the lake, the one was here before I got busted for smackin' that loudmouth?"

"Yep," Luther said. "He takes that yacht of his around the lake a couple of times a week. He stays over to the Prescott's now."

Corliss turned. "Is that right?"

6

August 25

Looking out his cabin window at the lake sparkling in the morning sun, Lee forgot he was supposed to be writing, his mind circling back to Sydney. Her sprained ankle was almost healed, but she was too quiet, the incident in the woods still on her mind. It hurt him to see her like that, the psychological wound affecting her worse than the physical one. It bothered him Corless Creed was unpunished.

And then, there was the Dr. Kane and Jessica situation to consider.

He had spoken with Red last night about it all, telling him how he thought Jessica's and Dr. Kane's story about developing a new sonar system did not seem quite right somehow; Red coming back with, "That's all you got on your mind? What about Corliss and that trap? Been a week now an' he's still free as a daisy."

"I haven't forgotten him. I told you what Sheriff Gordon said."

Sheriff Gordon thought it would do no good to press charges, no way to prove the Creeds had set the traps or hold Corliss on a parole violation. Anyway, Corliss had vanished, not seen since the incident. That was okay, though, his time would come.

Red's response: Not damn near soon enough.

All right, Mr. Redmond, consider this: Sheriff Gordon said Dr. Peter Fraily was a potential murder victim. The coroner had found evidence of blunt trauma to the head. Also, Greenbough Energy won't comment on Fraily's death, and Prescott Scientific claims they did not have a "Dr. Kane" in their directory.

Red: Forget it, man, and pass me another beer. That's the corporate way, clam up like that. Find Corliss, bust his ass. That's what you want to do.

Staring out the window now, wondering where to find Corliss, find him before the freaking snow flies. Summer was winding down fast, yeah, with two strangers coasting up to the dock in a bass boat.

Damn.

Lee picked up the big Nikon zoom.

One of the strangers was tall and heavy, the first telltale layer of middle-age flab swelling around his waist, some flecks of gray in his close-cropped black hair and mustache. Red nylon shorts, tan fishing vest, and white canvas sneakers. An olive drab boonie hat shaded the man's eyes, eyes hiding behind polarized sunglasses. Despite the man's fishing outfit, his skin had the appearance of a golf course tan rather than a one gained from the open water. His friend, dressed in a similar manner, was smaller, leaner, and moved with a light step, handling the boat lines.

Lee put down the camera. He had noticed too, that Dr. Kane's houseboat was not anchored off the dock, the doctor out supposedly testing his secret project.

By the time he reached the stone steps to the dock, the strangers had just finished tying off their boat, a green Ranger. They waited, seeing Lee coming down. Under his fishing vest, the big man's blue tee shirt read, "Bait my ass, that's my catch" and had a cartoon man holding up a fishing rod with a dangling minnow attached. The smaller guy had a crooked nose dabbed with white sun block, a black ball cap on his head with SOX on the front, the guy a Chicago White Sox fan. They stood on the dock wearing their dark sunglasses.

Lee stopped a few feet away from them, saying good morning. He glanced into the boat. Nothing out of the ordinary there, a cooler and some fishing rods.

The big man took the briefest moment to size-up Lee before stepping forward and extending his hand. "Good morning, I'm Howard Gardner."

He would have sung in the bass section. His hand was soft but strong. This guy, Lee decided, was not just a walk-on character. The folksy fishing attire did not hide the underlying sense of authority about the man. Lee thought he might be a police officer or other professional used to dealing with people. Then too, he might be a player, one of Jessica's industrial spies.

"Lee Picket," he said, dropping the man's hand. "I

work security here."

"Great. This is my colleague Bill Stokes."

The smaller man touched the bill of his SOX cap and said, "Security?"

"Yes. Look, Mr. Gardner, you've caught me at a bad time. I don't mean to be blunt, but I'm in a hurry. Do you have business here?" He wanted to get rid of these two, fast.

"We're down from Kansas City, doing a little fishing this weekend, and I'd heard about Jessica Prescott's lodge through contacts at work. I thought I'd drop by and look it over." He grinned, showing some teeth. "From time to time I'm responsible for setting up corporate training and retreats. I thought this place might be a suitable location for a future event. Is Ms. Prescott here?"

Jessica's MG was still in the little parking lot up at the lodge, but these guys did not need to know that.

"It's a bad time for visitors," Lee said. "You want to call Sydney Tatum to see about any business arrangements. You have something to write with? I'll give you the number."

"Hey, it won't take a minute just to look around," Howard Gardner said. "That way I won't waste my time or Ms. Tatum's coming down to look at a facility that may not be suitable. Really, just a quick look is all I need."

Strange, the guy knowing Sydney was a woman. About a fifty-fifty chance of that at best, if he was guessing. "What company did you say you were with?"

"Universal Traders," Bill Stokes said. "It's a trading conglomerate. We contract some of our needs with Prescott Scientific Solutions."

"I'll let Ms. Tatum know you stopped by. But, unfortunately, there are no visitors allowed on the property at this time."

"Sounds serious." Howard Gardner gave him a wide grin, teeth shining under the mustache. "Really, I won't be a minute, no trouble at all."

"Mr. Gardner, do you mind if I see some identification? Your driver's license will do."

Gardner and Stokes looked at each other briefly, their eyes hidden behind dark lenses. Lee was beginning not to like these two at all, that intimate polarized glance adding a creep-factor to them.

"I don't believe this," Gardner said, the bonhomie fading from his voice. "I'm just asking about some business arrangements. What's going on here?"

"You know," Lee said, "I think it best that you leave now."

For a moment, the man stared at him, the anonymous dark glass in his shades giving him a vaguely insect-like appearance, and then he turned, motioned to Stokes who released the boat's stern line from the dock cleat without a word. Gardner started for the bowline.

Lee said, "I'll get that."

Gardner shrugged. He stepped from the dock to his boat, stumbling a bit as he landed, perhaps not familiar with the craft. Stokes dropped into the boat as easily as a cat. Lee untied the bowline and tossed it into the boat. Gardner started the motor. Stokes settled himself in a seat, staring across the lake as if he had already lost interest in the situation.

"This is a hell of a way to run a business," Gardner said, pushing the boat from the dock.

"It's not a business. I think you know that."

Gardner shook his head and shoved the throttle forward, roaring away from the dock in a boil of blue and white water, his wake rocking the pontoon boat and Bayliner in their slips. Lee watched the man adjust his course toward New Le Beau. He waved when Stokes looked back, the sun block like a white rose petal stuck on his crooked nose.

"Universal Traders, my ass," Lee said.

He leaned on the rail, checking the blue sky, the water—and remembered the houseboat was missing. Dr. Kane was supposed to let him know when he would be out.

Lee took the steps up two at a time. He needed to find Red.

***

He could do her, Corliss decided, standing on Jessica Prescott's houseboat in the shade of the blue canvas canopy. Yeah, looking at those legs with that salon tan, he could do her, but he'd have to stuff a rag in her mouth. Jesus, what a yapping bitch. Their little meeting, all he was trying to do was get his share of the pie, these people looking for the mystery container they'd stolen and didn't want to share now. Shit, you'd think he'd held them up for a million bucks instead of the twenty-thou he was asking. But, no, little Miss Bitch Mouth was getting herself all in a lather, cutting into him with words he didn't even understand but judging by her tone weren't complementary. He spit a stream of brown tobacco juice over the side of the boat and took a step toward her.

"You want to be more respectful, Miss Prescott," he said, looking straight into her eyes and meeting her go-to-hell blaze. "There's more things can happen to you than just getting busted by the law."

That got her. He liked the way fear shimmered—just for second—in her eyes. Yeah, he was getting to her. He could smell her sweat.

Dr. Kane said, "There's no need for threats. But, twenty-thousand dollars is . . . you know . . . *too* much. We simply don't have that kind of money. I'm sure Dr. Fraily did not offer you that much."

"Oh?" He had them talking deal. Couple of soft shells here, breathe on 'em hard and they crack. "This is a new

120

sich-iation. Miss Prescott here, prob'ly has that much in her underwear drawer. Ain't that right, Sweetpants?"

"As you said, Mr. Creed, I think a little more respect is needed all around." She looked at the old man, the doc looking concerned inside his print shirt. A level tone replaced the ice in her voice. "I don't think the amount is out-of-line, provided he helps find the project."

"If you, ah, think so, Jessica."

"Yeah," Corliss said, "I can help. I know just where it's at."

He could not believe it. They were going to go the full amount. They must be in a world of buzzard puke for sure, pay that kind of coin. Maybe he wasn't asking enough. He worked the cud of tobacco over to his right jaw, rolling it with his tongue and clamping it there, squeezing some juice out for a spit. Yeah, he'd get the twenty first, and then pinch them for more. He spat and pulled the tip of his white straw cowboy lower on his forehead.

The Prescott bitch was staring at him. Wrinkled sunlight reflected off the water and danced on the canopy over her head in fractured white slashes.

"That's good," she said, and crossed her arms under her tits, bunching them up against the deep blue cotton tank top she wore, her seamless tan flowing over her flesh and plunging with mouth-watering smoothness into her cleavage.

Corliss felt the snake stir in his britches. Yes, by God, he could—

"But it's got to be worth it," she said. "If you don't produce, you don't get paid."

"I can take you where it is, right now."

The old man stepped forward. "Where?"

"Contain yourself, Doc. Damn. We'll get there." The old dude getting himself all excited, sportin' a woody for the thing. That was good, though.

Prescott's hands were on her hips now, balled into fists. "Before we go any further, I want to know exactly what happened that night, what happened to Fraily, and how the project was lost in the lake."

The *Project*. It was a fucking barrel on skids, some extra science gear stuck on it. Educated people couldn't call a spade a spade.

"I'll tell you how. Something or another went wrong, switches or something got flicked while we was moving it." The memory was still strong: the moonlit lake, his old runabout tied behind the scientist's big houseboat, the container's weight making them ride way low in the water. Hell, *he'd* flicked the switches, just playin' around, jerkin' the guy's chain. "He opened a door on it and then started screamin'."

The old man looked at Prescott, his thick eyebrows raised over his eyeglasses. His voice was hushed. "He must have accidentally activated the nanite cell."

Corliss spat over the side. "Yeah. That's what *he* said.

Anyway, he's slappin' at his hands, then starts on his face, rippin' at it like a mad man." *Then he staggered back, screaming for help, his face coming off, dissolving in little bits and pieces, the sinews and bone showing white in the moonlight.* Corliss felt the fear again and the impact of the paddle as he hit the guy, scared of what was eating at him, then hitting him again when he reached out for him. "Something was on his face, eating it away. He was stumblin' around. We was low in the water. 'Fore I knew what was happening, we was sinking. That container thing of yours must weigh a good ton. It took my boat down like a stone."

"Five-hundred-sixty kilograms."

"Hunh?

"The container, the *tank*. It weighs approximately five-hundred and sixty kilograms, fully loaded, about twelve-hundred pounds."

"Well, it was fuckin' heavy. That's my point."

"What happened to Fraily?" Prescott asked. She had taken a step closer to him, her eyes fixed on his.

"That's it. He got himself tangled in somethin' or another and went down, too. I never seen him again." She kept looking at him, as if she wanted more, or did not believe him. "I swum back to shore and had me a good toke and a nice long pull at the bottle. What was in that thing, anyhow, to eat a man up that way?"

The old man said, "It was, ah, a type of acid."

"Damn sure works."

A boat came around the point, heading for them, white water curling away from its bow in a brilliant "V." Corliss nodded at it and spat over the side again. "Ain't that your Bayliner?"

*   *   *

At the houseboat, Lee tied off the Bayliner in silence, Jessica and Dr. Kane watching him, waiting in the canopy's shade. Their silence told him he had come at a bad time, interrupting some type of private business, just the opposite reception he had expected with Corliss Creed onboard. Creed stood by the far rail, staring over the lake, his shaggy hair in his eyes under his crumpled cowboy hat, a lump of tobacco knotting his jaw. Lee climbed over the houseboat's handrail. Red started to follow him, but Jessica stopped him.

"That's okay, Red. Mr. Picket won't be staying long."

"You know you're in bad company," Lee said, nodding at Corliss who glowered at him.

Jessica made a dismissive gesture. "Mr. Creed just dropped by to apologize for Ms. Tatum's unfortunate accident."

"What?" Corliss said.

"That was no accident," Lee said.

"Well," Jessica said, coming nearer, "he apologized. That's what counts."

"I doubt Corliss is prone to attacks of conscience," Lee said. "So, what's the program here?"

Jessica took his arm and tried to guide him back to the rail. Lee did not budge. His arm was rigid under her hand.

"I need an answer," he said.

Jessica recoiled. Her mouth worked open and shut twice before she found the words. "This is my boat! I say who goes and who stays. It just doesn't pay to be civil with you, does it? Get off my boat, *Mister* Picket."

"Sure." Lee nodded at Corliss. "As soon as he does."

Corliss spat into the lake, his glance skimming over Red in the Bayliner. He turned his empty black eyes on Lee. "I got me an invite, boy."

Lee noticed Corliss had his hunting knife in a belt sheath.

Suddenly, Jessica was all Lee could see. She pressed close to him. He moved back to keep her breasts from touching his chest, wanting to keep the distance from her. Her voice was low, repressed emotion forcing her words through clenched flawless teeth.

"Lee, please go. I know what I'm doing. You can only make things worse."

"The man's a sociopath. I don't want him near you or

Dr. Kane."

Corliss snorted. "Soci-o-path. Listen to him."

"I can handle him." Jessica touched Lee's arm. "I'll explain later, okay?"

She seemed sincere. This was the first time Jessica had been anything but arrogant or patronizing with him. Lee looked at her. "Well—"

"Whyn't you do that, boy?" Corliss said. "Run along like the little woman says. Go play hide-the-weasel with that girlfriend of yours and relax. I ain't gonna trouble you none. Leastwise, not for a while."

"Corliss," Lee said, "you're just not real bright, are you?"

"What? Her ankle not up to a little hump an' bump yet? Shit, man. Just tie it up out of your way, truss her up like a hog." He grinned. "Some of 'em even like it like that."

Lee eased Jessica aside. Here was the man responsible for injuring Sydney now laughing about it. He tried hard to keep the smile on his face, hoping it was disarming enough to conceal the anger he felt rising within him like hot smoke. Corliss moved from the rail and stood with his left foot forward, his arms loose, getting ready for action. Lee held his hands out in supplication. The trick was to get the man's knife out of the way before he could use it.

"Don't jump, man. I guess Jessica's right. It's her boat and her business." Lee extended his right hand. "Look, it's my job. You understand."

Corliss did not offer his hand, but relaxed his guard in surprise just enough for the police capture maneuver to work. Lee stepped beside him, fast, and slipped his arm between Corliss's arm and side. Turning behind him, he trapped the man's arm against his own back. With his free hand, he pulled Corliss's hunting knife from its sheath and flung it into the lake, then reached over Corliss's head, knocking off the cowboy hat, and hooked two fingers deep into the man's nostrils. He yanked back hard to show he offered no mercy, the leverage lifting Corliss onto his toes and bending his back. With his head pulled back at the extreme angle and his arm locked between his back and Lee's chest, Corliss was helpless. Heat lanced through Lee's injured back as he took the man's solid weight. He ignored it.

Corliss Creed stank of stale sweat, testosterone, and wet tobacco. The stench coated Lee's nostrils like oil.

"I have had enough of you," he said, and kept a strain on Corliss's nose, which was slimy with snot. "You're going to get in your boat and go. Got it?"

Corliss breathed noisily through his mouth. He coughed out a word that Lee decided to take as an affirmation.

"Good." He leaned close and whispered so only Corliss could hear. "I'm done playing. You understand that?"

"Fuck you, man." Clear as a bell.

Lee pulled hard; he felt cartilage snap in the man's nose. "Get in your boat."

He released Corliss without warning and stepped back. Corliss turned, holding his nose with his good hand. Trickles of blood seeped through his fingers. He shook the arm Lee had pinned. He took a step forward, black lightening flashing in his eyes.

Lee shifted his feet, kept his hands ready to block and punch. "Do something stupid, Creed."

"Lee!" Jessica was behind him, alarm in her voice.

"It's up to him," he said, keeping his eyes on Corliss. He was sure he could take him. There was a scuffling noise behind him as Red climbed aboard the houseboat.

"Let's all stay calm, now." Dr. Kane inched forward, moving into the far corner of Lee's vision. "There is no need for violence."

Slowly, Corliss reached down and retrieved his battered hat. Drops of blood splattered on the deck. He placed the hat on his head, tilting the brim low over his eyes. He reached up slow and wiped the blood and snot from his nose, cleaning his fingers on his jeans.

Lee nodded toward Corliss's stinking Johnboat, dead minnows sloshing in the open bait well. "Let's go."

"Lee, stop it." Jessica was beside him now, touching his arm.

Corliss moved with care toward the rail, watching Lee.

He opened the rail gate and stepped down into his boat. Lee stepped closer, watching.

Corliss looked up at him, his eyes shaded by shaggy hair and his dirty white hat. "You owe me a knife, boy."

"Just go, Corliss."

Corliss turned and yanked on the starter cord of the small outboard engine, ripping it three times before it caught and the engine burbled to life. He untied the bowline and cut the tiller away from the houseboat. The boat crawled away toward the open water.

Lee turned, feeling the adrenalin dissipate and leave him weak. His back ached. Dr. Kane and Jessica stood looking at him, their expressions neutral. Red was grinning.

"That," Lee said, "was for Sydney."

***

Celia thought she had never seen her daughter so angry, Jessica calling this impromptu meeting because Lee Picket's spying had gotten under her skin. Apparently, Lee had given Corliss Creed his due today.

"He's crazy, Mother." Jessica stood in front of Celia's business table, a half-empty gin and tonic in her hand. The ice cubes clinked against the glass as she gestured erratically. "There is no excuse for what he did this afternoon."

Celia looked at Lee. He sat on the couch nearby, his arms spread across the top cushions, his legs splayed, relaxing at the cocktail hour. If Jessica's accusations bothered him, it did not show. She looked back at her daughter, still trying to sort it out, what had happened on the lake with Corliss Creed.

"I still don't understand why Corliss was with you on the boat. You said he wanted to apologize for trapping Sydney, so you let him onboard? Really, Jess, that wasn't very smart, knowing his reputation."

Lee took a sip from his beer and sat it back on its coaster. "I think there's more to it than that," he said.

"How dare you!" Jessica swung toward him.

"Stop it!" Celia turned to Lee. "You had better explain yourself."

"When Red and I got there, they were as cozy as a box of kittens, all three of them." He leaned forward. "I don't see conspiracies behind every bush, but I know one when I see it. It's in the body language, in the tone of voice, and in the lack of eye contact. I've seen it a hundred times on the street, in drug deals going down. They were up to something very private."

"Jessica?"

"He's paranoid, Mother, and violent. He has manhandled me, and now a guest onboard my boat. You've hired a maniac. How much more proof do you need?"

Celia looked at Lee. Were his eyes glassy? She wondered if that was his first beer of the evening, and if perhaps there was some truth to her daughter's accusations. The man shrugged.

"Some guest," Lee said. "Men like Creed understand one language—violence. He has to believe I'll go to the mat with him, every time. If he doesn't, then he will continue to do as he damn well pleases. No, this afternoon had the all earmarks of a deal going down."

Jessica took a gulp of her drink. "You're delusional."

Celia pushed the control lever on her wheelchair, coming away from the table and rolling to a smooth stop between the two combatants. "Lee," she said, "I believe you are right. However, I find your tactics unsettling. Please, no more wrestling people about."

"Sure."

Closer now, she noticed his eyes *were* glassy, the pupils black dots rimmed with brown. Still, she felt a breath of sympathy for him, knowing his past. She turned to Jessica, who had returned to her seat at the table.

"And you," Celia said, "what have you gotten yourself into? I want answers, right now."

"I'm a grown woman. You can't talk to me like that. I—"

"Jessica," Lee said, "that spy showed up this morning.

He asked about you."

The color faded from Jessica's face. "What?"

"I'm pretty sure it was the same guy at the city dock last week, asking Red about you and Celia, and the lodge. This morning he stopped at our dock, tried to bluff his way into the lodge, pretending to be a fisherman. He said he'd heard about the lodge through business contacts in Kansas City, and he might want to use it for training seminars. He was lying, too."

Jessica's hand shook as she put down her drink. "What did he look like?"

"Late thirties, black hair and mustache, clean fingernails, a corporate type."

Celia said, "Do you know him?"

Jessica shook her head. "He must be a spy. He must be trying to find Dr. Kane and his project."

"Corporate spies make you turn pale, do they?" Lee winced as he sat back, spreading his arms along the couch again.

"I've had a rough day. I'm not used to being around a violent madman, and I mean you, if you are too drunk to work that out for yourself."

"All right!" Celia slapped the arm of her wheelchair. "Stop this bickering."

Jessica frowned at her drink, holding it with both hands

if it might escape. Lee took a sip of his beer and studied the opposite wall.

"Are you going to tell us why you and Dr. Kane are involved with Corliss Creed? Does it have something to do with your project or the man on the dock?"

Jessica remained silent, staring into her glass. Her fingers turned the glass around its axis.

Celia said, "Jess?"

"I need time to think." She looked at Celia. "I need to talk to Dr. Kane. This . . . spy showing up may change things."

"That," Lee said, "is a good idea. Why don't we all talk to Dr. Kane. I'd like to find out more about him. I'd like to ask him about the radio gear he keeps on the boat. Why would a sonar experiment need that?"

Jessica stared at him.

"What else I'd like to know, is his real name, and if he knows anything about piranha or alligators in the lake."

"What?"

"You've heard the rumors? Liz Jordan's latest article reports another bite victim in the hospital."

"You are crazy. And, Kane is his real name."

"Unh-huh."

Lee left the couch and went to the table. Celia noticed he moved with care, and eased himself into the chair beside Jessica as if his lower back hurt. He leaned close to Jessica, his voice low and gentle. "Enough cat-and-mouse. I know all about Dr. Peter Fraily, but I'd like to hear it from you. How, exactly, did he wind up in the lake? Was it you or Corliss who knocked him in the head?"

Jessica's eyes widened. "Oh, God."

"I'm sure *He* knows, but your mother and I don't. Why don't you tell us about it?"

***

Luther followed the faint blood trail across the bridge from his family's island and into the Prescott Sanctuary, not sure just what he was tracking. The ground around the barn had been too dry and hard to find a set of prints, so the only clues left were the occasional bent weed and drops of blood that were getting few and far between. There had been a struggle, for sure, one of the wire hog panels on the farrowing pen was tore loose and bent-up, and the old sow had been bleeding from a dozen deep scratches around her head and shoulders. He paused on the other side of the bridge, looking for the next sign, and found it, another drop of blood on a stone in the middle of the road, like a small red bead sitting on a plate. A thrill of fear shot through his heart.

Maybe the ghosts came and got the piglets.

He shook his head. No, that could not be right. It had to be a bear, or maybe a panther. Southern Missouri had a few black bears, and though he had not seen cougar sign in several years, one could show up at any time.

But, three piglets? How could a bear or cougar make off with three twenty-pound piglets? Ever what it was, it traveled without leaving a sign. Luther felt his neck hairs rise. It was a spooky thing, the critter that took them.

He crept forward, feeling the ground under his bare feet before putting his weight down, moving twigs aside with his toes when he needed. The woods whispered around him, the collective voice of leaves rustling in the treetops, the occasional creak of a branch, and all around, the cicada bugs droning away. Every once in a while, a tree frog would start-up. Yet, as he got further down the road, Luther sensed a dead spot ahead, a void in the musical fabric. He pulled his skinning knife, wishing now he would have brought his rifle. The killer, he knew, would be in the center of the dead spot.

He left the road and eased through the sparse undergrowth, crouching low. He just wanted to get a peek at the culprit, and then he would know what kind of trap to set.

As slow as darkness, he moved through the trees, their leaves and trunks spackled gold by the rays of the declining sun. It took him twenty minutes to move as many yards, doubling back to the ghost road. Through a last screen of sassafras saplings, he heard little grunts and lip smacking punctuated by wet, tearing sounds. Luther parted the leaves.

The Cats, as he thought of his new family members, were sitting in a loose group, all five of them, devouring their kills. Their skins were patterned and colored with browns, greens, and grays, matching the old roadbed beneath them. If they had not been moving, Luther might have had trouble spotting them. Sometimes he wished they had taken to the clothes Mama had wanted them to wear. They were hard to see when they took a notion, and he suspected it was a game to them, to see how close they could come to being stepped-on before someone noticed them. The one named Jubal (who was *not* his Pa, no matter what Mama said), had his own piglet. Uther and Jessie shared one, as did Horace and Hank, Horace getting the head and shoulders, Hank getting the hind-end.

Luther stepped from cover, sheathing his knife. The Cats jumped and turned, their arms out for action, their hard fingernails red and dripping. They all growled in surprise.

"I cain't b'lieve it's you," Luther said, relief and puzzlement sweeping through him. "Don't you'ens get enough at dinner? Y' ain't got to go killin' piglets."

The Cats stared at him, and then relaxed. Jessie, Horace, and Hank went back to their meal. Uther pulled the entrails out of his piglet and appeared to study them. Jubal put his piglet down and watched Luther.

Luther came forward.

"Oh, Mama's going to be mad. She ain't gonna like this, not a bit."

Jubal came over to Luther, his golden eyes unreadable.

He stopped in front of Luther, almost able now to look him in the eye. All of the Cats had done a good spate of growing.

Jubal took his hand. Luther felt hard muscle and tendons under soft calluses. Jubal's skin tone shifted. Luther loved to watch that, as if the skin was a critter all to itself. The mottled earth tones ebbed to gray, then to a faded blue, reminding Luther of the denim overalls he was wearing. In fact, as he watched, Jubal's skin mimicked the overalls, the straps over the shoulders, and the green patch on the one knee. Luther's mouth fell open. A skin tone that matched his covered the Cat's arms, neck and face, mirroring his own appearance.

"Hey," Luther said, "that's a good trick. When did you learn that?"

Jubal stared at him. His golden eyes never left Luther's face. Horace and Hank tossed the remains of their feast into the brush. Jessie kept eating. Uther stopped studying his piglet and listened, watching Jubal and Luther.

Jubal tugged at Luther's hand and pointed to his half-eaten piglet. He squeezed Luther's hand, just ever so slightly. Maybe it was the flesh tone Jubal wore now, making him seem more human, but Luther thought he had seen that same look on Corliss's face about a hundred times when they were kids, and a few once they had grown up, Corliss warning him not to tell—or *else*.

Luther took his hand from Jubal, feeling stickiness from the drying blood. He shook his head.

"I guess I won't be tellin' Mama."

Jubal stroked Luther's arm, still gazing into his face.

***

"My real name is Chilson, Dr. Montgomery Chilson."

It was nearly nine o'clock at night. Celia had drawn the curtains against the night and any prying eyes that might be floating offshore. They sat around the table in Celia's apartment, Lee, Jessica, and Celia, listening to Dr. Kane's confession. Lee silently congratulated himself on maneuvering Jessica and the good doctor to this point.

Dr. Chilson removed his eyeglasses and polished the lenses on his shirttail. He put them back on and clasped his hands on the table. "I work for Prescott Scientific Solutions. For the past six years, I have been working as a contractor on a secret project for the Biological Division of Greenbough Energy."

"How secret?" Lee said.

Dr. Chilson looked at him over his glasses. "Very secret."

"He has trouble with that 'secret' concept," Jessica said.

"Jessica," Celia said, "try not to be yourself."

"Prescott Scientific, that is, Douglas, your husband, and I, designed the instruments and machines for the project. He and I were old acquaintances, professionally speaking." Dr. Chilson looked at Celia. "His passing saddened me."

Celia nodded.

Dr. Chilson continued. "Greenbough decided to take the project in a new direction, one Douglas and I thought inappropriate. We began planning a way to remove the project from Greenbough's control. Then, Douglas died. When I began to suspect my days with the project were growing short, I approached Dr. Peter Fraily, the Assistant Director of Biological Research at Greenbough, with the idea of stealing the prototype. I knew him to be unhappy— he had heard rumors they were replacing him soon—and needed his help and brilliant mind. I agreed he could sell off small bits of the technology to the private sector, provided he was discreet. With Jessica's help, we planned the, ah . . . *acquisition.*"

"Wait," Lee said. "I missed the part where Jessica became involved."

"Dr. Chilson and Fraily approached me after Father's death," Jessica said, "and told me of their plans with him. About that time, Greenbough filed a patent suit for many of the Prescott designs and informed us our contract would not be renewed. So, I decided to steal the program and prototype. It is what Father wanted, and he was wise to risk it."

"You keep talking around it," Lee said. "Secret

prototype of what?"

"Yes, what is it, Jess? We must know if we are to help you."

Jessica glanced at Dr. Chilson, and then back at Lee and Celia. "It is a new bio-fuel process, one that has the potential to end U.S. foreign oil dependency."

"That's a big one," Lee said. "How does it work?"

"Oh, I'm sorry, Lee," Jessica said. "It's that pesky secret thing again."

"Okay. So you stole this pesky secret thing because that's what Dad wanted, not for fun and profit?"

"My father developed the technologies with the understanding that once Greenbough had recouped its investment costs, they would share in the profits. As the project neared completion, it became obvious Greenbough had other intentions." Jessica looked at her mother. "I think the accident that killed Father and nearly killed you was not an accident at all. That is my final motivation. Greenbough will never get the project back as long as I am able to stop them."

"Jessica!" Celia placed a hand at her throat.

"So," Lee said, "you did all this to spit in the dragon's face."

"If you say so."

Dr. Chilson said, continuing as if his narrative had not

been detoured, "But things went wrong. People were killed at the lab. The explosion there was an accident. We came to the lake with the prototype intending to hide here until we could leave the country. However, Peter, according to our Mr. Creed, attempted a double cross. I imagine Peter found Creed in a bar, someone to help him move the prototype process tank."

The little old man stopped, lost in thought, staring into space. Lee tried to prompt him. "So, after you killed all the project scientists and the double-cross went bad, Fraily . . .?"

"*Fraily* set the explosion," Jessica said. "Let's get that straight."

"Of course. What happened with Fraily?"

"Apparently," Jessica said, her tone glacial, "there was an accident while he and Corliss were loading the process tank onto another boat, stealing it from us while Dr. Chilson was ashore on an errand. Fraily drowned, and the tank was lost in the lake. Now, Corliss says he has the tank."

"And he wants money," Lee added.

Jessica nodded.

"How did he find it, if this thing sank in deep water?"

"I borrowed an amphibious robot, a rover, to find and retrieve the process tank."

"I'm getting lost here," Lee said. "An amphibious robot. Huh. And you borrowed this from . . . ?"

"Prescott Scientific. Oh, don't look surprised, Mother. The stakes are more than you can imagine. Besides, we own the damned thing, and the project was mothballed after we lost the grant and contract to Honeywell."

"I'm sure your shareholders would approve," Lee said.

Celia settled back in her wheelchair. "Go on, then."

"Well, that's it. The rover found the tank but we lost its radio signal. Corliss, somehow, found them."

"Or," Lee said, "he's trying to make you think he did."

Jessica looked at him, her eyes empty of reaction. "Perhaps."

"I believe the rover's communication system was damaged," said Dr. Chilson. "I have received several signals since we lost contact, but they have been weak and momentary."

"Radio doesn't work underwater, Doctor."

"Low frequency radio functions through water. However, the rover deploys a retrievable float. This float does double duty as a radio antenna and a solar charger."

"Oh."

"The rover is itself a prototype," Jessica said. "It has operational issues as such. We cannot rely on another GPS transmission. So, it is imperative we deal with Corliss Creed. The men you spoke with on the dock may be Greenbough operatives. The moment they have proof that the tank is here, they will send in a recovery and clean-up team. The only reason I took the doctor with me today was to keep Corliss from pulling anything."

"I meant to ask you," Lee said. "How did Corliss contact you?"

"He approached me in town. I was standing by the drugstore waiting for the light to change. Corliss steps up from behind me and says, 'Want to buy a robot?' Then he asks if I want to know what happened to my partner, and tells me to meet him on the lake, in that cove."

"This is incredible," Celia said.

Lee nodded. "Interesting. A clean-up team? Is that what it sounds like?"

"Dr. Chilson and I, once I am implicated, are potential risks to Greenbough's plans. They will not let us live."

"Jessica!" Celia reached toward her daughter. "Are you serious?"

"Unfortunately," Dr. Chilson said, "she is correct. Under their present leadership, Greenbough will stop at nothing to recapture and protect this project."

"How dramatic," Lee said.

Jessica looked at him. "I am sure they killed Father. And, we have betrayed them. Global Contractors is the enforcement arm of the company. You've heard of them?"

The name sounded vaguely familiar to Lee, from the

nightly news, maybe. "Para military outfit, works in the Mid-East?"

"And now, Africa. They have contracts with several governments."

"My God," Celia said, "What have you gotten yourself into, Jessica?"

"Don't be too upset, Celia," Lee said. "This fairytale has enough holes in it to make a tuna net."

"I am not sure," she said.

"Believe me, Mother. It all happened. Dr. Chilson and I need to find the process tank if we can, and get out of the country."

For a moment, no one spoke, and then Lee sat back, looking at Dr. Chilson. "You keep talking about prototypes. How about some details, so I know what it is we're dealing with."

"The tank," Jessica said, "is self-explanatory, as is the amphibious robot. At least, to most people it would be."

Dr. Chilson spoke quickly. "The algae samples cell resembles a large, insulated tank resting horizontally on skids, or rails. One end houses the battery compartment, nutrient cells, environmental pods, and other process devices."

"Even you couldn't miss it," Jessica said.

"Heavy?" Lee asked, ignoring her.

"Yes. The hold is flooded with a fluid cushion."

"The reason it sank."

Dr. Chilson opened a notebook in front of him and passed a manual to Lee. "As far as the rover is concerned, this summary should answer your questions."

Lee flipped the manual open, but stopped on the first illustration he saw. He had been expecting some kind of wheeled or tracked vehicle, a blocky, cumbersome thing. Prescott Scientific's amphibious robotic rover, designed for utility service along coastal regions, was streamlined, had legs, and looked like a black lizard. It was constructed in segments of various sizes.

Flipping the pages, he stopped and studied a section briefly. *Length*: twelve feet, 3 inches. *Weight*: 1,236 pounds. Heavy, most of it batteries, Lee thought. Buoyancy foam lined its aluminum skin like a layer of fat and ballast tanks to let it sink or rise. Strong legs served by independent motors raised the belly sections, the main battery housings, off the ground.

"It was modeled after a salamander," Dr. Chilson said. "Like its biological models, the rover's legs fold to its sides when it is in swim mode. It is shorter, now. I removed most of the tail to accommodate a snatch-hook to retrieve the process tank. The modification means the swim mode is lost to us."

"So," Lee said, "how does it get around?"

"The rover has been dragging it along the lake

bottom to a secluded take out point."

"You must have known it would take a long time to retrieve the tank that way," Lee said. "Why didn't you just get a diver to attach a rope and wench it up when you found it?"

"Jesus!" Jessica said. "It's secret! And besides, the doctor and I needed the robot to help load the tank into a truck, take it to a chartered plane."

Celia looked at Lee, her eyes questioning. He shook his head.

"They're not telling us everything. I don't like it."

"I think she's told us enough."

Lee shrugged and looked at Jessica. "She's the boss. Make your arrangements with Corliss Creed. But, I'm in on every detail, yes?"

Jessica's gaze remained cool. "Of course."

7

August 26

Lee made a cast sitting in the deck chair, glad Sydney had come down to the dock, taking his mind off Corliss Creed, robots, and bio-fuel after a long day of getting nowhere with any of it. Leaning on one of the dock pilings, Sydney watched the lure arc over the water and land far out in the lake with a minute splash. Her legs were long coming out of the tan cargo shorts she wore. A fading yellow bruise showed under the strap of her dainty sandal, her ankle finally pain free now. Lee leaned back and worked the lure into the dock slowly, the action automatic to him.

Dusk softened the air and tinted the sky with purple hues. In the distant southwest, the sun's last rays shone on the tops of a line of thunderheads, illuminating them with brilliant, glowing light, giving them life, like cloud giants marching on the far horizon. He stared at the phenomenon, lost in the distance and beauty. As he watched, the light grew dim, dulling the clouds from white to blue. His lure came out of the water, dripping and unharmed. He stared at it, his mind still in the clouds, looking for answers.

"That was beautiful," Sydney said.

"What?"

"The sky. What just happened."

"Oh. Sure. Every once in a while you see it, that backlighting effect." He made another cast, giving the lure one more chance.

Sydney turned toward him, still leaning on the piling, giving him a better view of her charms, charms he was starting to covet more and more these days. She had a way of making him feel good no matter how crappy his day was; she could take away the sting.

"You seem distracted," she said. "Want me to go?"

"No. It's just that I have a lot on my mind." Should he get involved with her or not? If it didn't work out, staying at the lodge would be awkward. "The Creeds. My writing."

And stolen bio-fuel secrets and ruthless multi-national corporations.

She moved around behind him. He felt her fingers on his neck and the top of his shoulders, probing. Her scent, light and compelling, distracted him.

"You're very tense," she said. "Why don't you relax for a minute?" She began kneading his neck, her fingers surprisingly strong, dissolving the tension he had not known was there.

"Oh," he said, wondering if her gesture was simple compassion or if she had other intentions.

"When I started college, I thought I wanted to be a physical therapist. Massage was the fun class."

He closed his eyes and let the rod and reel idle, let the lure take care of itself out there. Sydney pinched, squeezed, and prodded, her nimble fingers ferreting out every bit of torque in his shoulders and neck.

"And, after college?"

Sydney remained quiet for a moment, and then said, "Let's just say I'm one of Celia's projects. Two years in a bad marriage, domestic abuse."

"I'm sorry to hear that."

"I've been three years with Celia."

"Prescott Lodge and Sanctuary."

"Don't make fun of me. You are the first man I've told."

Lee wondered how bad it had been for her. Maybe the massage cost her more effort than he knew. "I'm not. It's just that Sanctuary seems to be the operational word for several of us here."

She pushed his head forward, making him look at the lake again. Her fingers kept working, tireless. "Actually, I thought I'd pry some information out of you. What's with all the meetings with you and Celia, Jessica, and the doctor? Those meetings yesterday? Celia always has me in the loop, but this time she won't tell me a thing. It's not like her."

"Hey," Lee said, "you want me to betray a confidence?"

"I just worry. Have I done something wrong I don't

know about?" Her fingers kneaded deep into his trapezes muscles. "Don't tense up like that."

"It's nothing like that. Celia thinks you're an ace. Beyond that, I plead client privilege."

"If there is anything I can do to help, let me know."

He looked up at her, Sydney close and feminine there in the gathering dusk, the sun now down for the count under a smear of dark purple.

She stopped massaging him, ruffled his hair and stepped back.

He turned, and they stared at each other. Sydney pushed a strand of hair from her face.

Water slapped the dock pilings and at the boats in their slips. Footsteps sounded from behind them. He turned to see Jessica coming down the dock steps, the nightlights glowing around her feet.

"I'm not interrupting anything, am I?" she said, coming on anyway.

"As a matter of fact," Lee said, "you are."

"No, no," Sydney said. Her voice held that differential tone people used when talking to a superior. "We were just talking."

Jessica was with them now, a physical and emotional presence in khaki shorts and a black polo shirt. "Anything important, Sydney? If not, I need to talk with Lee. It's rather urgent."

"Um. That's fine."

"Good. Then, would you mind?"

Sydney gave him a brief what-can-I-do look where Jessica could not see. "No problem. I was just going up, anyway. Bye, Lee."

"Goodnight, Syd."

He watched her go up the steps. Jessica watched him watching Sydney. When Sydney disappeared over the short bluff, he turned and nodded to the small cooler beside his chair. "You want a beer?"

Jessica came close enough he could smell her perfume. The light at the end of the dock clicked on. "This isn't a social call."

"Suit yourself."

"If we should find the process tank," she said, "I don't want Mother to know. I want to keep up the pretense that we are still searching for it."

"I don't get it."

"There are already too many people involved with this. I can't believe how many. From here on, everything is a need-to-know basis. If Corliss Creed delivers, we pretend to the rest of the world that he didn't. If Greenbough is watching us, it will appear that nothing has changed. Do you understand?"

"That's a good idea. No problem."

"I'm not comfortable bringing Redmond in on this, either. I don't like that at all."

"I can't work it alone."

"That would not be necessary if we would just pay Corliss in full. The money is not a problem."

"Jessica, Corliss Creed is like a wild animal. If you keep feeding him, he'll keep coming around for more. But, he's not a cute little squirrel that means no harm. We've got to discourage him from dealing with us. Hell, he's going to get ten-thousand dollars as it is."

"I don't know," she said, doubt in her voice. "He thinks he's getting twenty. What's to stop him from going to the law? If we piss him off, what has he got to lose?"

"He won't go to the law. He'll try to figure a way to get the rest of his money."

"Oh, that's better."

Lee reeled in the lure, forgotten these past few minutes out there in the water, and put down his fishing rod. "I thought we had this settled."

She shrugged. "He makes me . . . nervous."

His laughter escaped before he could stop it. "I'm sorry. It's just that you're dealing with one of the biggest technological secrets in history, hiding from a ruthless organization, but it's Corliss Creed makes you nervous."

"There is something missing in that man. He, he's . . ."

"Degenerate?"

She let out her breath. "Yes."

Whip-poor-wills began calling to each other in the timber. Ensembles of frogs and crickets began tuning up. The air smelled wet and organic. It all gave Lee a sense of time and place, as if he were in a painting by some classic pastoral master.

"And he bothers you more than Greenbough? Strange."

"That's different. Whoever they send out will be all business."

"Hmm. Let me ask you this. Is your exit strategy still in place?"

"Yes. But you don't need to know about it."

He thought about that for a minute. Finally, he said, "Fine. Just give me the time table."

He would let her hold a few cards; let her think she was still in control.

August 27

The willow pool, Corliss thought, smelled just about normal as he stood there beside Jessica Prescott and her buddy, Doc Kane. The last time, when Luther had brought him over, the area had that oversweet, dead smell hanging over it, just enough to make him feel like he was on the edge of losing his lunch. But, the dead things, all the little mice and birds and shit caught in the funny gray algae, had all dried up or had sunk in the water. A redwing blackbird called in the willow thicket surrounding the pool, and *that* was different. There had not been any birds, live ones, anyway, near the place the last time. Reflections from the willows rippled across the dark water, reaching toward them like pale fingers. Remnants of the gray algae, most of which had dried up, coated the shoreline and willow trunks. He stepped on a swatch of it; his boot crunched through the thin, scabrous stuff.

"This is where your robot and tank was, here in this pool," he said. "You can see the tracks it made coming out."

Corliss pointed to the wide path still visible in the weeds. The tracks led from the water into the woods, a trail that held a constant, four-foot width, the larger bushes and windfall branches crushed and snapped, the smaller, springier weeds upright again. "I wondered if the lizard legs on that thing would work on land. I reckon they do. Look there, it motor-gated right over that big log."

"The Salamander drive, yes," the old man said. He

stood looking at a small hole in the water willows. He turned, and the black backpack strapped loosely to his narrow shoulders shifted with the movement. Excitement edged his voice. "And you say you found the rover with the tank, right here?"

"I said I did, dint' I? I judge that robot came through the willows there at that lil' opening, coming out of the lake with it."

"Extraordinary!"

Jessica Prescott toed aside some weeds, uncovering the sunken remains of some animal. Corliss thought it was a raccoon. "Ugh," she said, and backed up. "Can we get on with the search?"

"This here's the goop that burned my brother's hands and made him sick when he messed with it," Corliss said, and spat tobacco juice onto the dried algae to make his point. Mum's the word on the other critters. He would get paid for the robot and tank first, keep the critters a separate deal. "You can see it killed some mice and shit got caught in it, and maybe Mister Coon over there."

"Algae?" The doc knelt to examine the coating, his paper-thin slacks pulling tight against his bony legs like pale green tissue paper. He adjusted the glasses on his nose. "Truly? Was it always this color?"

"Far as I know, Doc." Corliss looked at Jessica. Her legs were covered by a pair of designer jeans, but her boobs rode up nice and high under a low-cut sports top, all tight against her body like they was trapped in a coat of purple paint, shiny in the afternoon sun. She wore her hair up off her shoulders, tied back in a ponytail, the first time he had seen that. She looked good. If he could figure a way to get rid of the doc and get the other half of his money, the ten-thousand dollars she still owed him, he would ride that snub queen, shove her face in the dirt and—

"Stinging algae," Dr. Kane said. "It must be a mutation of the original model. How did it escape the ETU?"

The little dude seemed right interested in that. Corliss wondered what he would think if he knew that tank of his had made a bunch of other things, like the ones Mama and Luther had brought home and were trying to pass off as kinfolk. He would play a card, see if he could build the pot for later.

"They was other things here," he said. "My brother said there was things like big eggs in the water, all covered with this slime. I reckon they either sunk or hatched out. If any of them lived, you think they'd be worth anything?"

"A fortune, I imagine." The doc looked at the pool. "Amazing, development capsules, your *eggs*, Mr. Creed, protected by a colony of toxic algae. It seems to have a short life span and limited, or perhaps conditional, reproductive abilities."

Corliss looked at him, deadpan. "Yeah, that's what I thought." The fruity bastard, talking shit like that to him.

"Doctor! We are not here to elucidate Mr. Creed. I am more interested in who opened the ETU and its current whereabouts." Jessica had started a short way down the robot track, peering down it.

"This is a *crèche* or nursery of some sort," the doc said.

Jessica came back to the shore. "Oh?"

"According to Mr. Creed, his brother discovered several development capsules here. They seemed to have disappeared."

"What's a 'kresh'?" Corliss asked, looking around. He did not see what they were talking about.

Jessica's voice dropped to a whisper. "You mean, we have a yield?"

"Brilliant." The old man stood, wincing as his knees flexed. "The GX system adapted to the local environment. It is possible the uncontrolled nutrients in the lake water accelerated growth. However, I did not program the nanites to alter designs, to construct stinging algae as a group protective measure. I wish I had brought some collecting jars. I would like to study this residue."

"GX?" asked Corliss.

"Nothing you need be concerned with," Prescott said.

They stared at him, their faces expectant. He spat again. "We gonna find this robot today, or stand here talkin'?"

"You will get your money," Jessica said. "Doctor, he's right. We need to get going."

"Fuckin' 'A'," Corliss said. His boot heel crunched into something hidden in the weeds on his way to the path. He looked down into empty eye sockets and macabre grin of a bobcat skull. He had stomped through the rib cage.

***

Lee hurried back across the wooded point, ignoring the briars and other underbrush that caught at his legs. The game, as Sherlock Holmes would say, was afoot. Corliss had led Jessica and Dr. Chilson to the place he claimed to have seen the rover and what they were calling a bio tank. Chrome and water glinted through the trees ahead—Red waiting for him on the lake. He took the see-through camouflage netting from his head and tucked it in a pocket of his camouflage hunting pants. Breaking from the trees, he splashed through the shallows to the Bayliner, handed the heavy camera to Red, and then pulled himself aboard.

"They're leaving," he said, sitting and pulling his boots off, up ending them to let them drain. "Let's give them a few minutes and then go around."

"Where they at?" Red wore his camouflaged do-rag again and Lee's other camo-shirt with the sleeves rolled up.

"There's a willow thicket on the other side." It was hot. Lee rolled up the sleeves of his own shirt. "Corliss took them into the woods. They stood around talking for a few minutes before they took off."

"You didn't see the gizmo?"

"No gizmo."

"You tell if our boy was packin'?"

"He was too far away. He might be."

"Glorious."

"Your enthusiasm is overwhelming."

Red shrugged. "I'm enthusiastic about payday."

"If it goes by the numbers, you can take the rest of the day off."

"I'm overwhelmed."

For a time, they sat in silence. Lee watched Red fidget, smoking a cigarette, polishing the dials on the boat's instrument panel. He could not tell if Red was excited about the thousand-dollar bonus he would get for helping to rip-off Corliss, or if something was bothering him.

Red watched him wash down a painkiller with a swig from a water bottle. It was the second one today.

"I'm okay," Lee said. "It's just that my back hurts."

"I said nothing." Red turned his eyes to the lake and drew on his cigarette.

The minutes passed.

Lee had argued long with Jessica about bringing Red

into the secret. Finally, she had listened to logic: To ensure success in the scheme, they needed another player, both to cut Corliss from his deal and to help with the bio tank. She had never taken time to get to know Red, though, and thought of him simply as "the help." In the end, she agreed, but Red would know only the bare minimum about the tank, that it held expensive biological research. Lee did tell him about Greenbough without Jessica's knowledge. The man had not seemed too surprised. All he had said was, "No shit."

"That boat," Red said suddenly, "it's been here as long as we have."

Other boats plied the lake, most of them bass boats with one or two graying men in them. The weekend would bring out the younger generation who would crowd the water with ski boats and jet skis. The nearest boat, a standard bass rig, had anchored out from them. Two-hundred-yards distant, the angler was a dim shape. Lee appreciated the privacy. The last thing he wanted was to make pleasant small talk with a passing fisherman.

"I think he's all right." Lee checked his watch. "It's been twenty minutes. Let's go."

"You're the captain."

Red started the engine and brought the Bayliner around the point, going slow, giving Lee a chance to scan the far timber and willow thicket with the zoom lens. The lodge's pontoon boat nuzzled into the shore near an impenetrable willow pool.

Red asked, "They gone?"

"Looks like it, but I can't see through those willows from this angle. That's where they were."

"You want to go in?"

"Yeah. Let's chance it. Head for that gap where the willows stop."

"Aye, aye, Captain."

Lee reached for his boots, hoping most of the water had drained from them.

A short time later Red killed the engine and coasted into the shore, grounding the Bayliner beside the pontoon boat, running the hull onto the mud and breaking loose little rainbow bursts of swamp gas at the waterline. Frogs moaned at the water's edge. A horsefly buzzed in from the trees, wings glittering like diamonds, and nailed Red on his exposed arm. He slapped at it.

"Son-of-a-bitch!"

"Quiet!" Lee whispered.

The horsefly zoomed off, vanishing into the trees. Red examined the welt rising on his skin.

"You got any more of that repellant?" he said.

"I don't think it works on horseflies." Lee jumped to shore, sinking a couple of inches into the wet earth.

"Son-of-a-bitch." Red stayed in the boat, rubbing at his arm as he stared into the trees.

Lee did not care much for the set up either, the way the woods, dark and creeping with hard shadows, rose above them. Cicadas and other insects screeched their lunacy in the trees, the Beast of a Thousand Eyes. Corliss could be watching too, waiting in ambush. Not knowing, taking the first steps on faith, was the worst part of the plan. Did they have the element of surprise, or did the enemy have that advantage?

"That pick handle," Lee said, "looks like it wants to come along."

Without speaking Red handed down a yard-length of hickory, the wood smooth and hard, shaped flat on the edges the better to fit the human grasp. Lee had chosen it from the rack of implements in Red's shop, sliding off the steel pick.

"I still think you should've brought that pistol of yours," Red said.

Lee thought about that, remembering the cold, sick feeling he had in his cabin, looking at the Colt automatic. He could not forget he had killed a boy with a pistol, had lost a partner killed by a gun. Beneath all of that, he could not forget the shock and pain of his own wound.

"Corliss knows a firearm is an automatic ticket back to prison," Lee said, "He's not going to carry unless he feels he has to. This pick handle will take care of his knife if he gets cute."

Red jumped to the shore, his do-rag flapping around his neck. In one hand, he held a tire iron, with the other he raised the tail of his shirt revealing the butt of a slim automatic pistol tucked into his waistband.

"Corliss doesn't impress me in the wit department. I hope you don't mind I packed this equalizer."

"It's okay," Lee said, feeling conflicted by relief at having a gun with them just in case and concern about having things get out of control. "Just don't skin it if you don't have too."

"I keep thinking, what if he's got his family up there waiting for us, cousins and all? We wouldn't know."

"That's possible," Lee conceded, "but unlikely."

"Man, you know, I'm just sayin'. It starts looking like *Deliverance,* I'm changing the play."

Lee took the anchor from the bow, stretched the rope taut and dropped the anchor. He stepped on it, mashing the dull points into the soft earth. Red followed him to the edge of the willow pool. A patchwork of footprints decorated the shoreline.

"What's that gray crap all over the place?" Red whispered. "Looks like Godzilla blew his nose."

"I don't know. Algae, maybe. I'm more interested in what made that."

The mingled footprints of their quarry left the lagoon and vanished down a wide track crushed into the weeds and damp earth. Here and there, a large four-toed print shaped much like a lotus blossom appeared in the earth. The tracks and a drag trail led up the ridge, into the trees.

"Come on," Lee said, slapping the pick handle in his hand. "It's time to make Corliss's day."

***

"A baby could follow this track," Corliss said, taking off his cowboy hat, wiping the sweat from his forehead and setting it back on, tilting the brim just so, still mindful of his style.

Jessica Prescott and the doc did not answer, the woman and old man going up the trail. But, yeah, you could see the trail plain as grits, how the weight of the tank the robot was dragging crushed down weeds, broke branches. Going up over the ridge, the robot's fancy—what did the Doc call it?—*salamander* drive system had kicked rocks as big as mush melons out of the ground.

Corliss stopped at the top of the ridge to let them rest, in an area where the earth wore thin and broad shelves of naked rock pushed through, moss and lichens growing on them like green pelts. The doc looked like he appreciated the break, breathing a little heavier than normal. Prescott seemed okay, though, her tits rising gently with even breaths. He judged she likely worked out. A beam of sunlight cut through the trees and made the sweat on her chest glisten, highlighting the swell of her cleavage. Corliss licked his lips.

"It's close in here, ain't it?" he said. "Usually this high, you get a breeze."

"It is hot."

"Maybe we ought to leave him here," Corliss said. "He don't look too good."

"Not an option." Jessica's voice was level, her eyes flat. "For one, we will need him when we find the rover."

"Just a few moments rest," the doc said. "I am just not used to this kind of exertion." He brushed aside some twigs and leaves from a rock shelf. A locust buzzed off the rock and into the trees, not wanting to get sat on.

"What's 'For two?'" Corliss asked. He opened his foil pouch of tobacco and put a good dose of chew in his mouth. He poked an escaping tobacco leaf back between his lips. "You said, 'For one.' What's 'For two?'"

Prescott put her hands on her hips. "You and I will never be together alone."

Corliss smiled. "Don't trust me, huh?"

"Not the way you've been looking at me, no."

"Come on, I don't mean nothin'. You're a good-looking hammer, is all, and it's of a manly nature to want to look."

"Mr. Creed," she said, her eyes still flat, "when we find

the rover and tank and see it all safely loaded on the boat, I will pay the remainder of your fee. After that, our association is finished. Is that clear?"

Swear to God, he was close to stepping forward and swatting the bitch. He got himself under control at the last second. There was another ten grand on the line. Would not do to lose that over a moment's satisfaction. Besides, there was always later. He smiled and touched the brim of his hat, smooth, the way he had seen it done in a hundred cowboy movies.

"Yes, Ma'am."

He would tend to her when the time was right, and there were no witnesses.

She pulled a water bottle off her belt and offered the doc a drink. While he rested, she worked the straps of the backpack off his shoulders and slipped them on her own.

"Besides that controller," Corliss said, "what you got in that pack?"

Jessica looked at him. "Just the controller. Why?"

"Just wondering about my money."

"You'll get it. Don't worry."

When the old man had rested, they followed the path down the other side of the ridge. The going was steep and led often to the edge of small bluffs with drops between ten and twenty feet. Loose leaves made their footing slippery.

"How in Christ did that fuckin' robot drag that thing this far?" Corliss said. "And, why would it want to?"

Neither one of them answered him, either saving their breath for the hill or just being snotty.

The machine had slipped over an eroded bank and landed upside-down, wedged up against an oak tree belly up, its funky feet dull and worn with dirt. The tank rested in the leaf-litter beside the robot, busted open like a stepped-on milk carton. Corliss saw the innards of the thing had some kind of white fiber honeycomb in it, what he took to be a baffle system of some kind, the honeycomb holes in different sizes, large ones on the bottom and small ones toward the top. Maybe a couple hundred little plastic tubes ran all through the honeycomb.

"Oh, my," the doc said. "I was afraid this would happen."

Corliss spat a stream of tobacco juice off the bank and watched it splat on the robot in a small brown explosion. "What's that?"

"That it had broken open," Doc Kane said.

Prescott, frowning, said, "Let's get down there."

Corliss skidded down the crumbling bank while the other two walked a ways to the end of the bank and came back on the level. Sweating in the heat, Corliss used his new hunting knife to cut a strong sapling and trim it to a ten-foot long pole.

"Don't go near it," the doc called. "There may still be some danger of contamination."

"You ain't got to tell me." He still woke up in a cold sweat dreaming of the night he and that fruity scientist stole the tank from the houseboat, the guy getting his face eat off. Dumbass.

The doc stopped several yards away and studied the robot, shifting around twice to get a better look at particular parts of the thing. Finally, he walked up and bent down to get at a hatch.

"Any reason," Corliss asked, "that thing looks like a lizard instead of havin' wheels?"

"Um, optimum mobility." The doc patted the robot. "It deactivated itself. Good."

"What does that mean?" Jessica asked.

"It has gone into sleep mode. A fail-safe if it should encounter a situation such as this to save power." He ran his hands over the robot's metallic shell. Where it rested against the oak tree, there was a slight dent. Then, he went to the tank and checked that out. Corliss saw his shoulders slump.

"Gone," the doc said, "all but the upper tier."

"So we still have some embryos?"

"The smallest ones. If they are still viable."

Prescott chewed her lip and studied about that for a minute, finally saying, "It doesn't matter, we can salvage the

ETU. We can replicate the complete cargo from the program profiles."

Doc Kane returned to the robot. "If we can retrieve them. Mr. Creed, do you think we can right it?"

Corliss pushed a rock into place to use as a fulcrum and jammed the end of the pole under the robot. He nodded at Prescott. "If she helps."

Jessica gave him a look, but said, "What do you want me to do?"

***

Lee ducked behind the rock he and Red hid behind, waiting to spring the trap on Corliss. He could smell Red, a mix of sweat, antiperspirant, and insect repellant. Up on the ridge, the afternoon heat carried sporadic and uninspired bug song from the woods around them.

"What?" Red whispered. He had perked up along the trail. The excitement of hunting another human being seemed to have quelled his doubts. He was in the game now.

"Corliss may have seen me. He looked straight up the ridge."

"Not cool."

"I'm not sure, though. Peek around your side—not over the top! Around the side."

Lee waited. Loaded with heat, the limpid air weighed against him, seeming to press the sweat from his body. The voices of the people below echoed, indistinct and fragmented, among the trees and rocks. A large wood ant wandered across the camouflage pattern of Red's shirt like an erratic windup toy. Lee flicked it off before it could cause any mischief.

"Well?" he said in a low voice.

Red kept watching and spoke over his shoulder. "He ain't lookin' now. He's jus' standing there, watching Dr. Chilson and Jessica fool with the thing."

"Rover," Lee said.

"Yeah, Rover, Fido, whatever . . . they got some kind of computer or remote control out. Chilson's working the keyboard . . . Jessica's trying to pull a stick or something out of the, uh, rover. Looks like it was caught in a joint. Damn thing's got *legs*. You see that?"

Lee looked around his side of the rock again.

Corliss Creed stood just uphill from Jessica, Dr. Chilson, and the rover, his hands in his pockets, his cowboy hat low and tight on his head. The leaves and ground around the rover were scraped and disturbed, as if some forceful action had taken place.

"They must have had an accident," he said.

"Yeah, something ain't—look! It's moving!"

The rover jolted to life. It *stretched*, and then moved forward, its long metallic body flexing side to side as it moved. The rover's four legs moved up, forward and back, appearing to feel out the way.

"How can they make it do that? Looks like a giant lizard," Red whispered. "The hell are those things by its head?"

"They look like mechanical tentacles."

"Man, they must've been stoked when they tricked this one out."

Dr. Chilson walked behind the rover and tank, holding the control board, and Jessica behind him, carrying a three foot rail, what appeared to be a piece of the rover or ETU. Corliss stood still for a moment, his eyes dark shadows under his hat, and then he too, followed. His gaze seemed to focus most often on Jessica's backside.

Red said, "They're coming this way."

"Yeah, heading back to the boat. I don't think Luther is in on this, or else he would've put in an appearance by now."

"Be my guess, too. When do we shock Corliss?"

Lee watched the rover crawl through the woods. There was something fascinating in its movements, the way it moved without wheels or tracks, just that reptilian motion, its legs lifting it over small rocks and logs as it toiled up the steep hill through drifts of leaves, slipping some, but moving ever-forward like a single-minded automaton intent on a mission. "We'll stay just ahead of them," he whispered, reaching for the pick handle. "Let's go."

***

Corliss cursed under his breath and stopped. He had been so busy watching Prescott's trim ass moving in front of him and dreaming what he was going to do with the money, he was damn near to the water before he noticed the lodge's Bayliner parked next to the pontoon boat.

"Son-of-a-bitch," he said again, his teeth clenched. He scanned the weedy shoreline, looking for fresh tracks. Wrong place to look; the sound of crackling leaves came from behind him. He turned.

Pulling a camouflage head net from his face, Lee Picket stepped from behind a tree. The black dude from the lodge came out from a small willow thicket several yards away. Both men were cammied-up like they were turkey hunting. Picket had an ax or pick handle in his hand. The black dude held a tire-iron.

"Corliss," Picket said, "it's time to renegotiate."

"I knowed it was you." Heat flared up inside him. His nose was still tender where the man had rammed his fingers up there, shit, yanking like a son-of-a-bitch.

The doc stopped the robot at the waterline and

turned to watch. Jessica had turned. Her eyes flicked from Corliss to Picket and back again. Neither the doc nor Jessica seemed surprised at the ambush.

They had set him up from the start. He glared at Prescott. The treacherous little bitch stared back at him, her face as still and composed as a tombstone angel.

Picket stepped forward. He stopped about twenty feet away, his eyes deadpan. "You've kept your word, and I appreciate that, but I think twenty-thousand dollars is too much. You're just not in that league."

"What are you . . . you cutting me out?"

"You've got ten grand in your pocket, Corliss." Picket took another step toward him. The pick handle dangled at his side. "If I had my way, you wouldn't have that. Fortunately, for you, Ms. Prescott there feels ten thousand is the price of doing business. But I've got no use for you. I ought to turn you in as a suspect for the murder of Dr. Peter Fraily."

Corliss stared at him, wondering how-the-hell Picket could know.

"The autopsy showed blunt trauma to his head," Picket continued.

Oh.

"I don't know nothin' about that," Corliss said. He looked at the doc and the robot, both of them at the water's edge, the doc watching him, the computer console in his hands. "Anyway, you got no proof, and if you tell that lie it would bust up your little secret, here."

"That's the only thing saving you now."

Jessica walked toward Picket and the black dude, her expression still placid. She said, "Corliss, just take what you've got, and go."

All business. Corliss made himself calm down and adjust to the development. The wheels were turning, big wheels.

"But, we ain't done yet, darlin'. You owe me money."

"It's not her," Picket said. "It's me. The best thing you could do, take the money Jessica already gave you and count yourself lucky you're not in jail instead."

The black dude stood beside Picket now. A horsefly buzzed around the black dude's head. He jerked away from it, fucking city boy, nervous about a bug. Despite his efforts, Corliss felt his anger building again, this asshole trying to cut him out of his due. "I want my money, boy."

"You've got all you're going to get," Picket said. "Do you want me and Red to help you find your way home?"

Corliss stared at Picket, burning his features into his memory, hating every angle in the guy's face, his superior attitude. He put his hand on his new hunting knife. Picket lifted the pick handle.

"You think I'm scared of your little stick?" Corliss said. "I ain't. You step over here and I'll show you how to work that son-of-a-bitch."

"You're coming out of this all right, Corliss. You want to keep it that way."

"You owe me ten-thousand dollars, boy, and I swear by the feud I'll get it."

Picket stared back at him. "Just go."

Corliss looked from Picket to Jessica, hot. "That goes for you, too, bitch."

With that, he turned and walked into the woods. It was going to take all afternoon to get home through the woods, but that was all right. He did not even feel the ground he walked on, thinking about his revenge. Picket and his goddamned pick handle.

***

Looking at the rover and tank sitting in the gloom, Lee felt he had earned his pay. It had been a bitch getting it loaded on the pontoon boat, using makeshift wooden ramps, then off again at the lodge without being seen, Jessica paying Celia a visit to keep her occupied.

Red brought down the garage door and turned on the lights. "Welcome to the bat-cave," he said. "My refuge from the world."

Mowers, garden tillers, and other lawn equipment ranged in a neat line near the door, various ladders hung on the walls. A workbench stood against the wall, fronted by a table saw and drill press and flanked by racks of lumber. Opposite the workstation, a mini-maze of storage shelves rose head high, each one stuffed with paint, cleaners, or spare parts. The building smelled equally of motor oil, saw dust, and fertilizer. At the end of the building, half hidden by the shelves, a crude lounge was set up around a scarred dinette table. A refrigerator leaned against a grimy deep sink, Miss December two-thousand-thirteen held to the faded olive door by magnets salvaged from old small engine magnetos.

Lee dropped into a frayed patio chair, numb from stress, and watched Dr. Chilson flutter around the rover and tank, happy. Dr. Chilson talked as he went, Lee sometimes not sure exactly who the old man was addressing.

"Yes, we will have to repair that circuit. I see you have kept your power up . . . good. What has happened to your umbilical? Are those teeth marks? Of course, mice . . . or perhaps, rats, some small animal . . . after the embryonic proteins?"

A touch of unreality washed over Lee. For the first time, he had a chance to think of the bio-fuel science, what this whole mess involved. He scratched his chin.

"You said, 'embryonic proteins.' I thought this was about algae?"

"Hmm?" Dr. Chilson kept opening small hatches on

the tank, peering inside them. "Oh, yes. Well, this tank contains genetically manipulated strains of high energy yielding algae. Development capsules contain the various strains that the tank feeds through a nutrient process. One of our research techs called it embryonic fluid because she thought of the capsules as embryos, and the term stuck."

"Seems I remember hearing some of that GMO stuff, like corn and beans, mutates on its own." Lee said. "I just want to know one thing, Doc. Is it safe?"

"What?" Dr. Chilson peered at him over the top of his spectacles. "Safe?"

"Yeah, the algae or the acid Corliss said hit Fraily, is this thing safe now?"

"Oh, yes. The tank has lost its nanites, unh, the acid that Mr. Creed mentioned. It is quite harmless now."

Red crossed to the refrigerator, rummaged, then handed a beer to Lee and popped the top off one for himself. He took a swig and stared at the tank. "It lost what?"

"The GX, ah, that is, the *process* nanites," Dr. Chilson said, wiping his hands on a rag, "they are missing. At least the bulk of them are out of their canister. There might be some few million scattered in the compartment, but without a microscope, it is impossible to determine."

The beer foamed in Lee's mouth, tasting like a small metallic explosion. "I don't believe you've told us about nanites. Are you saying that this rig has nano-technology?"

"What nanites?" Red asked.

"Oh, well." Dr. Chilson paused, looking uncertain. He removed his glasses and polished them on his shirttail. "These prototype algae samples do not reproduce naturally, so they must be replicated in-lab. The nanites facilitate that process. Some of them assist in nutrient delivery and cell replication."

Neither Lee nor Red spoke. Dr. Chilson continued.

"The nanites, in this case, are hybrid cybernetic mechanisms built on the molecular scale and programmed to assemble proteins into adaptive connecting mechanisms between the various bacteria to form a minute processing plant. It is all in the final experimental stage."

"We've come that far?" Lee said. He thought of the science-fiction movies he had seen, where the microscopic robots and genetic manipulation were common. He also suspected the doctor was somehow shining him on, something about the doctor's explanation not ringing true.

"A colleague of mine developed, well, stumbled upon, actually, a semi-organic process of creating the nanites, a happy accident, as they say. It *is* fascinating. A base of silicone molecules is combined with—"

Red set his beer down hard on a table. "How did they kill Fraily, man? You're tellin' us this tank is safe. It killed a man."

"Oh. Well, some of the nanites salvage raw materials from their environment, for the organic material needed for the assembler, as well as nutrients for the embry—ah—development capsules. However, without a designated supply, the nanites will use whatever they, uh, find. Human flesh is no different to them than any other suitable material."

Lee sat up, a tingle of alarm working its way through his fatigue. Killer nanites, now. Considering the cutting-edge rover and the bio tank, it was not difficult to believe the ultimate technological wet dream was sitting before him. He said, "Doc, I'm having a rather nasty vision, microscopic army ants pouring over the ground, devouring everything in their path. Tell me I'm wrong."

"Yeah," Red said, eyeing the tank. "Tell him he's wrong."

"The Gray Goo Theory," Dr. Chilson said, nodding. "This is the idea that, once created with self-replicating capabilities, nanites will grow exponentially, eventually consuming all living matter on earth."

Lee stared at him. Red took another step back. Dr. Chilson replaced his glasses and continued.

"That is not the case here. These nanites require a liquid medium to travel. Water is the design element."

"So the army ants," Lee said, "if they are on land, are laying on their backs, kicking their little legs in the air?"

"They actually have a combination of cilia and a device similar to a whip, but essentially, that is an accurate analogy. These nanites, however, are not self-replicating. They function approximately for three months."

"Their batteries go dead?"

"They are powered by a hydrogen process, a readily available fuel. No, their components breakdown, heat, friction, oxidation, and even the ultraviolet rays of the sun all act as destructive forces on these nanites."

"Finally," Lee said, "some good news."

"About time." Red sat on a bar stool, its green vinyl skin bandaged with gray duct-tape. He lit a cigarette. "So, you sayin' this thing is all safe now? No radiation, any kind of shit like that?"

"No radiation."

Lee shifted. "What about the lake?"

"Hmm?"

"You said the nanites travel in liquid. What about any nanites that are still in the lake?"

"Oh, I do not think the swarm will hold together in that environment. They will be too scattered to be dangerous and will expire at the end of their life-cycle."

Lee watched Dr. Chilson continue his inspection. Something about the nanites and algae story seemed out of place, but what did he know? After several minutes of silence, Lee took a last swig of beer, set the bottle down and looked at Red. "I don't know about you, but I've had enough science for the day."

"Damn straight on that." Red watched Dr. Chilson. "This is some serious shit, man. We need to get this out of here. I feel like . . ."

Lee raised his eyebrows, waiting for him to finish.

"I feel like," Red said, "this thing is carrying the plague. You know what I mean?"

"Yeah. I do. This whole situation is wrong." A thought occurred to him. "Doc, if this system can make algae, how long before it can make other things, like higher life forms?"

Dr. Chilson paused, looked at him over his glasses. He returned to his work without answering.

Martin Woodward

8

September 2

"These guys that have been watching us the past few days," Lee said, leaning his elbows on the table to ease the pressure in his back, "are setting up a routine."

Late afternoon sun slanted through the big windows of Celia's apartment, its rays cutting a warm swath in the air conditioning, highlighting floating dust motes. Celia, Dr. Chilson, and Jessica sat, attentive, around the glass-topped table. No treats or beverages this time, the table was cleared for business.

Lee continued. "Two men keep their boat within sight of the lodge pretending to be fishermen, likely the same two that dropped by our dock. At night, they turn the boat over to another man. This third man stays all night, and then they swap out again in the morning. This has been going on for two days."

"Greenbough," Jessica said, her expression grim, "gathering enough information to make the kill."

"I had a friend in KCPD run their auto tags. They register to Global Contractors. That's the subsidiary of Greenbough you're so worried about, right?"

182

Dr. Chilson nodded. "So, they have found us."

"God," Jessica said, then, looking at Lee, "why the hell didn't you tell us before now?"

"I wanted to make sure who they were before I raised the alarm.'"

"It doesn't matter," Celia said. "What can they do, storm the lodge?"

Jessica and Dr. Chilson said in unison, "Yes."

"That being the case," Lee said, "What are they waiting for?"

"I surmise they believe we do not have the, uh, bio tank in our possession." Dr. Chilson placed both hands on the table and appeared to study his fingertips.

"Why would they *not* think we had it?" Lee said.

"If they have been watching us, if they have been watching me drag the lake with my sonar, they would wonder if somehow the bio tank had become lost to us. The fact that we are still here would declare something was amiss with our plans. They would not think us so stupid as to stay in the country once we had stolen the golden goose. I think they may be confused and are waiting for more information."

"That may work for us," Celia said. "When you find the damned thing, give it to them and swear to keep your mouth shut."

Lee felt a pang of guilt. As a security precaution, they had not told Celia about recovering the bio tank. If the situation became bad, if Global moved on the lodge, that knowledge could be a liability. There was no need for her to know, not yet anyway, despite her influence and position.

"I don't think they would go for that, Mother. They are thorough, not reasonable."

"What is to keep us from going to the press?" Lee said. "Expose the secret and we're done. Cat's out of the bag."

"Greenbough is powerful, and the core group we are dealing with is merciless," Dr. Chilson said. "The likely scenario is, ah, while we are awaiting trial for grand theft and industrial espionage, we would vanish without a trace or become victims of tragic accidents. Either way, Greenbough would take the tank into custody and the truth along with it. You are a writer, Lee. Use your imagination."

Lee considered. There would be a hundred ways to spin the story.

"You've missed the point as usual," Jessica said to Lee. "We have decided to give this gift to the world. No more wars over energy. However, the trade secret must make it into the right hands. That will take more than a press conference."

"The internet," Lee said. "What's stopping you?"

"We don't have the all the programs," Jessica said. "That's one of the reasons we took the prototype tank. Some we may have to reverse engineer."

"You guys should stick to your day jobs," Lee said. "You're lousy thieves."

Celia gripped the arms of her wheelchair. "Tell me when you find it. I have some influence in certain circles. They will listen to me."

"You don't know these people, Mother."

"You cannot run for the rest of your life!"

"Okay, maybe Celia's right," Lee said. "What if they find out, or even just think, that the rest of us know their little secrets? They going to do us, too? You said they were thorough, but would they murder the entire lodge?"

Jessica stared at center of the table. "I don't know."

Lee waited. No one spoke.

"Okay, look," he said finally. "First things, first. You two find the bio tank. Celia and I will start working on a way to persuade these guys to go home. That suit everybody?"

Dr. Chilson nodded. His mild, serious eyes betrayed nothing behind his glasses.

"I guess it will have too," Jessica said, standing. This charade had been her decision, her very determined decision, to keep her mother out of the loop. "But let me say again, you cannot deal with these people."

"I think we will find a way," Celia said, and gave Lee a curious look.

***

Liz Jordan took photographs of the scene with her digital camera, wondering if the little flash she was using in the shade cast by the pine trees was enough light. There was not much to photograph: two splashes of blood and a churned up drag trail that led into the lake. She stood at the edge of the yellow police tape stretched between the trees to block off the crime scene, the mute water lapping the shore near her feet. Try to make sense out of the story; try not to gag when she thought too deeply about how *big* the red splashes were. Wondering, Dear God, what had happened here? Thanks to her police scanner, she had arrived in time to get the gist of it before the sheriff had bundled Stacey Harlow off to town, a tearful, shock-white high school cheerleader.

The story was simple: Stacey, age seventeen, and her boyfriend Travis Christian, also age seventeen, had been down by the lakeshore not far from Lookout Park's boat ramp, their blanket spread on the ground for an after-school petting session in a secluded nook. Stacey left to visit the park restroom three hundred feet away. When she returned, Travis was nowhere to be seen, only what looked disturbingly like blood on the ground. She thought he was playing a joke on her. As the shadows lengthened and Travis did not appear to deliver the punch line, she thought more and more about how real the blood looked. At last, trying to control the panic she felt rising, her stupid cellphone not getting a signal, Stacey used the parking lot payphone to call her mother, a secretary for a local law firm. The county machine had taken over at that point.

Liz lowered her camera with a sigh and turned to the deputy beside her. They were the only ones left, waiting on a State evidence team to arrive from Branson.

"You think this could be a prank, Bob? Maybe that's pig's blood or something?"

"I doubt it." Bob, sixteen years with the Sheriff's Department, a tall, slow talking, mustached man with dark, serious eyes, pushed his Smokey Bear hat back on his head and rubbed his jaw. Bob smoked a pipe. He took the pipe from between his teeth now, a tendril of fragrant smoke spilling over the rim.

"The boy was getting lucky with his cheerleader girlfriend. I can't see him taking off—can you?"

"I guess not." She stared at the blood. "What's your take?"

"I don't have one yet."

He too, looked at the blood, now a congealed mess in the dirt and leaves. The last of the late summer flies buzzed around it. Sick.

Liz said, "Looks like something dragged him into the lake."

"Somebody, you mean."

187

"A little girl caught a piranha in the lake this summer, Bob. The Missouri Department of Conservation confirmed that. And, the one witness to that boy who drown after falling off his skis, said the victim was pulled under by what looked like an alligator. An alligator, Bob. Why didn't they find that poor kid's body?"

"It's a deep lake."

"Something's in the lake, Bob."

"I'm not touching that, Liz. You want a quote, you go talk to the sheriff."

"Off the record?"

Bob shook his head, his eyes neutral and dark. "Not even that way."

"I'm just a girl trying to do her job. C'mon, what do you think?"

Bob shrugged, frowned at his pipe. A blue jay screeched in the distance, its raucous voice loud with irritation.

Liz stared at Bob, not wanting to let him off the hook. Wanting him to admit, damn it, something dangerous stalked the lake. "Well, what now?"

The deputy looked at the water for a moment before he answered, blowing a long puff of air through his lips. "We'll probably drag the lake. We'll check to see if Travis Christian had any enemies, or was having problems at home."

"Duh."

"Hey, you asked." The pipe went back into his mouth.

"Thanks for nothing."

***

A taste of fall weather had come without an invitation. Lee shifted on his seat in the bushes at the end of the town's marina, one of those three-gallon plastic coolers shaped like a tall footstool, and wished he had brought his windbreaker jacket. The sun was going down, allowing the first true hint of autumn to slip in with the purple darkness. It was seven o'clock. He had been there since three-thirty, watching and waiting, monitoring the Greenbough goons. His back, despite a painkiller he had taken earlier, ached deep down.

At New Le Beau's city dock, the photocell-controlled lights came on and glowed like small space ships hovering over the man waiting for the incoming boat, the boat now only a good stone's throw from making the landing. The man wore a dark blue windbreaker.

Lee shivered. A windbreaker. The son-of-a-bitch.

The boat came in, a big one like the lodge's Bayliner, and the two guys tied it up, Lee sure they were the ones he had shooed away from the lodge dock. One of them, the big guy who claimed to be Howard Gardner, spoke face-to-face with Mr. Windbreaker, gesturing back across the lake, emphasizing something he was saying. Mr. Windbreaker got into the boat and stowed his pack.

Gardner and his smaller associate waited while Mr. Windbreaker backed the boat from the slip and turned the bow toward the distant lodge. If they followed their usual routine, they would get in their Ford and drive to their franchise motel out on the highway. About thirty minutes after that, they would eat at The Chatter Box Cafe, stop at Randy's Liquor, and finally return to their room. Lee thought that tonight he would let them go un-chaperoned. His back ached. Gardner and his sidekick watched Mr. Windbreaker a moment longer, then walked up to the parking lot, got into their Ford and left, leaving the marina, hell, this end of town, deserted.

Yeah, their standard operating procedure.

The wind crossed the lake and chilled him. Lee stood, feeling an odd tinge of loneliness, and keyed his hand-held radio.

"Mud Puppy to Red Dog," he said.

Up the hill, Main Street, a four-lane avenue lined on each side with shops terminating at the docks, was preparing for night. The day shoppers and retailers, insurance peddlers and so forth, had gone home. Cars were still parked at the Main Street Cafe, and farther down at John's Bar and Grill. John's served only hot and cold sandwiches, nothing more complicated than burgers, but they were sirloin and piled high with garden goodies. His stomach growled.

The second time he called, Red answered, his voice distant in the static.

"This is Red . . . *Dog*." Red was not too thrilled with radio call signs, what he thought of as Hollywood bullshit.

"One hour."

"If I feel like it."

"I'll buy you a bottle."

"I'll be there."

"Out," Lee said.

"Cool."

Red would pick him up at the city dock in one hour. The radio contact they kept to a minimum, just in case Gardner and his goons were monitoring the radio waves. Red had scoffed at this; Lee said hey, the National Security Agency has computerized programs all they do is search the airwaves for key words and listen for a few minutes to see if the conversation concerns national security. Suppose, the goons had enough pull they could have this area under electronic surveillance. Hell, they could have satellite infrared spy cameras watching everything you do. Red said, the problem with him, is he thought too much.

Lee stowed the binoculars in his small backpack and shouldered it, left his cooler in the bushes to retrieve later, and headed for John's Bar and Grill. He should have thought to tell Red to bring a windbreaker. That boat ride going back would be chilly.

***

Liz locked the front door to the newspaper office just before eight o'clock and was just about to start her old Pontiac, when she saw Lee Picket down the street leaving John's Bar & Grill, a backpack hanging off his shoulder. He wore faded jeans and one of those camouflaged hunting shirts, a thin pullover, which she thought was odd. She did not think he was the backwoods type, to be wearing that in town. Besides, it was too chilly for just a shirt. He moved at a leisurely pace toward the city dock, passing through the cones of streetlight. Set to go home, she debated for a moment, and then left her car parked beside the newspaper office. If Lee Picket were not up to something, she would turn in her press pass. Even if he was not, he might have some gossip or actual news from the Prescott Lodge. Besides, he was attractive and good company.

She followed him, notepad in hand.

***

Lee searched the lake for running lights, did not see any, and dropped his backpack on a concrete bench just uphill from the city dock. His cooler was still in the bushes, but no hurry. He would get that when he saw Red coming.

The place was absent of anglers or anyone else, the parking lot empty of trucks and boat trailers, everybody in for the night. Figuring Red would not begrudge him a snort, he took a pull off the bottle of Royal Crown John had sold him. The dose added to the warmth of the double he had drank with his cheeseburger. Lee stowed the bottle in the backpack, stretched his legs and crossed his arms. Red would be along in a few minutes.

A bat flitted through the streetlight.

Lee checked his back trail. The public restrooms just a few yards behind him were half dark, the light over the men's room door not working. Had it been working earlier? He could not remember. Beyond the restrooms, up the street where the businesses began, a woman in a skirt was coming toward him, still about a block away.

The door to the men's room creaked softly. Lee turned.

A man left the restroom and walked toward him, his features indistinct in the shadows. Lee stood, about to greet the man, who was close now, coming into the light. The man wore a dark ski mask. He kept his right hand behind his back.

Lee took a step back.

The man's baseball bat came around in a swift, vicious arc. Lee dodged, managing to escape the full force of the blow, but felt his legs jelly as the bat glanced off his up-raised arm, breaking bone and pinging off his skull.

Too slow, he thought. Too much Crown.

Dimly, he heard a woman scream somewhere up the street.

He swung at the man with his good hand. He could see the slow motion of it, his fist taking its sweet time drifting past the man's face. The eyes in the mask followed it. They were dark eyes, familiar eyes, Lee thought. Then the man shifted his grip on the bat and hit him again. This time, the blow caught him in the belly, the business end of the bat rammed up and in with great force. Lee fell to his knees, unable to breathe, feeling something like broken glass in his gut.

The next blow did not quite catch him with full force either, glancing off his shoulder as he twisted to avoid it. Just the same, it connected with the back of his head, striking red and white sparks in his vision. On the ground now, Lee saw his nemesis standing over him with the bat, dull light from Main Street backlighting him in silhouette.

C'mon, Lee thought. Finish it, you bastard.

***

Jessica watched Dr. Chilson tinker with the Embryo Transport Unit; he had two computers plugged into it and some of its insides were out, strung across Red's workbench in a snarl of multicolored electrical wires and circuit boards. The bench was covered in butchers' paper, fastened with gray duct tape at the corners, the best she and Red could do to stop the good doctor from whining about laboratory conditions and clean rooms. They had covered the floor in heavy black plastic and made a curtain wall with seven sets of shower curtains. Now, everyone pulled blue paper booties over their shoes at the curtain. Looking at the disemboweled embryo tank and the curtains, some of them patterned with fish, frogs, and seashells, the maintenance shop resembled a theme park ride gone mad.

A cuckoo clock Red had resurrected shattered the silence suddenly, the little plastic bird leaping out and screaming hysterically "Cuckoo! Cuckoo!"

Jessica jumped. It was, according to the idiot bird, ten p.m.

"Are you listening, Doctor?"

"Hmm?" He stared at a computer screen, his eyeglasses perched high on his nose. She had been trying to tell him about the getaway plans for several minutes, and he would not take his nose out of that damned machine.

"I said, 'What's so interesting?'"

"Oh, yes. The eight embryos. We lost two more overnight, but the remaining four are strong and stable. They are mid-tier, so I suspect they are near yield point. Their growth was slower than the ones lost in the lake, perhaps because they remained on the unit nutrient support."

She did not care what tier the embryos were, as long as she had a living sample to show to the buyer. Mr. X would be easier to handle once he had seen the success of the program with his own eyes.

"Well, this is good news."

"However," Dr. Chilson said, "I found some of the program files. Peter must have been in a hurry and just deleted them. They are still on the hard drive. The computer is damaged. But, with care, I think an expert could retrieve all files. As it is, I have be able to access portions of the data base."

"Great." Finally, things were going her way. "What are they?"

"I have some project systems. One file is the current production catalog. It seems Peter, along with Singh and Azar, have produced several species, including one that develops into a dominant life-form."

"A dominant life-form?"

"It will be a competitor for the top of the food chain, an apex predator." He turned. His eyes were intent behind his glasses. "Due to the partial access, I cannot determine the species' particular characteristics, or the full inventory."

She stared at him. The chill that stroked through her at his words was a hard blue presence in her veins, like chips of glacial ice. Her mouth was dry.

"Why, why would they do that? *How* could they do that? Fraily said they had managed only a few flatworm types and a Franken-frog."

"*Proto*-frog. And, he lied to us. Obviously, the Genetic

Xenomorphic Project was far more advanced that I was allowed to know. I was design, he and his team were production. They fed me, and Greenbough, false progress reports. However, I suspect Greenbough discovered what Peter and his team were up to and decided to take the GX Project under its weapons division. They intended to replace Peter because he lied, not because they had found someone more qualified. Peter kept these spectacular advances secret. They could no longer trust him."

"Neither could we, apparently. Okay. This really doesn't affect our plans, does it?"

"If the lost embryos do not survive, no." He looked at the computer screen, then back at her. "But if they have, it may have tremendous impact on human-kind. The ramifications could be dangerous."

"Screw the ramifications! This is an isolated area. What's the worst that can happen? Billy-Bob comes into town one day with a strange carcass tied over his hood? Meanwhile, we're safe and comfy on our little island. I'll have a nice tan, and you will have a new lab and whatever those embryos become." She relaxed. "It really doesn't matter."

"Perhaps." Doubt still lingered in his voice.

"What?" she said. "It's not gray goo, is it?"

"No. The Gray Goo Theory involves nanites."

"Well, what is it?"

"The dominant life-form, they tagged it as a Category IV. That means they used human DNA."

"Christ. Reproduction?"

"Again, I cannot access the design specifications or matrix. If Peter choose to make this creature largely mammalian, then offspring yield would range from, oh, say from one to four. For example, canines typically have litters of up to eight pups. Humans, on the other hand, commonly have only one infant, with multiple births beyond twins being the exception."

"And the other options?"

"Introduction of reptilian DNA could produce a hybrid mammal that bears young in greater numbers and matures at a much faster rate. There could be endless variety."

"Terrific." Jessica chewed her lower lip, thinking hard. Finally, she looked up. "It doesn't matter. We are leaving in three weeks. Can you have a smaller transport unit ready by then?"

"I should have one operational several days before the deadline. Mr. Redmond is a man of great resource."

"Good." She paused. "Doctor?"

"Yes?"

"You know to keep this new development just between us? This is still about bio-energy and Mother does not know we have recovered the ETU."

"Of course."

At the far end of the building, beyond the shower curtains, the door opened and closed quickly. The sound of footsteps moved toward them, someone coming fast and purposeful.

Jessica tensed, if it was someone other than Lee Picket or Red, their secret was finished. She moved to the curtain wall, intent on forestalling and deflecting the person if need be. Too late. A section of curtain snapped aside.

Red Redmond stood looking at them, one of those ridiculous bandanas on his head. The mercury light from the overheads carved Red's face into an ebon mask, his eyes wide and intent.

"Damn it, Redmond!" she said. "Knock, the next time."

Red stared at her. "Lee's in the hospital. Somebody jumped him at the city dock."

**

Beyond the warm sleep, there was pain. Like fog, it hovered in the background. Sometimes it came forward and blotted out the voices of the angels Lee heard. The pain threatened to take him to a red place filled with agony. He hated and feared that place, and in the beginning, he had to fight hard to stay free. Gradually, with help from the angels, he found it easier to resist the red place. He felt certain the ephemeral beings who came and went through the swirling mist were angels. They would push the pain back as far as it would go, sending it away with soft commands and silver needles. He loved the angels. At some point in his sleep, they left, and he missed them, their glowing whiteness and quiet, wordless voices.

People came in their stead. Some of the people he knew and some he did not.

Sydney appeared for a time, and Red, too. They spoke to him, but some of the pain came back, and he could not understand them.

A man with a mustache and a silver badge spoke to him, asking about what happened at the dock, who else was there. This puzzled Lee. He had no idea what the man was talking about.

The other people were strangers. At times, Lee knew they were doctors and nurses and that they were there because something had happened to him. Other times, he forgot who they were and tried to ask them what they were doing.

There came a point when he opened his eyes and the fog was gone. Night pressed against a window to his left, the window set in a stark hospital room lit by soft night-lights and the status lights on the gizmo that was plugged into him, IVs and wires.

God, he was thirsty.

"Water." His voice rustled like tissue paper.

The figure at the end of the bed, a dark-haired woman in a white uniform who was busy with a tray of something, looked at him. "Awake?" she said. "Great. I'll get that water for you." She left the room on little cushioned feet. Darkness found him again.

***

Lee realized he was conscious, floating up through a dark blue dream to reality. The world outside the window was dark; the atmosphere had that peculiar late-night quality. He focused on a silver badge floating on a khaki shirt beside his bed.

"How long was I out?" He hurt all over, but it was a kind of numb hurt.

"Three days. It's September fifth."

Lee thought about that. Three days on the River Lethe.

"He really worked you over, son." The man stroked his gunslinger mustache, looking at him with bright brown eyes. "Besides some scrapes, your buddy left you with a concussion and fractured forearm. If Liz Jordan hadn't come along, I doubt you'd be alive."

Lee stared up at him.

"Concussion," Lee said, trying to concentrate, "what's that mean, exactly."

"It means you were under a watch to see if your brain was bleeding. Fortunately, you seem to have a hard head. You'll just have to take it easy for a while, and you should be all right. I'm Sheriff Gordon, if you don't recall."

Lee moved his hand, weak, so weak. His left arm was trapped inside a cast that seemed to weigh several tons. "Yeah, from the Fraily investigation. I remember."

Sheriff Gordon reached over and handed him a plastic cup. Lee sipped through the straw, trying to wash away the pasty sickbed taste. The sheriff looked almost dapper in his polished cowboy boots, jeans, and tailored shirt, one of those guys you could roll in a pile of coal dust and he would come up spotless.

"Who?" Lee said. "Who worked me over?"

"I peg Shorty McGinty. We found his ball bat at the scene. Of course, he swears he didn't do it.

"Shorty?"

"Shorty McGinty. Owns and operates Shorty's Bar and Fish Camp at the edge of town. The reason I wonder if it might be him is he made a trip to the emergency room the same night you got dusted. He claims somebody smacked him from behind in his parking lot and took his wallet."

"I don't know Shorty. What's he look like?" It was difficult to think. His thoughts fell away almost has soon as he had them.

"You'd know Shorty. He's about six and a half feet

tall, near three hundred pounds. Ugly, mean, and nasty. Has a glass eye."

Lee thought back, trying to find his memory of the incident. Fragments came to him: the guy coming from the dark restroom doorway, swinging the bat, the lights, the sound the guy's feet made on the sidewalk. How big was the guy? Six, six? He did not think so.

"You okay, Picket?"

"Yeah. Just tired."

"See," Sheriff Gordon said, "I thought you two might have mixed it up or had a falling out of some kind. Thought you could have put out Shorty's lights behind his bar, then he woke up, tracked you down to return the compliment."

Lee sensed the mixture of drugs in his system, a pharmaceutical sludge that made him feel heavy and slow, and competed with the splintery, fragile thought process. "I don't know him. Sheriff, I'm having a little trouble . . . concentrating."

The same dark-eyed nurse he now remembered asking for water stepped briefly into the room. "You're real popular, Cowboy," she said. "There's two ladies waiting to see you, after the sheriff."

She vanished into the hall, a whirl of white uniform and brown hair. Sheriff Gordon turned his attention back to Lee.

"You sure? He says someone stole his baseball bat, the one you met at the marina. That bat is well known in this area, at least in the certain circles. You probably didn't get a chance to notice, but he's burned notches into it for the number of heads he's busted breaking up bar fights. Looks like you'd be notch number seven."

"This guy wasn't anywhere near that size. I'd remember that."

"Are you sure?"

"We going to play games, now? I'm really tired, Sheriff."

"All right." Sheriff Gordon shrugged. "For what it's worth, Shorty says he has never heard of *you*. I just wonder how many answers you're holding to what's been going on around here."

"I don't . . . understand."

"You were a police officer. Do you still believe in coincidences?"

"A true coincidence? Not when people are involved."

"Well, check this." Sheriff Gordon used his fingers as a checklist. "One, I've got Lee Picket coming to the Prescott Lodge, a local landmark of wealth and privilege, to write a book after getting himself shot in the line of duty. Two, said writer, the ex-cop, discovers the body of a biological engineer in the lake not long after he arrives. Three, said engineer worked for Greenbough Energy, a major corporation that just happened to have had one of its research labs in Kansas City blow up earlier this summer, killing a dozen or so people. Are you with me?"

"I'm tired, Sheriff."

"Four, this writer, that's you, to refresh your battered memory, at some point becomes Celia Prescott's security man or private investigator or whatever-the-hell title you like, and starts agitating the Creed family. And just lately, he has taken to tailing a small group of tourist fishermen whose license tags run back to Global Contractors. This Contractors outfit, a heavy security provider, is a subsidiary of Greenbough Energy, the same company that lost its lab in the mysterious explosion just weeks before one of its engineers turned up in my lake *after*, so says the medical examiner, he suffered a blow to the head."

No moss on the sheriff. "That it?"

"Nope. I've lost five people in or around the lake this summer, and had two people bitten by something that has impressive dental equipment—also in the lake. The most recent M.I.A. is a teenage boy. Maybe you've read the newspapers? Liz Jordan covered the story real nice. She mentioned several times how the blood trail led into the lake."

"I'm sorry to hear that. I didn't know."

"We don't think the boy's alive. So now, Mr. Lee Picket, the cop-turned-writer-turned-gumshoe, gets himself beaten half to death at the city dock with a ball bat belonging to a local bar owner, an ex-Army ranger."

Lee waited. He thought the man was having a good

time, showing off his detective skills. He also thought the man liked to hear himself talk.

"Now," the sheriff said, "I can't help but think that at least some of these incidents are related."

"I told you, I don't know Shorty."

"Yeah. Liz Jordan said she thought your assailant was about your size. She thinks she would have noticed a monster like Shorty. But, you know how things like size and color can get distorted in the dark, especially when you're taken by surprise."

"You mind telling me what happened? After I went down, I mean."

The sheriff grunted. "Whoever you were in discussion with was shy. He took off when he saw Liz, or heard her screaming for help."

"I owe her one."

"Yes, you do. I think your attacker left you for dead. He just didn't have time to hang around and make sure."

The sluggish feeling in his mind and body made it difficult to concentrate. Sheriff Gordon's quick little brown eyes did not make thinking any easier. The man would pounce on the first mistake Lee made.

The sheriff stroked his mustache. "If it wasn't Shorty, who is you next best suspect?"

"No one that comes to mind."

"Corliss Creed?"

Lee remained silent. They stared at each other.

Finally, Sheriff Gordon said, "I don't think you're a criminal, Mr. Picket. However, I do think you are involved in whatever is going on around here. I'll put the pieces together at some point. Be sure you're squeaky clean when I do."

"What movie is that from? Sounds familiar."

They stared at each other some more.

There was motion and a light knock at the door. Lee turned his head slowly to keep the room from spinning. Liz Jordan stood in the doorway, her purse in her hand and a camera slung from her shoulder. She wore a green skirt with a matching jacket. Something in the material made it sparkle just a bit when she moved. Her smile was tentative.

"Hi," she said. "If I'm interrupting, I can come back."

No, it's fine, Liz. We were finished, anyway." Sheriff Gordon looked at Lee. "Weren't we?

Lee nodded.

Liz came in and stopped at the side of the bed.

The sheriff paused on his way out the door. "I'll give you some advice, son. Get out of it, whatever the hell it is."

"Sure."

"Liz," the sheriff said, "don't wear this boy out. I just took him over the hurdles."

"I won't." She smiled and winked at Lee.

When the sheriff had gone, she said, "You look like hell."

"Feel like it, too." He raised his hand and she took it, careful of the IV set taped there. "They tell me you saved my life. I want to thank you."

"I just happened along." Her hand was warm and soft in his. "I'm glad I did."

"Me, too."

She released his hand. "Do you feel like talking?"

"I can talk, but I don't feel up to another interrogation."

"Sure. I just wanted to know if it was Shorty McGinty that put you here."

"It wasn't him. Not if he's as big as the sheriff says."

"I didn't think so."

"Sheriff Gordon seems to like his job."

"He's a little rough about it sometimes, but he's a good man and a good sheriff. I've covered quite a few cases with him. He may look like a Wyatt Earp wanna-be, but he is quite impressive. I'd hate to have him on my ass."

The comment made Lee grunt with humor, which hurt

something deep inside him. He groaned.

"Oh," Liz said. "Are you all right?"

The pain subsided. "Yeah. Just don't make me laugh."

"Sorry." She studied him. "You're in no shape for this. One more question, then I'll leave, okay?"

"Shoot."

"What were you doing with binoculars?"

"Bird watching."

Liz made a face at him, patted his hand. "Thanks for nothing."

Sydney Tatum walked in moments after Liz Jordan left. She kissed him on his forehead.

"Hey," Lee said.

Tears slipped out and ran down her cheeks. She wiped at them with a tissue. "You had everybody scared there for a while."

"So I hear. It's good to you see you, Syd."

"The doctor thinks you can come home in a few days. We all miss you. Celia says don't worry about the doctor bills or anything. She's taking care of it all."

"Kind . . . of her."

"She thinks you getting hurt, uh, had something to do

with whatever it was she had you doing."

"I can't say, Sid. Listen, I'm getting tired."

She kissed him on the forehead again. Her perfume made him dizzy. "I'll come tomorrow. You want anything?"

"Just your company."

***

Arletha Creed looked over the dinner table with satisfaction. Everyone but Horace and Hank had come to supper with their best manners. The platter of fried pork chops was empty, all the boys digging in soon as she set it down, Corliss and Jubal having a spate of competition over the largest chop before it tore in two, making Jessie laugh in that strange snuffling way of his. Uther was the little gentleman; he used his fork instead of his fingers to reach the chops and he did not tug and paw at his shirt the whole meal through like Jubal and Jessie did. Jubal and the others had forgotten how to wear clothes. She reckoned it would take a while for them to get used to them again. Horace and Hank seemed the slowest when it came to taking on new ideas, just like they had been in their first life. She could hear them every once and awhile, smacking their lips where they had taken their dinner plates out onto the porch, likely eating with their fingers. Maybe some things, like a person's nature, were eternal.

Dirty overhead light from the solitary kitchen bulb cast a dim glow on the table, which was now a litter of empty dishes and serving bowls. Arletha shook her head. "Boys, I'd be obliged if you'd clear the table. I feel my years this evenin'."

Corliss, picking his teeth with a matchstick, nodded his head at Jubal who sat listening attentively. "Whyn't you have him to do it? He's the one made all the mess, him and the other monkeys."

"Corliss, I told you about calling them names. An' that ain't no way to talk about your pa." She sucked a particle of food from the empty socket where once she had a molar. "I expect when he gets his full size he'll take you to task. You 'member that time he whupped you clean around the barn?"

"I do!" Luther leaned forward, his eyes bright. "I remember. Pa had him dancing and screamin' ev'ry step of the way. Corliss, you screamed like a little girl."

Corliss shot his brother a hard look from under his hair. "What do you expect? I was nine, ten-years-old, and Pa had a hickory switch after my legs. You'd fuckin' scream too, you ignorant shit-stick. I still got scars."

"Corliss!" Aretha said. "Boy, that ain't no kind of language for the dinner table."

"You were *twelve*-years-old, anyway," Luther said. "An' Pa had caught you smoking in the barn."

"Do you remember that, Pa?" Arletha watched Jubal, hoping this time he would recollect something from his past.

Jubal studied her face, his eyes empty of recognition. He looked almost like his old self tonight, she thought. He was getting better at coloring his skin to look like it ought, but it still held a slight golden shimmer when the light caught it just so.

Corliss snorted. "Hell, he don't know left from right. How much longer 'fore you see these ain't Pa and the others? They's just some kind of freaks."

"You quit talkin' like that or you can sleep in the barn tonight." Arletha felt her heart sink. Why did life always have to be so difficult? The most natural thing in the world, a boy recognizing his own flesh and blood, and Corliss could not see it. "Maybe you ought to sleep out there anyway, 'til you come to understand the pure miracle of them coming back, your Pa and the others."

Corliss stood quickly, the feet of his chair squawking on the wood floor. He pointed his matchstick at her. "I ain't sleepin' in no barn."

Jubal tensed and made a low noise in his throat, taking his hand from Arletha. He watched Corliss with unflinching eyes. Maybe, Arletha thought, Jubal would be sending Luther after another hickory switch.

"That's it," Corliss said, "growl at me, you little shit. I'll bag your ass up and carry you to the nearest sideshow."

Corliss paused, looking past Jubal now as if he could see through the walls to a distant horizon. He put the matchstick back in his mouth and shifted his gaze to Jubal, speculation joining the anger that still snapped in his eyes.

Luther leaned back and slapped his knee. "Haw! I'd pay to see that."

"You shut up, too," Corliss said. "I ain't foolin' Ma. I've had enough of your crazy notions and these little bastards. It wasn't your witchin' brought them here. They come out of that thing in the lake. Luther knows they ain't our kin. He's just playin' along 'cause he's always been under your apron."

"Son," Arletha said, "you break my old heart."

"Aw!" Corliss spun and struck the back of his chair sending it clattering across the floor and into her grandmother's hutch.

Jubal, Uther, and Jessie sprang from their chairs and froze, staring after Corliss who now had his back to them, heading for the door. A peculiar low moan came from them, so faint she barely heard it.

"Easy, Pa," she said. "You know he's always been that-a-way."

The screen door slapped behind Corliss. Jubal, Uther, and Jessie relaxed. Their skins shimmered for a moment. Corliss's voice leapt through the door.

"Get out of my chair, you fuckin' baboons!"

Hank and Horace bumped into each other as they came through the door. Horace dropped his plate. They turned and looked out the door, then Horace picked up his plate and they came to the table. Jubal moaned at them, saying something in that odd way of his.

Arletha stared at the door, seeing the empty sky darkening beyond. "How'd I raise a boy so mean?

Not having time to ponder that in full, she looked at Luther. "I want you to find me a copperhead, a rattlesnake would be better. I'll be makin' up a witchball for Celia Prescott, and I want some poison. She thinks she can run us, she's wrong. Sendin' her men after you."

"Snakes are hard to find this time of year, Ma."

"You go to the caves, I 'spect you'll find them. You ought to know that."

"Corliss is growing his stuff out there an' he don't like nobody messin' around."

"Don't pay him no mind. What's the matter with you, anyway? You act like you don't want to he'p your old Ma."

"Well . . . I figure maybe if we leave them Prescott's alone, maybe they'll leave us alone."

Arletha stared at him. Jubal and the others were listening attentively. She knew how Jubal would feel about that idea. "Boy, what kind of talk is that? These are the people killed your pa an' uncles, an' them standin' right here, listening to you. They ain't ready to take up the feud, so we have to carry it 'til then. Look at them. Tell your pa right now that you don't want to fix the folks what killed him and his brothers. Go on, tell him."

Luther's eyes flicked over to Jubal then dropped to the

table. His voice was quiet. "I'll . . . go find you a snake."

"That's better." Arletha reached over and pinched his stubbly cheek. "Make it a big one."

9

September 6

Jessica Prescott was the last person Lee expected to see standing at his bedside. She wore pale green slacks and a brown cashmere sweater shot with gold threads. Her hair was down as usual, delicate emerald earrings peeking out from beneath it, her green eyes serious behind minimum mascara.

"So, how are you?"

He detected a hint of unease in her casual tone.

"Fair," he replied. Actually, he still felt pretty-damned banged up. His head still spun if he turned it too fast. Sometimes, dreams and reality seemed to overlap. His arm ached and itched in the new cast. "The doctors think I'll be out of here in a few days."

"That's great." Her gaze wandered over him then traveled without intent around the room. "Are they taking good care of you?"

"Not bad."

"You really know how to make conversation."

"Just wondering why you're here, Jessica."

"I suppose if I told you I cared about you that would be too much?"

"I don't know."

"Then I won't tell you that. Let's try this instead. Corliss sent me a letter. It looks like a fourth-grader wrote it, pencil on that wide-lined notebook paper. He wants the rest of his money plus interest. I don't know what to do about it."

Lee thought about that. "Give it to him."

"What?"

"Give it to him. Get him out of the way for now. I'll deal with him when I get out."

"He wants *fifty*-thousand."

"What? Why is he so greedy now?"

"How should I know? I guess he's mad you screwed him over the first time."

Lee nodded. "His penalty interest on the ten grand we owe. He should be a banker."

"I thought you were against giving him money. Remember, that stray dog theory you mentioned?"

"Jessica, they've got me held together with duct tape and picture wire. I feel like I have loose glass sliding around in my head. The doctors tell me I'm out of commission for week at least. What is it you want me to do? He's got us over a barrel."

She dropped into the visitor's chair, her hands falling between her legs like dying birds.

"Okay," Lee said, feeling moved, this woman doing better than most under incredible pressure, "how soon before you and the doctor can travel?"

"Not anytime soon."

"Okay, pay Creed the ten grand we owe him. Tell him it will take time to get the rest together."

"I've got a fifty-thousand-dollar limit on my corporate card alone. Do you think he's that stupid?"

"Yes, I do. How does he expect delivery?"

"I am to put the money at the end of his dock at midnight tomorrow."

"Take Red with you."

"Red? He's liable to knock me in the head and take the money himself. He's from the Kansas City streets, for God's sake."

"You really believe that?"

"I don't trust him. He's just another stray Mother has taken in."

"I disagree. That's an act he puts on. Besides, you don't trust anybody."

"It works for me."

"Then, take Sydney, too."

"Sydney?" She stood and stared at him. "How am I going to explain it to Sydney? 'Hey, come with me, I'm dropping off a charitable donation for under-privileged sociopaths?'"

"You're a smart girl. Figure something out, or don't take her."

"Thanks for nothing. What are you going to do when you get back?"

"I'm still working on that."

"I feel so much better."

He watched her face. One of the small muscles at the corner of her mouth twitched.

"The Creeds are the least of your worries, now. Who do you think put me in this bed?"

"I don't know. You're so adorable. It's difficult to think anyone would want to hurt you."

"The sheriff asked me if I thought it was the "fishermen" I was tailing that did it. I told him, no. But, who else could it be?"

She shook her head. "They're pros. If they wanted you beaten as a warning, they would not have come so close to killing you. If they wanted you dead, then you would be dead."

"Maybe you're wrong."

"Have you thought that Corliss followed you to town? He hates you."

"I don't think he's got that kind of nerve. I see him as more of a back-shooter."

Jessica looked out the window where the rain clouds had crept closer. After a moment, she whirled, took two steps to the bed and patted his hand. She wiped away a tear that spilled suddenly from her eye. "I've got to go. I'll do something with Corliss."

Before he could reply, she swept from the room.

Jessica's performance in replay: Was it real? She seemed to be a soulless corporate player, a spoiled Daddy's Girl who fought him at every turn. It was convenient not to like her. Now that she had shown her vulnerability, it was difficult to keep his sympathy in-check. He owed her, anyway. He had let her down, should have been able to control Corliss, and not let him get to her the way he did.

Owed her.

Drowsy, fading fast, he realized he had meant to ask Jessica if Dr. Chilson's little project could have anything to do with lake monsters or alligators. He looked out the window. Outside, lightning ran through a cloud like a strobe light firing in a brown paper bag.

September 7

Celia had not slept well during the night's thunderstorms. This informal luncheon, she decided, had been just what she needed to perk her up. Sydney was always upbeat, and Liz Jordan ever surprising and irreverent. At zenith, the sun's rays cut through the arbor, now only half-clad in its yellowing late summer coat of grape leaves, and warmed the flagstone patio beneath. Listening to the other two talking, Celia felt the warmth on her back radiating from the lodge's rock wall and for just a moment forgot about all the storms in her life.

"So tell me," Liz said to Sydney, pulling a grape from the small bunch on her lunch plate, "is it true you've got Kyra James coming to the charity?"

Sydney glanced at Celia. She nodded "go-ahead."

"Well," Sydney said, "she's only dropping in for a photo-op, but she agreed to do a couple of songs before she leaves, just for the kids. We were lucky. She's playing a gig in Branson, kicking off her new album, and we're only twenty-minutes away by helicopter. Otherwise, we wouldn't have her."

"That's great," Liz said.

"But," Sydney added, "that's confidential, Liz. No leaks in the press, or we'll have a blockade of fans clogging the dock and storming the beach. You're welcome to try for an interview while she's here, but nothing before, okay?"

Liz crossed her heart. "On my honor."

"I mean it," Sydney said. "I'll have Lee throw you into the lake."

"If he ever gets out of the hospital. Are there anymore celebrities coming?"

"Calm yourself, Liz," Celia said. "All in good time."

"Celia, out here in the sticks, I get one, sometimes two chances a year to cover something more interesting than city council meetings and who-grew-the-largest-squash contest. This summer has been the exception, all the missing people and a possible lake monster, but I'd still like to know if I'll cap it off with another big Celia Prescott Party. Come on. You've got to know your events are like the Academy Awards around here. They draw a big interest."

Celia pushed her plate away. A feeling of unease began to thread its way up her backbone. Her wheelchair held her like a prison. "I am not sure. I . . . Syd, who else is coming?"

"Celebrity-wise? You have Alan Ricky from that TV show, 'Harper's Row,'" and Laura Munroe from NPR News."

"Radio?" Liz said. "That's for illiterates."

Sydney looked at her. "It's *National Public Radio*."

Liz smirked. "You're right. Who listens to that?"

"Oh, you're just jealous," Sydney said, smiling.

Celia rolled herself back from the table, unable to shake the sense of impending doom that now loomed like an approaching storm in the back of her mind. The women looked at her curiously.

"What is it?" Sydney asked.

Celia shaded her eyes and studied the tree line. With the sun overhead, the woods were full of shadows, solid dark shapes that skulked amid the kaleidoscope screen of leaves. "I feel I need to move. There is something . . . coming."

Sydney stood. "Would you like to go in?"

Liz turned her gaze to the woods. She gasped.

A cold hand squeezed Celia's heart. At the edge of the woods, mottled by shade, an apparition stood watching them.

Liz said, "My God."

The figure shambled from the shadows towards them, hitching along in a determined manner, a scarecrow in faded cloth leaning on a gnarled walking cane with every step. Sunlight landed hard on the apparitions' weathered, wrinkled face.

Celia whispered, "Arletha Creed."

Sydney moved beside her and placed one hand on her shoulder. Celia scarcely felt it. Liz did not move; her eyes were locked on the approaching woman.

Arletha's shapeless housedress hung on her like a tattered battle flag, torn and stained, a gray memory of too many campaigns. Her hair was a matted nest wrapped about her head, lifeless and dirty. She moved across the yard in a jerking, mechanical way, her body hard, gnarled and nut-brown like the walking stick she stabbed into the earth at every step. Her eyes burned with dark intensity.

She stopped at the patio's flowered border, turning her head to see each one of them. Her nearly toothless mouth gaped. She inhaled noisily.

Liz Jordan said, "Oh!" and covered her nose as the air current carried the woman's odor to them, a rank miasma of unwashed body, wood smoke, and stale grease.

"Prescott," Arletha said, her voice harsh as a crow's, "you old bitch. I come to put the death hex on you."

Celia could not move. It was as if a giant hand pressed her into her wheelchair. She could not find her breath.

"You know why!" Arletha continued. "Don't you be looking shocked."

Sydney took an uncertain step toward her. "You leave her be, you hateful thing."

"Settle down, Sassy-frassy. I got no truck with you." Arletha jabbed her stick in Celia's direction. "Only this one, this liar, *this killer bitch* living past her time."

"Get off this property," Sydney said. "You are violating the restraining order."

"Ha!" Arletha tapped her stick on the ground in apparent mirth and spoke into the air. "Little hussy, you go back inside and play with your dolls afore you get hurt. Heh, heh, little hussy thinks she's fierce, heh, heh. She don't know. She don't know."

Celia found her breath and her voice. "Creed, you do as she says. Leave. You have no business here."

Arletha fixed her black eyes on Celia, her toothless mouth open for air.

"I got business." She reached into the pocket of her stained apron. "Your man killed my husband an' his brothers. Your man stole our land, cheatin' us when he knowed we was down on hard times. And you held his hand ev'ry step o' the way, wanting it just the same as him."

Celia gripped the arms of her chair, wondering if the woman had a pistol in her apron. "Sydney, call the sheriff!"

Sydney turned. "You want me to leave?"

"Oh, for heaven's sake," Liz said, pulling her cell phone from her purse. "I'll call. I have his number on speed-dial."

"Don't fox me," Arletha said. "Them things don't work out here."

She pulled her hand from her apron and in one motion

tossed a small black ball over the patio table. It landed in Celia's lap.

Celia looked at the object lying in the valley of her dress, a confused knot of black hair, grease, and god-only-knew what else. It was similar in size to a tennis ball. She felt its dead weight.

"That's it, now," Arletha said, "I've put the hex on you. You'll be dying soon, I s'pect. That witch ball will do the trick. I made it special for you, Prescott."

Celia snapped her dress taught, launching the odious ball. It landed on the flagstones with a small thud and rolled to a stop against a planter of bright mums. She looked at Arletha.

"You demented old bitch!"

"Ha!" Arletha turned and hobbled toward the woods. She spoke without looking back. "Ha! Call the sheriff—he cain't stop it. Sic your boys on me—they cain't stop it! Nobody can."

They all stared at the departing woman, watching her grow smaller until the woods swallowed her in a leafy gulp. A blue jay screamed in the trees there.

Sydney said, "Who was that with her? Did you see? Someone came to meet her."

"Someone?" Liz said. "Some*thing*. It was a big dog, or at least, I think it was."

Celia took a drink of her iced tea, trying to regain her

composure. The ice clinked in the glass as she set it down. She could hear her pulse in her ears.

"I have had enough of that woman," she said, and looked at the grotesque black ball resting against the planter. "Sydney, bag that disgusting thing. It is exhibit 'A'."

***

The night seemed unusually sinister to Jessica. Darkness pressed around them, almost a physical beast, greedily sucking at any light source. Red brought the Bayliner up to speed and headed for Creed Island. Rushing after them, the darkness beast gobbled the dull white tear of the boat's wake just a few yards behind them. In a continuous groan of wind, the night swept past smelling of water and the coming autumn. She shivered and drew her sweater around her. Sydney Tatum, more insurance against Corliss doing something violent, looked at her from the other seat, her face putty-colored in the weak light of the instrument panel.

"I still think you should tell your mother," she said over the sound of the motor and wind. "I mean, midnight intrigue and sacks of money is a little drastic."

They had boarded in the dark, not using the dock lights, and Jessica had ordered Red to keep the running lights off for the duration of the trip. Both measures were precautions against surveillance by Greenbough or her mother.

"I told you," Jessica said, "She would have a fit if she knew I was even considering this. But, I am sick of this endless feud she has with the Creeds. It has been going on my entire life. If paying them to stay away is what it takes to end it, then that is what I will do."

"I'm just not comfortable with this."

"Are you comfortable with having Arletha Creed come to lunch again?"

Today's lunch incident had caused quite a commotion at the lodge. Celia had everyone on alert now and frequently scanned the woods with her telescope. She had Red patrol the lodge perimeter twice a day and was talking about getting guard dogs. However, Arletha's visit had provided the perfect cover for recruiting Sydney for the money drop.

Sydney stared across the lake in silence.

Red, who knew Corliss was the real reason for the payoff, grinned. "I get overtime for this action?"

"There may be a little something extra in your Christmas stocking."

In the darkness, Creed's Island drew closer. Her heart beat faster. The naked way Corliss always looked at her made her uneasy, and he was there, crouched on his night-shrouded island like a predator at a water hole, waiting for them. She shivered.

They arrived at the island without further conversation. The bones of the old dock emerged out of the night. Red cut the throttle and let the boat drift on momentum.

"Here we are." He turned to Jessica. "How you want to do this? Slow an' easy, or stroke it an' go?"

"Fast," she said. "Let's get this over with."

"You got it."

Red pushed the throttle forward, and the boat surged ahead.

"Sydney," Jessica said, "would you put the box on the dock. I don't want to set foot on Creed property."

"I might as well do something." Sydney moved forward, brushing past her toward the bow.

Red backed the throttle at the last minute. The boat bumped against the empty dock. Sydney leaned over and held the boat close to the rough timbers.

With the motor now idling at a low grumble, the silence of the night again pressed against them. Frogs, scattered in the trees and along the shore, murmured with hushed, almost sly voices. Jessica found herself standing, straining to hear anything beyond them. She watched the far end of the dock where it thrust from the inky woods, half-expecting Corliss to rush from the shadows.

"Sydney," she whispered, and leaned forward with the cardboard shoebox that held ten-thousand dollars in one-hundred dollar bills. The cardboard felt damp and surprisingly light.

Sydney took the box. "Where do I put it?"

"Put it anywhere," Red said. "The dude's got to be watching right now. He ain't gonna lose track of it."

Jessica snapped her attention again to the wall of dark trees looming above the shore, searching for any movement. She kept her gaze there, peripherally watching Sydney lean far over and set the box on the dock. Red put the boat in reverse and backed it away, gently. They had spent less than a minute in the maneuver.

In silence, Sydney made her way to the backseat and sat down.

Jessica stared at the box, the crappy, common little shoe box, sitting like an abandoned puppy at the end of the dock; distance and darkness soon cloaked it. The desperate and preposterous birth of the mission hit her then, how film Noir the operation had been, with the cash pulled from three different accounts and a final midnight drop-off to a ruthless blackmailer, hushed voices in the night. She clapped a hand to her mouth to stifle a burst of dark laughter.

Red turned the boat toward the lodge. "You say something?"

"Just clearing my throat." The dock vanished, swallowed by the night. "I thought he might show."

"He ain't interested in us, tonight," Red said. "He jus' wants the cash."

Jessica watched the dark hump of the island slowly

defuse into the darkness. "I hope so."

September 8

Energized by his new plans this morning, Corliss took a toke from the jay and passed it back to his life-long buddy and partner-in-crime, Darryl Hicks. He gulped an air chaser after the toke, putting more pressure on the smoke in his lungs, pushing the magic into his system faster. His hair tingled at the roots, making him push the cowboy hat further back on his head. He leaned against the couch, comfortable inside the softness of his old gray sweatshirt, the collar rib cut vertically a couple of inches at the front because he did not like things tight around his throat.

Darryl's place was deep in the woods, the only house down a half-mile of broken gravel road the county had forgotten years ago. From where they sat on the decrepit front porch, kicked back on a raggedy-ass couch that smelled of dog and mildew, Corliss could just see bits of lake through the pale burn of early autumn trees. Darryl's dog, a rangy blue tick hound named Reefer, lay on the boards beside his master, pissed-off because they had taken-over his couch. Late morning light filtered through the hickory and oaks that crowded the weathered little shack, finding its way through yellow and rust-colored leaves. A ramshackle shed, what used to be a smokehouse really, was falling down slow, leaning against one of the massive oaks by the rocky drive where the rusting hulks of two ancient Chevys were pushed to the side like road kill, Virginia creeper clinging in scarlet wreathes over them.

Darryl had himself a mini-toke. Corliss could see him working over the proposition in his mind, weighing the yeps and nopes. Darryl stroked his thick cowboy mustache, a pale ragged thing yellowed by nicotine, and pretended to study the end of the joint like maybe the little ember did not suit him. Despite the coolness in the air, Darryl was barefoot; his dirty feet stuck out of his faded blue jeans like strange, anemic animals. His toes curled on the rough porch planks.

Corliss let the smoke out of his lungs in a great huff. The pot heightened his senses. The air, sweet and soft with the season, was marred by the whiff of smoldering garbage from Darryl's trash heap just to the side of the house. "What do you say, Bro?"

Darryl seemed not to hear him.

Corliss gave him a minute, knowing Darryl took his time with things. Finally, he said, "Well, how about it?"

"I dunno, man." Darryl went to hand him the joint but Corliss waved it away, not wanting to get too high. Darryl studied the tip of the joint again. A Jonsered chainsaw ball cap, once red and now faded to a splotchy pink, kept Darryl's stringy hair, the same washed out color as his mustache, from falling into his face. "I dunno. I got me a purty steady business with the pot. So do you. I don't get why you want to branch out. If you got all this money from Prescott, why do you want to work? Why don't you take your ol' partner to Branson and we'll party down, get some girls?"

"Man. Meth is here to stay. Makes twice as much scratch as pot." Corliss made a wide gesture. "Lost as this place is, we could cook it by the barrel and nobody'd know. I'll take it to this guy I know in Kansas City for distribution. We make enough of it, we can carry it to Saint Louie an' Little Rock. We can get rich, man, *rich*."

"I ain't opposed to that," Darryl replied. He took another mini-toke. His eyes, a watery, dreamy blue, settled on Corliss. "It just sounds like work. And, ain't that shit dangerous to make?"

"If you're an idiot. But, I know how to do it safe. C'mon, what do you say? It's not much different from what you're doing now, an' more money. Look, we can use that old shed there if you're worried about blowing up your house. I'd make it at my place, but Ma would bust a garter."

"Shhh." Darryl sat up straight. "Somebody's comin'."

Corliss looked around to see a sleek brown Crown Victoria moving slow and careful down the rutted drive. The windows were tinted light gray, obscuring the occupants.

"Pinch that joint out, Darryl," he said. "They got the look and feel of real cops."

Darryl complied and dropped the dead joint into his shirt pocket. He capped the bottle of Kentucky bourbon resting between his legs and set it on the floor. Reefer raised his head and watched the car approach, raising his nose to catch the scent. Corliss stuffed his snub-nosed .38 between the seat cushions. Darryl looked at him.

"You're carryin', with *your* record? Man, they catch you with that, you're gone five-to-ten."

"I got to protect myself. Besides, they got to catch me first."

The sedan stopped behind Darryl's old Dodge pick-up. After a moment, two guys got out. They were dressed in good clothes, but common, both in jeans and pullovers. One of them, the biggest one, wore a beige sport jacket and pilot's sunglasses. The smaller guy had creases pressed into his jeans—who the fuck did that? They were cops of some kind, for sure, their hair cut short and smooth.

"Good morning," the big one said. He had a wide, flat face, just a hint of jowl starting to show, and an air of readiness about him. He and the other guy walked right up to the porch like they had an invitation.

From the bottom step, the smaller guy, who had a crooked nose, nodded at Reefer who was watching them with suspicion in his eyes. "Is he okay with strangers?"

Darryl said, slowly, "Depends on the strangers, I guess."

"Well," the stranger said, "I can't take a chance like that."

The guy brought a pistol out from nowhere and shot

Reefer twice, the pistol only making abrupt whapping sounds, like somebody clapping their hands. The dog yelped once, kicked, and then lay still.

With a cry, Darryl leaped from the couch and cradled Reefer in his arms.

Stunned by the unexpected attack, Corliss knew it was too late to go for his gun hidden in the seat cushions. The new guys had the jump. The new guys were pros.

Darryl looked up, shouting. "What the fuck? What the fuck're you doing?"

"Looks like," the big guy said, bringing out a silenced pistol of his own and pointing it at them, "looks like he's killing your dog."

"He din't do nothing!"

Reefer stiffened. A sigh escaped him, and then the hound's body relaxed.

Blood pooled under the dog. Reefer's eyes closed. The tip of his tongue poked from side of his muzzle like a piece of pink bubble-gum. It was too bad for Darryl. Reefer was a pretty fair coon dog.

"Corliss," the big guy said, "may I have your attention?"

"What?" This guy knew his name.

"We'd like a little information, please. We'd like to know why Jessica Prescott is making midnight runs to your dock."

"I don't know who, or what the fuck you are. And I don't know what you're talking about."

The other guy, Crooked Nose, said, "You don't know much, do you?"

"Fuck you," Corliss said. The thought that these dudes might be after his money crossed his mind. Sure, what else? Crooked cops. Nasty ones, too.

Darryl crawled to the couch, moaning. Before Corliss could have the idea to stop him, Darryl snatched the snub-nose from the cushions, spun, and fired at the two strangers.

The silenced pistols barked twice each. Corliss heard the rounds hit Darryl with smacking, thudding sounds. His stomach turned. He wanted to run.

Darryl fell back against the couch, his eyes going wild, looking at everything, some kind of question in them as he saw Corliss. The front of his shirt spilled blood from four neat little holes. Air sucked into one of them, a wrong, wet sound.

Corliss half rose to reach him, but stopped. The shooters might think he was going for the snub-nose and smoke *him*.

Darryl's eyes cleared then, and had the steel in them Corliss knew Darryl could find when things got rough. When his daddy was alive and drunk, he beat Darryl with a tow strap and Darryl would take it, that same look in his eyes.

"Bessie's home," Darryl said to him, his voice weak and constricted. "Bessie's home."

"What?" Corliss said, then he remembered, and a thrill of hope fired through him. *Bessie.*

Suddenly, the light left Darryl's eyes. His body went limp. Corliss fancied he saw a little wisp of smoke drift up through the mustache. The stench of fresh excrement filled the air; Darryl had crapped himself.

The little revolver rested on the planks beside Darryl. The big stranger, from behind his pilot's glasses, said, "Are you going to do something stupid, too?"

Corliss looked at him, his heart pounding in his rib cage, pounding so hard it hurt. "Not me."

"What was he saying about Bessie?" Crooked Nose had a touch of excitement in his voice, maybe a little breathless, a fucking kill-freak. He was looking through the open door into the house.

"It didn't make no sense," Corliss said. "Bessie's been a long time gone. His old girlfriend."

"Touching," the big guy said. "Now, about Ms. Prescott?"

Corliss stood, thinking hard and fast. He had to play the next cards just right, or he was going to be as dead as Darryl and Reefer. "Can I get off this porch? I cain't bare to see this."

The two guys looked at each other, a silent message passing between them. The big guy came up the steps, still covering Corliss with his quiet pistol. "We'll go inside," he said. "Any surprises in there?"

"Might be," Corliss said, struggling to keep his cool. He put his hands up and moved through the open door slow and easy. "Darryl wasn't much for housekeepin'."

The house smelled much like the couch on the porch, but with the tang of wood smoke from last night's fire leaking from the old iron stove adding to the aroma of dog and mildew. Corliss walked through the living room towards the kitchen, all of which was one room, really, past a bare-armed couch and a dusty, battered television that was playing with the sound turned down. Looked like a Clint Eastwood western on. He waited for the guys to stop him, but they let him go to the scarred Formica table in the kitchen. The table was the old-fashioned kind, with the wide chrome trim that dropped from the tabletop as a short skirting. He went to the far side and faced them.

The smaller guy, who had been looking around the house, nodded at the chair. "Okay."

Corliss pulled out the chair, a chrome job scabrous with rust, and sat, feeling the torn vinyl cushion scratch against his rump. He put his hands on the table, keeping them where the jerk-offs could see them. The big guy raked back the chair across from him and sat, putting his pistol under the table, an unseen threat likely pointing at Corliss's belly. Crooked Nose stood to one side, his bent honker wrinkled.

"You weren't bullshitting about the housekeeping," he said, and turned back to Corliss. "You jokers are big operators, is that it?"

"Not anymore."

Crooked Nose smiled. "Check this one. He's got a sense of humor."

"That's good," the big guy said. "He might need it."

Corliss stared at them. "You gonna tell me who you are? If you're cops, you're the crudest motherfuckers I've seen."

"We are not cops or motherfuckers," the big guy replied. "We are corporate investigators who have come to recover stolen property."

"I ain't got it."

"Got what?"

"Your property. Prescott's got it." Corliss figured these two would brook no pissing around and decided, live or die, that he could at least get even with Jessica Prescott by siccing these assholes on her. "A big fancy tank, right? Science stuff inside?"

The two looked at each other again, some kind of inside joke going on. Seeing it was getting to be a little creepy. He wondered if maybe they were showering together. They looked back at him.

"I found it in the lake," he said. "A little while later, the

Prescott bitch shows up looking for it. I sold it to her for ten-grand. Bitch still owes me five."

Maybe he could buy them off cheap if it came to that.

"That's too bad," Crooked Nose said.

Corliss dropped his head into his hands and sobbed, starting out fake but surprised to find it turn real. He snuffled and got himself under control, then looked up, dropping one of his hands under the table. "Jesus, is that it? You gonna kill me now?"

"You never know." The muzzle of the little guy's pistol had not wavered from Corliss's chest. "I'm curious though. Was it you put Lee Picket in the hospital?"

These guys got around. "Yeah."

"Just wanted to thank you for that."

"Sure," said the big guy. "We ought to put you on our payroll, taking care of our light-work for us."

"That right?" said Corliss.

Crooked Nose said, "Picket was a minor irritation."

Corliss looked dead in the sunglass lenses of the big guy across from him, seeing himself there, his white cowboy hat shining like a western-wear halo. "You guys" he said, "are minor irritations."

The smile left the face of the big guy. Corliss squeezed the first trigger on the double-barreled sawed-off twelve-gauge shotgun Darryl had holstered to the bottom of the table, the snake charmer he had nick-named "Bessie." Darryl, always a little paranoid, had business partners, new and old, sit in that chair where he could use Bessie if things got out of control.

The far edge of the table and a portion of the big guy's belly exploded in a thunderous red clap of sound and debris. The shot slammed the big guy backwards, his chair going over, dumping him to the floor.

Corliss threw himself to the side, pulling the shotgun with him. What felt like a big bumblebee punched him in his left arm. From the floor, he fired the remaining barrel at ol' Crooked Nose, spinning the dude around and down in another explosion of blood and bits.

Shaking, he got to his feet. Big Guy wasn't moving; coils of his wet purple guts spilled out, twitching on the gritty linoleum. Crooked Nose did not move either. His face had been replaced by chopped red meat in a bowel of shattered, gleaming white bone. Have to call him No Nose, now, Corliss thought, his heart still pumping hard.

He looked at the shotgun in his hand. "Crap! What'd Darryl load in this thing?"

He shoved the shotgun into the dirty dishes on the counter and stared at it. What it had done to those guys, even though they had it coming, was too much.

He felt a sting of pain in his arm. Crooked Nose had almost nailed him. The bullet had carved a nick, small and neat, from the flesh below the round of his shoulder.

Freshets of blood ran down his arm. Not finding a dishtowel in the kitchen drawers, he ripped down one of the filmy, rotted drapes from over the kitchen sink. Using his teeth to help, he managed to tie the drape around his arm and stop the bleeding. When he stopped to view the carnage again, he realized for the first time that his knees were weak.

Darryl's house reeked of gunpowder and the slaughterhouse stench of raw meat and guts. Corliss walked out of the house not looking at dead Darryl and Reefer, walking up the road a ways. The air cut clean and sharp into his lungs. He felt every pebble that crunched and turned under his boot heels.

He was alive, fucking alive! Took on those city assholes, two to one, and came out on top. He almost laughed, but thought of Darryl being dead and that put a crimp on the feeling. He had lost a good partner there; but that was the breaks. Now, down to cases.

He tried to think of all possible ways to deal with the situation. The law was getting too freaking good at solving murders, all that CSI shit they had now, and this messy little scene would doubtless involve the state homicide unit and maybe the Feds as well. Darryl, he knew, was not unknown to the DEA boys in Springfield. After several minutes, he decided there was no way he could cover up the fact that a fourth party (himself) was involved. He thought of burning the house, but the smoke might attract attention. He would leave it as is. When the probation officer came out, or a deputy, maybe in a week or so to find out why Darryl hadn't shown up for his meeting, it would look like a deal gone bad. Any of his fingerprints they found could be explained: Hey,

Darryl was my friend; we visited.

He found keys to the Crown Vic in the big guy's pants pocket, took the wallets from each of the dead men, pocketed slightly more than three hundred cash, and kept one of the silenced pistols and the shotgun. On the porch, Darryl lay staring at the mud-dauber nests clumped on the porch rafters. A bottle fly perched on his nose. Corliss retrieved his snub-nosed Colt, stuffing it into one of his back pockets, all the other guns he held making the job awkward. He looked at Darryl again, studying him this time, seeing how death had made his features and body sag and droop.

"I'm sorry, man, but the county will take care of you." He stared at Darryl a moment longer, his thoughts skimming the surface of something sad and achy. "Maybe, they'll bury ol' Reefer, too."

The car was sweet, a 2012, the last of its kind. It had leather upholstery, a good stereo system, man, all kinds of accessories. There was a guy in Howell County who could get rid of it for fifty-cents on book value. Damn, he was making money like a charm. About time his luck turned.

Before he left, Corliss went down to the rickety dock and flung Ol' Bessie, wiped of prints, far out into the lake. He doubted the law would look that far out. Then, he took the little Evenrude kicker off his boat before pulling out the drain plug. Slowly, the steel boat sank out of sight. Corliss headed back to the car, going to put the little outboard motor in the trunk and scat. He would have to hear about the lost boat from Luther, but shit, he would buy the boy a whole new one, maybe a fiberglass job with a steering wheel. But, he had something to do before he went shopping. Coming out of the jaws of certain death had given him new energy, a new attitude. The wind was changing, boy, starting to blow his way now, and he was going to ride it like a hawk.

***

Lee looked up as the nurse stepped into his room.

"There's a Mr. Redmond to see you."

"Great. Send him in."

He put aside the book he was reading, a James Lee Burke novel, and looked with pleasant anticipation at the doorway. Today was the first time he actually felt like having a visitor, his head not feeling full of broken glass.

Corliss Creed walked into the room and closed the door. He tilted his white straw cowboy hat back on his head and stood at the foot of the bed, a grin on his unshaven face and a gleam of triumph in his black eyes. He grasped the foot rail with both hands and leaned over the bed, exuding animal strength and feral odor.

"Imagine that," he said. "Me usin' that nigger's name and gettin' in to see you."

Lee tried to keep his voice calm, which was tough, lying weak and completely vulnerable before his enemy, his heart beginning to pound. He thought of yelling for help.

"You think I wouldn't see you if you used your real name?"

"I wanted to surprise you."

"What's on your mind, Creed?"

Corliss leaned back and forth on the rail. The heavy motions made the bed shift and creak.

"I come to cut a deal. Some of your friends visited with me yesterday. They shot one of my buddies when they come. Poor ol' Darryl. They shot his dog, too. Used one o' them quieted pistols. What you call it, a silencer?"

"I'm sorry for your loss. What makes you think they were acquainted with me?"

"They knew all about you, an' pretty Jessica. They wanted to know why Jessica paid a visit to my dock the other night."

"Did you tell?"

"Hell, yes." Corliss stopped and grinned. "I figured even if they wasted me, I'd still be nailin' her ass to the barn."

"So, they know about the robot and tank?"

"It's what they were lookin' for. I even added a little touch of my own to make it good." He smirked. "Told them Jessica Prescott was laying some leg on me."

"Stupid. Telling these guys anything was a mistake."

"They won't trouble me no more." Corliss grinned. "Jeez, Hoss, you don't look so good. Looks like somebody danced a little with you."

"You wouldn't know anything about that, would you?"

"Me? Naw, don't know anything about that. I'll let you in on a secret, though, one I didn't tell them other boys."

"Why are you going to do that?"

"Because them other dudes were killers, stone cold. You ain't. You ain't going to waste me just because you feel like it."

"If you did this to me, don't count on it."

"I don't count on nuthin'." Corliss walked to the window where bright sunlight glowed. He came back to the foot of the bed. "I got me some critters. They come out of that tank. I figure Miss Snub-Queen an' Dr. Four-Eyes ought to be inner-rested in them."

"Critters."

"Yeah. Sumbitches about this tall." Corliss tapped his chest. "Look a little like a cross between a person an' a cat, with some other shit thrown in. They're smart little bastards. Oh, an' they can change their skin differ'nt colors. They got to be worth something."

"And they came out of the tank?"

"Where it sat out in that willow pond. My brother found them. Said they was in egg sacks or something."

Monsters in the lake.

"Why come to me? Why not Jessica and Kane?"

"You're the one callin' their play. Why waste my time?" His face lost animation and his voice dropped low. "I want fifty-thou apiece for them."

"Apiece? That's steep even for the Prescotts."

"That robot and tank were stolen. The funny thing is, I ain't seen a sign about it in the newspapers or on TV. Ain't heard a whisper about it on the radio. Those ol' boys who came to see me were serious as could be about getting that machine back. Looks to me like some super-secret shit is going on here. Prob'ly make quite a splash if the news ever got public. Might be a reward an' maybe a spot on a TV show for the guy breakin' the story."

"You want to be famous?"

"I want to be rich."

"You go public with any of this, Corliss, and I expect you'll end up like your friend and his dog." Lee could not shake the presence, the intensity of the man. It was like being caged with a wolf. "I've got to talk with Jessica and the doctor about the creatures."

"I ain't got a lot of time. I'll call tomorrow for my answer."

"That's not enough time."

"Tough shit. I got schedules to keep." Corliss stared at

him. "You decide by then or I'm selling to them other boys still hangin' around the lake."

"The same bunch who tried to kill you? I'm sure that would work out." Lee felt his anger rise, straining through the medications, Corliss trying to push him. "You have anything else, Creed? It's almost my nap time."

"Oh? You are gettin' a mite cranky." Corliss stepped around to the IV machine. He brought a syringe full of a translucent liquid from his jacket pocket. "Here's something for your dreams."

He stabbed the needle into the IV bag and injected the syringe. Briefly, the IV solution swirled with the new substance.

Lee sat up in alarm. The movement brought sudden pain to his injuries and sent his mind reeling with vertigo. The pain and shock of the attack jolted him like an electric current.

"You have a good nap, now." Corliss laughed and patted Lee's leg. "I'll tell the nurses not to disturb you."

Without looking back, Corliss left the room, closing the door behind him.

Lee stared at the IV, and then started. He snatched at the IV needle in the top of his hand, ripping it out in a gasp of adhesive tape. The IV stand crashed to the floor and leaked solution over the tiles. Blood seeped from the small puncture in his hand. He held his hand to stop the blood flow and the sudden throb of pain.

When he got control of his breath, he called for the nurse, loud, and snatched up the assistance buzzer, clicking the call button repeatedly.

10

September 9

Liz Jordan snapped a photo of Wally Bean of Gasville, Arkansas and caught his face in semi-profile, a red bump on the bridge of his nose, his powder blue porkpie hat set at a rakish angle on his balding head. Wally, a retired plumber, piloted the bass boat into a narrow cove. She lowered the camera and studied the shore. Thick timber grew to the edge of the lake, with steep banks and a small bluff rising from the dark water. At the very back of the cove, the steep ground relented and settled at a gentler angle. Wally slowed the boat and steered around a sunken tree. Tree branches, boards, plastic bottles and other flotsam studded the water here. She wiped sweat from her brow. The sun could still mean business this time of year. Wally reduced speed to a crawl and angled the boat toward the back of the cove.

"This is where I found the fish back in June," he said. "It was the gawd-damnest thing."

"Right," Liz said quickly, hoping to head off yet another account of the bug-fish story, "and where did you see the monster?"

"Right here, same place. Like I told you, I been comin' back here off an' on all summer tryin' to catch that fish again, 'cause nobody believes me, an' yesterday I saw the monster. I been followin' your stories in the paper about folks being bit in the lake an' that missin' boy. I thought it was time to talk to you."

"Uh, huh. Exactly where did you see it, Wally?"

"Right over there. See that bluff?"

The wooded bluff rose as high as a second story roof above the water, the trees casting shadows on the water at its feet. Between the shadows and the silence, the place had a definite sinister atmosphere,

Wally opened the cooler at his feet and took a beer. "You want one?"

"I've got water, thanks. Do you have a depth finder?"

"Naw, I don't need no gadgets to tell me where the fish are."

"How deep do you think it is here?"

"Deep. An' full of snags an' crap." Wally popped the beer open and took a long pull, his Adam's apple bobbing in his scrawny throat. "Anyway, I got the idea maybe there's a cave up under that bluff, an' that's where it lives. I got to say, I ain't real easy about being here."

Liz thought again about Wally's character and habits. They had been on the lake for less than an hour and that was his second beer. She was sure his red nose told no lies; the man liked to tipple. He also seemed convinced he had caught a strange fish and just yesterday, had seen another strange creature. After careful and discreet examination, she had decided this was Wally's first obsession, and that he had not previously been out chasing Big Foot or flying saucers. Still, she hoped she was not wasting her time.

"Tell me again," she said, "what it looked like."

"I just caught it from the corner of m' eye, just as I was comin' into the cove." He took another swig of beer and pointed with the can at the bluff, which was growing near as the boat coasted forward. "Seemed to me it come down off the rock."

"What, climbing down?"

"No. I believe it dove off the top."

"And, you say it looked like a dragon?" The man stared at the bluff, squinting. He took a swig of beer.

"Wally, you wouldn't pull my leg, would you?"

"Not 'less you wanted me too." He chuckled, took another swig and wiped his mouth. "Aw, I'm gettin' too old for that anyway. Sorry, sweety, you're out of luck."

"Really, though, a dragon?"

"It happened so fast I didn't see for sure what it looked like. Only it was big, an' about the color of the rock there. I say 'dragon' 'cause that's just the impression I got."

"How big?"

"Big as a horse at least, maybe bigger. It made a good splash when it come down."

They reached the bluff. Heat radiated from the rock in a dry wave. Liz looked at the dark water around them and felt a ribbon of unease tighten around her heart. Could there be a monster down there, a monster that had dragged poor Travis Christian into the lake? Was that what happened to the other missing persons here? If just a kernel of truth originated the rumors of strange lake creatures, then she had a story. She just needed proof. One photo would do.

"Wally, I'd like to get a shot of you against this bluff. If we find something, it will make a dramatic picture and set the story."

"I ain't real eager to get near that bluff. Wouldn't it be best to get a photo of the monster?"

"It would, but I'm thinking beyond the newspaper right now."

"Hunh?"

"Wally, if there is a creature unknown to science here, do you have any idea how important a find it would be?"

"Oh. You're figurin' on writing a book."

"Something like that. Anyway, you'll get the credit for the discovery if we find it."

"Ever'body will have to b'lieve me then, won't they?"

"You bet."

Wally dropped her off across the cove where the hills met in a narrow gully. The shore there was soft mud. The air stank of rotted vegetation and stagnant water. Angling under the trees, the sunlight revealed a faint path running away from the lake and up the gully. Liz felt pressure on her bladder. She should have gone before they left. Thank God, she had tissues in her purse.

She said, pushing the boat's bow off the shore, "While you get into position, I'm going to go for a short walk."

"A walk?" He caught her look. "Oh, right. Listen, where exactly do you want me?"

"Park it near the center of the bluff."

Wally backed the boat away, the propeller churning up clouds of mud in the water, his mouth set tight.

She watched him steer his way through the floating debris, and then turned into the woods.

***

Minutes later, Liz stood on the shore, watching in disbelief as Wally's empty boat motored slowly out of the cove, nudging aside the occasional piece of flotsam in its wandering path. Quickly, she scanned the water between her and the bluff—no Wally.

"Wally!"

It could not have taken more than ten minutes, going down the path and taking care of business. Yet, it was enough time for something to happen. She moved up and down the narrow strip of mucky shore watching the water, alarm building within her.

"C'mon, Wally. Come on!" She caught herself wringing her hands and stopped. "Oh, Wally, where are you?"

Gone. He was gone. She felt it.

Maybe the monster got him.

She shook the thought away. No, he had an accident and fell overboard. He no doubt had been drinking even before he picked her up, and half-drunk, slipped and fell, could have hit his head or became trapped under a floating tree. Sure, because there could not really be a monster. She had just been indulging herself when she set out, desperate to land a big story, find some proof to bolster her something-in-the-lake theory. An alligator track, that was what she really expected to find, proof someone had dumped his growing pet into the lake this summer.

Liz fumbled in her purse where it hung from her shoulder and took out her cell phone. The screen flashed, "Searching for signal." She returned the phone to the purse.

"No shit."

She crossed her arms and willed herself to stand still.

If Wally was playing a joke, he was willing to lose his

boat to make it happen.

So, joke or an accident? Could anything else have happened?

She could not think of any reasonable scenario.

The facts, ma'am. Get the facts.

Okay, here are two facts. Wally is apparently drowned in the lake, and I'm stranded.

She had met him only this morning, but she had liked the old man well enough at arm's distance, a harmless boozing fisherman, coasting away the remainder of his years. Tears welled in her eyes. She fought them back, unsure if they were for him or herself.

Now what?

Maybe the boat would come back.

No chance. The boat was now past the cove's mouth and heading into open water.

Still, somebody would find it. Surly, they would report it to the police or water patrol, and there would be a search. That would be good, because nobody knew she was out.

Oh, no.

Stunned, Liz realized she had not told a soul what she was doing. She had come on this monster hunt on her own time because Ed Price would never waste a good reporter on such a ridiculous story. And, Wally was a life-long bachelor from out of state. How long before someone looked for *him?*

Stupid, stupid, stupid.

She had a mirror in her compact. She could flash a signal off the sun to a passing boat, but the cove had a narrow mouth. She would have to go around and climb the bluff to get a good view of the lake and any boat traffic. That meant a good thirty minutes at least, humping it through the woods over rough, steep terrain. By then, the sun would be near setting, setting on a weeknight after the summer boating season, school in-session, all the recreational boaters done with the lake until spring. She might get lucky and attract a die-hard angler like Wally.

Her shoulders sagged. As tough as it would be, crossing to the bluff and trying to signal was her best chance at rescue. She started down the trail into the woods.

Something splashed in the lake behind her. She whirled.

A large ring of expanding ripples grew halfway between her and the bluff. She watched, but saw nothing more.

"Wally?"

Gradually, the ripples extended and diminished, and finally, like her hope, vanished.

Liz stared at the lake, unable to move. The unthinkable pushed at her mind like a sly beast testing its cage.

It could have been the monster.

Or, a fish. A big fish.

But, it could have been the monster.

She looked across at the bluff. Wally had claimed to see his monster leap from the top. If, *if*, mind you, there were such a creature, the plan to signal from the bluff might put her in danger.

For several minutes, she stood debating. In the end, mad for spooking herself with childish imagination, she decided to get away from the lake entirely. If she followed the trail and kept heading east, she knew she would eventually find a gravel road and there be rescued. With luck, she could find a road by nightfall.

Miserable with herself, sick at the thought that Wally was dead, she headed inland.

***

Colonel Solomon Grue, the Chief Tactical Officer with Global Contractors, watched the light from the setting sun angle lower through the trees, fracturing into golden shafts through the leaves, the light striking a momentary glint off an empty brown pint bottle of whiskey half hidden in the new fallen leaves. He sat in the open door of his Ford sedan; his number one operations man John Miller sat beside him. Miller kept a finger pressed to the communication bud in his ear, waiting for a progress report and staring through the trees, intent on their mission; they were looking for Dennis Johns and Mark Forrester, the two investigators who had not returned from this minor mission. They were parked on the long rutted caricature of a path that passed for some Ozark hillbilly's idea of a driveway.

The domicile of Darryl Hicks was not visible from here; it was down below, hidden by the dappled trees. Solomon glanced at his watch and noted that nineteen minutes had passed since Miller and he had dropped off the two-man reconnaissance team.

Miller tilted his head, and nodded, turning to Solomon. "They found Johns and Forrester, sir. Both of them dead. It's a slaughter house down there."

Solomon watched a blood red leaf detach itself from a tree overhead and flutter to the road where it lay still, as if it had never possessed motion or life.

***

I must have taken a wrong turn, Liz thought, the trees look familiar. Somewhere in the ups and downs of the wooded ridges and failing light, she had lost her sense of direction. She had tried to find trees with moss growing on them, because she had heard moss always grows on the north side of a tree. The few trees she found with moss had it growing all around their trunks because of the ever-present shade. Now, with twilight pulling deep shadows from the trees, she realized she was lost. There was an hour left at most before night fell full upon the woods. She could not travel in the dark without risking a turned ankle or worse, falling off a bluff. Then too, though summer was blending into autumn, the temperatures still accommodated snakes. Copperheads, she knew, were chiefly nocturnal and resented people stepping on them.

Liz tried her cell phone for the tenth time, and again found no signal for transmission. She leaned against the rough bole of a hickory and stared into the gathering gloom. Panic rose on fluttering wings within her.

"Keep cool, babe," she said to herself. "At worst you've got an uncomfortable night in the woods. You can handle that."

Unless, the monster gets you, follows your trail and—

Stop it!

Thoughts of the monster had been with her since the lake, dogging her footsteps, snapping twigs and rustling bushes behind her. Each time she jumped, her heart freezing in her chest, she would chide herself for such thoughts, because monsters do not exist. Poor Wally fell overboard, that was all. She could have gone to the bluff to signal and been perfectly safe. In fact, how was she going to explain in the light of day why she left the lake and went into the woods with the sun going down? They would find poor Wally in the lake snagged underwater by fishing line or something, and then the word "monster" would seem so very silly. Telling people how, right now, with dusk pooling between the tree trunks and the whip-poor-wills starting their lonesome night calls, monsters could be real, because you are alone and lost and losing hope, well, that would be useless.

Liz looked around. The steep slope she was on was not suited for an overnight stay. Carefully, she made her way to the bottom, picking her path through the rocks that cluttered the forest floor and lurked like traps beneath the leaf litter, waiting to turn under the unwary heel. The bottom of the slope ended in a narrow gully stitched by a dry streambed. She walked along the stream keeping watch for snakes. After some minutes of traveling, she stopped against a tree, thirsty and tired, her clothes torn by green briar and snags, her feet aching from the uneven ground.

Darkness walled off her back trail. Ahead, though, she thought the light was stronger, as if perhaps a clearing broke the trees. A clearing would be better than the streambed where the trees seemed too close about her. Liz shoved herself off the tree and moved toward the lighter area.

Closer now, she saw there *was* a break in the trees. She fought her way through the barrier of thick underbrush that encircled the clearing, making enough noise she hoped to scare away any snakes in the vicinity. She yipped when a blackberry thorn caught her thigh.

The clearing was small. She thought she could almost throw a rock to the other side. The ground looked as if it had been cultivated. Scraggily weeds lay in thin tangles or sprouted uncertainly over the disturbed earth. Someone had been there recently, doing something, maybe harvesting . . . she did not have to finish her thought.

Across the way, hidden in the overhanging trees, a long, rusty shed roof leaned against a short bluff. Thick rows of harvested marijuana plants hung upside down from poles tied in the rafters.

"Just great," she whispered.

For several moments, she watched the clearing. A bat flitted over the empty field, dodging after a flying insect in an erratic dive, and was gone. Crickets started again in the surrounding brush, their numbers and music diminished by the passing of summer. It appeared that she had the clearing and the rough shelter against the bluff all to herself. Eager to situate herself and rest, Liz started across the clearing.

***

Corliss could not believe his eyes. He had been sitting there, finishing up a jay, when he heard what sounded like a wounded buffalo coming through the woods on the other side of his patch. He had like to shit himself trying to hide, figuring it was the law coming to bust him. Now, he was looking at this woman walking across the patch, heading straight for the drying shed as if she was in bad need of a toke. As she came closer, he recognized her from the courthouse. She was a reporter for the local paper. He could not remember her name, though. He watched as she came to the shed and stopped, checking out his crop, probably figuring its street value and patting herself on the back for finding herself a scoop story.

His heart sank. All summer he had tended that patch, hoping the State Pukes would not spot it from the air, or some asshole squirrel hunter would not stumble across it and decide to be a hero. Now this busybody news reporter had found his patch, and he was going to lose it all. He felt the dull throb of anger building, tightening round his head like a strap wrench. It wasn't just the money he was going to lose, it was the principal of the thing, all that work down the tubes because this bitch wanted a three column story in her piss-ant paper.

He noticed her condition for the first time. She looked like she had been rolled in the pigpen. Her clothes were torn and streaked with dirt. Dried mud caked her running shoes; her hair was mussed and threaded with twigs. She had a look on her face, too, that didn't mesh with busting a story. Plus, she was alone.

The bitch was lost.

***

Liz decided she would stay the night under the shed roof and not risk getting lost in the dark following the faint path she had found leading out of the clearing. She was getting hungry and the temperature had dropped, but she was comfortable enough sitting on a lone, dusty hay bale with her back against the warm rock bluff. The smell of the marijuana drying overhead was earthy and powerful, and sparked memories of her youth when she was Little Miss Counterculture and believed smoking pot made her a political activist. She shook her head. Naive little girl, partying under the banner of social revolution.

That was a long time ago, she thought. How did I ever get here?

She watched the light die in the clearing and the first faint stars of the evening glow in the sky. Yes, she could stay here the night, stretch out on the ground when she absolutely could not keep her eyes open anymore. No real predators inhabited the Ozark woods, and she would be safe enough.

Urine spurted into her panties as a voice spoke from practically beside her.

"Mercy me. You look lost."

She jumped up and whirled, and looked straight into the black eyes of Corliss Creed.

Corliss shifted a knot of tobacco in his mouth and spat a stream of brown juice into the leaves. He stood at the foot of the bluff, wearing work boots, faded jeans with the knees worn out, and a sleeveless green western shirt. A black Harley-Davidson bandana confined his shaggy hair. She let her gaze drift past him to a narrow path that twisted between the tumbled rocks at the bluff's base.

"Yup," he said, "lucky for you I come along, else you'd have to spend the night alone."

She tried hard to think through her panic, through the sound of her own blood booming in her ears, but Corliss stood there looking impossibly lean and fast, so inescapable, she found only frozen thoughts in her mind.

"What?" he said, and spit again into the dry leaves. "Why you looking at me like that? You don't think I'd leave you in the woods, do you? There's all kinds of ferocious beasts out here, jus' waitin' to pounce on anybody happens along."

She found her voice. "I'm . . . not alone."

Corliss made a show of looking around the clearing. She jumped aside as he stepped over and lifted the hay bale she had been using for a seat. He turned back to her and shrugged.

"I don't find nobody. Where they at?"

"We were separated. There were two deputies." The words rushed out, artless and weak. "They know about this field, Corliss. They're on their way to destroy it. You should run while you have the chance."

He appeared surprised. "That right? Whyn't I hear you calling to them, then? You're lost, ain't you? Two big, stud deputies should've made it here with you. Where they at? I think somethin' must have happened to 'em. You know, anything can happen out here, anything at all."

"Corliss . . ."

"That's another thing." He took a step closer. "I'm jus' flattered all to hell you know my name, but you got the drop on me. What's yours?"

"Liz. I write for *The LeBeau Examiner*."

"Liz, I'm glad to meet you." He stepped up, grabbed her right hand and shook it. "Why, you're tremblin'. You cold? Well, don't you worry none. Ol' Corliss will keep you warm."

He pulled her close, his grip like the jaws of a trap. She smelled the rank tobacco on his breath and the smoke in his clothes. His presence was feral and frightening.

"Nunnh!" She brought her knee up into his crotch and tried to break free. He was ready, though, and turned his hip so her knee glanced off his thigh.

He shook her, hard. His strength shocked her into submission.

"Here now!" he said. "None-a-that. We got to be friendly towards one another, 'cause you're gonna be with me a day or two."

She stared at him, his words sinking into her like concrete into a pool. Corliss grinned at her.

"Oh, don't worry," he said. "Just a day or two, while I get my crop to town. Just a little vacation for you. I wouldn't want you comin' back tomorrow after you found your deputies."

"I wouldn't," she said. "Let me go. I won't tell, I swear."

"Uh-huh. But, I'm kind of takin' a shine to you. For an older broad you look pretty good." He reached down and massaged her buttocks. "Yeah. We gonna get to know each other real good before I send you back."

This time her rising knee made contact. Corliss doubled over and clutched his groin. Liz staggered free, shocked it had been so easy. She ran for the edge of the clearing, toward the path she had seen earlier.

Corliss tackled her at the edge of the clearing. She hit the ground hard, knocking the breath from her lungs. He rolled her face up and slapped her hard across the face. The impact made her see stars. She raised her arms to protect herself from another blow, still struggling to get a breath. He grinned, his face flushed and triumphant.

"What's the matter with you?" He straddled her, pinning her with his weight. "You ain't a lez-bo, are you?"

He tore the front of her shirt open with one convulsive wrench, his fists twisted in the fabric. Cool air rushed against her exposed skin.

"This can't happen," she told him. It could not. Because things like this, being caught in the woods and manhandled by a brute intent on rape, were impossible. Moments ago, her worse fear was staying a night in the woods alone, and this was just unfair. It was unfair.

Corliss looked at her. His face was becoming indistinct

in the dusk. He shook his head. "You dumb bitch."

Liz screamed. All the terrors and injustices of the day leapt from her mouth in a high-pitched rip of sound that echoed through the trees. Startled, Corliss jerked back. She windmilled her arms at his face, her fingers like iron claws slashing at his eyes. She did not consciously will the action; instinct had taken over. His skin peeled away beneath her manicured nails.

"Aggh!" Corliss pitched sideways, his hands on his face.

She rolled over, kicked free of his leg, and stumbled to her feet. *The woods.* She could lose him in the woods in the dark and be safe. Panting with adrenaline, she staggered into the trees, blindly seeking escape in the gloom.

She ran into a tree, catching it with her shoulder. Turning from the impact, she saw Corliss getting to his feet. He had lost his bandana and his hair now hung in his face. Her heart quailed. Moaning with despair, she scrambled up a rise thick with trees, zigzagging around rocks and deadfall branches, her pace maddeningly slow.

Corliss's voice followed her, wild with rage. "I'm gonna get you!"

The ground rose quickly. Rocks turned under her feet. Many times, she grabbed at saplings and low branches to keep from falling backwards. Nearing the top of the ridge, larger rocks and huge boulders forced her to thread carefully through their maze. By the time she reached the top, her heart was pounding painfully and her breath came in great ragged gulps. She leaned against a tree to recover, watching behind her, downhill where the shadows grew deep.

Several minutes passed. Creatures of the night, the crickets, frogs, and whip-poor-wills, resumed their lonely communications. In the distance, an owl hooted. Liz found her breath slowing. Corliss did not seem to be following. Maybe, and her heart leapt at this, *maybe* she had really hurt him and he would not follow. Quietly, she turned and made her way along the ridge.

She glimpsed the half moon rising through the treetops. Its beams glowed through the canopy. She realized now that she was following an old roadbed that ran along the top of the ridge. Her spirits lifted. If she stayed on the faint path, it might lead her to a real road. She strained to listen beyond the soft rustling her own steps made in the leaf litter. The surrounding woods were alive with a million furtive cracklings and flutters, soft betrayals of insects and small animals, a bird shifting on its roost, a mouse scurrying across the leaves. There was no sign of Corliss. The air was cool. She pulled her damaged shirt together and held it as she walked, her feet aching and bruised from the rough terrain. She cast frequent glances behind her.

She would keep moving through the night, she thought, and put more distance between herself and Corliss. Attempted rape aside, she had found his pot patch and was not sure he would stop at abduction and rape. To keep his secret safe, he might decide to kill her.

Moonlight shone through a break in the canopy, illuminating the woods ahead. With a shock, she realized a figure stood on the trail, silent, watching her approach. Her feet locked in place automatically. She stood immobile.

The figure moved toward her. Moonlight fell upon the face of Corliss Creed.

"Evenin,' Bitch," he said. "I figured you'd follow the ridge."

Liz whirled and ran from the path. A branch slapped her in the eye, stinging and half-blinding her. Still, she ran, dodging the rocks and stumps that jutted like gravestones around her. The sound of Corliss giving chase, his heavy footsteps pounding behind her, spurred her to greater panic. She ran full speed then, reckless and erratic in the night, until the ground dropped without warning from beneath her feet, and she screamed.

Cool wind rushed past her ears as she fell into the darkness, the sickening pull of gravity a cold knowledge in her stomach, a scream in her throat. Twisting in midair, she glimpsed the hard white moon through the trees, saw Corliss in silhouette at the bluff's edge. Then, she hit the rocks at the bottom and saw no more, forever.

***

Tonight, in Lee's hospital room, Red wore a black and white do-rag styled in the symbols Yin and Yang. Lee motioned to close the door.

Red complied and then returned to the visitor's chair. "What's up?"

"Corliss." The name left an oily taste in his mouth. "He paid me a visit yesterday afternoon."

"You jest."

"Nope," Lee said, "he was here. I would have called you sooner, but, I couldn't get my head together over all this."

"All what?"

He summarized the surprise meeting with Corliss: his alleged run-in with Global Contractor types, how Corliss wanted to sell creatures he claimed came from Chilson's tank, and his dramatic departure, injecting the IV system with who-knows-what. By the time he finished, Lee found his mouth was dry. He took a swallow of water while Red pondered the new information.

"That's some shit," Red said. "The man comes here with a price like that, fifty large each for some kind of bogus monkeys. He knows you won't go for it. He came to shake you, Marshal. Dude's letting you know the game's still on. He's checking out his handy-work, too. Ten-to-one he's the one booked your bed here."

"Maybe. He's more hard-core than I thought. I think Corliss somehow took the two players he met at his friend's house off the board. He spoke about them in the past tense. But, I think others are still in town."

"No, man, it was him." Red tapped a cigarette from a pack in his shirt pocket. He put it in the corner of his mouth but made no attempt to light it. "You know he wasn't trying to kill you with that IV stunt. Not with you wide awake and watchin' him."

Lee tried a smile. "I had a hell of a time explaining that to the nurse. I told her I knocked it over getting up for the bathroom and accidently ripped it loose from my hand."

"The man's either going to let you think about it for a while and come back with a new deal, or he was just jackin' you, letting you know he's got your number."

"Yeah."

"They're putting the heat on, Aletha visiting Celia, now Corliss yankin' your chain."

"What a pair."

"So, what are you going to do?"

"Get out of here, for starters. Tomorrow, with your kind assistance."

"You got it. Then, we go Creed hunting, right?" Red took the cigarette from his mouth and kept it between his fingers. "Those people are getting out of hand. They need some tuning."

"Yeah, as soon as I can manage it. Tell me again what happened with the old woman."

"Simple. The bitch came out of the woods and threw

this nasty homemade ball at Celia's patio party. Said she was getting even for all the grief Celia and her husband had brought her family."

"What is that, tossing a ball at someone, some kind of Ozark hurling of the gauntlet?"

"Beats me. That ol' woman's supposed to be a witch of some kind. Be my guess she was puttin' the hoo-doo on Celia."

"When I get back, I want to look at that ball."

"Nothing but some horse hair and a bunch of gunk. The sheriff's got it."

"I'd still like to know what it is and why she threw it."

"It's psychological." Red studied him for a moment. "The ball was thrown by an enemy. It looks evil. It smells evil. The move is calculated to strike fear and doubt in the mind of the victim. At least, that's my guess."

Lee looked at Red, amazed. His lips moved, but he heard nothing.

Red said, "What?"

"I said, 'Who the hell are you?'"

"Oh. I didn't tell you, man. I have a bachelor's in sociology from your old Alma Mater. I can psycho-babble with the best of them."

"What? I'm a little confused. What happened to the

street guy?"

"I grew up in the streets. Most people speak how and where they were raised unless they have to keep up an act."

"Hunh. If you have a degree—"

"What am I doing chasing turds down clogged toilets and changing light bulbs?"

Lee nodded. Redmond had duped him completely.

"I decided society is doomed. All is smoke and mirrors. The multinational corporations influence outcomes always in their favor regardless of the cost in human suffering. They get their puppets in office, and the world bleeds." Red put the cigarette back in his mouth. "Anyway, I liked what Thoreau said about living deliberately. So, I went back to my roots, stopped putting my degree on my resume, and try to live as it pleases *me*. You grasp?"

"I understand. Seems to me The Prescott Lodge is a long way from your roots, though."

"I have a daughter in college. Natasha. She's a sophomore at Kansas City Metro, be transferring to Mizzou next year. Celia pays half 'Tasha's tuition, and has a pension plan for me, matches me dollar for dollar." Red shrugged. "I don't get into trouble down here, keep my mind clear. Deliberate, natural me."

"You're having a mid-life," Lee said, wanting to ask about Natasha's mother but deciding now was not the time since the man had not volunteered the info. "Living like a monk until it passes. Your secret is safe with me."

Red turned and looked out the window. "Seems we're both hidin' out here in the woods."

Lee stared at him. Red gazed out the window. Voices and crepe-soled footsteps moved past the door while a minute ticked by.

"So," Lee said finally, "can you bust me out of here tomorrow?"

Red said, without turning, "You call, I'll be over."

***

Luther, who had been heading toward the bellows and screams coming from Corliss's pot patch, stopped on the moonlit ghost road when he heard the last, hopeless scream cut short. The others, Jubal, Jesse, Uther, and Horace and Hank, stopped on his heels. He figured he knew what had happened.

"She run off a bluff," he whispered to them.

Jubal looked at him, his eyes large, almost luminous in the moonlight. The way the light struck him and his brothers, the way they shifted their skin in mottled shades of light and dark, made them almost invisible, like ghosts.

Ghosts on the ghost road.

"Let's stay quiet," he said, keeping his voice down, "an' see what all Corliss is up to."

They moved into the woods, Luther avoiding noisy leaves and branches by intuition and scarcely making a sound. Jubal and the other Cats, barefoot like they were, did not make any noise at all. Spooky, he thought, how quiet they could move. A low branch caught in his 'coonskin cap and spun it on his head, turning the tail to dangle in his face. He put it back right.

It took them several minutes to reach the bluff. Corliss was not there, but Luther could hear the rustle of leaves and the snap of a twig coming from below. He got on all fours and crept to the edge. Jubal and the others imitated him. They all lined along the edge like squirrels on a limb.

The moon threw a good bit of light onto the forest floor. Thirty feet below, Corliss crouched over a woman, feeling of her throat, then her neck. Luther felt sad for the lady, running off the bluff and killing herself that way. He wondered what Corliss could have done to her to spook her so.

Jubal touched Luther's shoulder, caught his gaze and looked down below, then back at him. Luther shrugged.

"I don't know," he whispered. "Let's watch an' see."

The lady was on her back, staring up, her face a pale oval in the darkness. Luther was pretty sure she was dead. Corliss sat on a rock beside the lady, his chin on his fists, studying her. For a long time he sat like that, not moving except to wipe tenderly at his face every once and a while.

Finally, he reached down and tugged the strap of her purse over her head where she had looped it across herself. He found something, money, Luther guessed by the way he seemed to count it, and stuffed it in his pocket. The lady lay on the rock, sprawled out like a big rag doll, her shirt torn open and her brassiere shining white as bone in the moonlight. Corliss seemed to be staring at it. After a moment, he looked around the ravine each way, finally looking up and scanning the bluff.

Luther stood.

"Here, now," he said. "Why'd you kill that lady?"

Corliss jumped up. "Luther! I ain't done nothin'."

Luther walked along the bluff to where it crumbled and sank in a wide crevice that allowed entry to the clearing below. Jubal and the others got up and followed, murmuring among themselves, indistinct as mist in the moonlight.

Luther said, "She's dead, ain't she?"

"Yes, but I din't kill her."

Luther reached the crevice and started down, watching his step in the dark. "Sounded like you was after her."

"Listen, shit-for-brains, it ain't what you think. You tell anybody that lie and I'll stick a blade between your ribs, brother or not." Corliss stared past him. "That the critters? What the fuck d'you bring them for?"

Luther reached the bottom and walked toward the lady where she lay atop a large flat rock. Jubal and the others spread out behind him, still moving quietly, but intent on Corliss. He could feel the distrust they had for his brother.

"I come to tell you," he said. "The sheriff come an' took Ma away."

"What?"

"For throwin' that witch ball at Miss Celia. The sheriff come and got her."

"She did . . ." Corliss appeared to be thinking. "Son-of-a-bitch."

"You got bail money?"

"What? Yeah. How'd you find me?" Anger rose in Corliss's voice. "You been spying on me?"

"I knowed you been harvesting your weeds." The lady, Luther noticed, had a trickle of blood at the corner of her mouth. Her eyes were open. He thought they looked sad, reflecting the moonlight like big glass marbles. "Jubal and Jessie sniffed your trail, anyway. We heard sceamin' an' yellin' when we got near, an' then we spied, 'cause we didn't know what was going on."

"Well, now you do. She got scared and run off the bluff. I didn't have nothing to do with it."

Horace, or it could have been Hank, because it was tough to tell them apart anyway and here in the moonlight with their skins shimmering like that it was impossible, approached the dead lady. He bent low and sniffed at her mouth.

Corliss waved his hands at Horace or Hank, whichever one it was. "Get away from her, you monkey twat."

Horace or Hank moved back, growling softly.

Corliss turned to Luther. "Now that you're here, you can help bury her. Go on over to the patch an' fetch that shovel I got there. It's hanging on the back wall."

"If you bury her, how's her kinfolk to know what become of her? Whyn't we take her to the lake and set her on the shore where she can be found?"

"Because, we're going to bury her."

"Oh." Luther looked at her again. "Reckon what she was doing out here?"

Corliss stared at him, and then looked at the lady. "I forgot to ask."

Jubal and Jessie approached the body, their nostrils dilating. Jubal looked at Luther.

"It's a lady," Luther said. "She's dead, though. Corliss run her off the bluff."

"God-*damn* you. I didn't either."

Jubal touched between the lady's legs. He made an inquisitive sound in the back of his throat.

Corliss charged him and gave him a tremendous backhand smash across the mouth. Jubal fell back with a cry of surprise and pain.

"Get away from her, you fucking pervert!"

"Dang, Corliss!" Luther rushed over to Jubal, who leapt up and growled at him. Luther backed off and turned. "They's just animals."

"I don't give a *shit*." Corliss picked up a rock the size of a tennis ball. He threw it hard, hitting Jessie who stood crouched and wary beside the lady. Jessie howled, clutched his arm and retreated. "They want their jollies, they can hump on each other."

A rock hit Corliss in the side, smacking into him with a meaty thump. He grabbed the spot and yelled.

Uther picked up another rock. Jubal bent, fingers searching through the leaf litter, and did likewise. Horace and Hank found rocks. Jessie watched, still holding his arm.

"What the hell?" Corliss said.

Luther watched, happy amazement trickling through him. "I b'lieve they's mad at you, Corliss."

"Nobody pegs me with a rock." Corliss drew his hunting knife. Moonlight gleamed along the blade like water. "Least of all these cat-faced sons-a-bitches."

Jubal launched his rock at Corliss; Luther heard it buzz through the air. The rock struck Corliss in the thigh. Corliss danced in-place.

"God-*damn!*"

"Yep," Luther said, "they's mad at you."

Corliss, his knife held low, darted at Jubal who was closest to him. Jubal skittered back and away, dodging the clumsy attack. The knife sliced through empty air.

Another rock flew out of the darkness, then another, Horace and Hank letting fly. Both rocks whistled past Corliss without doing damage but were close enough to make him dodge and twist.

"You little shits," he said. "You're lucky I ain't got my guns with me or I'd splatter your guts all over these woods."

Jessie and Jubal picked up more rocks. Jubal growled.

Corliss looked at him. "Go to hell."

Jubal brought his arm back, ready to launch his rock. Jessie did likewise.

Corliss looked at Luther. "You just goin' to stand there? Help me out."

"Don't know what I can do." He shrugged. "'Sides, you started it. And, Mama sets a good store by these critters. I ain't gettin' crossways of them if I don't have to."

"I'm your *brother*. You ain't going to help me?"

"Best you go, Corliss."

Jubal took a step closer, his rock still raised. Corliss took a step back.

"This ain't right," Corliss said.

"If they was lookin' at me, the way they's lookin' at you, I'd be leaving."

"Well," Corliss said, edging back toward the bluff trail, "this ain't over, brother, not by a damn sight. I ain't forgetting this."

"What about the lady?"

"Let her rot." Corliss sheathed his knife. He paused at the footpath that led up to the bluff top. "I'm done with all this shit, you and your freaky friends. And Mama. She's going crazy, or don't you know that?"

"She's doin' the best she can. We need to get her out of jail." Luther looked at the lady. "I'll bury her, I guess. It ain't right to leave her out."

"Fuck her for all I care. Maybe you and your buddies here can pull a train on her."

Corliss turned and made his way up the steep trail. Jubal, Jessie, and the others, watched him in silence. Luther stared after him, too.

When his brother reached the top, Luther shouted after him. "You're jus' mean, Corliss."

Corliss continued walking. The night swallowed him at the top of the bluff.

Luther looked at Jubal. "I got to go get that shovel."

When he left them, Jubal and the others were standing around the dead lady, looking at her in silence.

11

September 10

Out of the hospital at last, Lee sat in a lawn chair in front of his cabin trying to keep his mind out of gear and absorb the cool evening, the sounds of the cicada's and crickets, and the rich scent of the trees. He saw Red cutting across from the lodge and knew his break was over. As much as he wanted just to relax and recuperate, he had to move with the events. It was time to check in with Dr. Chilson.

Red stopped at the edge of Lee's little flagstone patio. He wore a black polo shirt and black jeans. Clean white cross-trainers sheathed his feet.

"No do-rag tonight?" Lee said.

"Didn't feel like one." Red nodded at the lodge. "You heard about Mama Creed? Sheriff Gordon picked her up on that restraining order."

"Good. That's one player off the game board."

"Until her boys bail her."

"That will keep at least one of them busy for a while." Lee looked at Red. "Thanks for coming."

"Hey, I wouldn't miss it. You know how much I like this science stuff."

"Is he there?"

"Little dude almost sleeps with that thing. Yeah, he's there."

Lee stood, did a quick self-inventory. The dizziness had not returned, but his arm itched in the cast. His back had that twinge that would appear when he shifted wrong, no real pain. He was okay. "Let's go see the good doctor."

***

"It's cool," Red called out as they entered the maintenance building. "It's me and Lee."

The overhead lights were off at the entrance, but glowed with bright intensity beyond the shower curtain partition at the other end. Dr. Chilson's voice drifted over the barrier.

"Um, very well."

Red locked the door behind them.

Lee walked through the rows of lawn equipment and parts shelving and stopped at the box containing the blue booties. He shook out a pair and prepared to don them.

"No need for the booties," Dr. Chilson said from behind the curtain

Lee and Red looked at each other and replaced the booties.

"That's more like it," Red said.

Dr. Chilson sat on a bar stool hunched over his computer keyboard beside the tank. The robot rover rested beside him. When they entered, the robot's face or what Lee thought of as a face, lifted and turned toward them, its lens and sensor screens glittering in the light. For the first time, the thing gave Lee the creeps.

"Sometimes," he said, "I think that robot is alive, Doctor."

"It reacts to its environment. I understand you were badly beaten," Dr. Chilson said. "I hope you have recovered."

Lee held up his arm, showing the cast. "I still have a few minor glitches."

"Um, yes, glitches. I have repaired the transport unit, with Mr. Redmond's help, but the repairs are temporary. Why are you here?"

"We came," Lee said, "because your esteemed backwoods partner, our special friend Corliss Creed, came to me with an odd proposition. He claims he has some unusual creatures for sale. He wants Jessica to buy them or he will offer them to Greenbough."

Martin Woodward

He waited for a response. Dr. Chilson sat still on his stool. His eyes lost focus behind his glasses. "Doctor?" Lee said.

"That is interesting. What type of, ah, creatures is he offering for sale?"

"He said they are nearly man-sized and look like a human with a cat face. Or, something along those lines. And as he put it, they are 'smart sumbitches.'"

"Hmm. Unusual. Why would Mr. Creed concoct such an outlandish story? You don't believe it, surely?"

"Ordinarily, no. But he said these creatures came from your tank there." Lee watched him closely. "What aren't you telling us, Doctor?"

Dr. Chilson pulled at his thin mustache. He seemed to shrink two shirt sizes. "Cat-like humanoids, you say?"

"That's what he says."

"Oh."

Lee nodded. He had been hoping Corliss was lying, but he could see Dr. Chilson had yet another secret. "Time to tell the truth, Doctor."

"Yes." Dr. Chilson turned on his stool. His hands trembled as he tapped instructions into his computer keyboard.

"I mean it," Lee said. "I'm sick of being lied to by people I'm supposed to be helping. You come clean or I'm

286

through. I'll throw you to the wolves."

Dr. Chilson turned back to them. "I had hoped Peter had not created a Cat IV. I found the model on his private design list. I have not been able to access the production files to see what designs were actually developed."

"Okay. What's a cat-four?"

Beside Lee, Red shifted closer to the doctor.

"The bio fuel algae we told you about, would be a Category I life form. Once Peter and Edward, Mr. Prescott, thought it was possible to design higher life forms, Peter categorized the concepts. A Category IV creature," Dr. Chilson said, "was hypothetically any design creature with human DNA composing the bulk of the genetic coding. A Cat IV will tend to resemble humans in basic form and function."

"Are you telling me . . ." Lee's head swam with the implications of what the little man was saying. "What are you telling me?"

Dr. Chilson pulled at his mustache. "Peter and our team created a fully equipped genetic assembler. The assembler can, or could, produce life using both existing DNA patterns and engineer-designed patterns by molecular manipulation. This project is the height of synthetic biology."

Red said, "Crap."

Lee tried to grasp the concept. "Designer animals?"

"Peter's genius. Here." Dr. Chilson turned the

computer monitor so Lee and Red could see the screen. He tapped the "enter" key. "This is the presentation used by the lab to explain the project. It is very general, geared toward educating non-scientific parties about the GX, that is, the Genetic Xenomorphic system. Peter and Edward put this together to show to our, ah, benefactor."

The program played, showing first bits of DNA that tumbled into center screen and formed a single stand rising from a circle. "The circle represents the genetic pool," Dr. Chilson said.

Narrated by a voice that sounded to Lee a little like Morgan Freeman, the animated program began by showing how nanites were made and how they worked, explaining that the problems of sub-atomic friction and power had been solved allowing the construction and manipulation of the molecular robots, essentially hybrid bio-silicon machines. The program continued, showing how the nanite multitudes were modeled after natural insect colonies such as ants and bees, with task-defined nanites taking the roles of workers, scouts, and soldiers, all governed by a swarm intelligence program. Lee felt a disturbing sense of wonder settle over him.

"I was right," he said, "about the army ants."

"Closer than I could admit at the time," Dr. Chilson said.

The next section explained how the nanites, now housed in an assembler, guided restriction enzymes to cut and paste DNA into new genetic models. The video went on to explain accelerated organism growth but lost Lee almost immediately, his mind numb with shock. All this took place in what Lee could only think of as a primordial soup vat of genetic elements. The program ended with the summary stating that this genetic construction was, at present, only possible with extremely simple life forms like single-celled animals, but advances were expected, as the process was refined and improved. One day, multi-cellular organisms would be possible.

Lee stared at the screen. The DNA icon revolved slowly. He discovered his mouth was dry.

Red said, "This is some bullshit."

"It is quite real, Mr. Redmond, all true."

"You should have told us," Lee said. He rubbed his mouth, thinking. No time for recriminations. "This says the assembler can only create simple life. These Cat 4s are a big stretch beyond that—if they exist."

"Peter made the design break-through three months before we stole the embryos. We did not tell Greenbough because our plot to steal the project was forming, and we did not want additional security or team members complicating the operation. Peter convinced the other team members to remain silent, selling it as a big surprise for the Board. Then, he killed them all in the explosion."

"Jessica knew all this?"

"No, not at first. It was only recently that I discovered Peter had actually created anything but Category I and II creatures. Jessica has only just learned about the higher prototypes."

"Treachery at every turn. New species? Do you realize what that could lead to, Doctor?"

"In the proper hands, it is worth the risk. Think of it, Mr. Picket. The world loses hundreds of species per month to so-called human progress. With this technology, we could replace those losses and, given time, we could develop species that would make the need for habitat destruction unnecessary, perhaps design pollution-eating organisms. We could create a veritable Garden of Eden."

"Doctor, technology never stays in the 'proper hands.' You must know that."

"If I have time, I can assemble a group of colleagues to help modify the GX system. We would introduce safeguards, of course."

"I think you should seriously consider destroying the program," Lee said.

"What?"

"Damn straight," Red said. "Pull the plug before it makes a Cat 5 and really jacks us up."

Dr. Chilson glanced at Red sharply. His eyes narrowed behind his glasses.

Red said, "Uh, are there Cat 5s?"

"Look," Lee said, "the development lab was destroyed.

So were most of the people working on the project. Who else in the world can put this all together?"

"Very few."

"Then, I think you should consider it," Lee said. "This is just the beginning, and the technology has already gotten away from you."

"Yes, but because of one individual, Peter Fraily."

"All it takes is one," Red said.

"It seems to me your project was out-of-control at conception," Lee said, "if what you've told me about Greenbough is even half-true."

"And, who would you rather have develop it?" Dr. Chilson's voice was quiet and firm. "The Chinese? Russia? Or, perhaps one of those pleasant Middle Eastern countries that are so often in the news?"

Lee drew back, not prepared for the doctor's calm sarcasm.

"Someday," the doctor continued, "someday someone else will develop this capability. If it is an unscrupulous regime, the world is doomed. If we have a chance to advance this technology first, perhaps when that time comes we will be able to counter that scenario."

"Maybe," Lee said. "But destroying it now would at least buy us time."

Suddenly, Lee felt the tension he had been holding in

his shoulders. He let them sag. Dr. Chilson had risked his life to steal the tank and destroy the Greenbough lab. He was not going to quit, fanatics never do. Maybe Dr. Chilson had a point. Perhaps it was better for the "good guys," whoever they were, to perfect the technology first. He would think it over. He still had time to act, destroy the tank if it came to that.

"All right," he said. "What do we do about the Cat 4s, assuming Corliss isn't bull-shitting about something completely different, and they exist?"

"What choice do we have?" Dr. Chilson's eyes grew behind his glasses. "We must buy them."

***

Luther did not care for the county jail one bit, waiting for the deputies to get Mama from beyond all those bars. He saw it as a giant trap, all brick and concrete and steel. He wished Corliss was with him, but Corliss was still mad at him about the dead lady. Corliss got meaner every year, but Luther decided he could put up with that just now, smelling the pine disinfectant supposed to mask the stiff odor seeping from beyond the bars, the bars painted green and chipped in places, showing about a million coats of different colored paint.

The deputies on duty sounded like leather creaking when they moved. They smelled of fried food and hair tonic, except for the one lady deputy. She smelled like baby powder and was as beefy as an old bull. Luther thought she might creak even without her duty belt.

He waited on the bench in the tan-colored lobby, his hands on the knees of his faded overalls, and tried not to look at the deputies in the office next to the gate. Once a police officer brought in a woman, her hands behind her back in metal cuffs, her voice thin and stringy like her hair, dirty jeans falling off her hipbones. She had asked Luther what was the name of his pet coon, talking about his cap. She stared at him while the officer checked her into the jail, asking if he had a girlfriend, things like that, if he had cigarettes. He had not liked the woman, sensing something sick and wrong with her. Eventually, the lady deputy took the woman through the gate. He hoped Mama would come out before somebody else like that woman came in.

She did.

Mama's hair was in her face. Luther figured they did not allow hairbrushes in the jail. He stood, seeing Mama come through the gate clutching a plastic bag with her old purse in it, the lady deputy who smelled of baby powder escorting her, passing Mama to him without comment, her eyes like gray stone. He put his arm around Mama, feeling her light but tough in her old housedress, the dress whiffing of the same sour smell leaking out of the jail.

"Mama," he said. "Are you all right?"

"I'm fine." She started for the door, walking right out from under his arm. "Where's Corliss?"

"He didn't come, Mama. Jus' me."

"What's become of that boy? Wait until Jubal gets a hold of him. He'll wear him out."

They went through the double glass doors and stopped on the sidewalk. The square, the old courthouse in the center stacked high in dusty red brick, was busy with working people going home, other people strolling, window shopping. Luther saw the clerk that had taken the bail money and arranged for Mama's release leave the courthouse, a woman about his age built like the fireplug she was passing. She had seemed to be not a patient type of person, snapping her words at him, acting as if he should know how to fill out the forms and get his mama out of jail, which Luther figured maybe he should if he was not so slow-witted. He waved at her, feeling sorry to have put her through such trouble.

"That's the clerk-lady helped me with the bail papers, Mama. There, in that green dress. I don't guess she saw me wave."

"Don't be a fool. How are we to get home?"

"We got to hitch a ride to the dock at New Le Beau. I got lucky on the way here, hitched all the way on the back of a post truck."

"Ain't this fine?" Mama peered around the square, maybe looking for someone to give them a ride. "She'll pay double, when the time comes, havin' me arrested, puttin' my family through all this. I been studyin' about Prescott, boy, when an' how to fix her. I b'lieve I know what I want to do."

"What's that?" Luther had a cold feeling in his belly, not really wanting to know.

"We'll give her to the lake, the same as her husband did to your pa an' uncles."

September 16

Celia's apartment seemed too warm this morning, all that sunlight pouring through the windows. Lee shifted in his chair. His arm under the cast itched. His head ached. He and Red had gotten deep into his rum bottle last night, talking until the wee hours about the GX and Creed situation. This morning's meeting with the boss had been frustrating. Celia, even knowing now that Greenbough was closing in and they had supposedly killed one of Corliss's friends, would not cancel her charity event or let him hire additional security. She did not want her party in the middle of an armed camp. Red could help, if Lee liked.

"They would not dare arrive in the middle of such an event" She sipped her coffee and placed the cup back on the saucer carefully. "However, if the situation deteriorates, we can reconsider."

"If it deteriorates any more, the game is over." Lee closed his eyes and pinched the bridge of his nose. Jessica had finally made travel arrangements to get the ETU and Dr.

Chilson shipped off to their mysterious patron. He needed to hold it together for another three days.

"I have aspirin in the medicine cabinet," Celia said.

"S'okay." He looked at her. "I guess we're done, unless you have something else."

The phone rang. Celia frowned and picked up the handset, listened, and said, "Sydney, you know I'm in a meeting."

Lee stood up to go. Celia motioned to him to wait. He sat down again. Celia made terse demands into the phone. What? When? Are they sure? Out the window, the lake had taken on a lighter shade of blue. Celia's conversation continued: No . . . no, I have not seen her . . . I will. A boat moved across the water at slow speed. He thought it might be the Greenbough goons, but the boat was too far off to tell. Celia hung up the phone. Her face was pale.

"Elizabeth Jordan is missing."

"Liz?"

"She has been missing for two days." Celia put her hands on the wheels of her chair as if she wanted to go somewhere. "That was a deputy. He wanted to know if I'd seen her, or if she mentioned a trip or other plans during her interview with me last Friday."

"Had she?"

"No. They have no clues where she might be, or what may have happened to her. Ed Price became antsy about his star reporter when she did not come to work and did not call."

Lee felt the sense of doom creeping from the corners of his being, getting familiar with it by now, ready to give it a name, go out and have a few beers with it. A thought edged past the doom. "Liz witnessed both my attack and the confrontation you had with Arletha Creed. I wonder . . . if there is a connection."

"Do you think Corliss or Luther was the one who assaulted you?"

"I don't believe it was Luther. Corliss, on the other hand, is a different story." He had not told Celia about the Corliss visit or spilled the beans on the real GX Project, not wanting to upset her or complicate things.

"Do you think he would harm Elizabeth to keep her quiet?"

"Murder over an unproven assault? I doubt it. He may have intimidated her though, chased her off." He thought of Peter Fraily, that bash on his skull found during the autopsy. Maybe he had misjudged Corliss.

"The deputy said all of her clothes and luggage were still at her apartment."

"That's not good." He thought for a moment. "Two days is nothing, though. Maybe she ran off to Branson and is just really letting her hair down."

"That is a nice thought, but she would have called the

paper. She is a very responsible person. And besides, how many reporters fail to answer their cell phone?"

Lee stared out the window again. Liz Jordan was missing, and he had business with Corliss Creed later on. A sly question or two to Corliss might be in order, find out if he knew anything about Liz. Out the window, the sky did not seem so bright anymore.

***

The sun was a good ways into the western sky by the time Luther got back home from his walk, trying to get the smell and memory of the jail visit off him. Corliss was sitting on the front porch leaning back in his old chair, his feet propped on the rail. The stink of the hog lot and burn-barrel chased away all the sweet smells of the woods Luther liked so well. He got closer to the porch, smelled Corliss had been smoking his weed again, Corliss leaning back in his creaky cane chair watching him come up, his eyes glassy, the last wispy curl of smoke dying above his head. Luther clumped up the steps and set his rifle, a little .22 caliber bolt action with the split stock he had repaired with rawhide laces, against the wall by the door. He laid two young fox squirrels over the railing, their eyes closed in death.

"These 'uns will be nice and tender," he said. "Mama can fry them up tonight."

Corliss grunted and shifted his eyes across the yard to

the cellar door. The door stood propped open in the dusty evening sun. "She's down there, with the critters."

"That so?" Luther sat down on a nearby bench, took off his coonskin cap and wiped his forehead, feeling the cool air find his scalp. "Comin' home, I seen two rabbits playin' in the dust up on that north ghost road. I 'spect we'll have some rain tonight."

Corliss drifted his gaze to the western sky. "I don't see no clouds."

"But, the rabbits was playin' in the dust."

"That don't mean shit. When you goin' to learn that?"

"You don't pay attention to no kind of sign, Corliss. You never did."

"It's all bullshit. Where you been, anyway?"

Luther nodded at the dead squirrels. "Been huntin'."

"I see what you been *doing*. I want to know where you *been*. Where'd you take them squirrels?"

Luther thought about lying, but he was getting fed up with the way Corliss was at him lately. "I was out by that north patch of yours."

"I told you not to go out there no more." Corliss frowned at him, his eyes red and intent. "We got to stay away now."

"I go where it suits me." The words were out before he

could stop them. Suddenly, he was scared, but excited at the same time. Luther felt as if he stood on the edge of a great bluff, so high it took his breath. Emboldened, maybe a little crazy with the feeling, he went a step further. "I put flowers over her an' made a lil' cross out of hickory sticks an' bittersweet."

Corliss let his chair drop. His boot heels hit the dusty planks with a hard crack of sound. "You what? You marked her grave?"

"Yessir. It wasn't right, her layin' out there all alone. I even said some words, jus' like Reverend Hickey would have done."

"You dumbass! They got law in three states lookin' for her an' you mark her grave?" Corliss stood. His fingers twitched. "Great. Just great. Now I got to go and fix that before some wanderin' fool stops to take a piss and finds it."

Luther decided he liked the new feeling, letting Corliss know about things, how they really stood. "You didn't care what happened to her when you killed her."

"I didn't kill her. You quit sayin' that. Anyway, I was mad. Them critters had me riled."

"You chased her off the bluff. It's the same thing."

"The hell's getting into you? You think I can't kick your ass?"

With care, Luther set his coonskin cap beside him on the bench and stood. "Corliss, I don't care to hurt you, but I will."

Corliss's jaw dropped. A full minute must have passed before he spoke. "How's that again? You think *you're* goin' to hurt *me*?"

"If I have too, yep."

They stared at each other. For the first time, Luther looked right through the emptiness in his brother's black eyes, and it startled him. Way deep down in those eyes, a kind of pitiful thing, a dark, sick, scared little thing, twisted and cringed. For a moment, Luther felt sick to his stomach, but his eyes did not waver.

"I'll be god-damned," Corliss said. "It's a fine thing when your own blood threatens you."

"You take her marker off, I'll make another."

"Oh, that's good. You want me to go to jail? I'll tell them *you* killed her. That's right. 'Sheriff Gordon, my poor idiot brother run her off the bluff tryin' to catch her for sex.' Now, who do you think they'll b'lieve?"

"I reckon I'd take that chance."

"Well . . . You're a dumbass, then."

They stared at each other another minute or so before Corliss stomped off the porch and headed toward the bridge. Luther watched his brother out-of-sight, wondering about the nasty little thing he had seen in his brother's eyes. He stood still, letting his feelings sort out and settle, then put his cap back on and adjusted it so the coon's tail was hanging just to the left. The pure golden feeling inside him, he realized, was happiness. He had told ol' Corliss to go jump in the lake.

***

Lee took the ghost road slowly, easing the ATV with care over some of the roughest places and around saplings growing in the way, trying to minimize the jolts to his back. The declining sun, where it cut through the trees, was warm and bright. The air was cool and dry, and smelled of loam and leaves. By the time he reached Creed's bridge, his back was aching, and a dull pain pulsed in his skull where the ball bat had struck him. His arm, for once, did not itch under the cast, and did not pain him at all. He turned the ATV around ten yards from the bridge and stopped, killing the engine but positioned for a quick get-away. Silence rushed in, the sudden quiet almost a tangible presence in his ears. Dismounting, he stood and looked at the bridge, the cow skull and childishly lettered 'no trespassing' sign giving him pause, reminding him what kind of people lived beyond, isolated by the water that surrounded them, their moat against the world of computers, shopping malls, and civilization.

The air around the bridge seemed fragile, as if the scene were painted on a pane of glass. He wondered if the pain medications he was taking had something to do with that. A crow cawed in the distance, mournful, calling three times. The smell of the lake was strong here, wet and organic. He stepped toward the bridge, the envelope with the instructions in his hand.

A low voice from the woods said, "That's far enough, boy."

Lee stopped.

Corliss.

Twenty feet away, the man stepped from the trees, a small automatic equipped with a silencer in his hand. He kept the muzzle pointed at Lee's midriff.

"Reckon I ought to shoot you," Corliss said, "just to keep you from mischief."

"That's a nice piece you've got there, Corliss. Where did you get such a professional rig?"

"Never mind that. What took you so long, makin' me wait near a week?"

"I just got out of the hospital."

"I was about to offer them critters to those other boys."

The dark hole in the silencer, like the fixed gaze of a viper, never left him. Lee could feel heat building in his guts right where the bullet would go. He decided the questions about Liz Jordan could wait. "Jessica wants to meet about the deal."

"What's she want?"

"She wants to see the creatures."

"I thought you were in-charge."

"It's her money. She wants to see them tonight."

"Just like that? It ain't like I got 'em penned up."

"I'm just telling you what she wants."

"Huh. She comin' over here?"

"Meet her on the trail by that rusted-out logging truck. You know where I'm talking about?"

"Yeah, on the ghost road, about halfway to Prescott's. When?"

"Midnight, of course."

"I don't want you there."

"Red will be with her."

"That black boy? Well." Corliss frowned, scratching his jaw. "She goin' to have the money?"

"Come on, Corliss. The way it's done, you show her your animals, agree on a price, then make the trade."

"My price is fifty-thousand apiece."

"That's between you and her."

"What about you?"

Lee looked off into the woods. "It's not my money."

He could feel Corliss staring at him, the man's mind running over the possibilities.

Corliss spat. "Sure. She slapped you down, didn't she? Or did her mama kennel you up?"

"I'm just out of it." Lee looked at the ground. "That's all."

"Shit. They nutted you like a pig." Corliss grinned, shaking his head. "You're up there with all them women, and you pissed 'em off somehow. Didn't you?"

Lee looked into the trees again, wondering if he could get an Oscar for his performance.

Corliss chuckled. "Yeah, boy. That's what you get, working for women. You come on all badass but cain't handle the women, shit, scared to treat 'em rough, show 'em who's boss. Been me? I'd have knocked 'em around some, bent 'em over a time or two."

"You're a real man, Corliss."

The mouth of the pistol rose. Lee felt the hot spot in his chest now.

"That's right, boy. I am."

Lee waited in silence. Sweat trickled into his cast; his arm began to itch.

Corliss scratched his chin. "Tell you what. I'll have *one* of them critters at that wreck tonight. You tell Miss High an' Mighty to have her ass there on time or I'm sellin' to them boys' been floating the lake. Oh, and make sure you stay home. I don't want none of your pussy ways to rub off on me."

"That it?"

"Yeah. Now, carry your ass on out of here."

Lee moved with care to the ATV and heard Corliss over his shoulder.

"And, boy?"

Lee turned. Corliss still had him covered with the silenced pistol.

"Don't come back here, ever."

Without responding, Lee climbed aboard the ATV, started it, and rolled slowly down the ghost road. When he rounded the first turn, out of sight from Corliss, he smiled.

***

Seventeen people arrived on Red's evening boat run, a bright, noisy bunch in the cool twilight. Lee met them on the dock with Sydney and Anita, the maid, checking them off on his guest list as they disembarked. Several were event volunteers. The rest were a mix of philanthropists ranging from a wealthy widow from Memphis, Tennessee, one of Celia's close friends, to a strident heiress from Washington,

D. C. While the boat passengers had an air of celebration about them, they all seemed focused on their mission to raise money for handicapped children.

In the midst of all the loving people, Lee felt guilty about his evening mission to kidnap Corliss Creed. No, not guilty, he decided, but ashamed. He felt like an impostor. These people were on a peaceful, compassionate mission. He was wrapped in deceit and treachery. Yet, Corliss had to be taken out of the game. He was a wild card, too big a variable. The trick was to minimize Corliss without being entangled with the law or Greenbough.

With a sigh, Lee picked up a suitcase with his good arm, wincing as the pain in his back bit him, his price for the ATV ride to Creed Island. He brushed close to Jessica who was smiling and talking with her mother's guests. Lee thought the smile looked a little forced, her tone a bit strained.

"See me as soon as you can," he said and gave her a meaningful look. "Before eight."

She nodded. Lee moved on, carrying the suitcase up the dock steps. Sydney appeared beside him, also muling luggage.

"So, when do I get to see you? Do I need an appointment too?"

"Syd, it's a security matter I need to discuss with her. Don't read anything into it."

Sydney bit her lip. "That's getting a little difficult to

do. Now you have a rendezvous with the boss's daughter. It makes me wonder."

"Don't." They topped the steps and continued on the walk, the lodge lights glowing softly in the dusk ahead. "Jessica's strictly business. Okay?"

***

Kidnapping, Lee decided after several hours of straining his eyes and ears in the dark, his attention focused on the ghost road and the hulk of an ancient truck where Jessica and Red waited by the ATV, was not his cup of tea. He was about to give up waiting for Corliss when he heard the sounds of someone coming through the woods from the lake. Corliss had taken a boat around and used a short cut through the trees. He came in without a light, missing Jessica by thirty yards, but not bad for navigating woods and rough terrain in the dark. Lee could see Corliss pause on the road, getting his bearings. After a moment, the man walked confidently toward Jessica and Red, the moonlight filtering down through the tree branches.

It was wrong, of course, all wrong. Corliss was supposed to come down the road with a creature of some kind. Corliss appeared to be empty-handed. Crouched behind a nearby tree, peeking from one side, Lee tensed for action.

Corliss slowed, peering ahead, and stopped when he

saw Jessica and Red where they leaned against the rusting hulk of the old truck, Corliss without his cowboy hat. "I got the goods down at the lake," he said.

The Goods. Man, the guy watched too many old movies.

Jessica said, her voice icy in the moon shadows, "The deal was, as Mr. Picket explained it, that we were supposed to meet here."

"We're here, ain't we? You want to see the critter, it's in a boat down at the lake." He looked at Red. "What's this guy doin' here?"

"You can't 'spect the lady to wander around alone in the woods at night," Red said, cool, wearing a black doo-rag, suitable headgear for night ops. "Why don't I help you carry the animal up?"

"Not fuckin' hardly," Corliss replied. He spat a stream of tobacco juice into the leaves. "Little bastard weighs near a hundred-fifty pounds. You want to tote that through the brush?"

Jessica crossed her arms. She wore designer jeans, hiking boots, and a goose-down vest over a thick dark sweater. "I am not going to the lake."

"No sweat off my balls. I'll just give them boys been snooping around a peek at it. I got a feelin' they might be in the market. You know what I mean?"

"Those men will pay you in lead."

Jesus, Lee thought, now *she's* spouting bad movie lines. He stepped from behind the tree, drawing the Colt automatic holstered at the small of his back. Being beaten half-to-death had gotten him over his gun-shyness.

Corliss jumped, started to reach for his beltline.

Red drew a pistol from his light jacket and favored Corliss with the muzzle. "Don't."

Corliss froze. Lee walked toward him. Maybe it was the man's stance, something in his shape or attitude, but suddenly, Lee knew it was Corliss with Shorty's ball bat.

"Come on, Corliss," Lee said, his voice tight with sudden emotion. "Hands on top of your head and turn around. I'm sure you know how it goes."

Corliss locked his fingers on top of his head and turned. "I got my brother watchin' in the woods. I call out and he'll blow your guts in the leaves."

Lee took Corliss's pistol—the one with the silencer—from the man's waistband, engaged the safety, and then wedged it inside his own belt. As far as Luther went . . . "Strange I didn't hear him. He must move quieter than you." Anyone walking through the carpet of dry, freshly fallen leaves would make some noise. Jessica moved out of the way. He pushed Corliss toward the ATV. "Put your hands on the truck and step wide."

As soon as Corliss complied, Lee holstered his pistol and grabbed Corliss by the belt with his left hand, feeling the new cast like armor on his forearm. "You come off this machine, I'll break you in-half." Lee pushed hard enough in the small of the man's back to let him get the idea.

"Fuck you, man."

Corliss spat into the leaves. His body was a block of tense muscle as Lee patted him down, searching for other weapons.

Red said, talking street, "Man, we should just shoot this ignorant cracker. Let me do it. I ain't never shot a white boy before."

"Maybe later," Lee said. He snapped a handcuff around Corliss's wrist, pulled both arm's back and cuffed them together quickly, before the man had a chance to think about fighting it. "Right now, we are all going down to the lake to see if Corliss really has something for us."

"What the hell you doing cuffing me? I don't know what kind of game you think you're running, chief," he said, "but you're fuckin' up hard. All of you."

"Why is that?" Lee asked. "Is your brother down at the boat? He waiting on us?"

Corliss stared at him. His jaw worked on the tobacco, giving an audible grinding sound.

"What about it, boy," Red said, "your friends come with you?"

"You'll just have to wait an' see, won't you?"

"Do I have to go to the boat?" Jessica said.

"That would be best," Lee replied. "I think if anyone came with Corliss, they stayed at the boat. But, there's an outside chance Luther might have crept in before we arrived and is watching us now. Why take risks?"

"Shit."

Lee motioned to Corliss. "Let's go. You run, Red's gun is liable to go off. Understand?"

Without a word, Corliss led them into the trees.

***

They came out of the trees to a narrow strip of rocky shore. The lodge lights gleamed to their left at the distant point. Creed's island was a dark hump in the water far to his right. Twenty yards in that direction, a new bass boat waited at the shore. Moonlight gleamed on its chrome trim.

"Looks like you moved up in the world, Corliss," Lee said. "I want you to walk slow and easy to the boat, but stay off of it."

"Sure," Corliss said. "This is a business deal—for now."

"Red's going to keep you covered just the same. I think he wants to shoot you, so be careful how you move."

"I'll only shoot him a little bit," Red said.

They spread out at the boat, standing around the bow in a semi-circle. A ragged tarp covered a large lump on the interior deck. Ready for betrayal, Lee cover it with his pistol and jerked back the tarp with his other hand.

At first, he thought he was looking at a person, somebody Corliss had kidnapped and bound with wire and duct tape, but the hairs on the nape of his neck rose when he looked closer. The humanoid creature stared up at him, moonlight glinting in its feline eyes, its mouth taped shut. It wore a pair of faded jeans, cut at the ankles, but was otherwise naked. Long, powerful muscle tensed under the creature's skin, the skin different shades of gray in the moonlight. It was about the size of a large-framed teenage boy. Corliss was right about its weight; Lee thought it would weigh around one hundred and fifty pounds, maybe a little more.

The creature breathed slowly, watching him.

Red said, "God damn."

Jessica took a step back. "What is it?"

"It's a critter," Corliss said. "Now, tell me that ain't worth fifty grand."

"You say this came from Dr. Chilson's tank?" Lee said. That unreal feeling still prickled his scalp, the creature before him as strange and non-sequitur as if his mirror reflection had suddenly spoken to him.

"Pretty sure of it." Corliss spat a stream of tobacco juice high in the air. It landed on the creature's face. "What do you think?"

The creature jerked in its bonds and glared at Corliss.

"I think," Lee said, "you'd be in trouble if it got loose."

"This isn't right," Jessica said, staring at the creature. "Fraily could not have made *this*. No way. He did not have the technology."

"That's not what the doctor says."

"I thought he was just . . ." Jessica shook her head. "I don't know what I thought. This is incredible."

"Yeah, yeah," Corliss said. "You want this thing or not?"

She nodded.

Lee said to Red, "Pay the man."

Red, who had stepped closer to Corliss, ostensibly to look at the creature, brought a blackjack down across the base of Corliss's skull. Corliss collapsed on the shore, unconscious.

Red tucked his pistol in his jacket pocket. He bounced the blackjack in his hand.

"That was satisfying," he said. He looked at Lee. "Can I keep this? There's a few other people I know could use a stroke or two."

Lee took the blackjack. "If I didn't know better, I'd

swear you've done that before."

"Beginner's luck."

"God," Jessica said, looking at the creature. "Do you realize what this means?"

"It means we better get this thing to the lodge," Lee said. "We can ponder the philosophical ramifications later."

Talking in calm tones to the creature, telling it he meant no harm and being careful not to touch it, Lee rummaged around in the boat and found a roll of duct tape in a storage compartment under a seat. He tossed it to Red.

"Hands, feet, and mouth. And anything else you think needs it."

"My pleasure."

Red went to work on Corliss, wrapping the man up like a cocoon.

***

Corliss was caught in a forest pool, the water black as used motor oil, dead branches and tree limbs under the surface catching his legs and pulling him under. He could not move his hands to help himself. Overhead, through the charcoal branches of overhanging trees, he saw the sky growing brighter, the light shafting through the trees making his eyes hurt just before he sank beneath the surface for what he knew would be his last time. He tried to hold his breath, but at last, even knowing the black water would rush into his lungs, he gasped for air—and woke up.

White light and water filled his eyes. He shook his head to clear his vision. His face, shit, his whole head and chest were wet. Lee Picket stood over him, an empty water pitcher in his hand.

Corliss tried to move but discovered someone had wrapped his ankles and knees with duct tape, and he was still handcuffed, though his arms were no longer behind his back. A length of galvanized chain tethered him from the cuffs to a steel support pillar bolted to the floor and ceiling. No-nonsense padlocks secured both ends of the chain. He looked around. He was on the houseboat the old doctor used, in the dining nook with the table and chairs missing.

"The fuck's going on?" he said. His head ached like a son-of-a-bitch, right at the base of his skull. His neck was stiff there, too, and hurt when he turned it. "The hell'd you hit me for? You're some kind of double-crossing son-of-a-bitch, Picket, you know that? Thought we had a deal?"

Picket turned and sat on an overstuffed chair. He stretched and put the water pitcher on the counter. "I am detaining you for security reasons, Corliss. Also, I don't make deals with bottom-feeders like you. Where are the other creatures?"

Corliss laughed and immediately regretted it. A bolt of pain shot through his head, followed by a wave of dizziness and nausea. But, he said, cool as can be, "You know what you can do."

Something bumped against the boat at the waterline, then footsteps down the deck. A moment later, there was a peculiar knock at the door, three raps followed by a pause, then two more. Picket said over his shoulder, "Come in."

A key turned in the lock and the door opened; Jessica Prescott entered the cabin. Corliss caught a glimpse of blackness as she closed the door and locked it behind her. It was night, then. Prescott wore the clothes, the designer jeans and dark blue sweater he had seen her in last. Still the same night, then. He glanced around the room and found a digital wall clock that read 2:52 in pale green numerals.

Jessica dropped the key on the end table, nodded to Picket, and then turned to Corliss, crossing her arms and staring at him. Her eyes were red and puffy, but still held venom.

"Corliss was just about to tell me where we could find the other creatures," Picket said, sounding like they were passing time on a park bench.

"Don't let him fool you none," Corliss said, wondering how the Christ he could get loose. "We was talking about how sweet you would taste."

He saw a muscle tighten in Picket's jaw. Jessica Prescott showed no real reaction, but maybe dropped another degree in her frosty eyes.

"I'm trying to keep it reasonable here, Corliss," Picket

said. "But, it's your choice."

"Knockin' me on the head and chaining me like a dog is reasonable?"

"Where you are concerned, that's reasonable. However," he looked at Prescott, who reached behind the counter and brought out a short-barreled twelve-gauge shotgun, "however, I can become unreasonable if that's the way you want it. Jessica would probably like that."

"My brother's going to come after me. You want to talk unreasonable? He'll skin you alive."

"Jessica," Picket said without turning, "what is going to happen at the first sign of anything going amiss here?"

She answered as if she was reciting from memory. "Corliss attacks whoever's onboard and is shot in self-defense."

"Right," Picket said, nodding, "because he was caught breaking and entering, this dangerous, convicted felon."

Corliss stared at them, his head hurting. Not able to think of a comeback, he remained silent.

"You're on the houseboat, of course," Picket said. "You can tear that tape from your knees and ankles whenever you like. That chain you're on will let you get to the head there."

The pisser door was open. Corliss brightened. Maybe there was a razor or something in there he could use to escape.

Picket continued. "We've cleaned out anything you could use as a weapon or tool."

Crap.

"I'm going to leave now," Picket said. "If you get mouthy, give her any trouble at all, Jessica's going to radio me. If you don't want to spend your time here hog-tied with your mouth taped shut, I suggest you behave yourself."

Picket took the keys from the table and turned to go.

"Hey," Corliss said. "How long I got to stay like this? Jus' what're you trying to prove?"

"I've got to check on a few things," Picket said. "Make some preparations. I'll come back later and we can talk. How you leave this boat depends if you cooperate or not."

Picket opened the door. The black fabric of the night waited beyond. He said to Prescott, "If Corliss so much as makes you nervous, shoot him."

"No problem," she said, looking Corliss right in the eyes.

She would do it, too, Corliss decided.

Picket left. Corliss heard the key turn in the door, locking it.

Prescott, well out of his reach, sat in the chair Picket had used. She leaned the shotgun against the end table and picked up a magazine there. She opened it, ignoring him.

"What's he mean?" Corliss asked. "What's he mean, 'how I leave here?'"

She looked at him, and then let her eyes slide back to the magazine. "You figure it out."

***

The creature, which Lee was beginning to think of as a Cat 4, watched him as he entered the curtain wall separating the maintenance shed. Still wrapped with the duct tape Corliss had applied—a little irony, Lee thought, with Corliss now wrapped in the same tape—the creature lay quiet, strapped down on an old army cot Dr. Chilson used for naps. Dr. Chilson himself sat on a five-gallon paint bucket with a notepad full of spidery handwriting on his knee. He adjusted his glasses and looked at Lee. The air smelled of hot metal. The Cat 4 jerked as a burst of light exploded in an electric pop on the other side of the curtain wall, illuminating the bare steel beams overheard, the light followed by the peculiar tearing sound of a high voltage arc on metal. Red was over there, welding a cage together. The Cat 4 relaxed a degree when it saw that he and Dr. Chilson showed no signs of alarm.

Lee could not take his eyes from the creature, noting its confident golden eyes and a body that seemed to fade away in spots. He felt a little high, looking at it, as if reality had been turned a few degrees off-center. Maybe, it was the painkillers. He had taken two more for the ache in his back.

And, he was tired. "Everything, okay, Doc?"

"Quite. Our friend here seems to have the patience of Job and the constitution of the, um, proverbial ox. How fares our other guest?"

"He's a bit unhappy." The Cat 4's skin amazed him. Right now, it matched the faded green of the cot, as if the animal had melted into it. "I think he's worried Jessica might shoot him."

"That is a possibility. The skin is fascinating, isn't it?" Dr. Chilson adjusted his glasses and peered at the Cat 4. "Peter seems to have used chromatophores of some type in the matrix. There must have been a sample of cephalopod DNA in his library."

"Yeah. That's what I was thinking. What's a cephalopod?"

"An octopus or squid, and, um, cuttlefish. They use special pigment cells to change the color of their skin."

"Like a chameleon or something?"

"Chameleons, I believe, use hormones to effect color change. Cephalopod chromatophores are controlled by the nervous system, so the change occurs much faster."

"I thought your expertise was in computers and nanites."

"I do not believe that specialization in one field precludes a reasonable level of knowledge in other core areas."

A reasonable level of knowledge, Lee thought, skin pigment mechanisms.

Lee turned his attention to the creature. The eyes really got to him. They seemed to hold innocence and wisdom, to be young and old at the same time. And something else, a threat resided deep in the golden orbs.

Lee bent down. "Let's take the tape from its mouth."

"I am not sure that would be wise."

"We can always replace it." Slowly, he reached toward the tape on the Cat 4's mouth, speaking in soothing tones. "Easy there, amigo, just going to let you get a little more air. There's going to be some pain, but nothing you can't handle, okay?"

The Cat 4 watched him, body tensing, golden eyes steady and clear. His skin shimmered and turned gray, matching the color of the duct tape.

Lee paused. "Do you see this?"

"Fascinating," Dr. Chilson murmured.

Lee took a corner of the tape that had curled up. He felt the creature's body heat. At close range, it smelled of animal musk. "Sorry, fella," he said, and ripped away the tape in one swift move.

The Cat 4 gave a small woof and jerked his head away. Glaring, he bared his teeth at Lee for a moment, giving Lee time to appreciate the strong dental structure, especially the prominent canines.

"Sorry," Lee said.

The gray skin shifted colors again. This time it became flesh-toned, almost matching Lee's sun-browned arms. The golden eyes became watchful once more.

"It is a he, isn't it?" Lee asked.

"Its' musculature is heavy, and no mammary are visible. The over-all impression is that this is a male creature."

"I guess we'll find out when Red finishes the cage and we can get the tape off, see what happens when he drops his drawers."

Lee went to the battered fridge and came back with a bottle of water. He spun the top off and squatted next to the creature, holding up the bottle. "Thirsty?"

The Cat 4 dropped his jaw a fraction and allowed Lee to proffer the bottle and hold it while he drank. What gave the creature its feline appearance, was its nose, which was broad and flat, much like a lion's, and its upper lip area, which was thicker than a human's rising to the nose, just short of becoming a muzzle.

"This creature has definitely been socialized," Dr. Chilson said. "Yet, Corliss treated this phenomenal creature as if it were a common farm animal. Based on the Creed reputation, it is difficult to believe any of that family would not have killed it immediately."

Lee set the bottle on the table. The Cat 4 kept a steady

323

watch on him. Lee wondered at the intelligence behind those golden eyes.

"I can't say. The question we really need to ask is, where do we go from here? Do you take him with you when you and Jessica cut out? Do you leave him here? What about the others Corliss said were still on the island?"

"This one, we must take with us." Dr. Chilson frowned. "Hmm. Let me see. I will need some sort of tranquilizer for the creature. We will not be able to bring the cage Red is making . . . perhaps a large dog kennel, the type approved for air travel. As for the others, we cannot leave them to the mercenary Mr. Creed. You must capture them somehow and make arrangements to get them to us in exile. We cannot allow Greenbough or the world to know of their existence."

"Capture them." Lee thought about that and did not like the complexities he encountered. "Maybe I should just take a crack at bringing peace to the Middle East."

"You *must* capture them."

Lee stood and leaned against the counter, easing his back. He pinched the bridge of his nose and tried to think. His concentration scattered down a dark maze of ephemeral paths. When he opened his eyes, Dr. Chilson was watching him.

"I have no ideas," Lee said, and looked at The Cat 4. The Cat-4 stared back.

"You need rest," Dr. Chilson said.

"Can't.   I'm going to watch Corliss the rest of the night."

With a sigh, Lee turned from the Cat 4 and headed for the door.

12

September 17

His telephone was ringing.   Lee could hear it, almost see it in his mind ringing away, the handset jumping and twitching the way they do in the old cartoons. He ignored it, hoping it would stop. It did not. He rolled over and opened his eyes. Daylight, murky and cold, filtered in through the cabin's closed curtains.

Bad news about the Cat.

The digital numbers on his clock read 12:14.   The telephone was insistent. He sighed, rolled over and reached for the phone, his arm heavy in the cast.

Sydney's voice was soft in the receiver.   "Hey, Sleepyhead. You going to sleep all day?"

"Heaven forbid."

"Sorry, Lee, but Celia wants to see you ASAP. Something about storm preparations. And, I think Celia wants to show you off to her friends. They're having a party later, cocktails and finger food."

"Sydney, I've had five hours sleep."   He wiped at his eyes as a phrase in the conversation came back to him.

"What storm?"

"The one that's coming. Turn on your TV."

Instead, Lee got up and pulled back the drapes. A bank of purple clouds, long and low, bruised the western horizon. White caps appeared at irregular intervals on the lake, like scratches through a watercolor. The air held a cautionary quality, the sunlight diffused by a filmy overcast.

Charity event people crowded the dock, moving luggage about and talking. A broken chain of guests toiled up the stone steps, the older ones slowing the younger. The lodge maids, Anita and the part-timer Betty, were helping Red with the luggage. Déjà vu.

Greenbough's spy boat, with its faux fisherman, was nowhere to be seen, the water too rough to be safe in a bass boat. Good, Lee thought. Just give us one more day.

"Hey," Sydney said, "you still there?"

He let the drape fall back into place.

"Yeah. I'll be up as soon as I'm presentable."

"Oh, don't take that long."

"Everyone's a comedian."

He hung up the phone and stared at it, waiting for all the information to process, waiting for his mind to produce a priority list. Shower. A shower would help wake him up.

***

The guests were all inside by the time Lee arrived at the lodge, escaping the threatening weather. There were children, an even dozen staying the night, playing games, excited, in the lobby. Two were in wheel chairs. The rest used leg braces and canes. Seven boys, five girls; they ranged in age from nine to twelve-years-old. All of them, Lee knew, were orphans. There were quite a few adults present. He estimated about thirty people crowded into the lodge great room, but only three men in attendance. The men were silver-haired, well dressed, and flashed Rotary Club smiles at each other.

Celia wore a pale pink sequined sweater and a new perm, black slacks on her still legs. She was talking with two white-haired women, twins it turned out, from Cherry Hill, New Jersey who let Lee know with their first sentence that they had telepathic abilities with each other. They wore what looked like several thousands of dollars of diamonds on their fingers and ears. The charity event was a *wonderful* reason to visit their friend Celia Prescott. Their perfume and patter gave him a headache. He grew restive. The tingle beginning to creep up his spine was not from the old wound this time, but from that sense of impending doom.

Must be the storm.

"It is so exciting, don't you think, Mr. Picket?" one of the twins said, beaming over her martini, half her red lipstick on the glass.

"Very exciting. Very busy, though." He looked at Celia, wanting to make his mood clear. "When exactly is Kyra James arriving, and is there anything in particular you want me to do for her?"

"You are all business," Celia said.

He shrugged. "I just want to make sure it goes by the numbers. When is she arriving?"

Sydney appeared at his side, breathless, her eyes bright. "Late this afternoon or evening. Just be a presence. Let her know you'll keep her safe from Paparazzi and crowds."

"We've got Paparazzi?"

"Well, no. But you know what I mean. I hear she likes attention, but on a personal level."

"You want me to get personal with her?"

"Now who's the comedian? Tomorrow we will have more guests arrive for the event." Sydney looked clean and wholesome. Lee wanted to tell her so, but not in front of Celia and the other women. She frowned at him. "That will give us a total of fifty-two people. Remember, we covered this in the meeting?"

"I've slept since then."

"Just be there for her. That's all you have to do."

"Check." Lee looked at Celia. "Did you have something for me?"

Celia waved her hand. "Later. It can wait."

He pleaded duty and slipped away through the crowd. The need to check on the Cat 4 and Dr. Chilson pressed on him now. He would do that, and then check Corliss and Jessica on the Houseboat. Maybe it was all the activity at the lodge, but he had begun to feel that something was off, like the picture was tilted and would not level.

***

Corliss nearly had his right hand free. He lay on the couch working his hands slowly, twisting and pulling. At the kitchen table, Jessica Prescott was watching CNN on a small television screen, not paying attention to him, had not said ten fucking words to him since she took over from Picket. She would look out the window once in a while, check the weather, maybe give him a quick glance then. He thought she was still scared of him. Ought to be, after the way she had turned on him. Treacherous bitch.

It was uncomfortable, lying on his side trying to hide what he was doing, but damn he was close. He looked down. What he thought was sweat, was his blood. He must have scraped himself on the steel cuffs and had not felt it, his hands numb from the pressure he was placing on his bones. He looked up again; he was sick to death of watching the news about the Middle East and what the hell the stock market was doing, the goddamned business report. The bitch refused to change the channel to something worth watching. That was okay. Yes indeed, that was just all right. A little more time, a little more blood and sweat, he would change the program himself. Bet your ass, he would be changing the program.

***

"It's me!" Lee said. He closed the door of the maintenance shed behind him, keeping out the first pattering raindrops, the sky gray and ugly outside. Overhead lights glowed in the back where Dr. Chilson had his makeshift laboratory. Otherwise, the place was dark. Passing a box with various lengths of scrap wood trim, he selected a thin wooden dowel rod and slipped it under his cast—his arm itched like madness. He made his way past the equipment and parts, through the mixed odors of fertilizer and gasoline, oil and paint, and pulled aside the shower curtain screen.

Dr. Chilson and Red looked at him from the workbench. The robot crouched still and silent between two tall shelves of supplies, by the bio tank, what he now knew was an Embryo Transport Unit, or ETU. The Cat 4 shifted in the heavy wire hog-panel cage Red had welded together. With a shock, Lee saw the creature was free. They had removed the duct tape bonds from his feet and hands.

He nodded at the creature. "How did you manage to do that?"

Red held up a brown plastic prescription bottle and

shook it. "Mother's Little Helper. Two of these mixed with some raw hamburger."

"Risky," Lee said, thinking about the claw-like fingernails and sharp teeth on the Cat 4.

"Hey, the doc said we had to move it."

Dr. Chilson adjusted his eyeglasses. "The animal was showing signs of stress and fatigue. We had no way of knowing how long it had been bound. I thought it best to sedate him and free his limbs."

"You should have checked with me first."

Red gave a sharp laugh. "Man, I knocked on your door and tapped on the window. You weren't taking any calls, believe me."

"Well . . ." He could not think of a suitable reply.

Distant thunder rumbled outside the building. The Cat 4 shifted slightly in his cage, sparing them from his liquid gaze long enough for a glance toward the front door. His skin shimmered, flashed through several shades of blue, and then stabilized in a flesh tone. The creature looked at Lee and leaned against the heavy steel grid of his cage. Its fingers curled around the metal grid and flexed as he tried, almost casually Lee thought, to pull it apart.

"Better keep this guy sedated, Doctor," Lee said. "I think he's a player."

"A player?"

"He'd like to take us out," Red said. "I know that."

The Cat 4 shifted its attention to Dr. Chilson and Red. It cocked its head at them as if it were following the conversation.

Lee spent another twenty minutes there, studying the creature, talking with Red and the doctor, coordinating the logistics for tomorrow's escape. Red and Jessica would load the houseboat with a fake ETU as a decoy and head to a remote boat ramp, while Lee and Dr. Chilson took the real ETU, the rover and Cat 4 out using a rental truck and the gravel road. Finally, a particularly loud boom of thunder vibrated the tin roof and walls, reminding him of the world outside and his other cares.

"The storm will be here soon," he said. "I'd better check on Jessica, see if she's shot Corliss yet."

Red smiled. "Ain't no such luck, man."

***

As if it had been waiting on him, a burst of cold rain pelted Lee as he left the maintenance shed, the wind whipping it into his eyes, stinging his face. Hurrying to the dock, he spared a quick look up and caught a glimpse of white caps on the lake, lightning flashing. He did not notice the houseboat was missing until he was nearly at the dock. He stopped on the top stair, staring at the empty mooring in disbelief, ignoring the rain. His first thought was that the boat had broken its moorings, but the waves and wind would have driven it into the dock. Then, he noticed a new boat, a big run-about tied inexpertly to the dock where it bumped and bashed against the wood. A chill ran through him.

Greenbough was here.

Lee moved behind a stunted juniper. Crouched there, he studied the lodge. Two men wearing black masks and carrying submachine guns left the front doors and sprinted to the cabins. Submachine guns—serious armament. They both wore translucent throwaway plastic rain ponchos, the kind people kept in the trunk of their cars for emergencies. Lee watched them go into the cabins, using keys apparently, one by one. Finished with the cabins, the two entered the lodge by the front door.

Lee thought about his pistol, his chances of reaching the cabin without being seen. No. It was not worth the risk. He studied the boats down below, the lodge's Bayliner and pontoon boat, and now Greenbough's boat. Red kept the boat keys at the lodge in the key cabinet. Lee had no idea how to hotwire the ignition, something that seemed to be common knowledge for every television and movie hero.

Damn.

Briefly, he risked exposure as he dashed down the steps. Once there, he was below the view of the lodge. Greenbough's boat ignition was empty. The pitching boat complicated his search for weapons, which turned out negative.

He crept to the top stair and peeked at the lodge, feeling the chill of the rain now as it seemed to sink into his flesh. No goons about. Red and Dr. Chilson had to be warned. If he could only make it to the maintenance building without being caught, they may yet escape. Then, he could look for the houseboat and Jessica, and call the sheriff. Because, enough was enough.

***

Lee slipped into the maintenance building, locked the door and hurried through the shop to Dr. Chilson's shower-curtained lair. The doctor was perched on a stool, peering at a computer screen. He turned, his eyes large behind his glasses, a slight frown on his face. In the cage across the room, the Cat 4 shifted and stared at Lee. The creature's skin shimmered and changed from a light tan to a pale mottled red.

Dr. Chilson tapped his computer. "Lee. I have a bit of bad news. It seems—"

"So do I. Where's Red?"

"He left shortly after you. I—"

"Where did he go?"

"To the, um, lodge."

"*Greenbough* is here. Jessica's taken the houseboat to

safety, I hope, and we've got to get out of here, too. We need to take your tank with us if you want to keep it."

"Greenbough?"

"Global Contractors I'd guess. They've got guns."

"Where?"

"Come on, Doctor! They're at the lodge right now, taking prisoners at gunpoint. Now, how do we move this thing?"

"Well, I . . ." Dr. Chilson adjusted his glasses and looked at the tank. "I don't know, exactly. We would need some type of vehicle to transport it, a truck or trailer of some variety. Do you have the rental truck yet?"

"No. Damn it! I can't think of a thing." Lee looked at the Cat 4. "We have to do something with him, too."

"If we cannot move them, then perhaps we could hide them."

"Okay, where?"

"The ETU is repaired. I will send the rover with the ETU into the lake."

"Good idea. Do it!"

"Open that hatch, please," Dr. Chilson said. "The protein fluid has been lost and we need to replace its weight. We must flood the ETU to provide ballast."

"Wait! What about those last embryos?"

"They should survive a day, at least. Hurry, now."

Lee complied, jamming the indicated compartment open with a screwdriver.

Dr. Chilson opened a program on his computer and began typing. The robotic rover stirred. Its head lifted, the lens cover retracted, and it located the ETU. It stepped around in a small circle and backed to the ETU.

"Lee, I was not able to repair the back sensor array. You will have to attach the cable to the ETU. See, the snatch hook is right there. Hook it to the lifting tab on the ETU."

Lee pulled the hook from the robot, a heavy wire cable with flexible electrical conduit running its length, and attached the machined robotic hook to the ETU sled. He stood back as the robot pulled the cable taught, leaving about five feet of cable between itself and the ETU.

Dr. Chilson worked his keyboard. The robot moved past them toward the door, moving its legs with stately precision. Sliding with surprising ease, the ETU followed.

In his cage, the Cat 4 moved as far away as possible. His skin colors changed to match the bars and background. He almost vanished completely.

"Open the door, please," Dr. Chilson said.

Quickly, Lee crossed the garage and peeked out the pass door to make sure no goons were about. Finding the coast clear, he punched the garage door "open" button on the wall. The door rolled up with a grumble of gears. Wind and rain rushed into the opening. He stepped behind the sheltering wall as the robot went past, towing the ETU.

Dr. Chilson unplugged the control keyboard and let it operate on its battery. He came to the doorway, watching robot make its way across the narrow field separating the building from the lakeshore, the sled rails of the ETU sliding on the wet grass. "The rover is autonomous now, operating within a temporary mission parameter."

"Which is?"

"To seek and remain on the lake floor one-hundred feet from shore."

"Good."

Lee pushed Chilson back into the building and closed the garage door. The pass door he left open a crack to see out. He divided his attention between the robot and the lodge, anxious that some of the goons would see. The maintenance building sat at a severe angle to the lodge, only the front of the lodge visible from here. Someone would need to be in front of the lodge to see the rover moving, God, so *slowly*, across the field to the lake. Lee became aware he was holding his breath. He let out a huff and drew in a fresh lungful of air. Just as the rover entered the waves, two men emerged from the lodge and headed toward the maintenance building. They wore rain ponchos, ski masks, and carried submachine guns. Probably, the same men he saw before.

Lee said, "Here they come. Quick, back!"

"The rover. Did it make it to the water?"

"Yes. The tank, everything's underwater, now. Get back to the lab."

Lee locked the door. He turned out the main lights at the circuit breaker box. Only the lights in the makeshift lab provided illumination.

In the lab, the Cat 4 stared at them, tense. The animal still gave Lee more than a touch of apprehension, seeing the calculating intelligence in those eyes.

"He knows something's up," Lee said.

"He is not stupid." Dr. Chilson put the control console on the table and began typing again.

"What are you doing?"

"I am manipulating the data base, tricking it into thinking the ETU has not been found and that no communication is possible with the rover."

"Permanently?"

Someone banged on the front door, a no nonsense kind of bang. Lee brushed some residual rain from his eyes. Maybe it was sweat.

"No," Dr. Chilson said.

More pounding sounded on the front door. This time a muffled voice demanding entrance followed behind.

Lee looked at the Cat 4. "I'm letting him go."

Dr. Chilson stopped and looked up. "I am not sure that is wise."

"I don't want these assholes to have him."

"He may very well attack us."

"Yeah? Well, he may attack *them*. That wouldn't be so bad, would it?"

Lee ran to the front and bumbled through the yard tools on the wall. He came back with an ax. Behind him, one of the machine guns opened up, blasting the doorknob and lock assembly on the pass door to hell and gone. The door flew back on its hinges, knocked open by a strong kick and a gust of wet, heavy wind.

Lee sprinted to the cage. The Cat 4 shrank back, still trying to mimic the background. His eyes grew wide and wild at the gunfire.

"I wouldn't," Dr. Chilson said, backing away.

The intruders entered the building. Lee heard their assault boots crunching on the gritty floor. "We saw you go in," one of them called. "Come out or die!"

Lee whispered, "No choice."

He turned the key in the lock and swung the cage door open.

The Cat 4 stayed in the back of the cage, even with the

door open. From beyond the lab's shower curtains, the man repeated the ultimatum.

"Come out or die!"

Lee looked at Dr. Chilson and shrugged.

"Time to face the music. Just do what they say and keep your mouth shut."

The enemy had captured their flag. Releasing the Cat 4 was an act of defiance. Lee dropped the ax.

"You've got three seconds or we blast through the curtains!"

"Hold your fire," Lee called. "We're coming out."

He pulled the curtain aside, slow. Dr. Chilson went first, his hands raised over his head in the classic surrender position. Lee followed the same way.

Both Global Contractors kept their weapons trained on them, the short, lethal submachine guns pulled high and tight to their shoulder the way S.W.A.T. teams did, their eyes watching down the sight line. Their index fingers never left the triggers. They both wore black pullover ski masks and tactical gloves.

"Down on your faces!" Lee mentally dubbed this guy as Goon Number One. He seemed to be in-charge. "Keep your hands away from your bodies."

Lee and Dr. Chilson complied. The doctor moved slowly. Lee heard tendons popping.

"Anybody else back there?" Goon Number One asked.

"Just the cat," Lee said. The stained concrete floor was cold under his body as he lay down. He smelled the dark, burnt aroma of used motor oil.

"Funny. Search them, Five. This one first."

The man so ordered walked behind them. Under his clear plastic rain poncho, he wore jeans and an olive drab sweater. Just a regular guy, caught out in a fall storm. Except, he was a highly trained assault trooper.

Way down deep, beneath the grimness of his situation, Lee felt an urge to laugh. These guys had numbers after all. He grunted as the hard toe of Number Five's boot snugged into his crotch to prevent him from rolling or turning. Rain dripped from the man's poncho onto Lee's back.

Number Five said to him, "You're a cop. You know the drill. Move and I blow your brains out."

"I'm hip."

Lee submitted to the search, the guy's hand roaming with confidence into places a weapon could be concealed. The storm moaned around the building. Wind and rain maintained a constant assault on the shattered doorway. After frisking Lee, Number Five used a thick nylon ligature to bind Lee's wrists, then moved to Dr. Chilson and repeated the procedure. Finished, Number Five said, "They're clean and tied."

From behind them came a slight knock, as if someone

had accidentally bumped into something. Goon Number One covered the curtained lab with his machine gun. "Who's there?" he demanded.

Silence continued behind the curtain. All Lee could hear was the storm outside.

"Come out," Five said, "or we open up."

Lee cleared his throat. "Nobody's back there. Can we get on with this?"

"Check it out, Five," Number One said.

Cautiously, Number Five advanced to the curtain. He ripped aside one of the plastic curtains, tearing it from the supporting wire. He stood, menacing all points in the lab with his SMG.

"Nothing," he said. "Looks like a make-shift laboratory."

Number One strolled to the lab and took a peek. "What were you working on, Doctor, the ETU?"

"No. May I stand up?"

"Get them up," said Number One.

Five helped Lee to his feet, and then pulled Dr. Chilson from the floor and stood him next to Lee.

"You okay?" Lee asked the doctor.

Dr. Chilson nodded. His eyes were large and watery

behind his glasses.

Number One Goon spoke into a headpiece microphone. "We've found two in the maintenance building, Chilson and Picket . . . No, it's not here." He paused, listening, receiving instructions apparently. Nodding. "Roger that."

Five looked back in the lab and swung the barrel of his gun in that direction. "You hear that?"

"What?"

"Something's back there."

Number One studied the lab, and then shook his head. "I don't hear anything. Doctor, our boss would like for us to return with a control console. You know where I could find one of those?"

"Ah, on the workbench, there."

With the control console, they would find the rover and the remaining embryos. Lee tried not to let the gloom he felt show in his face. Maybe, though, he could keep the Cat 4 from them.

"We going to stand here all day," he said, "or are you going to take us to your leader?"

Number One came close and stared at him with cold blue eyes. The muzzle of his SMG pointed at Lee's belly. "All right, smart guy. You want to move, *move*."

Slowly, Lee walked toward the door, awkward with his hands bound behind his back. The wind coming through the door smelled fresh and wet, taut with ozone.

Five caught up with them. He carried the rover's control console with him. He had wrapped it in plastic. "What was in the cage, Doc?"

Already soaked in the rain, Dr. Chilson seemed small and defeated. A gust of wind pushed him back a step. For a moment, Lee thought the man had reached his limit.

"A raccoon," Dr. Chilson said.

Another small victory.

The lodge soon loomed above them, its windows vacant, rough walls slick with rain. Reaching the porch, Lee turned enough to glimpse the maintenance building. At least the Cat 4 could escape. For just a moment, he thought a blurred form crossed the building's front. He could not be sure.

"Picket!" Five grabbed him and shoved him toward the open door. "Get your ass inside."

***

The great room was clogged with people. It appeared Greenbough had been successful in rounding up all employees and guests, the people now together in a murmuring, tense, and tearful crowd under the guns of three more gunmen. In the far corner of the great room, the twins from New Jersey were playing some kind of game with the children, casting surreptitious glances at their captors. Lee spotted Red, and his heart sank. Red was bound, like him, by a ligature, and sat on the floor with his back to a wall. Blood streaked the side of his face, his expression stoic. In the lobby, the three gunmen had Celia and Sydney by the reception desk. Celia, in her wheelchair, looked calm under the circumstances. Sydney bit at her upper lip. Lee wondered if the gunmen were Two, Three, and Four.

One and Five conducted Lee and Dr. Chilson to the lobby area and stopped them in front of a tall, slender man dressed in slacks and a dark brown sport coat. Behind a black ski mask, the man's eyes, brown and steady, held a penetrating quality.

"Welcome to the revolution, Mr. Picket," he said in a faint bluegrass accent. "And you, too, Dr. Chilson."

The doctor stared at the man through his wet glass lenses, his thin face impassive.

"Revolution?" Lee said. Rainwater pooled around his feet.

"Oh, yes. When this is over, the survivors will be convinced this was a raid by the dark forces of Al Qaeda sympathizers. You understand?"

"It's your ball game."

The man nodded. "Yes? Let's play ball. Take them to the kitchen, Number One."

Lee did not like the sound of that. He and Dr. Chilson moved, prodded into action by Numbers Five and One, down the wide hall. There were too many sharp, pointy instruments in the kitchen, too much tiled floor with convenient drains to carry away whatever liquids might spill there.

"I'm really not hungry," Lee said.

Neither of the goons answered. They reached the kitchen door.

"I suppose a bathroom break is out of the question?"

"Shut up," One said. "God, you've got a mouth."

The kitchen that had once seemed so friendly and warm, full of good smells and Darla's simple good humor, now appeared dark and dangerous. Stainless steel counters and fixtures that Lee had never paid attention to now gave the room a clinical appearance. He tried not to look at the institutional-grade garbage disposal, its rugged barrel body squatting under the deep sink, an eager scavenger. Lee worked his hands behind his back. The cable tie was loose; the cast on his arm had prevented proper application of the device. He would not allow himself to be tortured. Better to die in a burst of gunfire. He stared at the goons. They stared back.

"This is fun," Lee said. Maybe if he acted cool, he could stay cool, keep his voice even. "When do you let the noncombatants go?"

"As soon," came a voice from the doorway, "as we

have the embryos in our possession."

Lee turned to see the slender man entering the kitchen, the man walking with a slight, gliding limp, but not really using the cane he carried. His eyes said he was the boss. Stopping near Dr. Chilson, he placed the rover's command console on the stainless steel counter top. Lee recalibrated his assessment; the man was not slender. His body was a light frame that supported long quick reflex muscles, the kind rock climbers and martial artists used so well.

"Dr. Montgomery Chilson," the man said. "Where is the Embryo Transport Unit?"

"I don't know what you are talking about."

Without warning, the man slapped Dr. Chilson across the face, hard. The older man fell to his knees. His eyeglasses skittered over the tiles and came to rest ten feet away.

"Come on, Doctor." The man spoke softly, a Kentucky or perhaps a Tennessee purr in his voice. "Don't be that way. Does Jessica Prescott have it?"

"Hey!" Lee said. Another hit like that could very well kill the old man. "He doesn't know anything."

The man turned to him. "Oh? Do you?"

Stay cool.

"I know the tank is safe at another location," Lee said. "I don't know where. Neither does the doctor."

"You want me to believe Jessica has taken the tank to a safe house and will contact you later?"

"That's it."

The man stared at him. "One?" the man said.

Goon Number One stepped over and snapped the butt of his SMG into Lee's unprotected midriff. Lee doubled over, gasping, his knees hitting the hard floor tiles. He struggled to draw breath against the ball of pain in his stomach. Distantly, he heard the man speak.

"One, turn the stove on. A single burner will do."

Lee, still fighting for breath, heard One move to the stove. The gas burner ignited with a distinct pop.

"We don't have much time, Mr. Picket," said the boss man, his voice warm and low. "Tell me where I can find the ETU."

Lee shook his head. "I told you. I don't know where Jessica has taken it."

Moving with care so as not to draw attention, Lee worked his wrists up and down. He felt the cable slip a little lower over his hand. The rainwater and now his sweat helped the process. Just a little more and he would be free.

"I almost believe you," the man replied. "Almost. Gentlemen?"

One and Five let their SMGs swing on their shoulder slings and moved to Lee. Five kicked him in his stomach.

Lee doubled over, again fighting for breath. They each grabbed him under his arms and dragged him to the stove where they held him, their grips tight.

"His face," said the boss man. "Start with his face."

Blue flames, bright and merry, danced under their iron grate. Lee smelled the heat. Beneath the range hood, the sound of the storm whispered down the chimney pipe, windy moans mixed with pings as the rain hit the metal flue cap on the roof.

Odd, he thought through the pain, the things you notice when someone is about to burn your face off. Inexplicably, he laughed.

One cuffed his head, hard. "Shut the fuck up."

Lee shook the stars from his eyes. He felt the glass in his mind, so recently glued back together, threaten to break loose again. Though weakened from the blows, he still had some energy. He was going to kick the hell out of one of them, damn the consequences. When they got him to the stove, he planned to be unconscious or dying. He tensed, ready to stomp on One's foot, break free for a follow-up kick to the *cajones*.

Celia spoke behind them, her voice tight with tension. "I know where she is."

Dizzy, Lee turned his head. Celia and Sydney had entered the kitchen. Syd stood beside Celia, her face pale. Celia held up one of the lodge's radios.

"Let him go," she said. "Corliss Creed just called. He says he has taken Jessica hostage."

The boss man appeared to consider the information. Lee, too, turned the information over in his mind, a part of him wondering if this development would get him off the hook—or at least out of the fire.

"Explain that," the man said.

"He just called on one of our radios," Celia said, her voice about to break. "He has my baby. He wants to ransom her."

Lee looked at the man, waiting to see how he handled the unexpected news. The man stared at Celia.

"Corliss Creed," he said. "The village idiot I keep hearing about? Interesting. How much does he want?"

"One hundred thousand dollars, and he wants to talk to Lee."

"What does he say about the tank? Does he have it as well?"

"He did not say."

"Interesting." The man looked at Lee. "And odd. Have you been playing both ends? Perhaps you have secreted the embryos for yourself?"

"That's not my style," Lee said. "And, Creed's the one damned-near killed me, put my arm in this cast. You think I'd go into business with him?"

"Still, how convenient it would be to supplement your income by sharing ransoms in secret partnership with the local bad boy. Why does he want to talk to you?"

"Maybe it's time you answered some questions. Just who the hell are you, and what do you intend to do with us?"

Lee prepared for whatever crude and painful response was coming.

"He who has the guns asks the questions." The man studied him a moment, then nodded. "But, all right, I'll share, since any mention of Global Contractors will bring up my name. I am Solomon Grue. I am a trouble-shooter by trade. If you cooperate, help us get our stolen property back, I will let everyone go. However, I suggest you do tell the authorities Middle Eastern terrorist sympathizers invaded the lodge. Besides, it will do no good to mention my name. The passports for my entire team are stamped to show us enjoying the beach in Rio for this time frame."

"No doubt," Lee said, thinking stamped passports were just a small part of the alibis evidence. "As far as Corliss goes, he hates me, probably just wants to taunt me."

In the silence, nobody talking, Lee felt a draft against his back as the storm pushed a gust of cold air down the stove's exhaust hood. The pain in his stomach faded. For the first time in what seemed like years, he was able to take a full breath without hurting. Nearby, Dr. Chilson was also recovering, but slowly.

The man calling himself Solomon Grue strolled around the kitchen, his cane hooked over his arm now. A roll of thunder reverberated in the room. He stopped in front of Celia and Sydney. Sydney edged closer to Celia, protective.

"Did you know your daughter stole Prescott Scientific's amphibious robot? She is quite a thief. And now, she has been stolen. I love irony. Anyway, Creed must have the robot as well as the ETU and your daughter. Call him, pretend you will provide Jessica's ransom," he said. "Get the trade-off location and time."

"What are you going to do?" Celia asked.

"Send men to capture him and find Greenbough's missing property."

"What about Jessica? I want her rescued!"

Solomon Grue bent and placed his gloved hands on the arms of her wheelchair. His voice glinted with ice. "Your daughter has betrayed a special trust. She has chosen her path, and now she must walk it. If they find her with the tank, my men will bring her back. Otherwise, we will not waste time looking for her. As far as I am concerned, your daughter is nothing more than a rogue agent. She is on her own. Do you understand?"

Celia struggled, trying to rise on her unresponsive legs. "You bastard!"

Sydney put her hands on Celia's shoulders and looked at Grue. "Corliss Creed is a monster. We don't know what he will do, if things don't go his way."

"Not my problem. Mrs. Prescott, make that call."

"Not until you promise to rescue Jessica."

"Celia," Lee said, quietly. "How much of this did you know when you hired me?"

"I suspected Jessica was involved with some kind of corporate skullduggery. I didn't know she planned to steal technology. I hired you as a precaution. I never expected something like this. I'm sorry."

"Great."

"Number One," Solomon Grue said, "we don't have any particular use for Mr. Picket here, do we?"

Number One looked at Lee. "Uh, I guess not."

"Shoot him. No, a shot would disturb the guests. Take that butcher knife and slit his throat."

"What?" Lee said, not believing his end would come in such a way.

Number One looked at the designated knife hanging from a magnetic utensil bar. "Sir?"

"Do it!"

Slowly, One took the knife, a stout seven-inch blade, from the bar. Five gripped Lee tighter. Lee closed his eyes for a moment. Deep within him, past the rising anger at being cheated of his life, floated an immense sadness, for the loss of everything good in life: his parents, friends, love, and the simple joys. He pushed away the sadness. He could not afford it. Lee tensed, ready for one last explosive action, what he knew would be his last moments on earth, dealing as much damage as possible to these predators.

Sydney gasped. "What are you doing? You can't . . . My God!"

"Yes, I can," Grue said. "The end justifies the means. If Celia does not make that call, then perhaps Mr. Picket's death will encourage her."

Sydney rushed to Lee. Roughly, Five thrust her away, but she rushed back. Lee smelled her, met her eyes for a moment and saw true horror in them.

Grue pulled Sydney from Lee, pushed her toward Celia, and said, "Well? Shall I sacrifice your security man?"

"I'll call him!" She looked at Lee, her emotions unreadable in her dark eyes. "There is no need to kill anyone."

"Good! Another pragmatist. Please, make the call."

Lee relaxed.

One looked at the knife in his hand, and then placed it back on the utensil strip. Lee saw a look pass between Five and One, their eyes serious behind their masks.

The radio crackled with static, but Corliss Creed's message came through. "I want Picket to bring my money."

Solomon Grue rubbed his chin and looked at Lee. Lee stared back for a moment, and then looked at the others. Celia held the radio, waiting, her face pale. Sydney looked up, tears on her cheeks, and Dr. Chilson now seemed in the moment. Lee, aware of Grue's unbroken stare, saw a way to get his hands free.

"I'll do it," he said. "I'll take the money to Creed."

"It's a trap!" Sydney said. "Don't you know he wants to kill you?"

"It's a chance to save Jessica." Lee turned to Solomon Grue. "You'd better deal with him."

The radio in Celia's hand crackled again, Corliss getting impatient. "I'm waitin'!"

"He has not mentioned *us*," Solomon Grue said, finally.

Number One said, illumination in his voice, "He doesn't know we're here."

Grue motioned to Celia. "Let Picket have the radio."

Five used the kitchen knife to cut Lee's bonds. Lee took the radio from Celia. He looked at Solomon Grue.

"Picket," Grue continued, "Do this right and you live. Agree to whatever terms he wants. Don't say anything about the robot or tank. Understand?"

Lee stared at Solomon Grue and keyed the mike button. "Corliss?"

"Well, Picket." The words sounded scattered, as if the storm wind had somehow managed to blow the radio waves around. "My old buddy. How you doin', buddy?"

"Put Jessica on," Lee said. "Show us she's alive and well and that you've got something to bargain."

"Kiss my ass, you son-of-a-bitch!" The words exploded from the radio, blowing away the static like cobwebs. "You bring a hun'erd grand up to my place in an hour or I'm gonna leave you a present you won't never forget."

"Do you have that kind of cash lying around?" Lee asked Celia.

"Don't be ridiculous."

"Gold? Jewelry?"

Corliss spoke on the radio. "I waitin', Picket."

"Stand by," Lee replied. "You've got to give me a minute."

"That's about all you got, boy. One minute."

Solomon Grue said, "Just tell him you've got the money!"

"I believe this is the same village idiot that smoked two of your men, Grue. But, have it your way." Lee keyed the radio. "Corliss, we'll get the money. Where do you want to trade?"

"I want you to carry it on up to the house. But, you be quick about it. I ain't got a lot of time."

"I'll be there," Lee said.

"And, leave that nigger at home. I see more'n one person, Miss Jessie's going to be in deep shit."

"Just me. That's all."

Corliss did not reply. The instructions were complete.

"Celia," Lee said, "I still want whatever you have for the ransom. It might buy us some time."

Celia turned her wheelchair. "Sydney, collect my jewelry please. You will also find approximately twenty-five-thousand dollars in the safe.

Sydney steadied Dr. Chilson against the counter for support. His knees trembled. "Free his hands, for God's sake," she said, "He can barely stand."

"Do it, Five, and then go with her," Solomon Grue said. "Make sure she doesn't find a phone."

Five cut Dr. Chilson's bonds, and then escorted Sydney from the kitchen. Solomon Grue looked at Dr. Chilson.

"Doctor, how do we control the rover?"

"The prototype," Dr. Chilson replied, "is at the bottom of the lake, not responding."

"How did Creed take the ETU, then?"

"The embryo tank is on the houseboat," Lee said, the lie coming easy. "We got it that far by main strength and a deck winch."

One jerked, his eyes going wide behind the mask. He took two steps toward the door and stopped.

"Yeah," Lee said. "The boat was gone when you brought us up. Didn't you notice?"

Solomon Grue looked at One.

"It was storming," One said. "I didn't see . . . I was watching my prisoners."

Dr. Chilson looked myopically at the floor. "May I have my glasses, please?"

One retrieved the eyeglasses from the floor. Dr. Chilson placed them on his face, his hands shaking. A single crack split the left lens from top to bottom.

Solomon Grue picked up the rover's command console. "So, this no longer works?"

"The console works. The rover does not."

Celia rolled forward in her chair. "You are all wasting time. Mr. Grue, go get your damned tank and let Lee find Jessica."

13

Something, tugging first at her hands and then her feet, woke Jessica. Consciousness came to her in stages: the tugging, the realization she lay on something hard and cold, a damp musty smell, and finally, the pain. Her shirt was wet. Her legs were bare. Her jaw and neck ached, the pain in her neck reaching to the base of her skull. Opening her eyes to dim light, she saw Corliss tying cord around the upright of a large set of rough wooden shelves laden with dusty glass preserve jars. Memories dropped into her mind, vivid and immediate. On the houseboat, she had heard Corliss make a noise behind her as she looked out the window at the storm. Turning, she found Corliss before her, free of his bonds and grinning, his eyes lit with triumph. Without speaking, he had driven his fist into her jaw, snapping her head back and exploding a wall of dark oblivion through her mind. Now, she was spread eagle on the dirt floor of what appeared to be a root cellar, tied hand and foot.

"What," she said. Her throat was dry. "What are you doing, Corliss?"

He turned. His clothes were wet, too. The light, from a kerosene lantern she now saw, coated his face with a sickly sheen. He tugged again on the rope that held her left ankle, testing it for strength. "Makin' money," he said, "an' havin' fun. Ain't that what life's about?"

He moved beside her and squatted with his arms balanced on his knees. After a moment's reflection, he pushed her shirt up and trailed a finger up her belly to her breasts. She stiffened. Corliss Creed had one idea of fun.

"I thought, after this business transaction I got, you an' me can get better acquainted." He grinned. "How'd you like that?"

"We were going to let you go, Corliss. We just needed to keep you out of trouble for a while. Nothing personal. Let me go and we can call it even"

He massaged her breasts through her wet bra, going from one to the other. She tried to ignore it.

Corliss smiled. "The things we can do."

"Let me go." She heard the edge of desperation in her voice and hated it.

"Business first, though. Lee Picket's going to show up with the money you cheatin' bastards owe me. I'm going to blow his brains out and dump his carcass in the lake. Then, I'm going to wear you out." His fingers drifted down her belly and toyed with the thin edge of her panties. "And you ain't going to say one fucking word about it when I let you go. You understand?"

Her resolve slipped. After he killed Picket and raped her—God knew how many times—he would kill her. Her body would follow Picket's into the lake. She knew that. Corliss would never let her go, would never take the chance she would go to the police. She had one chance, appeal to his greed.

"I don't know how much Lee is brining you, but I guarantee I can pay far more. I can make you rich, Corliss, very rich. "

"Uh-uh. We been down this road before. It's going down jus' the way I said it." His fingers slipped under her panties and brushed through her pubic hair. The contact sent a wave of loathing through her. Corliss kept talking. "By damn, I'm tempted to have a little fun right now, but I ain't got time. Picket'll be showin' up any minute."

Jessica arched her back, trying to get away from his probing fingers. Corliss grinned.

"Oh, yeah, you're a hot little bitch, ain't you?" Suddenly, he withdrew his hand. The elastic on her panties snapped against her skin.

"Animal!" Her voice cracked. "You're an animal!"

"Ain't we all?"

He took a roll of duct tape from the shelf above her head and removed a strip.

"No," she said, "no, Corliss. I promise I won't yell, I promi—"

She did not see the blow coming; it happened fast, a hard slap against her already aching jaw. Her vision grew black for a moment, shot with red sparks. The duct tape smelled acrid. Corliss stretched a band of it across her mouth, burning the tender skin of her lips. Hot tears spilled from her eyes.

He patted her forehead, and then stood. "Well, I got to go, Ms. Prescott. After I take care of your boy, I'll be back."

Corliss turned down the lantern's wick. The flame and light died.

Cold air rushed down the cellar steps as he opened the door up there, on his way out. She saw light, pale and watery, for a moment, and smelled rain, before the door closed. Jessica strained against her bonds. In the darkness, she pulled and stretched at them until at last, she lie still, exhausted, numb in mind and body.

***

Luther adjusted the cooking pot on his bedroom floor to catch the slow drops of rainwater seeping from the ruined lath and plaster ceiling where years of rainwater had eaten away the plaster. Satisfied, he lay back on his bed and, the storm outside being noisy, turned up the radio volume. His favorite station, KBYT, 1120 on the A.M. dial, was just now playing a Johnny Cash song about the Burning Ring of Fire. The ripples in the cooking pot that bloomed out every time a water drop landed there seemed to mimic the song. Luther could almost see the ripples aflame. He propped an arm under his head, comfortable in his clothes, a flannel shirt and his bibs. He had nearly dozed off when a commotion started in the front of the house.

Luther sighed and pulled on his boots. He found Mama and the Cats (their skins all shifting colors under the various bits of clothes they chose to wear) excited and milling around in the front room. In the middle of them, touching their faces and growling that funny talk of theirs, was Jubal.

Luther saw tears on Mama's face. She kept trying to hug Jubal but the others got in the way. They all ignored Luther.

"What happend, Pa?" Mama managed to grasp his rain-wet shoulders. "Where you been?"

Jubal growled at her, not mean, but in a tone that brooked no-nonsense. Mama let go of him.

Just then, the door opened and Corliss came in, rain funneling off his cowboy hat and army surplus poncho. He stopped when he saw Jubal, a look of surprise on his face.

With a low growl, Jubal launched himself through the air straight as a hawk at Corliss.

Corliss swung his fist and caught Jubal upside the head. Lucky, Luther thought, more than anything. Jubal crashed into the end table by the couch knocking a kerosene lamp and a full ashtray to the floor, the dirty ashes puffing up in a dusty explosion. Jubal sat still, stunned by the blow. Jessie, Uther, Horace, and Hank howled, and charged Corliss. Corliss roared back at them and snatched up a heavy kitchen chair. He put his back to the wall and threatened the Cats with the upraised chair.

"Stop it, stop it, stop it!" Mama got between them. "Stop it, every one of you!"

Corliss roared again, his eyes wide and bright. "Come on! I'll kill every one of you sons-a-bitches! Come on!"

Mama waved the Cats back. Jubal got to his feet, moving slowly. His golden eyes, Luther noticed, were filled with much the same light as Corliss's. Mama turned where she could see everybody.

"What's all this? I cain't b'lieve this is my family, carryin' on so. What's gotten into you all? Corliss, did you do somethin' to your pa?"

"For the thousandth fuckin' time, he ain't my pa, you crazy ol' bat! What the hell's wrong with you?"

Mama's eyes began to fill with light too, a strange light Luther did not like.

"Don't you talk to me so, Corliss. I'm your mama, and you got no right. Now, put down that chair an' apologize to Pa."

"He ain't . . ." After a moment, Corliss put down the chair, but kept an eye on the Cats. "Ma, look. It was the Prescott's took him, that Lee Picket and that black dude. I just found out about it and was comin' in to tell you."

"Why's your pa actin' the way he is, then?"

"I think they hit him in the head, Ma. He's got it all backwards."

"Jubal? Corliss says he's sorry."

Luther stepped up. "No, he didn't. He ain't said that, Mama."

Corliss looked at him. "You, shut up."

Jubal rubbed his jaw where Corliss had struck him, his eyes on Corliss. He growled.

"You going to b'lieve me, or that freak? I'm tellin' you, Ma, it was the Prescott's took him away."

Mama gathered the Cats around her, ran her leathery hand over Jubal's head. "It's always been them, and the time has come to settle all. We'll go now, right now, in the storm, and kill Celia Prescott."

"Ma!" Luther stepped forward. "Ma, you cain't do that. It's murder. It ain't *right*."

Cautiously, Corliss turned the kitchen chair around and sat astraddle of it. He crossed his arms on the top and rested his chin on them. Anger and hate still glazed his eyes.

"You crazy old bitch," Corliss said, his voice soft. "You go do that."

"Don't you call her names," Luther said.

"He's just getting so mean," Mama said. "He don't care if he breaks his mama's heart. But, you come help us,

Luther. It's a curse on our family, pure an' simple, an' we got to do this as a family to break it. Once Celia Prescott is dead, thing's will settle down. We let that woman live instead of putting her in the grave beside that evil husband of her'n. It's tainted our family."

The Cats murmured beside her, looking at each other, then back into Mama's face. Jubal skin flickered in brief reds and yellows; he moaned, growled, and muttered at the others. Jessie, Horace, Hank, and Uther muttered back. Their skins flickered red, and then settled back to people tones.

"I ain't goin', Mama," Luther said. "I ain't."

Corliss snorted. "What's that? You finally gettin' out from under her skirts, Big Brother? Don't you want to go and kill the old lady? Hey! Maybe you can skin her like you do ever'thing else."

"I ain't goin'."

"Luther," Mama said, "you come with us now. We got to do this as a family. It's got to be that away. We must each have a hand, or the curse will never lift. You come on. Bring your knife an' come on with us. You too, Corliss."

"Unh-unh. I got something workin', Ma."

"You break this ol' heart, son. Jubal, Uther. Horace, you too, Hank. Jessie? You come with me. Luther, come on, now. Come on with us."

Luther looked at Mama and Corliss. Their faces were

different now, as if they wore masks, or had just taken them off. Strangers stared back at him, evil lights glinting in their eyes. Jubal and the Cats stared just the same, waiting for him. "I ain't goin', Mama."

He walked into his room and closed the door.

***

The boat ride was pure hell. The gunmen One and Five crouched in the Bayliner's cramped cabin while Lee, exposed to the full strength of wind and rain, piloted the craft across the heaving lake. The boat leaped from wave to wave, each impact registering in Lee's lower back in small stabs of pain. He felt as if something were loose in his head again, all the slamming up and down jarring the fragile gray jelly contained there.

"Tell me something," Lee shouted over the wind. "Would you really have burned me or cut my throat?"

Number One sat in the doorway holding his SMG at the ready with a casual hand. His facemask clung tight to his head, soaked with rain. Lee imagined the man was damned uncomfortable.

"I would have burned you some. Not much. It doesn't take much."

"Would you have cut my throat?"

Number One did not answer.

"Your boss is psychotic, you know that."

"Shut up and drive, Picket. You just don't know the score."

At the Creed's dock, Lee tied up on the opposite side from the houseboat, no mean trick because the waves kept bashing the boat into the pilings. Rain and spray seeped in under his cast and tickled like madness. His feet slipped once, almost pitching him between the dock and the boat where he would have been crushed and drowned.

"Just leave the keys," One said.

Lee put the keys back in the ignition. Hell, it had been worth a try. He grabbed the small tote bag that held Jessica's ransom, about eighty thousand dollars in cash and jewelry. One and Five waited in the cabin door, out of sight from all but Lee.

"I don't see anyone," Lee said, "no movement on the houseboat or shore."

"Check the boat," One said. "If Creed is there, we'll get him while you distract him."

Lee looked at the houseboat. The rough water caused it to pitch and tug at its dock lines. Beyond the boat, Creed Island loomed dark and sinister.

"No shooting until I find where he's got Jessica."

"You don't give the orders here, Picket. The woman is

your problem, not mine."

"I could use that pistol of yours," he said to One. "I promise I'll give it back."

"Tough luck."

Lee stood, his head bent against the storm, and walked across to the houseboat. The houseboat thudded into the dock, smashing some of the trim along its unprotected gunnel. If Corliss was in there, he was taking a beating.

"Corliss?" he said loudly.

No response.

Lee jumped onto the houseboat's stern. The effort cost him. His head swam for just a second. He knocked on the cabin door using the edge of his cast to make sharp sounds over the wind.

"It's Lee, Corliss. I'm unarmed."

Still, there was no response.

"I'm coming in."

He closed the door behind him. The interior, gray with diluted darkness, felt empty. Quickly, he searched through the boat, confirming his suspicion. *No one here, Boss.* He took an eight-inch knife from the kitchen and slipped it in his belt at the small of his back, hiding it with his shirttail. The pilothouse was empty, but the ignition was not. Silently, Lee thanked the mysterious fates for the small gift. The little orange foam float on the key ring made a lump in his pants pocket.

Back on the dock, his face once more bent against the rain, he said, "They're not there."

One peered up through the storm. "What about the embryo tank?"

"Gone."

"How the hell did he get it off the boat?" Five said.

"Not my problem," Lee said. "I'm here to get Jessica back. You guys follow me whenever you're ready. Try not to shoot me if things get exciting."

***

Picket walked right up the dock path, his head bent against the cold rain, no raincoat, getting soaked. Peering out of the barn loft, Corliss shifted when he saw the small bag the man carried, the sweet reward. The path behind Picket stayed clear, nobody following. That was good. Anybody else coming along was likely to get shot. Corliss squeezed the grip on the silenced pistol he had taken from one of the dudes he had killed at Darryl's.

Here Picket, Picket, Picket.

He almost laughed.

Shifting, he peeked through another crack in the barn boards. He had a good view most anywhere he looked. He could see the dock where Picket had almost lost his ass when had he tied up his boat and then checked out the houseboat. The dumb shit—as if he would be on that bouncing thing. Corliss spat out his chaw of tobacco and sluiced through the million years or so of loose hay to the ladder. He tucked the pistol in his belt and went to the ground. At a convenient knothole, he stopped to check Picket again and saw the guy was standing at the edge of the yard, uncertain what to do next. Corliss tugged on his Army surplus rain poncho and took the pistol from his belt. The barn door was open. He stepped into the doorway and pulled his cowboy hat tighter on his head, seeing in his mind how it was all going to go down.

***

Lee, standing in the Creed yard freezing and wet, decided he would not have noticed the rain and wind stop, keyed up like he was, if the absence had not left such a tangible, sudden silence. The Creed house crouched in front of him, its naked wood darkened by the rain, every vacant window a threat.

"Corliss!" he called.

He heard a sound to his right. Corliss, draped in a stained green poncho, stood in the barn doorway, the white cowboy hat on his head and a silenced pistol in his hand.

"Not so loud, boy," Corliss said. "You'll wake my brother."

Lee faced him. "Where's Jessica?"

Corliss walked forward, never taking his eyes from him. "You got the ransom?"

"Right here." Lee bounced the bag in his hand.

"Where's that .45 of yours? You packin' it?"

"It's back at the lodge. I am unarmed."

"Unh, hunh. Lift that shirt and turn around."

Crap. Lee did as he was told.

"Funny," Corliss said. "Lose the knife."

Lee took the knife from his belt and flung it to the side.

Corliss kept the pistol trained on him. "Where's that nigger at?"

"I'm alone like you asked. Look, you beat me, Corliss. You beat all of us." Lee held up the bag of loot. "Here's what you asked for. There's twenty-five-thousand in cash, the rest in jewelry. Take it. Let me get Jessica."

"Open it," Corliss said, looking at the bag. He licked his lips. "Let me see."

Lee unzipped the bag and tossed it on the ground at the man's feet, its mouth open, the jewelry inside bright and colorful even in the gray light.

"That don't look like much." Corliss bent, keeping his pistol trained on Lee, and pawed inside the bag. "Goddamit! I'll have to fence this jewelry an' it ain't goin' to be worth shit, then. I won't get half what it's worth. This ain't a hunnert-thousand!"

"It's the best we could do on short notice, Corliss. You didn't give us much time. Where's Jessica?"

Corliss grabbed the bag and stood quickly. Under his cowboy hat, his eyes burned. "You want to see Miss High an' Mighty? Turn around an' head for that cellar. Well, go on. Move!"

Lee opened the door that led into the ground. He could not help but to think of the Morlock holes in H. G. Wells' *The Time Machine*.

"Jessica?" he said.

The steps disappeared into darkness and a feral, musky odor. The wind blew, and he shivered in his wet clothes. Where was the damned cavalry, One and Five?

"Go on, she's down there," Corliss said.

Lee turned to the man. A slight smirk twitched through Corliss's two-day-old whiskers.

"Yeah, boy. I jus' might be fixin' to shoot you. But you don't know that for sure, do you?"

"Is she down there?" The confidence he had earlier slipped. Lee hoped it did not show. If Corliss wanted to pop him, there was nothing he could do.

"Only one way to find out, ain't there, boy?"

Lee faced the open hole, the darkness before him.

"Watch your step, now," Corliss said. "Wouldn't want you to fall an' break your neck."

Lee took the steps slowly. "You having fun?"

"Oh, hell yes!"

***

Beneath the trees, the rain fell in fat, infrequent drops. Arletha pulled the worn raincoat tighter about herself, but rain seeped through the shoulder seams anyway. She leaned on her gnarled walking stick, her breath coming hard. She imagined they were about halfway to the Prescott Lodge, her family about her, all but Corliss and Luther. Tired and achy as she was, she felt a sense of elation. Years of wrongs would soon be set right. Celia Prescott would die by Creed hands. She looked down the ghost road. Jessie, Horace, and Hank walked a ways ahead of her. She had to stare solid for a moment to spot them. Like Jubal and Uther, they had shed their clothes and now had their skins mottled in russet, in yellows and browns, matching the autumn leaves.

Uther stopped beside her and looked into her face. Concern showed in his golden eyes.

"I'm all right," she said. "I just ain't used to such a

long walk."

Uther grunted.

Arletha looked around. It had been some time since she had seen Jubal. She squinted behind her but saw only wet charcoal tree trunks lining an empty road.

"What's become of Jubal?" she asked, and then answered herself. "Probl'y, he's gone ahead. Well, he's always been like that."

She shivered in her faded raincoat. The cold and damp seeped inside her clothes and wanted to settle in her bones. Her shoes were soaked through; her feet were like ice.

"Come on, then, Uther. We'd best set a good foot under us if we don't want Jubal and the boys to have all the glory."

***

The root cellar was dark. Dim light from the open door struggled to define the fetid hole, failing in the farther reaches. Lee made out the vague shapes of shelves filled with glass jars. An unlit kerosene lantern rested on a barrel by the entryway. My god, was Jessica down here? Lee sensed they were not alone, but could not see deeper into the cellar. Corliss stopped behind him.

"There's a jar of matches beside that lantern," Corliss said. Lee could almost feel the pistol muzzle at his back. "Think you can figure how to light it?"

Something stirred in the darkness beyond, a slight scuffling noise.

The cellar door crashed shut over their heads, flipped closed by a gust of wind. Lee jumped. Corliss laughed in the dark.

Lee quelled the urge to turn on Corliss; the outcome was too uncertain with the man holding a pistol. By touch, he unscrewed the lid from the jar and removed a kitchen match. He struck the match on the rough sides of the barrel, turned the wick up in the lantern and lit it. In a moment, yellow light spilled over the cellar.

Jessica lay stretched between two rows of heavy oak shelves, naked from the waist down, her shirt ripped and torn—and bloody. Her eyes grew wide with recognition. The duct tape that sealed her mouth muffled her voice when she began screaming, her body shaking and arcing with the effort. Lee rushed to her. She would not calm down, but bucked and tugged hard against her ropes with hysterical strength. With relief, he saw that her wounds, a dozen or so deep scratches on her shoulders and hips, were not life threatening. He turned, fists knotting, and stepped toward Corliss. For the moment, he forgot the man held a pistol.

"You son-of-a-bitch! You raped her!"

Corliss, at the bottom of the steps, shook his head, frowning. "I . . . ain't."

Lee almost believed the notes of surprise and puzzlement in the man's voice. They sounded so genuine. But, the skeptic inside him whispered words of caution and rebuff. This is *Corliss*; remember?

Anger, like lava, boiled up inside him, but he kept control. The man had them in the cellar, had a silenced pistol, and already had the ransom. If Corliss wanted to make them disappear, it would be a simple thing.

Lee turned back to Jessica. He realized that in his rage, he had not removed the tape from her mouth. Now, with her eyes wide, she stared at the darkness in the far corner. He saw nothing there.

"Jessica," he said. "I've come to take you home. Corliss is going to let you go. You're safe."

She jerked at her bonds with a violence that surprised him. Her eyes never left the dark corner.

"Jessica!" he said. "Calm down. I'm going to let you go, but you've got to calm down."

He would let *her* remove the tape. The thought of hurting her more, even that little bit, bothered him.

Ignoring Corliss, Lee took out his pocketknife, a pitiful inch and a half blade that was legal at most checkpoints, and sawed through the straining bond that held her left hand. Immediately, Jessica's hand flew to her mouth. She ripped the duct tape free.

"It's in the corner!" She choked. Spittle flew from her

lips. Her free hand slashed toward the darkness. "It's in the corner!"

The hairs on the back of Lee's neck stood up. Slowly, he came to his feet. "Raise that lantern, Corliss."

"Shh," Corliss aimed his pistol at the dark corner. "Listen."

The dim forms of more shelves and crates were all that Lee could see. He waited, then, he heard something. *Breathing*, faint, but discernable.

They were not alone.

"Luther," Lee said. "Come on out."

"T'ain't him," Corliss said. "He's up at the house, sleepin'. It's one o' them critters."

The truth rose and broke in Lee like a bubble of light. The Cat 4's had raped a human woman. The urgency of the moment stopped him there, short of pondering why. Slowly, he moved toward the lantern. "I'm going to put some light on it."

Jessica shrieked. "Kill it! Oh, my God, kill it!"

Spurred by the hysteria in Jessica's voice, Lee snatched up the light and raised it toward the corner. Corliss spat tobacco juice against the stone wall and steadied the pistol. It took a moment, but Lee spotted the creature. Crouched beside the largest crate that held a tangled mess of blankets was the same type of creature they had caged. Lee had the impression it was the same Cat 4, but it was impossible to tell; the creature was nearly invisible with its camouflaged skin.

"It's Pa," Corliss whispered. He took a breath, held it, and took a careful bead on the creature.

"Corliss, don't!"

Too late.

The silenced pistol jumped and spat in Corliss's hands. Twice.

Jessica screamed. The sharp smell of burnt gunpowder filled the cellar.

The Cat 4 burst from behind the crate, a nearly invisible blur in the foggy yellow light. The wailing blur launched itself through the air and smashed into Corliss, throwing the man backwards onto the steps.

Corliss yelled in shock. He beat at the creature tearing at him, using the pistol as a club. They raged at each other, locked together on the narrow stair. The white cowboy hat spun across the floor and stopped under a shelf.

As Lee looked about for a weapon, the cellar door yanked open and cold daylight spilled down the steps. A voice, Number Five, Lee thought, called down.

"Freeze! Throw down your weapons and come out!"

In an instant, the Cat 4 leapt from Corliss. He bounded up the stairs, his speed incredible, and vanished from sight. Lee heard the thud of hard bodily contact, a scream, and then the unmistakable spitting sounds of a silenced automatic firearm firing a ragged burst.

Corliss rolled deeper into the cellar and came to his knees. He held the pistol in front of himself like a talisman. From the world at the top of the steps, silence reigned for a moment; then another muffled burst from the submachine gun sounded up there. A voice floated down then, hoarse with shock and despair.

"My God!"

That's Number One, Lee thought.

Corliss seemed frozen but for his breath, which labored in deep draughts. The tip of the pistol barrel trembled. Blood trickled from a several deep scratches on the man's arms and face.

"Cut me loose," Jessica said. She clawed and tugged at the rope binding her other hand. "Cut me loose, cut me loose, cut me loose!"

Number One called down the steps. "Creed! You come out. I want your hands up and empty, or I'll shoot you dead. Understand?"

Corliss did not answer. His black eyes shifted to Lee, to Jessica, then back to the steps.

"Creed? Picket! Can you hear me? What's going on down there? What the fuck was that thing."

"Don't answer!" Corliss said. "I got to think."

"Cut me loose, cut me loose!"

"Creed, you don't answer me, I'm going to toss a grenade down there!"

Corliss stood, still covering the steps with the pistol. "Hold on! I'm comin' out. I got me a hurt woman down here. Jus' give me minute."

Lee, his body still trembling with reaction, set the lantern on the floor and cut the cord on Jessica's other hand. Immediately, she sat up and worked at the cords on her feet. Lee shouldered her back. With hard upper cuts of his knife, he parted the bonds. Jessica whimpered and rushed to the far back of the cellar where she crouched, her face distorted by terror.

"Get her over here," Corliss said.

"Where's my pants?" Jessica said. She covered herself protectively, crouching. "I want my pants."

"The hell with your pants," Corliss said. "Think this guy up top will wait? Nobody cares about your bare ass. Get over here!"

"I want my pants!"

Lee found her jeans rumpled on the floor. He handed them to her. She fell as she struggled into them. Lee moved to help her.

"No, you don't," Corliss said. "Get away from her."

The voice called down again. "Creed! Get moving."

"Goddammit!" Corliss covered Lee with the pistol, walked back to Jessica and grabbed her by the shoulder. "Stand up. You're comin' with me."

Jessica cringed. "It's out there."

"Come on!"

She screamed.

"Jesus!" Corliss cuffed her head with the pistol butt. Jessica went limp.

Lee stepped forward. "Hey!"

The pistol came up. "I'll kill you, boy. I got nothin' to lose. It'll take 'em months to figure out what happened here. Toss me that ransom bag."

Slowly, thinking hard for a way to keep Jessica with him, Lee complied. Corliss slipped the bag's strap over his shoulder. Lee watched him, gauging his chances of a successful sudden attack. They were not good, he concluded. He would let the scene play and hope for a better chance.

"You better quit what you're thinkin', boy." Corliss pulled Jessica up, got an arm around her. She was half-conscious. Corliss put the pistol muzzle against her temple. "Get the picture?"

Lee stepped back. "You got me, Corliss."

"You're right about that." Like a cobra, the pistol snapped in his direction. "Dumbass."

Lee began to move, raising his arms, sudden intuition telling him what was coming.

Fire flashed from the pistol. The bullet smashed through the cast on Lee's arm with the impact of a sledgehammer. He fell into the shelves, knocking loose boards and preserves to the floor, the glass jars shattering with heavy, liquid sounds. He registered a burning sensation in his right side. Stunned, he sat as he had landed, propped against a shelf leg. Amid the sudden smell of ripe peaches, he stared at Corliss in disbelief.

Lee shifted, felt his side. Blood. Sometimes you don't feel the pain at first.

"That's right." Corliss dragged Jessica closer to the steps and paused. "You're gut shot."

"Corliss," the voice from above called again. "You and Picket come up right now, or the grenade comes down."

Corliss grinned at Lee. "Die like a dog, boy. Think about me while you do it."

Lee held his side. He did not have the wind to speak.

"Ha!" Corliss looked up. "I'm comin' out! Don't shoot!"

Lee watched them go, Corliss dragging Jessica up the steps like a life-sized rag doll.

Corliss's voice came down the cellar steps, saying to Number One, "Back up, boy, or I'll shoot her head off!"

Lee took a more accurate status check on himself. His breath was coming easier, knocked from him by his own arm cast slamming into him from the bullet's impact. His probing fingers, much to his relief, found the wound along his ribs was not a puncture, but a gouge. Maybe the bullet had broken or cracked a rib. It felt that way.

He pulled away some loose padding and fiberglass from his ruined cast. His healing arm tingled and stung, but was otherwise intact. The bullet had hit the cast, deflected slightly, and burned across his side. To Corliss, it must have looked like a terrible hit, the cast blowing apart and Lee falling back into the shelves.

He stood. Now, the pain came, gnawing at his ribs. His legs wobbled. The floor felt insubstantial beneath his feet. Pale lantern light and gun smoke floated him to the stone steps where muffled voices and rain-washed air met him. How could he win, if he went up those steps? All his enemies were armed. He had done his best to help Jessica, and his best had proved pitiful and weak. What could he do now, unarmed and shaken, his injured ribs burning, his back aching from the fall, and the fingers in his healing arm still tingling and weak?

Try once more.

Lee bowed his head and closed his eyes.

Corliss's voice rushed across the opening, saying, "I mean it. I'll shoot her head off!"

Lee remained still, living in the darkness behind his closed eyes. His body gave a single, tremendous shiver, as if it could shake off his failure. In his mind, time stretched to eternity; his thoughts came in slow, solid blocks.

I've failed at everything, every time. The Creeds have beaten me. Greenbough has beaten me. And Jessica . . .

He tried to stop thinking, not wanting to finish that thought, but an unspeakable image, iconic in its emotional power, flashed unbidden in his mind, a wicked surrogate for the unfinished thought. He saw himself releasing the creature from its cage. Christ, he thought, blinking away the unthinkable.

Not the same creature.

But, it was.

He had to save Jessica.

Lee stood still, feeling his body to be an empty shell, nothing inside but smoke and mirrors, some kind of cosmic trick to make a man think that what he does, how he does, matters.

It matters. You can't let the bad guys win.

I'll die if I go up there.

So?

He opened his eyes and raised his head, slowly, the world still jittery around the edges. Looking through the open cellar door, gray clouds rushed past, swift, bleak, and low.

14

The cold and wet weren't the worst of it, Arletha thought, it was the pain in her side that tasked her. She held up on Uther's hand, stopping him. They had come to the end of the ghost road. The back of Prescott's lodge loomed just beyond the trees. She could glimpse portions of its limestone walls through the autumn leaves. Jessie, Horace, and Hank stood at the tree line, almost invisible with their skin looking like the leaves and branches around them.

"Patience, you all," she said. She grew light-headed and leaned on her cane. Her head ached. "I'm needin' just a spell to catch m'breath, then we'll call on Prescott."

Uther looked at her. He had grown enough he could look straight into her eyes. She fancied she could see his real face beneath the cat features he wore now, how he had looked when he had taken her in her daddy's barn, before Jubal had got serious with her. A tangled mix of emotions crawled up in her, some dark, some bright and sharp as an August day.

"Oh, Uther," she said. "Am I jus' a foolish old woman, bringing you all back from the dead? With me about to cross the river myself? Am I foolish to be puttin' my house in order a'fore I go?"

Uther squeezed her hand, and then wandered over to the others, spying on the lodge. She watched them. They were good kin.

After a minute, Arletha tapped her walking stick. They turned to look at her.

"Well," she said, "I don't guess Jubal is here, or he ain't going to give us a sign. Let's go see Celia Prescott."

***

Lee peeked over the root cellar's raised doorframe. Number One stood like a statue just a few yards away, his back to the cellar, the SMG raised high and tight against his cheek, its fat and silenced muzzle moving, tracking Corliss. Corliss held Jessica to him, his body molded against hers, his gun pressed to her temple. Jessica seemed only semi-conscious. Corliss backed away slowly, crossing the weedy yard, his black eyes never leaving Number One. If he saw Lee, he gave no sign.

Where the hell was Number Five?

"Look, Creed," Number One said, "I just want the tank. Tell me where it is and we're finished here."

"I ain't got the damn thing. I told you, that freaky ol' doctor took it."

Number One moved forward, his footwork careful and

precise, maintaining the range between himself and Corliss. "Strange. He said you had it."

Lee edged a bit higher to keep Corliss in view and in doing so, found Number Five. The man gazed up at him from beside the doorway. He was still, sprawled in final disarray, blood-soaked from a terrible wound in his throat. The sight hit Lee like an electric shock. The Cat 4 must have ripped the man's throat out, killed him in passing. He looked away from the ruined flesh, scanning the yard, the house, and barn for signs of the Cat 4. With that fantastic chromatic skin, Lee realized he would never see the creature until it moved. Corliss called out again, breaking Lee's thoughts.

"I ain't got your ol' tank, city boy!" He continued backing. "Just you go on and get out of here before you wind up like your buddy there."

"Just stop a minute," One said. "Just for a chat. I told you, I don't want you, just the tank. And, maybe you can tell me what the hell that was killed my partner."

Corliss stopped, his heels almost against a low, rotting platform in the weeds behind him. He peeked around the other side of Jessica's lolling head, Jessica still a lethargic manikin in his arms.

"The critter came out of that tank," he said. "Thought you'd know that."

"That right?" One said. He stopped, but kept his SMG trained on Corliss.

Lee wished he would not, with Jessica in the way.

"That's right," Corliss said. "Now that you got all you came for, you can get the fuck out of here. Go tell your boss the Creed's ain't got nothin' you want."

"I can't do that. I've—"

The porch door moaned open on rusty hinges. Luther stepped out, rubbing his eyes, Luther in his coonskin cap and overalls. One unfastened overall strap swung free behind him.

Number One whirled and sighted down the barrel at Luther.

Corliss took particular aim with his pistol and shot Number One four times. Lee barely heard the muffled shots, quick snaps of sound.

Number One jerked with the impact of the bullets, most of them hitting his torso, thudding against his body armor. A single round hit his face with a sickening, meaty smack. The man dropped his gun and grabbed his face as he fell.

Corliss whooped and slung Jessica to the ground. He danced a brief victory jig, stopped, and pointed the pistol at the dead man twenty yards away.

"How do you like me, now?" He turned to Luther, who stood dumbfounded on the porch. Corliss wiped blood from his face, from the Cat 4 scratches there, and bowed to him. "Thank you, Big Brother. You finally got something right."

"What?" Luther looked from Number One's crumpled

body to Corliss, to Jessica who had propped herself up on one elbow and was staring about with a dazed expression. Luther rubbed his face. "What's goin' on, Corliss? Why'd you shoot that man?"

A scream, as abrupt and chilling as a panthers', ripped the air. From the rusted hull of the Creed burn-barrel, a blur of dark colors flashed across the yard. Corliss turned, raising his pistol. He was too late. The Cat 4 crashed into him, carrying him back, tripping him over the edge of the platform. They landed with tremendous force on the loose covering of boards. Lee saw red bits of Corliss fly in the air as the creature ripped at him. So intense was the attack that Corliss had to drop the pistol to keep the Cat 4's lethal fingernails from his throat.

The sight riveted Lee. He had never seen such savagery.

Together, the Cat 4 and Corliss rolled and thumped on the creaking boards, Corliss trying to pin his opponent beneath him while the Cat 4 strained to slash Corliss's throat. For several seconds they struggled, and then froze face-to-face in a temporary stalemate.

"Get off me," Corliss roared, "you son-of-a-bitch!"

The Cat 4 snarled. Like a viper striking, it lunged forward. Lee saw the creature's teeth flash, its jaws snap together. Corliss screamed as the Cat 4 ripped away his nose and upper lip. Blood gushed over Corliss's face, choking him.

Corliss heaved up, rolled, and slammed the Cat 4 down

hard. Old and rotted, the boards beneath them gave way. Corliss and the Cat 4 vanished in mingled wails of despair and rage.

Beside the platform, Jessica screamed and staggered to her feet. She stumbled across the muddy yard. Luther rushed down the porch steps and caught her as she passed.

"Wait, lady!"

Jessica turned her head into his shoulder and screamed again, as if she could transfer her horror to Luther. Suddenly, she went limp. Luther staggered under the unexpected dead weight, his facial expression uncertain.

Ferocious growls and violent thrashing sounds echoed from the pit. Corliss screamed again.

Lee glanced down, saw Number Five's SMG lay in a puddle beside the dead man. Fired by the chance to arm himself, Lee surged out of the cellar but tripped on the cellar's raised doorframe. He landed on his injured ribs in the mud, igniting a burst of pain there. Desperate, he reached for the dead man's weapon, felt his fingers encircle the collapsible shoulder stock. Lee raised his head.

The sounds in the pit stopped. The wind picked up, muttering in the treetops. Luther, his voice small and subdued, spoke.

"C-Corliss?"

Luther stood motionless, with Jessica crumpled in his arms, staring at the pit's mouth. Lee followed his gaze.

The Cat 4, his movement fluid and effortless, crawled from the earth and crouched on the ruined platform. Gore spattered his shifting, watercolor skin. He saw Jessica in Luther's arms. His weird, golden eyes almost glowed. With a low growl, the Cat 4 rose to his feet and stalked toward Luther and Jessica. Blood dripped from his lethal fingernails.

Luther let Jessica, unconscious now, slip to the ground. He stepped over her body and drew a long hunting knife from the deep leg pocket of his overalls. He pointed at the Cat 4, who, now seeing the blade in Luther's hand, slowed its advance.

"You ain't my pa!" Luther said.

Lee crawled through the mud, his injured rib biting him. The silenced submachine gun, the metal cold, wet, and wonderful in his hands, was heavy. Lying in the mud, He snapped the bolt back, going to bring it to bear on the Cat 4, but the weapon stopped short, almost snatched from his hands. Startled, Lee discovered the SMG's carry strap was still looped around Number Five's shoulder.

He cried out in bitter surprise, feeling his chance slipping away. The Cat 4 spared him a quick look, and then crouched, ready to spring on Luther.

In mounting desperation, Lee tugged on the shoulder strap. With a final, savage wrench, it tore loose. Firing from the ground, Lee's first shots went wild, the jumping gun spitting its lead rounds high and to the right, into the home's clapboards, shattering the front window. The Cat 4 whirled, snarling. Then, its skin mottling as if confused, the creature dashed around the corner of the house. Lee sent a follow-up burst, now better controlled, chasing behind the vanished super creature.

Suddenly, the gun was too heavy. Lee relaxed and let its weight lower his hands. Tension left his body, and he lay in the cold mud, looking at Luther, wondering if he would have to shoot him, now.

Jessica had not moved. She lay with her face turned toward the house, a peaceful sleeping form at odds with the drama.

Luther spared her a glance, and then walked to the pit. At the edge, he looked down. His shoulders slumped. The heavy knife dropped from his hand, and he knelt, staring into the pit with bowed head.

Lee mustered his strength, got his knees under himself and stood, slowly. The dizziness that had threatened him earlier did not return, though he knew it lurked at the perimeter of his mind. He put the loop of the SMG over his shoulder but kept his finger near the trigger. The near invisibility of the Cat 4 made him nervous.

Moving with care, he went to Jessica. He turned her face from the mud. She did not stir. He had to get her to shelter and medical attention. Cautiously, he went to Luther, stopping behind the man, the SMG at the ready.

"Luther," he said. From where he stood, at this angle, he could not see the bottom of the pit. "Luther?"

The man turned his whiskered face. Tears streamed down his cheeks.

"Look what it done," Luther said. "Oh, look what it done."

Lee, sensing no threat in the man, stepped closer. At the bottom of the pit, ten feet below, Corliss lay dead atop the broken cover boards, half submerged in foul water, missing the lower half of his face. His blood painted the rock walls and boards. His head was tilted at an unnatural angle, opening wide the jagged wound in his throat. His shirt was shredded, exposing his blue-gray intestines as they bulged over his belt. Lee turned away, his stomach suddenly sour and weak.

"I cain't let Mama see him like this," Luther whispered. He still stared into the pit, what Lee saw now was a cistern, not deep enough to be a well.

"Where is your mama?"

"She's away."

Slowly, Lee knelt beside him. "Luther, I've got to get Jessica to a hospital. She might die unless she gets to a doctor."

His eyes still on the destruction of his brother, Luther repeated the word as if it was new to him. "Doctor."

Lee looked around the yard, checking the surroundings. The Cat 4 could come back at any moment. After seeing the damage the creature had wreaked on Number Five and

Corliss, he was not anxious to meet the man-beast again, sub-machine gun or not.

"Would you help me, Luther? We'll take her to town and get the sheriff. He'll get some people out here to help with your brother."

Luther shook his head. "I'll take care of Corliss. T'ain't our way to mix with town folk, 'specially Sheriff Gordon."

"But, that creature may come back. You're in danger if you stay."

"I hope he does."

"Then, will you help me get Jessica to the dock? I'm hurt. I don't think I can do it alone."

"Miss Jessica?" Luther turned to look at her. "I'll help."

Luther came to his feet and went to Jessica. He scooped her up in his arms. The man made it look easy, as if Jessica's tall, well-muscled frame weighed no more than a child.

"Watch out for Jubal," Luther said. "He might come back an' 'tack us."

"Jubal?"

"That critter killed Corliss."

His own concern re-enforced, Lee watched their back

trail, searching for the blur that would be the Cat 4. Every sound made him jump: the wind stirring in the trees, drops of rainwater pattering down from the leaves. He watched for Arletha, too. He did not know how long she would be "away," or what she would do, maybe bring out Granny's shotgun, if she saw them.

"Luther, where is your mama? Where did she go?"

"She went to kill Miss Prescott. I told her it wasn't right or good, but she went anyway."

"Miss Prescott. Celia?"

"'At's right. She took Uther an' the others, an' she's going to end the curse, she said."

"Who's Uther and the others?"

"They're the other ones."

"I don't understand. You've got more brothers?"

"Naw. Ma thinks they're our kinfolk, my uncles, but they's jus' critters. Like Jubal."

Lee's blood ran cold. The others, a small pack Cat 4's descending on the unsuspecting lodge full of women and children. Solomon Grue and his gunmen, it seemed, may be unwitting and ironic gifts.

All the way to the dock, he felt eyes upon them. He could not cover all the places the Cat 4 "Jubal" could strike from ambush. Finally, when his feet hit the rough planks of the dock, he relaxed. If anything came for them now, he would see it, even a Cat 4 with its incredible biological camouflage.

Lee stopped in shock. Half submerged and tethered only by the bowline, the Bayliner wallowed against the dock like a dying whale. Dirty waves knocked the boat into the pylons as the lake tried to swallow the boat stern first. Lee could feel the impacts vibrating through the wood. On the other side, Dr. Chilson's houseboat tugged at its own dock lines.

"Your boat got sunk," Luther observed. He held Jessica like a baby. "You want me to put her on the other one?"

The wind cut across the lake, chill and harsh. Lee looked beyond the houseboat to the lodge on the far point. Details, people or vessels, were impossible to see at this distance. The boat ride to safety would take forever.

"Let's get her onboard," he said.

To his surprise, Luther leapt aboard the houseboat with Jessica in his arms as if he had been practicing the maneuver, timing his jump with the tossing deck of the boat to land when it was at its high point. Jessica made a mewling sound, but did not revive. Lee followed with greater caution, still feeling light-headed. His landing jarred his back and ribs, causing him to gasp and sink to one knee.

"Hey," Luther said. "You okay, Mister?"

"Yeah." Lee stood, feeling his injuries burn, the animal darkness roaring in his mind. "Let me get that door for you."

Inside, the boat creaking and thumping around them, they tucked Jessica into the stateroom's big bed. Lee did not like the way she looked, so pale, as he pulled the blanket to her chin. He felt a sudden tenderness for her, seeing in her relaxed face the little girl she once had been. The room was cold, but he did not want to waste time figuring out the heating controls. His best bet was to push across the lake to town as fast as he dared, get her to a doctor. Then, find the sheriff.

"She'll be okay, Mister."

"Yeah. Let's go."

Lee found the keys in his pocket and stepped into the pilothouse. Though he had not been worried, he felt a small tremor of tension leave him when the engines turned over and caught. He turned on the running lights and reached for the marine radio to call for help.

Someone had cut the microphone cord. The mic was missing, doubtless thrown into the lake.

Corliss.

Luther stood in the doorway, the wind flipping the tail of his coonskin cap up and down. The loose strap of his overalls tapped and jingled against the frame. "I got to go, now.

Lee extended his right hand. Luther looked at it for a moment, his face blank. Suddenly, he brightened. "Oh!" He pumped Lee's hand up and down.

"Thanks, Luther, for everything. I still think you should come with me."

"Cain't."

"Cast me off, then, will you?"

Luther closed the door behind him and disappeared down the side of the boat. Lee throttled back the engines and waited. Soon Luther came back. He jumped to the dock and went to the bowline. He slipped the loops free of the dock post and threw the line onto the deck. He waved.

Lee moved the throttle ahead, slow. He lost sight of Luther as the boat moved forward. Soon he was in open water, thudding through the waves. Lost in vapors on the far shore, New Le Beau looked like a mythical city.

At New Le Beau, he would keep his story simple, get the sheriff and maybe the State boys out to the lodge, tell them terrorists were holding hostages there. As far as he was concerned, the jig was up. Keeping Chilson's and Fraily's fantastic creations secret had been a mistake. Let the world know. He would drag Greenbough's ruthless operations kicking and screaming into the light.

The boat rocked and shook with the waves. Lee held his course and let himself relax a degree. His only worry now was that Solomon Grue would see the houseboat crossing the lake and contact more henchmen in town. He picked up the radio he had taken from Number One and turned it on. The device remained quiet, which meant no one was trying to contact Number One. Whatever communications arrangement Solomon Grue had with them, he was not yet concerned with the mission progress.

The SMG hanging from his shoulder annoyed him. He slipped free the strap and tossed the gun onto a seat behind him. Jessica's condition and the automatic weapon should help convince the authorities that he was not just some kook with a conspiracy theory. Sheriff Gordon already suspected some kind of plot was afoot. Wait until he got a load of this one.

Lee grimaced. His back pain was getting to him. He eased down in the pilot's seat, favoring his back and injured ribs. His healing arm still tingled faintly within the remains of the shattered cast, remembering the bullet's impact. The wound in his side where Corliss's bullet had nicked him still trickled blood.

Jesus. He was a freaking mess.

Leaning back, holding the wheel with one hand, he closed his eyes, just for a moment. That was all he needed, a moment.

The door blew open, and cold wind crashed into the cabin. Lee gave a start. The area in the open door was wrong, some kind of visual distortion there as if a cloud of steam obscured the view beyond. With a shock, he recognized the strange phenomenon. Jubal, the Cat 4, stood there, dripping wet, his skin modulating in hues of blue and gray, attempting to match his background. His golden eyes burned into Lee.

***

Celia looked out the lodge office window, trying to ignore Sydney's desperate gambit. The storm appeared to be dying. White caps on the lake had diminished, and the rain had stopped but for a few scattered drops. She turned back, casting a glance in Sydney's direction. Yes! Sydney was offering Red, who still sat with his hands bound, some water. The nearest gunman was not watching her, his attention on the crowd. With hope, Sydney would succeed in cutting Red's bonds and escape detection.

Celia looked back through the doorway, into the small study where Solomon Grue was still interrogating Dr. Chilson, not letting up, insistent on knowing every detail of the theft and the people involved. Their voices, Solomon Grue's alternately harsh, then reasonable, and Dr. Chilson's, always weak and weary, carried to her like a sound track of an old melodrama.

Celia had changed her mind about Solomon Grue. At first, she thought he was giving a performance, pretending to be a ruthless killer. Now, she wondered if he was authentic. Yes, he would leave once he found Greenbough's stolen project and let her guests live—killing them would launch too intense an investigation—and they knew nothing of the technological secret. Yet, she was beginning to suspect that sometime later, a week, or a month from now, she and Dr. Chilson, Jessica, Sydney, Red, and Lee, any who knew too much, would find a sudden death. Some deaths would look like accidents, some like street crimes. Or, perhaps their bodies would never be found. She shuddered.

One of the masked men, a tall well-built man Solomon Grue called, "Number Three," came in from the crowded lobby, his awful machine gun in his hands. He brushed past Celia heading toward Solomon Grue. She keyed the control on her wheelchair. Its response was sluggish, and she realized it was overdue for a battery charge. Soon, if she did not find time to re-charge the battery, she would be forced to wheel the heavy chair by hand. Still, she followed the gunman to the office. The fact her captors allowed her such freedom and privilege reinforced her idea that they considered her no threat to them.

Solomon Grue turned to Number Three. "What?"

Number Three stopped and held up a hand-held radio. "They are ten minutes late for check-in. You want me to call?"

"Yes, do it."

"Three to One," Number Three said into the radio. "Do you read me?"

He waited, looking at Solomon Grue, then at Dr. Chilson who sat with his head in his hands. No response issued from the radio.

"Number One, respond, please.

But for the faint hiss of static, the radio remained silent.

"Number Five, come in."

Static.

He looked at Solomon Grue. "What now?"

"Keep trying every few minutes." He looked at Dr. Chilson, then back at Number Three. "But, keep an eye on our guests."

The man turned without reply and passed Celia. She watched him join another gunman who stood watching the great room where the hostages sat whispering or staring. The psychic twins from New Jersey were leading the children in subdued song as they sat on the floor.

Celia turned back. Solomon Grue appeared to be giving Dr. Chilson a break, his gaze steady on the control console the doctor had said operated an amphibious robot. She watched his face freeze in an attitude of extreme attention. He picked up the console, which looked very much like an oversized lap top computer with an antenna, and studied the controls. He pushed a button, and his expression changed. With a huff of exasperation, he tossed the console into Dr. Chilson's lap.

"Cute, Doctor," he said, "putting the console in 'test' mode. Now, activate command override and bring the rover and tank back from wherever you have sent them."

Dr. Chilson seemed confused. "I do not know where . . . I do not have its location. If the console is in test mode, it is accidental."

Solomon Grue stepped forward and took Dr. Chilson's left hand in his. Without preamble, he bent back the old man's pinky finger. Celia heard the bone snap, and her stomach turned. Dr. Chilson cried out in pain.

"You have nine more. Should I keep going?"

"Tell him, Doctor!" Celia gripped the armrests of her wheelchair. "If you can bring the damned thing back, do it. Do you not see? You endanger us all with your stubbornness."

Dr. Chilson bent over his injured hand, his eyes closed behind his cracked glasses. His breath came in small gasps.

"Listen to the lady," Solomon Grue said. "She understands the situation far better than you."

In obvious pain, Dr. Chilson positioned the console on his lap. With his injured hand held to his chest, the little finger jutting at an odd angle, he worked the keyboard with his good right hand. The console bleeped in response.

"Link established," he said. His words were barely audible.

Solomon Grue stood beside Dr. Chilson looking at the console's screen. He pointed to a sectional window frame. "What is that?"

"That is the rover's status screen. These are the last readings it transmitted."

"Exterior readings, Photon read out 3, Temperature 17.6 degrees Celsius, humidity, one hundred percent? What the hell?"

"It, um, I would say that it is in the lake."

"Clever. I had forgotten it was submersible."

Dr. Chilson tapped more commands on the keyboard. He sat back and watched, nursing his injured finger. After moment he said, "The transmission rate is very slow, intermittent, I would say due to the storm. We are lucky its antenna is deployed."

"That was not so difficult, was it?" Solomon Grue patted the older man's shoulder.

Celia rolled forward, the chair slow and balking, and stopped beside Dr. Chilson. She reached for his injured hand and took it into her own, gently. "Let me see, Doctor."

He relinquished his hand, looking at her over the tops of his glasses as she examined his injured finger.

"He needs a splint," she said to Solomon Grue. "Let me get to the first aid kit. It is there, behind you."

"It can wait. I want that robot and tank before anybody gets anything. No favors, you understand?"

Celia sat back, staring into his eyes.

Twenty minutes passed.

Solomon Grue looked out the window at the lake. "Where is it? What is taking so long? Doesn't that damn thing have video capabilities?"

"Strange, the rover is still sixty yards offshore," Dr.

Chilson said absently, examining his broken finger. "It should be much closer to shore than that. Yet another malfunction."

On the console screen, a small electronic map of the lake illuminated the top right corner. Celia recognized the point where the lodge stood, and New Le Beau.

"The old town," she said, quietly.

Solomon Grue looked at her. "What's that, Mrs. Prescott?"

"Old Le Beau."

"What?"

"Before the dam was built, the town was in the valley," she said. "All the old buildings are still down there. Perhaps your robot has trapped itself in one of them."

"You're telling me the thing could hang itself up in some submarine Hooterville?"

Dr. Chilson turned his eyes back to the screen. "The rover has excellent problem solving capabilities. Give it more time."

"Mrs. Prescott, how deep is the lake? Do you know?"

"They say it is about forty feet there."

"Forty feet," Grue repeated, not sounding happy.

She saw him stiffen, something out the window

catching his attention.

"Isn't that your houseboat, Doctor?"

Celia's heart leapt. *Jessica!*

Dr. Chilson looked out the window. He squinted and adjusted his glasses with his unharmed hand. "I cannot determine from this distance. It could be."

Solomon Grue spoke into his radio. "Number Three, report to me in the office."

Static crackled on the radio. "Coming."

Celia watched the houseboat rock through the rough waves. She had no doubt that it was Dr. Chilson's boat or that her daughter was onboard. With luck, Lee Picket, bless him, was taking Jessica to New Le Beau, going for help.

Number Three returned to the office. "Still no answer from the recovery team."

"For the moment, that can wait." Solomon Grue pointed out the window. "That houseboat belongs to our colleague, here. Take the boat—no, take their pontoon boat—and see who is captain. If it is Picket or Jessica Prescott, or our friend Mr. Creed, do bring them to me."

"Right." Number Three hesitated. "Uh, are there keys for the boat?"

"Check the key box in the office," Solomon Grue replied.

Celia stared out the window while the man complied. A few moments later, Number Three came back.

"No keys," he said. "The boat key slot is empty."

"Check the maintenance man," Grue said, looking at Celia.

The man stared across the crowd and located Red. He left on his errand.

Celia felt a sense of fatalistic doom settle on her. Was there no hope?

Solomon Grue frowned at Celia then looked out the window. "Strange. Whoever is at the wheel must be drunk."

Celia watched the houseboat. The course was erratic, as if the pilot was inebriated—or as if no hand at all steered the craft.

Where are you going with my little girl, Lee Picket?

The sound of shattering glass and screams behind her interrupted her thoughts. She keyed the wheel chair; it swung around slowly. Chaos reigned in the great room. One of the guards fired his machine gun at the shattered French door, the bursts made inaudible by the silenced muzzle and the noise of the hostages. The adults and children, screaming, rushed away from the shooting and windows, bunching against the inside wall. Celia could not see the source of the panic, but as she watched, the gunman who fired at the French door dropped his machinegun and collapsed to the floor, a look of disbelief and horror etching his features. Blood flowed in scarlet ribbons from his torn jugular, bright and wet against his black sweater. Over him, the air shimmered as if disturbed by a mirage.

***

Cold wind gusted through the pilothouse door where the Cat 4 braced against the rocking of the boat, Lee starting to see it now as *Jubal*, what the Creeds called it. The creature's skin settled to a uniform reddish color. It gave the Cat 4 a larger presence, made his eyes seem more baleful. That the creature had followed him onboard the houseboat made Lee certain the creature had an agenda. That realization ran down his spine and raised the hairs on his scalp.

The submachine gun lay on the seat behind him. Jubal dropped his gaze to the gun, and looked back at Lee. Lee doubted he could reach the gun before the Cat 4 reached him.

Jubal glanced into the interior, but looked back quickly.

It wanted Jessica.

Lee had no time to dwell upon it. The Cat 4 sprang at him without warning.

Lee twisted and lunged for the SMG, getting his hands on it but catching the corner of the seatback in his injured ribs. An involuntary yell of pain burst from him. Jubal crashed into him, crushing him against the seat. Lee brought the firearm around in a vicious arc. The hard metal stock cracked into the Cat 4's chin, sending him rolling to the floor. Even as Lee fired, Jubal sprang from the floor and grasped the silenced gun barrel. The bullets stitched into the ceiling.

Lee braced his legs and got his arm under Jubal's chin. Jubal raked him with his sharp, iron-hard nails and wrenched away the gun, flinging it aside. Desperate, Lee clubbed at Jubal's head with his free fist.

They whirled together in the pilothouse, Lee pummeling and punching, trying to keep the powerful hands away from his throat, Jubal growling, his rage seeming primal and eternal. Unguided, the houseboat continued on, its wheel wagging with the vagaries of the waves.

Suddenly, they broke apart. Lee found himself staring at Jubal, the Cat 4 braced once again in the open doorway. Jubal stared back. In that moment, Lee felt an understanding pass between them, an acknowledgement of quest and struggle, of kinship, of loneliness. He also understood there would be no prisoners. It was the way things must be.

Lee drove forward, hitting Jubal center of mass, carrying him out the door, the boat pitching, tipping them toward the water. Jubal locked his arms around Lee as momentum carried them over the lifeline. They fell together into the cold, crashing water.

Lee managed to keep the Cat 4 beneath him as they fell. The cold water almost sucked the breath from him. Jubal pushed and pawed at him in a panic, struggling to free himself. Hoping his lung capacity would win out, Lee gripped the Cat 4's arms and used his greater weight and position to drive deep into the darkness below. He kicked hard, getting down into a layer of much colder, black water. His lungs screamed with pressure. Jubal's struggles grew frantic, then weaker. The ringing whine of the boat's engines grew fainter, the boat leaving them behind. Finally, his lungs aching and desperate for air, Lee released Jubal and kicked hard, using his enemy's body as a launch pad to find the surface.

The wind seemed warm as it brushed his face. He gulped for air, turning, blinking the water from his eyes. The houseboat held its course, plowing through the waves toward distant Le Beau. He thought of Jessica lying helpless in the stateroom, oblivious to her danger. Less than two yards away, Jubal broke the surface, his miraculous skin gray and ghastly, his eyes like molten gold. Energized by the sight, Lee turned and swam for the shore and lodge. They were nearly half a football field away.

When his arms ached, when his lungs and injured rib begged for respite, he paused and spared a glance behind him. He kicked and rose as a wave lifted him. He did not see Jubal. He waited for another wave to raise him and looked again. There, far behind him, a disturbance in the water. Jubal was following him, not swimming well, but making progress. Lee turned again for shore, the waves assisting, running the same direction, a small gift from the Fates.

How many minutes in the water? God, he was cold.

His arms had become monstrous weights to swing above the water; the remaining cast on his arm was heavy, and he knew he kicked his feet, but felt little power there. He kept his eyes closed and swam blindly, letting the course of the waves guide him. At last, he heard the waves breaking on the shore and raised his head. He was just north of the lodge, not far from where the dock bluff dropped to the little scrap of crescent shore Celia liked to call, "the beach." At least he thought he was; his thoughts were becoming confused.

Exhausted, Lee coasted the remaining few yards on the waves until he felt the bottom under his shoes. He collapsed on the shore and rested a moment, shivering. His head began to ache. Strength, shy and tentative, spread back to his limbs from some last inner warehouse. Still, he rested there, hard pebbles pressing into his face, wind gusts raking over him with razor claws.

Get up, Picket. Get up now.

Just a few more minutes. I can't move. Hypothermia can wait.

Move, or die.

With a start, Lee rolled to his feet. Jubal still swam, his efforts awkward but strong, toward the shore. The Cat 4, the-thing-who-would-not-die, the merciless sum of all grade B movie monsters, would land in a matter of minutes. Lee stumbled higher, pressing through the brush line, finding the trail that ran along the shore to the lodge.

He had to get to Jessica before the houseboat met with

calamity. The pontoon boat: He had to find a way to start the pontoon boat, maybe find some forgotten keys in the boathouse or hidden on the boat itself.

But, wait. He was leading Jubal right to the lodge. Was it too much to ask that the Cat 4 would slink into the woods and forget about Jessica, about killing people? There were children at the lodge. Ah, but there were also men with machineguns.

Yeah, guns did you a lot of good, you and Number Five, his throat ripped out before he could fire a shot.

Jubal killed Corliss, too, Corliss in a watery pit, dead with a gun in his hand. Lee concentrated on putting one foot in front of the other, the only way he was going to make it.

The woods thinned and ended. He shot a glance at the lodge. Solomon Grue and his boys would be able see him on the open shore if they were paying attention. He had about two-hundred feet to the beach, then about the same as the beach rose to the little bluff at the other tip of the crescent shore. Once down at the boathouse, the bluff would hide his movements until he took the boat past the dock.

Lee looked behind him. Jubal was splashing ashore.

15

Solomon Grue took just a moment to assess the chaos in the great room before grabbing Dr. Chilson by his upper arm and pulling him from the chair. The command console fell to the floor.

"Come on, Doctor," he said, dragging the doctor past Celia, banging against her wheelchair. "You're staying with me."

They paused at the reception desk. Solomon Grue drew a pistol from his waist, a slim automatic. He shouted over the screams. "What's going on? Number Three! What's going on?"

Number Three dashed across the great room to meet Grue.

Celia moved the control lever on her wheelchair and rolled toward the lobby entrance, going slow as the battery became weaker. Red was loose, pushing Sydney away from the shattered window and danger. She waved, catching Red's eye as they moved along the wall. Celia motioned to him.

Come.

She watched as he skirted unnoticed around Solomon Grue and Number Three. Dr. Chilson stood waiting, a dazed expression on his face. Red paused to look at the room, where now most of the guests had crowded against the far wall. Sydney ran to help others who were trying to calm the children and a number of hysterical adults. One of the masked gunmen inched forward, his shotgun snug against his shoulder, toward where his comrade lie dead with his throat slashed open. Celia made it to the front door as Red caught up with her.

"Do you have the boat keys?" she whispered, watching Solomon Grue who seemed to have forgotten her. Her heart pounded with fear of being caught.

"The pontoon boat, yeah." Red looked around. "I think I can get you out of here, but we've got to move now."

"No! I won't leave my guests, but you must. Take the pontoon boat. The houseboat is heading towards town. Jessica may be onboard, but the boat is acting strangely, not going right."

"What?" Red looked out the door at the lake.

"Corliss Creed kidnapped Jessica," Celia said. "Lee went to rescue her, but I think something has gone wrong. Go, now. Catch the houseboat, see what is happening, then go for help."

"But those things are attacking, I can't leave you."

"For God's sake, Red!"

Solomon Grue and his gunmen were still in conference. Red turned, touched her arm.

"You've got to hide, Celia." It was the first time he had addressed her by her first name. "Get those kids somewhere you can lock up. The basement. No widows there. You get someone to carry you down, then lock the door."

"I will try. Now, go!"

Red looked out the door, and then back at her, uncertainty on his face.

"Go!" Celia said. She wanted to ask Red about the "things" that he thought were attacking, and how he knew about them, but time was short. She had a bad feeling she would find out soon enough what "things" were on the loose. She watched out the window.

Red slipped out the front door, moving quickly but with care, stopping to scan the yard around him every few feet. The care he took in looking puzzled her. The entrance to the lodge was quite free of hiding places for an enemy to use, and the lawn was open all the way to the dock, yet Red seemed reluctant to move ahead.

From outside, a preternatural wail arose, eerie in its wavering notes. Her blood chilled. Whatever was prowling the lodge, it had killed an armed man somehow, and now had Solomon Grue and the rest of his men excited and confused. Two of them went through the shattered side doors, guns at the ready. She could see Red was halfway to the dock bluff now, moving a little faster, though from confidence or fear, she could not tell.

One of the gunmen who had just gone out saw Red and shouted at him. Red froze for the briefest moment, and then ran hard for the dock. She barely heard the sounds of the silenced machine gun as it fired. She saw Red stumble and fall, clutching at his legs. Celia gasped in shock.

Before she knew what she was doing, she had rolled through the front door, using the last of the chair's battery power for the maneuver. She wheeled herself down the ramp to the driveway.

"Hey!" The shout came from behind her. "Hey, lady! Where do you think you're going?"

Red was curled in the yard far ahead, holding his legs, his jaws rigid with muscle as he clenched his teeth. She turned to see one of the masked men, Number Three, she thought, standing at the corner of the lodge, his machine gun pointed in her direction. The wind buffeted her, a chill breath against her exposed flesh.

"He's hurt," she called.

"He's lucky he's not dead."

A blur detached itself from the lodge's stone wall and swarmed over the gunman. The machine gun made little sound as it fired across the yard then up into the sky. The gunman went to his knees, fighting an indistinct *thing* that tore at him, turning his face and throat into red and bloody ruin.

Suddenly, the wind brought the whiff of wood smoke and body odor. A dry, withered voice spoke from behind her. "You ever meet Uther?"

Celia turned. Arletha Creed stood a step away, a gray apparition against the stormy sky. The wind raked tangled wisps of faded hair across her face, her black and shining eyes.

"No," Arletha continued. "I don't guess you did. Your husband killed him afore you had the chance. But that's him, over there, killing that boy."

"Arletha."

"That's right." Arletha stepped up and took control of the wheel chair, turning it to the asphalt path that led to the swimming beach. "Me an' the boys come to set things a'right between us. You an' me. My family an' your'n."

Celia could find no words. Her nemesis continued to wheel her down the path. Arletha's conversational tone skewed reality, as if they were old friends chatting over coffee instead of in the middle of this bizarre battle.

"Whew! It's a right good walk over here. My ol' legs like to give out on me." She pushed Celia on, going slowly. "Jubal an' his brothers came back. Did you know? They ain't quite themselves yet, but as soon as I put you in the lake, like your husband done them, set things right so to speak, everythin'll be jus' fine."

Celia pushed up, trying to throw herself from the chair. Arletha's boney fingers dug into her hair and snatched her down without mercy.

"You ain't going nowhere, sister, but in the lake."

"Arletha, this is madness. You must stop. The law will catch you. You won't be with your family. You will be in jail."

"No, I won't. But, justice is come'n due, all right. Don't worry about your nigger over there. The boys'll get to him when they're done with the rest. He won't suffer long."

In the middle of the yard, Red was sitting up now, taking off his belt and strapping it above his left knee. He spared a look at them, his expression set with concentration.

God, help him walk, Celia thought.

The lake ahead still tossed itself on the shore, breaking there in angry waves. In the middle of the lake, the houseboat still wandered toward New Le Beau.

Celia struggled to rise again. Arletha's iron grip, surprising in someone of her age, held her down.

"Arletha, let me go. You must let me go!"

"An eye for an eye, an' a tooth for a tooth." Inexorably, the wheelchair stayed its course, rolling toward the thin strip of sand she had brought in by barge to create the beach. "Should have done this years ago."

Celia gasped. Crossing the short beach in front of them was a creature from a nightmare. As large as a small man, it walked naked and upright in the sand. Its skin color shifted like oil under glass, grays and blues and blacks. However, it was the creature's face that unsettled her, vague feline features drawn with crude humanity. It plodded with single-minded determination to the rise of land that led to the boat dock bluff. She looked along the sweep of the crescent shore. Lee Picket came down the bluff steps and paused on the dock, looking at the pontoon boat.

***

Lee cursed at the pontoon boat's empty ignition slot. The dashboard compartment was keyless as well. He hurried to the boathouse, favoring his injured ribs, trembling with cold. Scanning the interior, he hoped to find a set of keys hanging on a wall hook. No luck. He rummaged through the small desk by the door, jerking the two drawers free and dumping the contents on the desktop. No keys hid among the collection of ink pens, fuel receipts, and paperclips. He stepped out onto the dock. The houseboat still plowed its way across the lake.

Faintly, he heard someone called his name.

He turned. At the opposite tip of crescent shore, Arletha Creed pushed Celia Prescott down the beach path, Celia waving and pointing at something above him. The vision was surreal. He turned to follow Celia's frantic direction.

Fifteen feet above, Jubal glowered at him from the bluff. The Cat 4 turned and headed for the dock steps. Lee noticed its skin had lost the camouflage ability, now shifting between unhealthy gray and blue blotches. Jubal still looked formidable, though, and his intent was clear. He was coming to finish the fight.

Lee spared a look at Celia and was just in time to see Arletha slap her hard. He ground his teeth. There was no way he could get to Celia, not with Jubal now at the top of the steps. Lee ducked back into the boathouse, looking for a club, a boat hook, anything to use as a weapon. He had been lucky before, keeping Jubal's sharp fingernails and teeth from his throat. The sound of the waves popped and slapped under the tin roof. He stepped out on the dock.

Jubal was coming down the steps. Arletha had Celia at the shore now, but was having trouble pushing the wheelchair through the sand. *Going to drown her?* Celia looked out of it; her head lolled on her shoulder.

Lee yelled, hoping to distract Arletha, but his injured rib bit at him, and his call struggled against the wind. His peripheral vision registered movement. Jubal stood on the dock, his eyes golden-red. Lee backed away, knowing the end, whatever it would be, was not far off.

"Lee!"

Red's head and shoulders appeared at the top of the bluff.

Crazy, Lee thought, why is he lying down?

"The tank, man, the tank. Get to the tank!"

At first, Lee thought Red meant the embryo tank, but

turned, following Red's direction. Near the end of the dock was the standing gas tank, the one Red liked to keep full for those times he was too rushed or lazy to fill the boats in town. Gravity fed, the five-hundred gallon tank dispensed through a ten-foot hose. A padlock kept the nozzle safe from gas thieves. Lee did not see the point about the tank, could not see why Red was excited.

"What?" he shouted. Jubal came on, cautious, watching both Lee and Red.

Something was wrong with Red. He wriggled forward, as close to the bluff's edge as possible.

"Get to the tank. Burn the son-of-a-bitch!"

Lee saw the idea then. He patted his pants' pocket and pulled out his cigar matches in their waterproof container. Inside the clear plastic, they rattled bone-dry. He rushed to the edge of the dock. Jubal was under the boathouse roof now, approaching with careful steps.

Lee pulled out his key ring and searched for the key to the tank padlock, aware that any second Jubal could charge him. But, the Cat 4 seemed to sense a trap. He was studying the distance between them, listening to him and Red. There: a small brass key. His fingers were stiff with cold. The padlock was cold and wet. It clicked when he turned the key. He took the lock from the valve.

Jubal growled. From the corner of his eye, Lee saw him tense, his muscles bunch for action. Slowly, not wanting to trigger Jubal into action, he pushed the valve lever open, letting the gas flow into the delivery hose.

Jubal charged. With a yell, Lee ripped the nozzle from its cradle and squeezed the nozzle lever. Gasoline spewed out in a fat stream, dowsing the Cat 4. Jubal recoiled screaming, swiping at his eyes. He turned and stumbled away, moving back down the dock blindly. When he was out of range, Lee stopped the stream of gas. For a moment, Lee thought the beast would fall in the lake.

Jubal stopped at the dock's edge, teetered for a moment, but then recovered himself.

Lee felt his heart pounding with adrenalin, with fear of what he would have to do next. He spun the cap off the match canister with his thumb and tried to get a match out with his cold, stiff fingers. Jubal turned, still rubbing his eyes but now trying to look at him. Lee dropped the nozzle and used both hands for the matches. Jubal stood a mere twenty feet away. Lee was trapped at the end of the dock, the gasoline-soaked planks between him and the Cat 4. He was out of options and out of time.

Send a card to Mother, he thought, and used his thumbnail to strike the match head.

Nothing happened. No spark, no flame.

Quickly, Lee tried again. The time he had spent in the water had softened his fingernails; his hands were still wet. With growing horror, he realized that *everything* was wet. The lake had soaked him, and it had been raining. Water dripped from his broken cast. Desperate, he shook another match from the container, spilling a few, and tried to strike it on the fuel tank itself. The match head softened, made damp by the moisture on the metal, and crumbled.

Jubal growled. He ceased rubbing at his eyes and took a step toward Lee.

"Lee!"

Red waved a small silver boxlike object in his hand—his Zippo cigarette lighter.

Lee readied his hands for the catch. Fifteen feet high, and fifteen feet out. It would be equivalent to a thirty-foot toss. And, Red was lying on his belly. They had just one chance to get it right.

"Do it!" Lee said.

Red aimed, moving the lighter back and forth along his sight line. Then, he tossed it.

The lighter came down to Lee's left, missing his desperate hands. It hit the planks, bounced twice, and then skittered down the dock, stopping at the edge. Lee rushed forward and snatched up the lighter, ignoring the pain it cost.

Jubal stood still, his baleful eyes suspicious, his body crouched and ready.

Lee backed away from the gas-soaked planks and rolled the strike wheel. Nothing. His vision collapsed until all he could see was that goddamned lighter, thinking Jesus, would nothing go right? He almost laughed. In desperation, Lee blew on the flint, trying to dry it, and rolled the wheel again.

Nothing!

Jubal slunk towards him, arms and hands spread wide, tears streaming down his blotchy, demonic face. The distance between them closed.

Fifteen feet.

Ten feet.

Lee tried the lighter with desperate repetition. A small spark jumped from the wheel.

"Come on," Lee said, every particle of his being willing the thing to FREAKING LIGHT!

Jubal set his feet. He crouched low, ready to spring.

Flame popped to life in the lighter.

"Yeah!"

Lee tossed the lighter at Jubal.

The explosion from the igniting gasoline knocked Lee into the lake in a blinding ball of hot light. The cold water absorbed the stinging heat he felt on his face and hands. Shocked from the sudden emersion, he kicked to the surface, gasping, blinking water from his eyes.

Jubal was a pillar of fire. His howl of agony cut the air, an unbearable cry that tore at Lee's soul. The Cat 4 staggered on the dock, beating at the flames as they ate him alive. For a moment, guilt buried the triumph Lee felt. He wanted to end the creature's pain. Jubal howled once more. This time it ended on a short note. He pitched forward, landing on the fiery planks with a dead thud.

Red's voice reached him, riding down on the wind. "Yeah, man!"

Another howl drifted over Red's head and floated down the bluff.

"What's that?" Lee shouted, treading water, his injuries numbed by the cold.

Red rolled on his side and looked toward the lodge. He rolled back and called down.

"That thing wasn't alone!"

With the little strength he had left, Lee swam for the shore. Weak, he dragged himself up on the rocks. He stayed still a moment, resting, feeling the hard rock beneath him. He had a micro-view of the limestone, close to it now, noting the grain and patterns in the rock. A thought tried to come forward, begging attention, but lost. Cold, man, he was cold. His head hurt, inside. A warm bed would be the cure. Sure, a hot shower, some rum, fix him up right.

That thing wasn't alone.

Lee struggled and sat up, the cold wind of reality rushing past him. Red needed help. And, Celia—Jesus! He had forgotten Celia!

He looked across to the little beach. Arletha had Celia in the lake nearly up to her neck. The waves broke over them, slapping Celia's face.

***

All was chaos. Dr. Chilson sat in the office, serene with the calmness that comes with many years of life, considering things. For some reason, the Category IV creatures had attacked the lodge. The fact they had attacked the armed men first, begged thought. That they had attacked *at all* needed even more thought. Was the attack planned and coordinated by a pack instinct, or did they arrive at the decision by thoughtful design?

He took stock of his environment. The guests, the women and children, scared, whimpering, but apparently unharmed, huddled in a corner of the lobby. Solomon Grue and one of his men crouched behind the reception desk, Solomon Grue speaking into his radio, his words indistinguishable but his tone tense and desperate. Celia had rammed herself out the door; what she thought she could do for her wounded maintenance man, he could not guess. Alone for the moment, he removed his glasses and cleaned the damaged lenses on his shirttail. He ruminated while he performed this automatic chore.

A beep sounded from the rover's command console. He put on his glasses and swiveled his chair to look.

A green icon flashed on the screen, signifying that a regular radio frequency stood open with the rover. The directional and other operational tags indicated it was coming out of the lake.

He rose and looked out the window. An old woman

dressed in a faded raincoat had Celia Prescott in her wheelchair and was pushing her into the lake. The stranger fought Celia's wheelchair against the stormy water and the lake's rocky bottom. As he watched, a shape emerged from the waves not far from Celia and the woman whom he guessed to be Arletha Creed. The shape, he saw, was the rover.

As the rover came out of the waves, it looked odd, something amiss with its shape. The embryo transport tank was missing, and some type of debris was trapped in its front array. Alarmed, he carried the command console with him to the front doors.

"Doctor," Solomon Grue called from behind him, "where do you think you're going? Get back in here!"

Dr. Chilson went through the doors without answering.

***

Solomon Grue watched Dr. Chilson walk down the lodge steps. With a start, he realized the old man carried the rover's command console with him. He grabbed Number Four's shoulder, Number Four covering the broken French doors with his submachine gun.

"Come on," he said. "Follow me."

Number Four did as ordered, still keeping watch on the

door. "What are we doing?"

"Our meal ticket is getting away."

Number Four glanced at the main doors. "You want to go outside? Man, we've lost contact with the whole team. We don't know what we're up against. We don't even know how many of these goddamned things are out there!"

Solomon Grue turned. "I don't care! We lose Chilson, we lose everything. You understand?" He brought his pistol up, aimed it straight between the man's eyes. "I don't have time for this!"

Number Four stared at the pistol muzzle.

Solomon Grue said, "He's getting away. What's it going to be?"

"Don't point the pistol at me again."

"That-a-boy."

They hurried to the doors, past the people in the lobby, one of them saying, "Where are they going?"

The creatures attacked them as soon as they cleared the doors. How many of them, Solomon was not sure; they were so difficult to see. They came from either end of the porch, seeming to step from the rock walls like living stone. Only their eyes were distinct, terrible, golden eyes.

Number Four brought his machine gun up, firing wildly. In the yard beyond, Dr. Chilson crumpled to the ground. Solomon fired at the shape leaping at him only to have the weapon knocked from his grasp. He turned in time to see two blurry forms hit Number Four, one high, one low, and bear him to the porch floor. The man's scream ended in a wet rip of sound.

Solomon stumbled off the porch, weaponless, his mind whirling with the devastating attack. Ahead of him in the yard, Dr. Chilson moved, feebly working his bloody fingers on the command console. Beyond the old man, an explosion of flame boomed over the edge of the bluff. The shock wave rippled the air, Solomon feeling it arrive with the roar of the blast. The yellow-orange light highlighted a prone form at the bluff's rim, the maintenance man protecting his head with his arms, his face tucked into the ground.

***

The chilling water, now up to her waist and washing higher with each wave, squeezed at Celia's heart and mind, reviving her. Arletha was trying to push her under water. Celia reached up and clawed at Arletha, desperate to stop her advance into the lake. Her manicured fingernails gouged ragged tracks through her enemy's skin.

Arletha slapped her hard against the side of her head. "Bitch!"

Celia shook her head, her ears ringing with the force of the blow. A wave hit, splashing against her breast, sinking its icy essence into her bones and leaping into her mouth.

She choked on the unexpected water. She heard yelling, Lee and Red calling to each other at the dock and bluff. A flash of brilliant light illuminated the lake. The air trembled with concussion as a fireball arose from the end of the dock. Where Lee picket had been, a roaring column of flame now moved, erratic and uncertain, a wandering firestorm on the weathered dock.

"Jubal's got your man on fire," Arletha said.

God! Was that Lee?

Behind her, Arletha gasped. The forward movement of the wheelchair ceased. Celia turned her head.

A few feet away, what looked like a large, nightmarish mechanical lizard was emerging from the lake.

It is the robot, Celia thought.

A wheelchair, slimed with rust, its cushions rotted away and strands of waterweed trailing from it, hung from the robot's structure. A snarl of barbed wire fencing spiraled from the chair.

Another wave broke against Celia. She sputtered and wiped the water from her eyes. "Danny?" Arletha said.

Fighting the waves, almost falling several times, the old woman waded to the rover.

"Danny, Danny!"

The robot stopped at the water's edge, its glass eye scanning the area. It seemed to focus on Arletha. A small mechanical arm near its head, caught in the wheelchair's frame, waved about as if trying to dislodge it.

"Danny, you come back to me." Arletha stood in front of the robot. She stared at the empty wheelchair, her hands raised as if to receive a gift. "We're all together, now. Your Pa's here, over on that dock."

Arletha moved closer and stroked the chair's armrest, oblivious to the slime and rust that came away on her hand. She laughed.

Danny.

Celia thought that was the name of Arletha's missing boy. Had he not been in a wheelchair like her?

Another wave burst through them and died on the shore. Celia gripped the wheels of her chair and tried to roll backwards, but her weakness thwarted her.

Arletha was trying to release the old wheelchair from the robot's arm, crooning, repeating the name Danny. For the briefest moment, the shimmering silver form of a little boy appeared to fill the ruined wheelchair, reaching for Arletha. Celia's breath caught in her throat.

***

From where he lay, Dr. Montgomery Chilson could see the rover in the lake, Arletha Creed in front of it, stroking what appeared to be a wheelchair caught in the rover's array. Celia Prescott struggled beside them, perilously close to drowning. The pain of his bullet wounds seemed distant, though their impact, like fists pounding into him, had made him lose consciousness briefly. That dark fog threatened his mind again. He was dying, he knew. He heard his mother's voice calling him to supper across the fenced, summer-green yards of Harrisburg, Pennsylvania in 1938. Times were hard, then. But, they were good times as well.

He pushed a last command into the console and lifted his head to see the results, but the edges of his vision dimmed. "Go, sleep in the depths."

The rover would station itself at the bottom of the lake and would not move until it received a coded command from him. The command would never come. The robot would cease to function when its battery spent its remaining energy. What had become of the embryo tank, he could only guess.

Now, the robot and the others had become dark, blurry forms in a black lake. Dr. Chilson lowered his head. As the last of his life drained away, he smelled fresh cut grass, and he wondered what his mother would have on the supper table.

**

Lee limped down the shore, back and ribs aching, weak, cold, so cold, picking his way through the rocks toward the place where the short bluff crumbled and sloped to Celia's artificial beach. For some reason, the robot had returned. It sat in the waves beside Arletha and Celia, a rusted wheelchair hanging from it. His feet continued to wander of their own accord through the rocks. He fell; his injured rib bit him. He pushed himself up again.

A scream rent the air above him. He looked back. Red was still lying at the bluff's edge, face down now, either dead, passed out, or playing possum. Something happen to him? It was not Red's scream. Lee was sure of that. He plodded on, hoping he had enough strength to pull Celia from the lake, hoping he would not have to fight off crazy Arletha.

Another scream, this one ending in a gurgle, called again to his attention. He looked toward the lodge.

***

Solomon stumbled forward and plucked the command console from Dr. Chilson's fingers, the old man staring through his damaged eyeglasses at the lake, a smile on his face. Solomon followed his dead gaze and saw Celia Prescott in the lake, and beside her, an old woman clinging to—the rover. As he watched, the rover sank deeper into the waves, backing into the lake. Behind him, the creatures were coming for him. He reached for his backup pistol, a little .25 caliber Beretta auto he carried in an ankle holster. A low growl came from behind him.

The force of the blow knocked the console from his grip and opened his flesh to the spine. He screamed. Three of the creatures circled him, skins shimmering, and in the distance, coming from the lodge, a fourth form, blurry and indistinct against the background. Solomon screamed again as they converged on him, their fingers hooking and ripping at his belly and face.

***

"Danny! Danny, you let go, now!"

The panic in Arletha's voice was shrill above the waves. At first, Celia thought the woman was following the robot deeper into the lake, but then she saw the wild strands of the barbed wire around her arm and waist. The robot continued, its head swiveled one-hundred-eighty degrees, looking over its back into the water.

"Danny, I din't mean to let you die. You cain't do this to me." Arletha struggled against the remorseless momentum. The barbed wire opened red seams in her arm as it tightened. Blood ran from the wounds, diffusing itself in a pink patina on her wet skin. "I'm your Mama, Danny!"

Struck still by the sight, Celia forgot for the moment her own peril, and clutched the turn rims of her chair beneath the water. The robot dragged Arletha deeper, its head vanishing in the waves. Arletha, up to her neck, turned to Celia, her coal black eyes brimming with the knowledge of her doom.

"Help me!"

Celia moved her hands, barely feeling the wheels in their grip. Then, the impossibility hit her, and she stopped. It was too late, anyway.

Arletha's last plea gargled out as a wave washed into her mouth. Celia watched as the robot tugged her under the water. Arletha's stringy hair floated out for a moment, like the petals of a ragged gray flower, and then vanished into the lake.

***

Lee turned to face the Cat 4s. Shimmering and indistinct against the background, they spread in a line and moved toward him. Celia called to him from the lake, her voice weak. Before he could help her, he would have to deal with the Cat 4s. They would be on his back as soon as he turned. He had watched them take down Solomon Grue; his body now sprawled beside a white, still form that could only be Dr. Chilson. Sadness, brief and aching, flickered through him. Lee picked up a rock the size of a baseball. It was the only weapon he had left. If he threw it, the effort would cost him dearly. The pain in his ribs would be excruciating.

The creatures stopped, murmuring to each other, blood painting their hands and faces, a contrast to their shifting skin colors. One of them pointed to the dock. Lee realized they had seen the charred remains of Jubal. The suspense of waiting for their charge became intolerable.

Lee bounced the rock in his hand.

"Come on, you bastards."

His words drew no response. He stared at them. They were no longer looking at the carcass on the dock, but into the sky behind him. He risked a glance.

A helicopter was flying across the lake, straight toward them, as swift and unerring as the flight of a dove. He heard it now, the beating hum of its rotors growing closer. A margin of hope arose in him.

The Cat 4s shuffled their feet. To his left, Celia still had her head above the waves.

Slowly, the Cat 4s backed away, then, when the helicopter circled and sank lower, their nerve broke. In a flickering, phantasmal pack, they loped toward the far tree line.

Lee saw the pilot's face as the helo swooped near and hovered. He could imagine the man's thoughts, seeing bodies, an old woman in the lake and a madman on the shore. He dropped the rock and beckoned, pointing to the open yard. The helicopter hovered a moment longer, the pilot speaking to someone, although whether to someone on his radio or in the cabin Lee could not tell. Finally, the pilot nodded at him. The helicopter set down in the yard in a deafening rush of wind and engine.

Lee hurried as fast as he could down the shore and

plunged into the water. He grabbed Celia's wheelchair and pulled. The lake sucked at her, unwilling to relinquish this last victim. His back and ribs flaring in bright new pain, Lee tugged at the wheelchair until Celia was safely ashore and black crows flocked thick in his mind.

"Thank God," Celia whispered. Then, her head dropped to her chest.

Alarmed, Lee felt at her throat. Her flesh was cold, but beneath it, a weak pulse still beat. He pulled the wheelchair up the beach, Celia still unresponsive, toward the helo.

The side door stood open. A man dressed in designer jeans and cowboy boots stood beside a woman Lee recognized as country music star Kyra James. They stood just outside of the slowing rotors, uncertainty on their faces. Kyra James pulled her sequined denim jacket around her.

The man said, "What the hell happened here?"

"Ms. James," Lee said, pausing as a sharp pain lanced through his side, "this is your hostess. She needs immediate medical attention. So do several others here. Can you get them to New Le Beau right now?"

"Of course." Kyra looked critically at Celia, taking the wheelchair grips from Lee. "Dick and I will get her into the chopper. Then we'll get your friend over there."

He followed her nod. At the edge of the bluff Red lifted his hand in a feeble wave.

"What happened here?" said Dick, his head swiveling,

eyes uncertain. "If there is any danger to Kyra, I need to know."

"There is," Lee said. "So I want you to call the sheriff and state police, tell them I've got a lodge full of children, and that we've been attacked."

"By who?"

Kyra James was already pushing Celia toward the helicopter's open door where the pilot now stood, waiting to help. Lee looked at Dick.

"Bad guys."

Epilogue

A green mist of early buds laced the trees on Creed Island, March not too far from becoming April. Lee had the impression someone, or some*thing*, had been on the shore, seen him and ducked into the trees as he approached. He dropped the Bayliner's throttle to neutral and coasted to the dock. Silence rushed around him when he cut the rebuilt engine. He made sure the .45 automatic was secure against the small of his back, and then climbed onto the decrepit dock, wrapping the bowline around a splintered plank. The tabloid's still ran an occasional sighting story on the Cat 4s, but he was sure, fairly sure, anyway, they were gone or dead, or had at least stopping killing people. However, against the possibility he was wrong about that, he decided the Colt would be good company.

At the foot of the dock, he felt eyes upon him and stopped, visually searching the brush. Birds began to sing again as they continued their interrupted spring courtship.

"Luther?" Lee said.

In the mud at the lakeshore, he saw boot tracks. They trailed along the shore then cut into the brush at about the same position he thought he had seen someone duck out of sight. Boots. Not Cat tracks.

"Luther, it's me, Lee Picket. I don't mean you any harm. We're still friends, right?"

He waited. That crawly feeling, the kind you might get if you suspect the crosshairs of somebody's riflescope are trained on your chest, began to creep over him on cold little feet.

The bare bushes rustled. Luther stepped out from behind a tree clad in his signature overalls and coonskin cap. Today, he sported a faded flannel shirt beneath the bibs, the colors perhaps once red and green. His eyes were bright and alert over a full beard, the beard dusty gray. He carried a twelve-gauge shotgun, a double barrel model, most of the bluing worn off the metal and showing the dangerous gleam of raw steel.

"I seen you," Luther said, the shotgun cradled in his arm. "I seen you over to the lodge. They going to open it again?"

"No. I'm just here, seeing how things are now." Lee eyed the shotgun. "How have you been, Luther?"

"Fine. It's different, being alone. I ain't sure I like it or not."

"I'm sorry about your mother and Corliss. I didn't want any of that to happen."

"I know you didn't. They made their beds. I reckon they had to sleep in them. It's jus' lonesome, is all, without them here." Luther looked across the lake toward the lodge. "Whatever happened to Miss Jessica? Is she all right?"

442

The runaway houseboat carrying Jessica had run aground near a private marina not far from the city dock. A startled bait shop clerk had called the police.

"She's well cared for. Her mother visits her every day. They're in San Diego, at a special hospital."

"California?"

"That's right."

"What ails her?"

"You know, she went through a lot. I believe that creature—"

"Jubal."

"Right, Jubal. I believe he made her hide inside herself, in her mind."

"He raped her."

"That's right."

Luther looked across the lake again, following a private thought. Lee put his hands in his pants pockets, waiting, giving the man time. After a moment, he cleared his throat and spoke.

"I wonder sometimes, Luther, if you've ever seen any more of the creatures. The investigators still think we made them up." The Feds, regardless of whatever agency they represented, stopped searching for the mythical creatures in November. Jubal's body had vanished, so they had been skeptical from the first about the Cats. They were more interested in retrieving the ETU than what appeared to be a stress-induced mass hallucination and contagious hysteria.

"I see 'em every day now."

"What?"

A sudden sparkle lit Luther's eyes. "C'mon. I'll show you."

Luther's rubber boots made little sound on the trail's damp earth as they walked up the path to the house. The tang of wood smoke trailed from the man and mixed with the pungent scent of moldy leaves and rotting wood.

I see 'em every day now.

"What are you doing these days, Mr. Picket?" Luther asked over his shoulder. "You still workin' for Mrs. Prescott?"

"No," he said. He had parted from Celia, and Sydney, too, their brief relationship dying from long distance. "I write freelance articles for newspapers and magazines, back in Kansas City."

They were almost to the yard. The house came into view. Excitement tingled to life in his belly like a small animal breaking hibernation.

"That's good," Luther said. "And, you came back."

"Yes." He could not keep it from his mind, all that had

happened here. Sometimes, a crushing sense of loss would descend on him and hot tears would stream down his face. It was not self-pity, but an emptying, a flood of unrelenting sorrow pouring forth from some deep, collective well. "I think I had to."

Luther nodded. "How's that black fella doin'? I heard he got shot-up some."

"He's fine, still working for Celia." Red had to use a cane now and was still in therapy to strengthen his legs where the bullets had damaged the muscle. One had shattered the fibula in his left leg.

The Department of Homeland Security had indeed classified the attack on the lodge as a domestic terrorist operation. They portrayed Solomon Grue as the ringleader, a rogue contractor conducting his own raid to support his renegade mercenary team with proceeds from stolen technology. DHS was using the incident as leverage for more funding.

They reached the weedy yard of the Creed homestead and stopped. Lee's eyes went first to the root cellar, scanning from there to the cistern and porch.

"Hey, you okay?" Luther said.

"Yeah. Just got a chill." Too much feeling hitting him. "That's all."

Luther studied him, a quizzical expression on his face, then turned and pointed. "Well, there they are."

Lee spun, his hand snapping back to the Colt in his waistband. He saw only the empty yard with its collection of decaying machinery and the dead stalks of last year's weeds. The barn stood quiet beyond. Panic clawed at him.

"Where?"

Luther jabbed his finger again, pointing to the barn. "Right there."

The barn wall: Luther's collection of critter skins. Amid the rag-tag and rotting pelts tacked to the weathered boards of the old barn, four new skins hung on display. Gray, almost transparent in the places where Luther had scraped too much, the skins looked like life-sized paper dolls pinned to the wood. The vision was grotesque. Yet, it was gratifying, seeing a mortal enemy vanquished and stilled in death.

"Their skin was only purty a day or two," Luther said. "Then it faded quick, to what you see now."

"How did you . . ." he could not take his gaze away from the skins. Slowly, he walked to the barn, fascinated by the horrid cutouts on the sun-bleached wall. "How did you get them?"

"They didn't come back after what happened to Mama an' Jubal. They took to livin' in that cave up to Corliss's weed patch, near where that reporter lady was buried. I took Horace an' Hank first. They was easy. Walked right up to my baited traps and—spang! They caught themselves in two bear traps apiece."

"How did you kill them?"

"Clubbed 'em like they was mad coons." Luther studied the skins on the wall. "Jessie an' Uther was diff'rent. They come for me, after that. Come right to the house. Uther stole my shotgun here, loaded it, too. But, he didn't know 'bout the safety, so I got to him with my knife a'fore he could shoot me. They jumped me 'bout, oh, two months after Sheriff Gordon brought me back from 'terrogation. That'd be, unh, first week or so in December."

"And Jessie?"

"I got m' knife into him, too, but lookit here what he done a'fore that." Luther pulled the tail of his flannel shirt out of the bib of his overalls and exposed his hard, white ribs. Three long scars, still red and angry, raced down his side from under his arm to his hip. "We tussled purty good for a while. Busted up the house some."

Luther tucked in his shirt with his free hand, still holding the shotgun with the other. Lee looked at the barn wall.

"I'm glad you got them." He scratched his arm; it still itched sometimes as if he still wore a cast. "Maybe you ought to take down the skins, though. Those government men might come back. That could start trouble all over again."

"I been goin' to do that, anyway. I figured the skins'd be purtier'n that." Luther scratched his beard. "Now I jus' got to trap that other critter, an' things can get back to normal."

Lee felt the back of his neck grow cold. "What other critter?"

"The one took my sow last night." Luther gestured toward the barn. "It come in an' took ol' Sally right through the pen. Din't leave not one single drag mark back to the lake."

"I don't understand."

Luther walked toward the barn. Lee followed him around to the pigpen. One section of the tough oak fence had been battered to pieces. Splatters of a dark substance stained the boards: drying blood.

"Sally weighed near five-hunnert pounds. Ever-what took her off was terrible strong. It's what I was doin', followin' tracks when you come in." Luther nodded to the mud in the pen.

Long, webbed, four-toed tracks overlay the almost dainty prints of the sow. The new tracks were huge; they would overlap a dinner plate.

Lee closed his eyes. He saw newspaper articles, Liz Jordan looking for a lake monster. He remembered Red and Dr. Chilson talking about destroying the embryos, Red saying, "Damn straight, pull the plug before it makes a Cat 5 and really jacks us up." Then, Red's worried follow up, "Uh, are there Cat 5s?"

The doctor had not answered.

Are there Cat Fives?

Lee opened his eyes and stared at the huge tracks. "Dear God."

"It ain't nothin' to worry with, Mr. Picket. You help me get another pig for bait, an' we'll catch this one, too." Luther scratched at his beard again and frowned at the tracks. "I'll jus' have to get a bigger trap, is all."

The End

ABOUT THE AUTHOR

Martin Woodward grew up among the clear streams and wooded ridges of the Missouri Ozarks. He holds a BS in Political Science from the University of Central Missouri and is a veteran of the U.S. Navy. Martin lives in the Kansas City area with his family and an assortment of dogs and cats, and the hope that one day the voice of reason and compassion will overcome the whispers of the sly, and the shouts of the fanatical.